2084

Mason Engel

STAY IN THE KNOW
If you would like to stay up to date with what Mason is working on
next, please check out his website at masonengel.com/future

DEDICATION

This story was directly inspired by "1984" and "Brave New World" by George Orwell and Aldous Huxley respectively. So here's to them: for doing it first and infinitely better.

Part I - The Seclusion

CHAPTER 1 – LENSES

The eyes of the students went white all at once, and the voice in their heads fell silent. Vincent Smith, squinting in a vain attempt to ward off the white, swayed as he stood from his seat. He started without pause for the hall, a breath caught deep in his throat, his hands wrung tightly into fists.

Moments later he was leaned over the restroom sink, and his Lenses were sliding from his eyes. He could feel the air opening up around him. His fists were unfurling into palms.

The respite would be only temporary, of course – the day's simulations were but halfway finished – but to Vincent, even if just for a few moments, it felt good to see something without the distortion of the Lenses. The narrow and asymmetrical face reflecting back at him, however, may have better remained distorted.

Someone outside tried the bathroom door.

Vincent felt a nervous lurch in his stomach. For students in their final year, like Vincent was, there was no punishment for removing one's Lenses, but doing so was as uncommon as removing one's eyes. Although, the difference between those and the Lenses that covered them had grown quite slim.

Vincent retreated from the mirror and leaned back against the stall door behind him. His eyes, feeling lighter now, twisted in their sockets for a few turns as if stretching, then settled their gaze on the far wall. Like everything else in the Seclusion, the wall had been scrubbed to a sleek shine so it glinted in the light. Its surface was sterile enough to have been bathed in bleach, but it left Vincent with a faint impression that a certain but implacable filth lay somewhere just beneath.

There was more impatient twisting of the knob.

Vincent sighed, then leaned forward over the sink once again with the first Lens already perched on his index finger.

Moments later he was holding the door open for the next occupant: a prim, surly-looking boy whose frail body appeared somewhat absurd under the baggy white uniform that clothed it. The boy's overalls, the legs of which would have fit snugly around Vincent's arms, were held up almost exclusively by the thin suspenders that hung from his shoulders.

On the off chance he might receive even some half-hearted expression of gratitude, Vincent held the door until the boy had passed all the way through. The boy said nothing, and Vincent turned away.

"Of course the simulations say that."

The voice was coming from down the hall. Vincent would not have needed to look to know who was speaking, but he looked anyway, as he usually did. It was Brian: a tall, articulate boy who seemed always to command the attention of at least a handful of admirers. Now, he was surrounded by a half circle of them.

"They don't want to scare us. But it doesn't change the fact that the Senate has no idea how to stop the attacks."

"And you think Newsight does?" It was one of the boys from the circle. His voice was eager, and his eyes were so wide Vincent could see the rims of his Lenses.

"My mom thinks so," returned Brian. "She says the new Lenses can help. With the right data. Newsight wants to…"

He trailed off when he spotted Vincent walking by within earshot. He paused, the other boys still hanging on his final word, oblivious, until Vincent passed. Seeming to regain his train of thought, Brian turned back to his small audience and resumed speaking, this time at a volume too soft to be overheard.

Vincent didn't strain to listen. Instead, he quickened his pace, and by the time he turned back into the classroom further down the hall, Brian's voice had faded. The rest of the class was already seated, tucked with obedient stillness in their white, wraparound desks, their feet fixed like tree roots to the white, seamless tile, and their Lenses and eyes behind glued to the white, undecorated wall ahead.

Vincent took his seat near the back – though not quite as near as he would have liked – and felt himself sink unnaturally deep into his chair, as if pressed down from above. The room's ceiling was far higher than necessary (the room was shaped the same as everything else in the Seclusion: as a giant dome), but to Vincent, it seemed to hang just a few centimeters too low.

Mrs. Farring, a terse, elderly woman whose age had cost her none of her full, straight-postured frame, entered the room through a door in the wall everyone was so carefully watching. Almost simultaneously, the frail boy from the restroom entered through the door in the wall opposite. Brian and the others followed close behind him.

"This is an important afternoon." It was Mrs. Farring. Her voice was shrill and sharp and cut through the air of the classroom with every syllable. "Today, we begin our examination of the Order."

Vincent sighed, letting his head dip a few degrees downward. He glanced around the class, hoping perhaps just once he would find someone to share in his boredom, but the only expression he could find that wasn't completely blank was the stern, scolding one worn by the girl to his left. When she saw he had noticed her, she huffed in disapproval, then turned from him so quickly her jet black ponytail curled toward him like a whip.

"Which, of course," continued Mrs. Farring, "is even more important…"

Vincent's spine straightened, almost involuntarily, when he felt Mrs. Farring's eyes on him.

"…today." With her eyes still on Vincent, she enunciated these last two syllables with cutting precision. "Now," she continued after a pause, turning to the rest of the class, "I have already transmitted the simulation. Please engage."

There was movement around the room for the first time as heads changed orientation in the slightest degree, tilting this way or that in time with the flitting of eyes across the insides of Lenses. Then everyone was still, and their expressions were even more vacant than before. Sighing once again, Vincent glanced down at the small message overlain across the bottom part of his vision – the message from Mrs. Farring – and the classroom disappeared. For a brief moment, his vision was black, decorated only with the emblem of Newsight – the white, rotating outline of an eye – as the simulation prepared to launch. When the eye disappeared, its dark backdrop was replaced by the typical white. Vincent spun around in his seat – they were in the usual classroom sim, one that depicted a room much like where their bodies resided, only in this room, if you turned your head too quickly, you could see the walls being rendered from miniscule black pixels.

"Let us begin."

Mrs. Farring was visible once more, standing at the front of the room, her voice no longer disembodied. She stood next to a massless screen that had been projected on the front wall from nowhere in particular. The screen showed a title Vincent found drudgingly familiar: "A History of the Order". Without hesitating, he glanced up and to the right with a quick flick of his eyes. The rendering lines of black on his periphery closed like a curtain, and the simulation disappeared.

He was back in the real classroom. Or, at least, half of him was. He had allowed his left Lens to remain engaged so Mrs. Farring wouldn't notice his absence. His right, however, was now nothing more than a thin glass window.

Mrs. Farring was still standing at the front of the room, but her usually sharp eyes had been glazed over with the vacancy maintained by the rest of the class. She, too, was in the simulation. There was no need to have the bulk of advanced technology in the physical classroom when that same technology could be simulated in a virtual one. That was all the same to Vincent; reality was much more difficult to escape from than the simulations.

"The Order formed some 50 years ago as a Newsight protest group," began Mrs. Farring, "but ever since, their attacks have grown increasingly similar to those of a terrorist organization. They have scarred the very fabric of..."

Vincent let her voice fade. He had heard the story several times before. His father and the rest of the Senate had been working against the Order for years. Every night, it seemed to Vincent, he received yet another lesson on the Order's history or its current state. Even if Mrs. Farring trialed the class with some sort of quiz, Vincent could afford his disattention. He was about to pull up a sim of his own to pass the time, when he paused. His eyes had been drawn to the girl sitting just in front of him. Her head was wobbling, almost floating as it turned back and forth, now and then staring at a wall off to the side instead of at the front of the room. In the simulation, of course, she was almost certainly facing forward, but the Lenses had a curious way of placing the wearer's body and mind out of sync. Vincent looked around at the rest of the room and saw evidence of much the same: heads were turned in odd directions; mouths hung slightly agape. Even those eyes that, for a fraction of a second, Vincent managed to catch didn't see him, but rather passed right over him, beholding some unseen element of the sim.

Entranced now, Vincent rotated in his seat to take in the rest of the room and nearly jumped when he noticed the girl to his left. She was staring at him – though not really. Her bottom lip hung apart from its counterpart above, and her eyes were completely relaxed in their sockets, unseeing, but pointing directly at Vincent. Vincent

5

stared back at her, with the impression of staring at a well painted portrait whose eyes seem glued to his own. And of this portrait, depicting the girl's tightly pulled ponytail and somewhat flattened face, he allowed himself a longer look.

The girl turned from him, slowly swiveling in the opposite direction until she faced the opposite wall. Vincent turned as well, already bored. Even the simulation's redundant facts about the Order would be more interesting than watching his blank-faced peers. But as he made one final glance around him before engaging his Lenses, he caught another set of eyes, only these were definitely not vacant. Brian too, it seemed, had exited the simulation, and now, instead of on the video, his eyes were trained on Vincent. Vincent stared back, too shocked to look away, then – or perhaps not; it happened too quickly to tell for certain – Brian flashed him a grin, and his eyes went blank. Vincent watched him a moment longer, but Brian's gaze had already started to roam.

"...and has continued to do so ever since its founding." Mrs. Farring's voice came back into focus, and Vincent turned, resignedly, toward the front of the room. With little else to do, he glanced down at the lower rim of his Lenses, and he was back in the sim. "In the past it has primarily targeted civilian populations in the cities." The video was showing gruesome footage of whitewashed hospital rooms overflowing with blood-stained patients. "But recently, the Order has released statements of intent against government structures that support Newsight, even those in Seclusions." The video changed to an aerial shot of their Seclusion: a hyper-developed expanse of stacked, igloo-shaped domes, spaced in concentric circles around a hub of buildings in the center, and enclosed on the perimeter by an enormous fence. "The Order's origins as a protest group have been lost in their transition to a full scale terrorist organization. Their attacks on the cities have..."

Vincent didn't bother stifling his yawn. Perhaps he should have settled for watching his empty-eyed classmates. He was only a few seconds away from letting Mrs. Farring's voice lull him to sleep when he felt his desk shudder. He looked down – the desk in the simulation remained perfectly still. Of course it had. Realizing his foolishness, he exited the sim. When the actual room returned, he had to twist to his right to look forward; he had been staring at the girl to his left.

Vincent's desk shuddered once again. He spun around in his seat, looking down, but no one had touched him.

Then he heard a rumbling – distant, but growing in volume. Some of the others were beginning to exit their sims as well.

Without warning, Vincent's desk lurched to the side, airborne for a split second as the entire room shook. The frail boy from the restroom flew from his seat, smacking his temple on the hard edge of the desk beside him.

Even Mrs. Farring was out of the sim now, staring at them accusingly, as if they were playing a joke on her. Vincent's knuckles were white from gripping the edge of his desk. He looked around, this time meeting eyes far more present than before. But no one spoke. There was silence, the kind usually conjured only in the moments immediately following some great noise.

A series of words began to scroll across the bottom rim of Vincent's Lenses. Mrs. Farring, with her eyes drawn close as if watching the bridge of her nose, seemed to have received the message as well.

"We are experiencing an earthquake," she recited, her voice hollow, monotone as she read the words aloud. "The students will take shelter until further notice."

The rumbling started again, louder this time, definitely louder. Mrs. Farring raised her voice only to be joined by a high, whistling shriek.

"The structural integrity of–"

There was a resounding boom and the entire class lurched upward. Mrs. Farring was thrown from her feet, and Vincent from his chair – along with the rest of his classmates. Instinctively, Vincent pulled himself back to his desk, underneath it this time, not bothering to climb up into it. The others did the same, their soft features pulled into looks of terror, their vacant interest in the sim forgotten.

The room shook once again, more violently this time. Vincent lost his hold on the closest leg of his desk. He scrambled back toward it–

The room went dark. Vincent could see nothing. He froze where he was, his eyes unmoving in their sockets, blind. The room was still, held there in absolute silence. The rumbling had stopped; the shaking had settled.

"Everyone."

It was Mrs. Farring. From the sound of her voice, she remained somewhere near the room's front. There was some rustling as she felt around in the darkness for her desk.

"The lights are on," she said. "But your Lenses are not. You will have to remove them."

Vincent didn't move. He didn't remember ever having taken out his Lenses in public.

"All of you," said Mrs. Farring, sharper than before. "Now."

Cautiously, and unsure whether or not he was being tested, Vincent reached up to his right eye and removed the Lens there. He could see the classroom – cut in half now with the darkness of his left eye – and the eerily black eyes of everyone inside it. He took out his second Lens, and he could now see Mrs. Farring in her usual spot.

"Would you rather walk around blind?" she snapped at them.

The rest of the class hesitated for a moment, as if considering these options. Then, slowly, they began lifting their hands to their eyes.

"The network must have been compromised by the earthquake," continued Mrs. Farring. "I will check with the neighboring classrooms to see if they are experiencing the same problem. Stay put."

She glared at them a moment longer before turning on her heel and disappearing through the far door. She need not have worried, though; no one budged. Without their Lenses, the class seemed incapable of movement. Even Vincent, who usually reveled in the precious few seconds he could spend with naked eyes, remained still. For as he looked down at his open hands, at the Lenses there, both of which were now completely black, he felt for the first time he was being watched.

******

"I'm glad you're safe, son."

Vincent nodded in response. He directed his attention to the plate of food in front of him, but he remained uneasily aware of his father's gaze from the left.

"We both are."

Vincent's mother, sitting straight ahead, caught Vincent's eye as she spoke. He humored her for the obliged glance of gratitude, then returned to his food. He resettled in his seat, shrinking in at the shoulders. Uttered over the sterile white surface of the table before them, the words of his parents seemed out of place, especially those of his father. They didn't pertain to the Order, after all, or to some new policy or heavy-handed lobbyist in the Senate. Those were the only sentiments of his that ever seemed truly genuine.

"Thank goodness no one was hurt," said Vincent's mother. Her voice carried even less emotion than her husband's had. The tone sounded off to Vincent – he felt certain he had heard a more animated version of it when he was younger. Of course, this was a near impossible comparison to make. Vincent's pre-Seclusion memories, all of them faint and fading quickly, weren't much use as a measuring post by which to judge things now. Before his father had been elected – or appointed, perhaps; Vincent wasn't sure – to the Senate, the one thing Vincent remembered for certain was a lack of white. Not in the way of darkness, simply not in the stifling way it existed now. Even in their own dome, in the curved walls all the way to the ceiling, in the bare, perfectly uncluttered tile floor, it followed them. It was present in every room without exception, especially in the room they occupied now. A kind of hybrid between a small kitchen, a dining area, and an area where one might sit in hours of lull to engage with one's Lenses, the Main was high ceilinged and perfectly round but for the two offshoot, smaller rooms linked to its perimeter. It played host to their nightly meal, at which Vincent now so painfully sat. Of course, dinner was slightly better than afterward when the table would sink back into the floor, the chairs would be spaced wider, and his parents would invite him to share a simulation. These invitations, to what seemed his parents' indifference, Vincent easily deflected with complaints of school work.

"You should be grateful, Vincent," said his father. "The cities had it much worse."

"They felt it too?" asked Vincent.

"Of course they did. They were the ones targeted."

Vincent's mother dropped her fork on the edge of her plate in surprise. "Father."

Vincent looked up from his food for the first time. Mother was aghast. Father opened his mouth then closed it again. He cast Vincent a nervous look.

"Targeted?" said Vincent. "By the earthquake?"

Father hesitated before responding. He looked across the table at his wife. Her stare was cold, admonishing, but she said nothing. She merely shook her head in disapproval before resuming her meal.

Vincent, however, never lifted his gaze from his father.

"What happened?" he asked.

Father cast his wife another look. She wouldn't meet his eyes. "It was the Order," he said, reluctantly. "The school didn't want to cause panic, but the Order has been growing more brash." His tone was no longer quite so apologetic. It never stayed level for long when he was talking about the Order. "The missiles were shot down not too far above the school. We're lucky they weren't nuclear or—"

"Father."

It was Mother's voice again, and it was sharper than before. Fathered deferred.

"Defensive measures have been taken," he said, adopting a more neutral tone. "There was a bug in the defense system that allowed them to get that close, but it's been patched. Nothing to worry about." He glanced at his wife, as if to confirm he had been convincing enough. After a pause, Mother nodded her approval.

"It's a good thing we were relocated to the Newsight Seclusion," she said. "Their people are so brilliant. After working on the Lenses, the defense system must have been trivial."

Father nodded in agreement, and Mother raised her lips in a tightly held grin. Vincent was staring up at them. He hadn't touched his food for the past several seconds.

"I nearly forgot to ask, Vincent," said Mother, her lips falling back into their normal straight lines. "Was everyone frightened when the Lenses went dark? How have you been?"

Vincent shrugged. He didn't want to talk about the Lenses. He wanted to hear about the attack.

"Terrified, of course," Father answered for him. "You too, Mother. Must feel odd."

As Father spoke, Vincent could see the corner of his right eye where the outer rim of a Lens was barely visible. The Senators had been given early access to the newest model. Their Lenses, it seemed, had been unaffected.

Mother finished chewing her current bite before replying. "I'm just glad you still have yours, Father," she said. "I feel safer because of it."

Vincent opened his mouth, then bit his tongue. Neither of his parents seemed to notice. Mother continued.

"And things will be back to normal soon, anyway. Mrs. Carsons says the recall has already begun."

"Mrs. Carsons," said Father, slowly, as if tasting the syllables on his tongue. "From Rearing?"

Mother shook her head. It looked odd when it wasn't moving up and down. "From Incubation," she said. "With me."

Father smacked the table in realization. Vincent jumped.

"Her husband is a Newsight man, isn't he?"

Mother nodded, looking natural again.

"I remember now," continued Father. "What did she say? How long until the recall?"

"It's already in process," said Mother. "Everyone will be shipped the newest model within the week. Mrs. Carsons said even the cities will receive the upgrade. Fatrem mandated it himself. Can you believe that?"

For a fraction of a second, Vincent saw something novel on his father's face. There was an upward twitch of his brow, a widening of his eyes, a slight parting of his lips, and then nothing. He was composed again.

"That is news indeed," he said. Mother didn't seem to notice his reservation.

"It's quite generous of him," she said. She was beaming – she could hardly speak of Newsight's beloved CEO without a smile. "Almost no one in the cities has access to Lenses. Mrs. Carsons mentioned something about an adjustment period, so not sleeping in them won't be an option." She shot Vincent an accusing look. Vincent looked down at his food.

"Well the old pair wasn't very comfortable, Mother," said Father. He cast Vincent a warning look. Mother glared at them both, her nose tilted ever so slightly upward. Father noticed.

"But when you get your upgrade," he said to Vincent, forcing sternness back into his tone, "you had better get used to sleeping in them." Then, deciding the matter was settled – though Mother's look said quite the opposite – he changed the subject. The glimmer of real conversation had been short lived.

"Speaking of Mrs. Carsons," Father resumed, picking up the prior thread, "you might tell her I'm a bit cross with the Newsight lobbyists at the moment."

Vincent perked up again.

"Really?" said Mother, frowning. "How so?"

Vincent fixed his eyes on Father. He could see remnants there of what he saw before: a look not so artificial as usual.

"The bill they've been pushing for comes to the floor tomorrow," said Father. "Perhaps I'm being old-fashioned; perhaps we all are, but I just can't see it ever getting passed."

"They're appealing the regulations again?" said Mother. Father nodded.

"All of them this time. Many of the cities have already conceded. In return, Newsight has used the data to fight the Order. The attacks *have* decreased for the cities that cooperate with them. It's just..." Father trailed off. He was in danger of exposing a real expression again. "It's worth considering the tradeoff."

"Well if it will stop the Order then I don't see why not," said Mother. "Is there much discussion about it?"

"It's all anyone has been talking about. Both parties are generally averse to it. There has even been a great deal of nonpartisan talks to make sure it doesn't get passed. We're collaborating closer than we have in years." Father paused, almost frowning, seeming to listen to the echo of the words that had just left his mouth, as if to ensure they had been his own. His face suddenly seemed lined with more wrinkles than Vincent had seen there before.

"Well," said Mother, pulling Vincent's gaze from Father, "whatever you decide, we trust you to make the right decision. Don't we Vincent?"

Vincent looked to her, then back to Father, whose face had closed to interpretation once again.

"Right," said Vincent.

Father looked up at this. Vincent stared back, searching Father's eyes for a look of confirmation, assurance, something, but all he could see were the tiny lines of the Lenses.

CHAPTER 2 – UPGRADES

The next morning, Vincent, still huddled into himself against the wind, stepped through the main doors of the school. Instantly, the cold in his muscles gave way to manufactured warmth, and the wintry howling in his ears to excited whispers and shuffling feet. Taking a moment to adjust to the light reflecting off the school's bleached interior, his eyes searched for the source of the sound. In the far corner of the room – in a space of congruent shape to the Main but of amplified size – a group of Vincent's classmates, nearly all of them, in fact, were clustered around a large opening in the wall where an uninterested looking man was passing out small packages. Vincent's peers clambered over each other wildly for their share, with an eagerness in their eyes Vincent had scarcely seen in them before.

"They can't function without their Lenses."

Vincent turned around, following the voice. He found its owner in the brawny, tall boy so used to being followed by the same crowd now clustered around the man with the packages.

Brian smirked. "I'm surprised they survived the night without them," he said.

Vincent glanced back at the group still fighting each other for – if Brian was right – their upgrades.

"They're already here?"

"They've been here for a while now," said Brian. "There's been a line ever since the doors opened."

Vincent continued to watch the crowd push and shove to get closer to the opening. "You got here early then?"

Brian shook his head. "Just a few minutes before you. I didn't have to wait in line. I got the new model as soon as I went home last night."

Vincent nodded, unsurprised. It made sense. He should have known Brian had a Newsight parent. Many of the kids in this Seclusion did – it was where the company was based, after all. Then again, the crowd of students was too large for everyone whose parents worked for the Lens creators to have gotten their upgrades early.

"Your parents work for Newsight?"

Brian nodded. Vincent motioned to the group at the opening. "And none of theirs do?"

"Some do," said Brian. "But none as high up as my mom." He

said the last part as something of a boast, but it seemed proud, too, genuine.

Vincent didn't say anything back. He was about to start over to join the crowd when the main doors pushed open a few meters off, dousing them with a sharp wave of cold. It was the girl with the dark ponytail. She cast the mob of students a quick glance before stalking past them and down the hall toward the classroom. Brian noticed Vincent looking.

"Our moms used to work together," he said. He sounded resentful anyone should have the privilege.

"Used to?" repeated Vincent.

"Her mom was Head of Product before mine," said Brian. "She was good at it, but she died only a year or so after getting the job." He finished with a blunt, detached tone, not quite cold, just matter-of-fact. Vincent, however, was more interested.

"So how does she already have her Lenses then?"

"Her dad still works for Newsight," said Brian. "Not nearly as high up as her mom was, but they still get taken care of. Everyone loved her mom."

Vincent fixed his gaze on the mouth of the hall where the girl had just disappeared. "What's her name?" he asked.

Brian watched him, wearing a hint of a grin. "Why don't you ask her yourself?"

Vincent shot him a look, his cheeks growing hot, then crossed over to the crowd of his peers to pick up his new Lenses.

******

Vincent blinked several times in quick succession as he dropped the second Lens onto his free eye. He squinted at himself in the restroom mirror. The new Lenses felt a bit thicker than before. The distortion, though undetectable, felt heavier now, like he had traded in a cotton blindfold for a leaden one.

For proper adjustment, please do not remove your new Lenses for the first three days.

The words scrolled across the bottom rim twice before Vincent could read them fully. Afterward, he tried to shift the glass with his index finger – he didn't like the idea of sleeping in Lenses – but it felt already fixed in place, held there as if by suction. He breathed out, heavily, and then yawned in the same breath. He had lain in bed last night with his mind spinning like a top, turning over and over again his father's troubled expression during dinner. Now, the Lenses would make sleep even more elusive.

Three small white numbers at the bottom of his vision began to blink: 8:00. He was about to be late.

Turning from the mirror, Vincent left the restroom. Moments later, just as Mrs. Farring was stepping through the door at the front of the class, Vincent lowered himself into the nook of his desk.

"Good morning, everyone."

The class responded in kind. Vincent called out habitually with them.

"We were cut short yesterday," continued Mrs. Farring, "so we won't waste any time this morning. You should receive my invitation shortly."

As the words left her mouth, a message began scrolling across Vincent's Lenses. Another sim. A second yawn rose up in Vincent at the thought, but he caught it halfway through when he noticed Mrs. Farring's eyes on him. The rest of the class, however, seemed all too eager to test out their upgraded devices. Expressions went blank faster than usual, and heads began to drift. Still under the careful inspection of Mrs. Farring, Vincent glanced down twice, and the classroom rematerialized in almost the exact fashion as he had just seen it. Admittedly, far closer to exact than had been managed by the previous Lenses.

The video screen was already hanging in midair at the front of the room, its picture frozen at some long-winded title, the first words of which made Vincent slouch in his seat.

"We'll pick up the Order simulation where we left off," said Mrs. Farring. "Today, we'll be covering the Order's presence in the cities." Vincent straightened slightly at this. He had never seen the cities before. Perhaps he would stay in the sim today after all.

But when the video began, with footage of a politician giving a particularly dry speech in the Senate, Vincent knew he would see nothing of the cities. It had been a fanciful hope to begin with.

Sighing, he leaned back and disengaged his right Lens. His head had been left facing forward and, for a second, the room was split seamlessly in two between the simulation and the real thing. Though now, seeing the two side by side, Vincent could easily have forgotten which was which; so closely had the sim recreated its mark. He chanced a look at Brian, half expecting, half hoping to see the larger boy disengaged as well, but Brian was looking in the opposite direction, his eyes glazed over with the telltale vacancy of the sim – the same as everyone else. Vincent turned to the girl to his left; she too was fully engaged.

Surely, Vincent thought, the cities had to be different than this. They had to be better. Even if they were completely empty, they had to feel fuller than the room of cold, blank-faces in which Vincent now sat. They had to be more exciting, too, though school didn't set the bar particularly high in that regard.

Vincent yawned once again, not bothering to hide it this time. Mrs. Farring always ended up watching the sim the same as the students. She wouldn't notice him. Taking care to position himself out of view behind the girl in front of him as a precaution, Vincent settled his face into his hands. He closed his eyes and began to listen.

"...only when the Order began dropping their warnings did Newsight take action. Stating it as their civic duty to protect the threatened, Newsight now provides defense networks to several major cities. These cities have consequently seen a drastic decrease in Order attacks, leading to a great migration to these cities by those seeking refuge from the Order. However, the Order's insatiable appetite for destruction leads them again and again to the unprotected outskirts. Where once families and children lived, there now are only ruins. The Order has..."

Vincent was starting to slip away, but his mind continued to linger on the narrator's last few words. *Where once families and children lived...* Vincent's memories from pre-Seclusion began to pry their way out of the dark once again. He remembered short square buildings with pointed roofs and none of the gentle curves of the Seclusion domes. He remembered the pungent smell of air not quite clean, of a thick black fog that clung to the clouds like a sticky film. He remembered the paths, the roads, and people walking down them, none of them dressed in white, and some shouting, some even smiling. And then he remembered the towers, slender and dark as they rose up from the stone paths that encircled them, reflecting rays of light with their story height windows...

The narrator continued to talk, but Vincent was no longer listening.

He was standing on the street, in front of a small brown house with a slanted roof. Behind the house were the towers, shadowed in gray light and fogged by the clouds that clung jealously to their edges. Vincent ignored the towers and started for the house instead. He pushed through the front door – it didn't slide open for him like it may have in the Seclusion – and stepped over the threshold. The entryway was floored not with tile, but with wood (the word, foreign to Vincent, sprang into his head of its own accord). The air in the house was warm but not stifling, cooled by a slight breeze through windows that had been left open.

Vincent closed the door behind him and stepped deeper inside. The space opened up into a joint kitchen and dining room, then into a larger area with comfortable-looking chairs around a flat black rectangle with a smooth, unmoving screen.

"Vincent?"

Vincent turned to his right, where the room with the chairs was linked to a hallway. A woman with a sharply sloped nose and wide, bright eyes was standing with her hands on her hips. It took Vincent a moment to recognize the woman out of her usual, collared white uniform.

"Mother?" he heard himself say.

"Will you set the table for us please?" she said. "For four. Grandpa is coming."

Vincent felt his head nod up and down. Mother smiled at him.

The next moment, Vincent was laying the last of the silverware on the table, a napkin under each set. There was movement behind him in the hall.

"Is it ready?"

Father – equally unrecognizable as his wife – walked up behind Vincent and clapped him on the back. He sat down in the chair closest to the kitchen.

"Coming," said Mother. She was pulling something from the oven. "I'm trying to find more dishes for you to do."

Father threw up his hands in mock despair. He rolled his eyes, and as they moved, Vincent could see no outline against their surface, no miniscule rim of glass to skirt the iris. Father wasn't wearing Lenses.

"Vincent?"

A third voice was calling for him from down the hall. It was kind, like his mother's, but male, and old.

"Vincent?"

Vincent stood from his seat.

"Vincent!"

Vincent's eyes snapped open and he was back in the classroom. Everyone was looking at him. Some even looked concerned.

He turned self-consciously in his seat. He caught Brian's eyes and was met only with a vague, unreadable look of curiosity. He turned to the girl. She was among those who had concern in her gaze. There was something else there too, something that made Vincent feel as transparent as glass.

"Vincent."

Vincent whipped around to face the front of the room where Mrs. Farring stood, simmering.

"You will stay after school to finish your simulation," she said. "Is that understood?"

Vincent blinked several times to clear the sleep from his eyes. He shrank into himself as the looks of concern on those around him turned to something closer to amusement. "Yes, ma'am." He said it in a small, defeated voice, and Mrs. Farring seemed satisfied by it.

"Good. Now, everyone else, we'll take our break a few minutes early." Without another word, she turned from them and disappeared through what seemed to be her own personal door. The rest of the class stood as well, starting for the door in the wall opposite. Vincent rose more slowly.

"You should be more careful, you know."

Brian had crossed over to him through the crowd. Vincent didn't meet his eyes.

"If you're going to fall asleep," said Brian, "do it in the sim. That's what my brother always told me."

Vincent looked up at this. He glanced around the class.

"He doesn't go to school here anymore," said Brian, noticing Vincent's searching look. "He's older, anyway." He glanced down at the desk where Vincent had just been sitting. "You were talking, you know."

Vincent wasn't surprised. He already had a feeling the looks he received had not been unprompted. "What was I saying?" he asked.

"Nothing really," said Brian. "Just telling someone you were on your way." Brian glanced around them. He lowered his voice. "You *should* be careful, though," he repeated. "Dreams are hard to hide."

In Brian's expression on these last words, Vincent could see the same shadow of a look he had seen during the sim the day prior, and something beyond it that seemed to leave words unsaid.

Brian turned away. Vincent stayed where he was, and as he watched the larger boy file out of the class with the few of their peers who remained, his breaths began to grow shorter. His Lenses felt suddenly tighter against his pupils. He started for the restroom.

The door was locked when he tried it. He knocked impatiently, and kept knocking until the boy inside stepped out.

"Just wait your—"

Vincent pushed past him and pulled the door shut as he went. He threw the bolt into place and leaned back. His eyes felt more constricted than usual, as if the stranglehold his Lenses had on them had finally been pulled all the way taut.

Trying to compose himself, he crossed over to the sink and leaned forward so his right eye, with its lid pulled all the way up, was within centimeters of the mirror. He dragged his index finger across the surface of the Lens, as he had done so many times before, but nothing happened. He tried again, pressing a little harder so his eye sank back a millimeter into his head, but the Lens remained. He leaned back so he was standing straight again, his eyes locked on his reflection. He blinked several times, then tried his left eye – still, nothing. Frowning, and sweating now, even under his thin, breathable overalls, he resumed his position up close to the mirror. He opened his eyes wide and inspected the white area just beyond the grayish green of his irises. He saw the rims of his Lenses the same as usual, but, amidst the irritated, spindly lines of blood next to them, he saw something else. Another set of lines, ones not his own, and nearly undetectable, stretched out from the edge of his Lenses and curled back under his eyelids.

The stranglehold felt by his eyes was nearing a breaking point.

Before he could go back to work on removing them, his Lenses started to flash white along the bottom rim.

11:28. It was time go back.

Vincent let his eyelids droop closed for a moment, though this didn't get rid of the numbers, and he massaged the area of his forehead just outside the tips of his brow. He stayed like that for a few seconds as he regained control of his breathing, then he left.

He pushed through the door back out into the hall and started for the classroom, but as he did, he saw movement behind him. All the way at the end of the passage, in the direction opposite the rest of the class, was Brian. The larger boy was walking rather quickly, hunched over at the waist as if hiding – as if bracing himself, too. He was probably feigning nausea to get out of the sim. It wasn't a bad idea.

The blinking numbers turned to 11:29. Sighing, and more out of habit than duty, Vincent turned toward the classroom, but only to come to a stop so quickly he nearly fell backward. The girl with the pony tail had just exited the girl's restroom, and he had nearly run into her.

"Sorry," he mumbled, looking down automatically. "Wasn't looking."

He stayed where he was, his eyes downcast, expecting her to twist around in her normal whipping motion, but she didn't. She stayed where she was, inspecting him with keen, wide eyes.

"I tried to take mine out too," she said, her gaze trained on Vincent's irritated right eye. "I couldn't get them out either."

Vincent started to raise a hand to his face, then caught himself. He glanced at the girl, then looked away again; her eyes seemed to stare straight through him. "I guess we're not supposed to be able to," he said. He forced himself to look up at her. It was an effort to hold her gaze. "They said we're not supposed to take them out for a few days."

"We're also not supposed to tune out of our sims," she countered. "But you do *that* anyway."

Vincent felt a familiar heat beginning to kindle under the skin of his cheeks. He glanced over the girl's shoulder at the open door of the classroom, longing, even, for the discomfort of his desk.

"How do you know that?" he asked.

"I can tell," she said, matter-of-factly. "I tune out too. When I do it, though, I try not to make it too obvious in case Mrs. Farring is watching. You, on the other hand, never hide it at all." She paused. Her inspection of him continued. "You watch me sometimes. A lot of times, actually." She said the last part without much expression, as if stating the obvious. Vincent barely noticed his lips part in shock. He tried to stammer some excuse, but nothing seemed to come. The girl grinned.

"Come on," she said, flicking her head back toward the classroom. "We've still got all afternoon." Unhesitating, and with far more confidence than Vincent could have mustered, she grabbed his hand and pulled him along behind her, back toward the classroom. With his full attention on the girl in front of him, Vincent almost failed to notice the whistling sound coming from above. Within seconds, though, the sound was undeniably loud. No rumbling to precede it this time, the whistle was growing to a bloodcurdling shriek. The girl looked up.

"What is tha—"

Her words were cut off as the whistle crescendoed in a deep, earsplitting boom. The ceiling above them cracked down the middle, leaking dust from above.

There was silence then. They were still, the girl's eyes fixed on the ceiling, Vincent's fixed on her.

Then they were flying backward. Vincent could hardly make sense of the colors spinning through his line of sight. There was a cloud of orange, hot with streaks of red, then plumes of black and gray, sprinkled with flecks of white that flew through the air in all directions.

He hit the ground in sync with the girl and skidded a meter longer from the momentum. When they came to a stop, the girl was dazed, and her arm was draped over Vincent's waist.

Vincent pulled himself into a sitting position – coughing up dust as he did so – and stared down the hall. Or, at least, he tried to. It was thick with a brown cloud of smoke and debris. The usually spotless white walls had been coated with grime, and the paint that covered them dripped from the heat of the flames that licked their perfect surface.

There started a second whistle. It seemed to snap the girl from her stupor.

"Come on!" she said, and she was on her feet, pulling Vincent up with her. "We need to get back!"

Vincent had barely gotten to his feet when there was another explosion and the ground lurched under them, sending them hurtling into the wall to their right. Vincent felt the heat much closer behind them now. Getting back to the classroom would be impossible.

"This way!" The girl dragged him in the opposite direction, her right hand still curled tightly around his, and her face dipped low beneath the smoke.

As they ran, the ground shook from yet another explosion. This one was followed by screams.

Doors up ahead were flying open on either side of the hall.

Teachers poked their heads out, their eyes wide with terror.

"You two!" one of the teachers shouted from his room. "Get in!"

They started for him but were thrown back yet again when the ceiling caved in between them. Vincent tried to come to a stop, his free hand covering his mouth from the debris, but the girl continued to drag him forward. Just when Vincent thought they would collide with the crumbled ceiling ahead, they dodged right. They had come to the high ceilinged room that led to the main entrance. The opening in the wall from which they had received their Lenses earlier that morning was now gone. It had collapsed, trapping the man inside so only his crimson-streaked torso was visible under the rock. The girl didn't seem to notice him. She had dropped Vincent's hand and her eyes were drawn close, as Mrs. Farring's had been when reading yesterday's message on the Lenses.

"We need to get out of the school," the girl said, still seeming to stare at the bridge of her nose.

Vincent looked through the glass of the main doors where the outside seemed tinted with a grim-looking red. "Out?" he said. "Are you sure we shouldn't stay here?"

She shook her head. "My dad just told me to get home as fast as possible."

Vincent turned around, staring at the ruined hall they had just been blocked from entering, then in the opposite direction where the blaze had grown even closer, and then out through the main doors.

"Vincent," the girl said, firmly, but composed. Vincent turned to her, and with her in front of him, his periphery seemed suddenly blurred, the smoke and dust and flames blissfully out of focus. The screams, too, sounded muffled and distant. When the girl held out her hand, Vincent hardly heard the explosion that sounded somewhere behind them. He looked down at the girl's fingers, steady, as they stretched out to him. "Trust me," she said.

And without really knowing why, he did.

CHAPTER 3 – NEWSIGHT

They came to a stop in front of a dome between the first and second rings. In a calmer setting – one without screams and smoke – Vincent would have had the presence of mind to be impressed. The prices of domes this close to the Center were astronomical. Typically, these properties had the best view of the upper levels of school, but now, the red haze of flickering flames that lit the horizon provided a view for which no one had paid.

The girl pressed her right eye up close to a palm sized screen on the door, and the screen shined green a second later. The door opened automatically. She grabbed Vincent's hand and started to tug him inside, but Vincent held firm. His attention had been drawn back to the horizon. When the girl saw what he was looking at, she stopped her tugging and turned around to watch. There was a streak of gold splitting through the sky. This one was brighter than the rest, with a thicker tail, and it was heading straight for the school's main dome. It moved with lethargic slowness as it fell down at an angle from above, lighting up the whole sky with a blinding, Armageddon-like glow. The object at the helm of the thing seemed to cut through the sky like a giant blade, its tip pointed resolutely at the last remaining remnant of the school.

In one final flash, it pierced its mark.

The dome hesitated for a fraction of a second, as if unsure what would happen, then shrank in at the sides and exploded outward with a giant pulse. The red haze above turned bright pink as the dome was engulfed from without in the same blinding white that had once decorated it within.

The sound reached them a second later, then the vibration. Vincent hardly noticed. His eyes were still locked on the cloud of smoke rising up from the Center.

"Vincent." The girl's voice was soft, but its edges had lost their usual calm. "We need to get inside." She tugged on his arm again. "Come on."

With his eyes still on the horizon, the pinnacle of which now seemed eerily empty, and with the image of the fire-tailed missile still seared into his mind, Vincent let himself be towed inside.

"My dad said he'll be here soon."

They were cast into darkness as the girl closed the door behind them.

"He told us to go to the cellar."

"The what?" said Vincent. He felt in a trance. His eyes were still trained on the horizon, though all he could see now were the unlit walls of the dome.

"The cellar," repeated the girl, as if that explained things. "This way." She tugged on his hand yet again, but he stayed where he was. The last hour seemed to register in his mind all at once.

"I need to get home," he said. "I need to find my mother. She works in Incubation in the school. She could have been—"

The girl caught his wrist when he tried to turn away. "Incubation is right next to the generators," she said. "It's underground. She's safer than we are."

Vincent pulled free of her grip. "I just need to – wait," he looked around them, noticing the darkness for the first time – the lights were automatic. "The power is—"

"We don't run off of the Center generators," said the girl, withdrawing, as if making a confession. "We have our own. They probably just shut off from the blast. Besides," she continued, sounding eager to change the subject, "the domes in the first ring had lights. The ones in the second did, too, other than ours. The generators haven't been hit."

Vincent tried to think back to their run here, but he had been too preoccupied to take in the sights. And he remained too preoccupied to think of anything but getting home. "I should still go," he said, and he turned away, starting for the exit. The girl didn't stop him this time.

"Where do you live?" she called after him.

"Just a few paths over." He was almost to the door.

"Really," said the girl. It wasn't a question. "I know for a fact you live on the other side of the Center."

Vincent stopped with his hand on the knob.

"You won't make it there for hours," pressed the girl. "If you make it at all. They'll send in the Guard. The whole Seclusion will be blocked off."

Vincent stayed where he was. Everything she said was true – even the parts she shouldn't have known.

"Wait a second," said Vincent. "How do you know where I live?"

The girl opened her mouth to answer, then paused, rethinking. "I...I've seen you leave school before. You always go in the opposite direction as me."

Vincent lifted his brow. "So you've been watching me?" he said.

Even in the lack of light, he saw the girl's face grow a shade darker.

"Walk home if you want," she said, turning from him. "I'm going to the cellar." Her body was cast into shadow as she started deeper into the unlit dome, but Vincent didn't follow. Not yet.

"Wait."

The girl paused where she was, sighing as she looked back at him.

Vincent spoke once again. "What is your name?"

The girl seemed taken aback. She hadn't been expecting this. "Jessica," she said. "Now are you coming or not?" Without waiting for a response, she turned on her heel and started deeper into the dome. Vincent watched her for a moment, then followed.

******

For the next few hours, Vincent and Jessica sat together in a small, underground room that was hidden beneath the master bed. The space was almost pitch black, lit only by burning, finger-width sticks Vincent had never seen before. The lack of white, too, was something novel. The room's walls and floor both, each damp and soft to the touch, were colored a dark, natural brown. No other dome Vincent had been inside had anything like it. Though, admittedly, he had been in only a handful.

A metallic rustling sound drifted down to them from somewhere near the ceiling. A second later, the trapdoor under the master bed swung upward, providing the cellar with only the rays of light slippery enough to slither by the man-shaped shadow above.

"It's safe," said the caster of the shadow. "You can come up."

Jessica rose without question. Vincent got to his feet more cautiously.

"It's ok," said Jessica. "It's my dad."

Vincent nodded in response, but he wasn't assuaged. A man with a hidden room underground and a dome that ran off of private power didn't call to mind a particularly trustworthy image.

Vincent followed Jessica up the steeply angled stairs toward the trapdoor. A few seconds later, they were back in the bedroom.

"In here."

The voice called out again, out of sight this time. They traced its source to the Main, where a short, grubby looking man with a rounded stomach was entering from a door behind the kitchen. As he did, the room brightened from somewhere overhead.

"Generator's back," he said. Vincent looked around with the aid of the lights for the first time. The dome varied greatly from the Seclusion standard. It felt more natural. The dining table actually looked used: strewn with articles of the day and scattered with flattened out cubes of bound paper, the likes of which Vincent had seen only in the simulations. Even the walls, usually the main source of the Seclusion's empty perfection, had been decorated, mostly with images of the same three people: Jessica, her father, and a woman Vincent didn't recognize. The sterile chill that seemed to follow Vincent around the Seclusion like a shadow was utterly absent here.

"You didn't say there was someone with you, Jessica." The round man who had entered from the kitchen stood next to the dining table, his eyes trained on Vincent with undisguised suspicion. He was short, only just taller than Jessica, with a face as round as his stomach and a nose so wide it must surely have haunted the lower edge of his vision.

"Vincent, this is my dad," said Jessica. "He's a developer for Newsight. He works on the software that runs our Lenses. Dad, Vincent is a friend from school."

Less tense now, but still never taking his large, beady eyes off of Vincent, Jessica's father extended his hand. Vincent stepped forward to shake it.

"Simon," said the man. "I trust my Jessica has been taking care of you."

Vincent nodded.

"And your parents," Simon continued, "they're safe?"

Vincent nodded again. He had received word from both of them while he and Jessica were in the cellar. The Lenses, though this attack had been far worse than the one before, had remained fully functional.

"Do they have a transport?" asked Simon.

"No, sir," said Vincent.

Simon grunted his disapproval but said nothing back. Jessica broke the silence.

"Can you take him, daddy?" she asked. She was still standing next to Vincent, but as she spoke, she stepped closer to Simon. The man's gaze softened as if by a switch, and his tenseness seemed to ease. Still,

Vincent didn't relish the idea of riding in a transport, let alone in the transport of the man who stood before him now.

"It's really fine," said Vincent. "Don't feel like you have to go through any trouble. Jessica has done more than enough already."

Simon seemed satisfied by the answer. He turned to Jessica. "Well you heard the boy. He'll be all right."

"Dad." She said the word in a parental kind of tone, almost scolding. Simon sighed in response, then looked away, running a hand through what little hair he had left. After a pause, he turned back to face them.

"Where do you live?" he asked.

Vincent didn't lie this time. "446 Ocean," he said.

"This side of the Center?" asked Simon.

Vincent shook his head. "Opposite."

Simon turned to Jessica, then back to Vincent. He sighed again, heavier this time.

"Come on then," he said to Vincent, flicking his head. "Out front." He turned and started for the front door.

"Uh…" Vincent stayed where he was. "I'm fine, really. I didn't see a transport out there, anyway."

"I called it around from the garage," Simon shot back over his shoulder. He was already at the exit.

"Go," Jessica cut in. "It's no trouble. He's always excited to drive."

"Are you sure?" Vincent watched, unconvinced, as Simon disappeared through the main door.

Jessica laughed. It was a pleasant sound, soft and sweet, and a pitch higher than Vincent would have expected.

"You're fine," said Jessica, still smiling. "You better hurry though."

Vincent took a deep breath. Surely this couldn't be worse than the explosions.

He cast Jessica what he hoped to be a confident look, then started for the door. He emerged outside a moment later where Simon was standing on the left side of a long, two-wheeled white contraption with an egg-shaped pod set in the middle. It looked barely big enough for two people.

"Get in," said Simon, motioning to the side opposite his. Hesitating, but knowing he didn't have much of a choice, Vincent stepped forward. He found a small button on the thing's exterior and pressed it, flinching slightly when the door slid to the side, deeper into a hollowed part of the pod. He climbed in and the door closed automatically after him. The interior was simple, just two plain seats, made of a sleek, slippery kind of material, positioned side by side behind a narrow dash where, in front of Simon, was a series of buttons and controls Vincent had never seen before.

Simon noticed Vincent's puzzled expression. "Your parents don't drive?"

Vincent shook his head. "My father doesn't trust transports. He doesn't think Newsight should have them all on the same network."

"Neither do I," said Simon. "Jessica's mother passed away in a transport accident. It was because of the network automation. This one will always stay off the grid."

Simon did something with his Lenses, then, so smoothly Vincent hardly noticed, the transport began rolling backwards. When it reached the street, it corrected itself with a half turn so it faced forward. They paused there, and Simon looked over at Vincent, amused. Vincent realized he had grabbed onto the inside of the door. His knuckles were nearly as white as the paint.

Turning from Vincent, grinning, Simon started the transport down the path and around the second ring. There were only four paths that connected any one ring to the others, and Vincent lived on the one farthest: North Ocean. It was a distance from them which, traversed by Simon's fragile-looking transport, left plenty of time for accident. But as they drove, Vincent's nerves began to settle. The ride was almost entirely smooth, and the sounds of the outside were completely mute. The Seclusion was eerily peaceful given the events of the day.

"Your father," said Simon, breaking the silence as if just remembering their earlier exchange. "He's not a fan of Newsight?"

"It's not that," said Vincent. "He's just…cautious, I guess."

Simon never shifted his eyes from the path ahead, but he didn't quite succeed in masking his interest. "What does he do?"

"He's a Senator," said Vincent.

Simon grunted at this. "Has his hands full at the moment then I suppose." His tone didn't sound convinced.

"Yeah, he does," said Vincent, firmly. "But he'll figure it out. He figures out all the attacks. He'll make the Order pay for this one."

Simon kept his eyes fixed straight forward. "They still think the attack came from the Order?"

Vincent frowned. It took him a moment to find his words. "Of course they do."

"So I assume they haven't launched an investigation then?" pressed Simon. "About the Newsight litigation?"

Vincent thought back to dinner the night before, to his father's comments about the lobbyists. "You mean about the data regulations?" Simon nodded. The transport tipped sideways as they banked to the right. Vincent grabbed onto the door once again. He could feel Simon's eyes on him. "Why would they?" he asked.

"Why would they not?" snapped Simon. "The government partnership for the new tech, the recall, and now the attack? If they let the bill through after all of that, then they're blinder than I thought."

Vincent frowned. "Blind to what?" he asked.

Simon opened his mouth, then closed it again. He shook his head. "If you don't see it, you're just as bad as they are," he said. "Unfortunately, you won't have to wait long to realize what you're missing. I expect the bill will be passed soon."

"Maybe not," said Vincent. Simon snorted, but Vincent continued. "You haven't heard what my father has been saying."

Simon perked up at this. "About the bill?" Vincent nodded. "What has he told you?" asked Simon.

Vincent shrugged, noncommittal. "Why do you think there should be an investigation?"

Simon stared at Vincent for a moment, eyebrows raised, then snorted again, under his breath this time. "If only the Senate were so curious," he said. They began to decelerate after these last words – they had come to a checkpoint of the Guard. A man in all white with his palm raised out in front of him stood in the center of the path, blocking their way. Behind him, a dozen or so more men of the same dress were huddled around the front door of a rather ornate-looking dome. Vincent hardly noticed.

"What should the Senate be investigating?" he pressed.

Simon glanced at him before turning back to the man outside. He shook his head. "You're just as bad as Jessica."

The Guard in front of them stepped out of the path, and they began to accelerate once again. Vincent held his gaze on Simon. The man was silent for several seconds.

"I'm not sure how the government partnership factors in," said Simon, after a pause, "but the recall and the attack are clear enough." He hesitated here, fixing his eyes straight ahead, seeming to deliberate whether or not he should continue. "The recall was nothing more than an excuse for Newsight to ship out the upgrades," he said. "The maintenance issues were all fake."

"What do you mean fake?" said Vincent. He was no longer looking out the window. His eyes were trained on the round-faced developer sitting next to him.

Simon acted reluctant, but Vincent could tell he wanted to keep talking. He had the same look in his eyes Father got when talking about the Order. "Did your Lenses go out today?" asked Simon. "During the attack?" Vincent shook his head. "But they went out yesterday, didn't they? From a little vibration. Why do you think that is?"

Vincent shrugged. "The upgrades are just more resilient I guess."

Simon wagged his right index finger, smiling. He seemed to be enjoying himself. "You think the inventors of the most advanced technology of the millennium would let their entire system go down from a little turbulence?" He snorted at the thought. "If you're anything like Jessica," he continued, "then you've tried to take out your new Lenses." Vincent nodded in confirmation. There was no need to lie anymore. "Well others have tried as well, and they've come up with the same result you have. No one can take them out. Newsight has released a statement saying it's because of the adjustment period, that the Lenses will be removable in a few days, but I'm not so sure. I don't think there was ever anything wrong with the old Lenses. Fatrem didn't send out a more resilient product; he sent out a more permanent one."

Vincent frowned. "Why would Newsight want to make the Lenses permanent?"

"The data they collect is only valuable if it's comprehensive," said Simon. "Otherwise, they only see what people want them to."

Vincent was shaking his head. "The Senate would never let Lenses be permanent," he said. Simon didn't argue – he seemed to know he didn't have to. "What about the attack?" said Vincent, changing the subject. "How is that a part of anything?"

Simon drove in silence past the next cluster of the Guard, seeming to consider how best to answer. "You can work this out for yourself," he said. "Look around. What do you notice?"

Vincent stared, dutifully, out through the oval shaped windows. "The Guard," he said. "They're going into—"

"Not the Guard," said Simon, impatient. "The domes. Who lives in them?"

Vincent hesitated at this, not sure if it was a trick question. "In the inner rings," he started, "mostly people who work for Newsight. Some Senators too."

Simon nodded. "That's right. But it's not just the inner rings; it's the whole Seclusion. Think. Who goes to your school? Who do you have class with?"

Vincent started fumbling for the few names he knew. "Well there's Jessica and Brian…I think there's a Sam. Or maybe it's…" He trailed off, painfully aware of how pitiful he sounded. Simon, on the other hand, didn't seem to notice.

"Right again," he said. "Newsight kids. And Senators' kids, too. All because of Fatrem's initiative some 10 years ago that brought them here. Why do you think he would want all of these important people in a single Seclusion?"

Vincent ventured a guess he was almost certain would be countered. "To protect them?"

Simon snorted. "Protection has nothing to do with it," he said. "It's all about leverage. Fatrem knew the Senate would never go for his bill. Whatever he's asking for in return for stopping the Order must not be worth it. After all, the Senators don't *really* care about stopping the attacks. All they care about is—"

"My father cares," Vincent cut in. He wouldn't have been so sure before saying it, but after the words left his lips, he knew them to be true.

"Maybe he does," said Simon. "But don't be ignorant. The majority of others in the Senate are only there for one reason: their paycheck." When Vincent didn't argue, Simon continued. "Fatrem knew if he wanted to get anything passed to 'fight the Order', the Senators would have to feel the Order for themselves." As the transport began to turn, twisting along the path around the Center, Simon flicked his gaze toward the window. Confused, Vincent looked out after him. He saw the Capitol where his father worked, the Newsight campus, and the patch of ground where the school should have been – that's what Simon was looking at. Vincent thought back to the hallway when he had run into Jessica. He had seen Brian there, too. Just moments before the attack, the other boy, the son of a Newsight executive, had known to leave

What Simon was implying came to Vincent in a rush.

"You think Fatrem let the Order's attack through," said Vincent. "You think he let the Senators' kids be killed just to get his bill passed." The words tasted filthy coming out of his mouth, forbidden. But to Simon, whose lips had sprawled into a broad, satisfied grin, they were as sweet as honey.

"It's looking less like a theory than a fact," said Simon. "But I don't suppose your father shares the same opinion."

The transport rolled to a stop – they had reached Vincent's dome. Simon turned to it and Vincent followed his gaze. Both of their eyes came to a rest on the front door, behind which, somewhere inside, was Vincent's father.

"He hasn't said anything about all that," said Vincent, turning back to Simon, "but he has said he doesn't think the bill will pass. The Senate is fighting against it. He says both parties are cooperating now more than ever."

"Cooperating?" Simon repeated the word, his eyebrows raised, his lips curled at the corners. "That's not a good sign. Cooperation leads to collusion, and collusion to conspiracy. At the end of it there won't be two parties at all. No government at all. Whoever controls the data controls everything. And a man named Alduss Fatrem controls quite a lot already." Simon paused here. His tone was no longer so gloating, his grin no longer so wide. "So I hope you're right, Vincent," he said. "I hope your father is right. Because if not, if the bill is passed…" he looked once again at the front door of Vincent's dome, "…we'll all be just another set of eyes for Newsight."

CHAPTER 4 – THE GRAY

The palm-sized screen in front of Vincent's right eye blinked green, and the door slid open. He stepped inside without looking over his shoulder. He felt as if Simon's words had weaved around him a fragile but constricting blanket, one whose threads were undeniable while in their grasp but easily broken when outside of it. Everything Simon had said had to be rubbish. It had to. Only now that he was outside of the man's two wheeled pod did Vincent realize how ludicrous it all sounded. Simon's words had carried the weight of treason with none of its merit. Fatrem was well-respected by everyone. Loved, even, by some. That he would betray his own people, his own admirers, was beyond the realm of reason.

Vincent collected himself and made sure the door had locked behind him. He was in the foyer, a small nook blocked from the rest of the Main and oftentimes the most private place in the dome. Now, though, he wanted privacy far less than he wanted sleep. He stepped through the second door and into the Main. The kitchen and dining area were empty, but there were voices coming from the master bedroom. Suddenly realizing he hadn't paged his parents ahead of time – they loathed surprises – Vincent flicked his eyes up and to the left. He started composing his mother a message, but as the words started to populate his Lenses, he began to hear the voices more clearly, as well as something in addition to them. It was a strange sound, one he had never heard before, and one he already felt certain he didn't want to hear again. Mixed in with the voices were deep, pained sounding sobs. Vincent stopped composing his message. Instead, he crossed the Main toward his parents' bedroom, his every step excruciatingly amplified by the unforgiving tile he contacted. After only a few of these betraying noises, he slipped off his shoes – a cardinal sin in the dome – and resumed his progress, silently this time. He felt himself spied upon by the walls around him as he grew closer, disapproved by the dome itself for sneaking as he was. But he kept going. Something about the sobs coming from the bedroom told him that the normal rules didn't apply to this particular moment.

He reached the bedroom door which, uncharacteristically, had been left ajar, held there by Father's briefcase which had fallen into its path. With breaths as soft and shallow as his lungs would allow, Vincent leaned in close and placed his ear to the gap.

"It's ok, Father." Vincent's mother was almost whispering. Her voice was calm. "It was the heat of the moment. You didn't know if he had made it."

"No. No." It was Father, though his voice was nearly unrecognizable. It carried none of its usual collected strength. It was shaking and weak, defeated. "I *did* know," he said. "And I wanted to vote against it, I did. I just…I was so angry."

Then the sound started again, the sobs. They were coming from Father. That's the way it seemed, at least, but Vincent could hardly believe it. He had never heard his father cry, nor, he was convinced, had anyone. It was a thing that didn't happen, that was never *meant* to happen. But still, the sobs continued.

Vincent peeked his head around the edge of the door and looked inside. He had never seen his parents' bedroom before, but he felt like he already had. It was plain, devoid of decoration but for the bed in the room's center, and stark white all the way from the curved ceiling overhead to the spotless tile below. Father was sitting on the foot of the bed, still in his collared, snow-colored uniform from the Senate, and Mother was sitting next to him, her right arm draped, a bit awkwardly, around his shoulders.

"Either way you have nothing to worry about," said Mother. "I'm sure it's for the best."

Father shook his head, puckering his lips like a small boy pouting, and lifting his gaze slightly so Vincent could see the red, puffy lumps under his eyes.

"It's not," he said. "It's too much." He clenched his teeth together. "We gave them everything. On a platter we just handed it over."

"I'm sure it will be ok," said Mother. Father interspersed her words with a series of "no"s and head shakes, but she kept on.

"It's Newsight, after all," she said. "Whatever you gave them, they won't misuse it. We're safe, Father. We can trust them."

"You're not getting it, Sarah."

Mother recoiled from him, her mouth agape, perhaps from hearing her own name. Vincent had no memory of it being spoken aloud. Nor, really, of the name at all.

"We can't trust them," Father continued. He had lifted his head from his hands, and now Vincent could see him clearly. His face was twisted into an expression Vincent was only slightly more familiar with than the sobs. It bore none of its usual composure, and it just failed to mask the fear underneath. Father's eyes, too, betrayed him, and not only that, they were too red to have been irritated just by the crying. Father had tried to take out his Lenses.

"I've been feeling different," said Father. "Since the upgrade. I've…" He held his palms out in front of his knees, facing upward. He stared down at them, wearing a look of disgust. "I've been feeling things. When we learned of the attack, I was so angry I could barely see straight." He looked back up at Mother. "It's the Lenses. I don't know how but it is. I tried to take them out…but they wouldn't move. I can feel them…" He bit back a sob with a grimace that made Vincent want to look away. "I can feel them strangling me." He shook his head, his lips puckered, on the verge of tears. "I've made a mistake, Sarah."

Mother didn't pull away this time. For Father, that seemed only to make things worse. He dropped his head once again, staring down at his palms. "I let us down," he said. "I'm sorry."

Mother's arm no longer looked so stiff as she rubbed her hand side to side in between Father's shoulder blades.

"We'll get through it," she said. Her voice had started to shake as well. "Together. Ok?"

Father nodded, barely, as he looked up at her, but the nodding stopped just as quickly as it had begun. He wasn't looking at Mother any longer, but at the door, where Vincent had been just too slow to pull back his head.

"Vincent."

This was the voice of Father's Vincent knew: stern and composed, without the wild, breaking fluctuations in pitch.

Vincent slid open the door and stepped inside. Father had stood up, seeming taller than usual.

"You need to go to bed." Father pointed out the door. "Now."

Vincent stayed where he was. He had never disobeyed a direct command of Father's like that before, but now his feet felt rooted to the tile. He looked from his father to his mother and back again, still trying to decide whether or not what he had just seen could be real.

"I said," pressed Father, his voice near a growl. "Now." He turned away, rubbing a hand over his face, looking exhausted. "I'll deal with you in the morning."

Vincent stayed where he was a moment longer. He remained until he caught his father's eye.

"Vincent," started Father, "I said to—"

"It's not your fault," said Vincent. It was an effort to keep his voice level. "You didn't let us down."

They were still for multiple seconds, Father's eyes fierce and Vincent's steady. And then Father was starting toward him, his posture large, powerful. Before Vincent could run, Father was on him, arms wrapping him tight, holding him there. Vincent tried to break free but stopped when he felt his shoulder growing hot and damp where Father's head was. Slowly realizing what was happening, Vincent raised his arms as well, and circled them around his father's back. They stood like that for several seconds, embracing for the first time in Vincent knew not how long. When they broke apart, Vincent looked up at his father, whose jaw was flexed, biting his tongue. Father gave him one last glance, then turned away. Vincent turned to his Mother next. She nodded at him, looking somehow stronger than usual, then turned as well.

In a daze, Vincent stepped back. He nudged his father's stray briefcase out of the doorway, and the door slid shut. He was back in the Main, and though it was empty save for him, he no longer felt quite so alone.

******

Vincent sat straight up in his bed when he heard the crash. It was the kind of sound that cleared the fatigue from one's eyes in an instant, even out of a dead sleep. It had come from the Main, from the foyer maybe. But as the silence endured, sitting in the air, its weight pressing down on Vincent from above, it felt impossible that such a sound could ever have disturbed him. He had almost convinced himself to lay back down when the crash sounded a second time. Only this time it didn't fade into silence. There was a sharper, fracturing pound, and then several smaller ones – footsteps, then shouting. Vincent had barely jumped from his bed when his door burst inward and two men in uniform rushed in after it. Vincent scrambled toward his bathroom, but his legs were weak with sleep, and the nearest man was on him in a blink. Vincent flailed his limbs in vain as he tried to break free, and then the second man was on him too. In a flash, both of Vincent's arms were pinned behind his back, forcing him to lean forward at the waist to keep his shoulders from popping out of socket. He continued to writhe against the men as they dragged him toward his busted door, but resistance was

36

pointless. The men had vice-like grips and seemed undisturbed by even Vincent's most violent struggles. They hauled him into the Main easily. Father and Mother were already there, struggling against their own escorts of uniformed, rough looking men. And now, in the light, Vincent could see the men clearly. They wore tight sleeves and collars up the neck like officers of the Guard, but they were clothed not in the normal bleach white, but in a dark, ashen gray. The only trace of white was stitched on their collars: the familiar outline of an eye typically reserved for the darkness of the simulations.

"Don't touch my son!" Father shouted when he saw Vincent being dragged into the room. "Don't you dare touch him!"

Father began to thrash against his captors. There were three men holding him, but they could hardly keep control. Wordlessly, the man who had first subdued Vincent crossed over to lend a hand. As Father's escort turned from three to four, Father grew still and the Main grew silent. But the calm seemed to have had little to do with the additional guard. Father had gone still not when he had been met with the extra pair of hands, but when his eyes had fallen in the direction of the foyer door. The door was out of Vincent's line of sight, but he could hear the footsteps crossing through it just the same, slow, deliberate, and ushering in with them a chill that seemed to slither down Vincent's spine.

"Hello, Mr. Smith." It was a man's voice, but it struck a pitch with each syllable that seemed to hover somewhere outside the normal masculine range.

"I have desired your audience for some time now," the voice continued – Vincent still could not see the man. "What a thrill it is to finally have it."

"Let my family go," said Father. It seemed to require of him a great effort to stay calm. "They did nothing."

More footsteps. The man had stepped closer to Father, and Vincent caught a glance of him for the first time. He was just large enough not to be considered frail, the skin of his face was pulled tightly around narrow cheek bones, and his features were sharp, his eyes calculating.

"You are right," the man said. "But thanks to you, I have plenty of data that says they have."

Father strained against his captors, spurred on by the man's taunting tone. His eyes were murderous, bloodshot, but the man merely turned away in response, his face now contorted with a smug grin.

"No," said Father, resuming his struggle. "No!" he shouted after the man, and the veins in his neck protruded as he strained against the men holding him. One of the men struck out with a club and made contact with Father's jaw.

"Dad!" Vincent cried out and tried to twist free of his captor's grip. The man tightened his hold easily. Vincent kicked out at him, making contact with the man's shin, but was rewarded only with a strike to the stomach by the man's fist. He hunched over at the waist even more drastically, his breath stolen.

Father saw the exchange, and something in him seemed to snap. "Don't you touch him!" he shouted through blood speckled lips at the man who had dealt the blow. "Let him go!" His struggle resumed with a renewed vigor this time as the men began to drag him to the door. With thrashing limbs he struck out in all directions, mostly striking nothing but air but occasionally making contact with flesh. The men continued to drag him in spite of it all, but they were losing control. Father was a man possessed by strength not his own, by mind, too, not his, but of an animal cornered and trapped. He managed to free an arm and ripped a club from the nearest guard's hand. He started batting with it madly, at arms, skulls, anything he could reach. One of the men holding Mother relinquished his hold and joined the others in the fray. But he had better fixed his hold on the woman he had just left. Mother kicked backward at her remaining captor so the heel of her foot made contact with the man's groin. The man buckled, hunched and holding himself. Mother turned, facing the man holding Vincent now, and lunged forward, lashing out with uncoordinated but vicious blows. Vincent twisted and writhed in the man's grip. The man pulled a hand from him to fend off Mother – Vincent wrenched downward with the arm that was still subdued – and he was free. He turned around to help.

"Go, Vincent!" Mother shouted at him and pushed him back just before the man grabbed her wrists. "Go!"

Vincent stood where he was, frozen to the spot, then looked to his father whose mouth seemed barely above the surface in a sea of gray uniforms.

"Go, son!" he shouted as he continued to struggle. And over the racket, Vincent heard the man Mother had kicked approaching in an uneven gate behind him. "Go!"

Vincent twisted around just in time to dodge the man's outstretched arms. He started for the kitchen, his eyes trained on the back door. He sprinted toward it, driven faster by the sound of the man's footsteps close behind. He felt a rush of cold air on his face when he threw the door open, and he kept running. By the time he reached the next ring of domes, his heart was pounding in his chest nearly as fast as his feet against the pavement. He chanced a look over his shoulder, then began to slow – the man had given up chase. Shrinking into the shadow cast by the dome at his back, he leaned up against the wall to catch his breath. His eyes were fixed on the back door of the dome he had just left, his dome, where his parents had surely been overwhelmed, and where their son had left them to their fate.

If only to numb himself of the shame quickly rising in his chest, Vincent felt the urge to take off running once again. He may have, too, had his Lenses not flashed white with the small message at their bottom rim.

Are you awake?

It was from Jessica. Vincent's urge to run began to falter. He started composing a message back, eyes fumbling over the letters as he went, but he only got halfway through.

They took my dad.

He read the message twice, hoping in vain its letters would rearrange themselves. If he had started running again, Jessica's dome would have been his destination. Now, it seemed, that was out of the question.

Vincent took a deep breath. He composed a message back.

Meet me in the second ring. East.

A feeling of dread planted itself low in his stomach as soon as he pressed send. After all, after everything he had learned, it was foolish to use the Lenses to communicate. It would have been decidedly more foolish, however, to let Jessica wander into a ransacked dome, the perimeter of which would surely be monitored.

Vincent took off at a jog through the relative darkness between the domes of the fourth and fifth rings, his eyes combing the depths of every shadow he passed. The gleaming white uniforms of the Guard would have been easy to spot. The smoke-colored ones of Newsight, however, would blend much more seamlessly into the night.

******

Vincent craned his neck around the edge of the dome behind which he was hiding. He stared down the path that cut through the second ring, half expecting an army of gray clad men to emerge from the shadows.

"Vincent!"

He spun around, his muscles tensed to run, but relaxed when he saw Jessica approaching around the dome next to him, opposite the path he had been watching.

"I thought you would come from the other direction," he said when she had joined him.

"I cut through the Center," she said offhandedly. Then, when she saw Vincent's surprise: "I didn't want to be predictable. And I made it here, didn't I?"

Vincent said nothing back. Making it, and making it without being detected were two very different scenarios, the difference between which would become evident only when it was too late.

"Are you ok?" Vincent asked.

"I'm fine," she said back.

Vincent didn't contradict her, though he could see, even in the dark, the slight shaking of her hands.

"When did they come?" he asked.

"A few hours after I went to bed," said Jessica. "My dad must have been right before yours."

She seemed to know what had happened without having to ask.

"Did he tell you about the bill?" asked Vincent. "Before he was taken?"

Jessica nodded. "He's *been* telling me," she said. "And now it's too late to do anything about it."

"It's not too late!" said Vincent. "People won't let this happen."

"People want blood, Vincent. The Order's blood. And Fatrem can tell them exactly where to find it. He can implicate whoever he wants."

Vincent shook his head. "But people will find out," he said. "People will try to stop him."

"Who will?"

Vincent frowned, confused at first, but as he let his eyes wander down the ring, scanning the unlit, peaceful domes that lined its either side, he saw what she meant: nowhere was there even the slightest sign of movement.

"It's the whole reason for the bill, Vincent," said Jessica. "If Fatrem had taken things by force, people would have resisted. This way, he's a hero. He'll take down the Order one by one. But the Order is whoever he says it is. Tomorrow there will be a press release saying our dads were part of it. And then leaders of the Guard will be found guilty. Then politicians. Then the whole Senate."

Vincent felt the reality sink in him like quicksand. "Then there's no one left to stand in the way."

Jessica looked down, silent. Vincent turned back to the empty path of the second ring. He found himself fixed with a mad desire to run from dome to dome, pounding on doors and telling people the truth, but he knew it wouldn't do any good.

Vincent turned his gaze a bit closer, on the first ring, where the Newsight families lived: the gentry, the unopposing of a revolution that would sit them atop the new throne. But, Vincent thought, perhaps there was opposition after all.

"I know where we need to go," he said.

Jessica turned to him. She too had been looking at the Center. "Where?"

"I..." Vincent trailed off. He didn't realize how ludicrous his theory would sound until it started to leave his mouth. But it was all he had to go on. It was their only hope. "I think I know someone who's fighting against Newsight."

"Really?" said Jessica, suddenly with a spark of hope. "Who?"

Vincent paused again. He thought back to the first sim about the Order, the one from which he had completely tuned out. In his survey of the room, except for Jessica, there had been only one other who had not been fully engaged. Vincent remembered the way Brian had caught his eye. The other boy had worn a grin, ever so faint a grin before his face had gone blank.

"Brian," said Vincent. Jessica deflated.

"Vincent his mom is a Department Head," she said. "Brian is the last person that would help."

"Your dad works for Newsight doesn't he?" countered Vincent. "And he knew the truth. He wanted to fight, and so do you. Why does Brian's family have to be any different? His parents could be–"

"*Parent*," said Jessica. "His dad isn't around. It's just his mom."

She took a breath to say something else, then hesitated, the pocket of air catching in her throat, held there by words she hadn't quite let go. "She was there when they took my dad, Vincent." It came out in a rush, and she panted slightly after she said it. She sank, too. She seemed to think the argument had been decided. Vincent wasn't so sure.

"You've met her?" he asked.

Jessica nodded. "When my mom was her boss." She paused, looking down, her cheeks sucked into her mouth. After a few seconds, she shook her head. "I just don't think it makes sense, Vincent. Brian's mom has almost as much to gain from this as Fatrem."

"But Fatrem will get rid of anyone who poses a threat!" said Vincent. He had to force himself to keep his voice near a whisper. His mind was racing. "She'll know that." Then he was thinking back to the simulation: to the day of the attack, when he had dreamed of the small brown house and the towers beyond. The words started to tumble from his lips now, as wildly assumed truths he somehow felt certain he could trust. "Besides," he continued, "Brian said something to me the day of the attack, when I woke up in class. He said to be careful, that dreams are hard to hide. Maybe he was talking about hiding from Newsight. Maybe he knew about Fatrem's plan." He looked at Jessica, hating the thin film of glass that covered her dark brown eyes beneath. "Maybe his mom told him about the attack," he said. "That could be why he was leaving – she must have figured out Fatrem's plan."

"Or maybe she helped come up with it," said Jessica.

The air went still between them. Jessica's expression was lined with doubt.

"Look," began Vincent, "I don't know why, but I'm sure of this. Brian can help."

Jessica looked away, shaking her head. She bit down on the insides of her cheeks. Vincent lowered his voice.

"I trusted you during the attack," he said. "Now I need you to trust me back."

She held his gaze for several seconds, then cast a glance behind the dome next to them. She breathed out, heavily. "Ok," she said. "I believe you."

Vincent released a breath of his own. In spite of everything, he allowed himself a small measure of relief.

"When should we go?" asked Jessica.

"Tonight." Vincent didn't hesitate. "We can't wait until the morning. Do you know where he lives?"

Jessica nodded. "I've seen him after school," she said. She turned to the Center. "They live in the first ring."

CHAPTER 5 – THE DOME OFF OCEAN

The stacked, ornate domes of the first ring were looming closer. They stood a good deal higher than their counterparts of the outer rings, higher, even, than those of the second and third. They concealed the Center behind them almost completely. Their plots, on which Vincent's dome could have fit three or four times over, were occupied so completely with sprawling expansions that the entire ring blended together at the sides, forming a single, impenetrable unit. As Vincent and Jessica grew closer to it, Vincent found himself stricken with the impression of having reached the outer wall of some giant cage.

"That's it," said Jessica. She came to a stop when she said it. Vincent stopped as well. They were in the narrow pass between the domes of the first and second rings, just a few plots off the main path.

"You're sure?" asked Vincent. He followed Jessica's gaze up toward the dome just ahead, the one closest to Ocean. It was a full four or five of Vincent's dome. The gleaming white hemispheres that formed it were stacked three high, with almost a dozen smaller offshoots. The additions hung out over the main stack as if hovering, casting so great a number of shadows as to shade a good majority of the dome's front face.

"Yes," said Jessica. "It's his."

Vincent drew a deep breath – as deep as he could manage, at least. His lungs had grown tight.

"How do you think we should get in?" he asked.

Jessica shrugged. "How else? We'll have to go through the front."

Vincent raised his brow. "Are you serious? Shouldn't we try to sneak in or something?"

"Don't be ridiculous," said Jessica. "We wouldn't be able to break into a dome in the sixth ring let alone the first."

Vincent looked again to the intricately stacked dome ahead. There were no windows, of course. Except perhaps on the far side facing the Center, but windows there would be far too high to access. There would likely be a back door, too, but if it was like Vincent's, there would be no method of opening it from the outside. Its surface would be undetectable, flush with the walls of the dome around it.

"We're already here," said Jessica. "We have to try. My dad wouldn't want us to just wait around. And neither would your parents."

As if the scene from earlier that night were replaying across his Lenses, Vincent saw his father's limbs flailing in a sea of gray, his mother's blood speckled lips parted in a soundless scream…

He blinked, hard, then again several times after. The images faded, but they didn't quite disappear.

He turned his gaze to the front door of Brian's dome. The greater portion of it was shaded by the overhang of the second story some three meters above. The palm sized screen on its surface was visible even from across the path. Vincent forced himself to focus on the small light there.

"Ok," he said, breathing in. "I'm ready when you are."

Jessica's posture grew straight. Her eyes were trained on the door the same as Vincent's. She nodded.

No longer shrinking from the lights overhead, they crossed the path together. In that moment, everything seemed almost natural. But just for that moment. In the next, they were standing under the flat overhang of the second story dome, completely still at the step of the front door.

"Look," said Jessica. Vincent followed her finger toward the palm sized panel on the door's surface. The light there was bright orange. "He must have been awake."

Vincent grew rigid, his spine straightening of its own accord the way it always did when he realized he was being watched. The orange light was to indicate the presence of the intercom. Brian could see them through the screen's front camera.

"What are you doing here?"

The voice was clear, ungarbled by the speaker that transmitted it, but it didn't sound as confident as usual. It wavered on certain syllables, and it shook in a way Vincent hadn't heard before.

"We want to talk to you." It was Jessica who answered. "Can you let us in?"

There was silence on the other end for a few seconds.

"You shouldn't be here," said Brian. He had forced some of the old boldness back into his voice. "The Seclusion is on lockdown. You need to go back to your domes."

"I think you know we can't do that," said Vincent, and from the silence he was met with, he knew he had been right.

"I don't know what you're talking about," fumbled Brian. "But you need to go back. You should be asleep."

"So should you," said Vincent.

The intercom went silent once again, for longer this time. Vincent was holding his breath. He had to resist the temptation to turn his head on a swivel to scan the shadows for gray uniforms. He kept his attention straight forward, his eyes locked, pointlessly, on the blank screen of the intercom, his ears perked for the slightest rustle of movement.

The front door slid open.

Vincent turned to the opening, frowning. The lower section of his stomach started to churn. He was almost disappointed. His nerves would have been much calmer had Newsight's charcoal gray uniforms streamed from the shadows. At least then he would have known what to expect. For the moment, however, that luxury had been withheld.

"Maybe you were right," whispered Jessica. The slight trembling of her lower lip betrayed a quite different sentiment.

Still frowning, Vincent turned back to the palm-sized screen to their right. The orange light had gone dark. Brian was no longer watching them.

"I guess we'll see," said Vincent. "Come on." He took the lead and stepped inside. To his surprise, the lights flicked on overhead.

If Jessica's dome was on one end of the spectrum, Brian's was on the end exactly opposite. The air inside the dome tasted so strongly of nothing that it made Vincent want to gag. The Main was dutifully barren but for two empty white chairs on either side of the kitchen table, the surface of which looked impossible to rest one's elbows on without slipping. Vincent felt as if he had just been dropped inside a giant, whited-out beaker in a private laboratory. Everything was eerily precise.

There was a soft thud from somewhere above. Vincent tensed, his mind once again filled with images of men in gray jumpsuits. Jessica shifted a touch closer to him as they looked up. The ceiling, instead of the dome's usual curve, was flat, and the pure white had been replaced by something not quite that, something almost see-through, opaque. Vincent could see a shadow; the thuds were footsteps of someone a story above. The steps grew progressively softer as the shadow drew farther away from them, deeper into the dome toward the far side, then went quiet altogether. Vincent cast Jessica a look, but she seemed as puzzled as he was. Neither of them spoke, waiting instead for the sound of the footsteps.

"This isn't a good idea."

Vincent and Jessica spun around in the same motion. Brian had just emerged through a door in the far wall of the dome.

"The raids on the Senators won't last much longer."

He was wearing white trousers, without suspenders, and a white shirt not so tight as the ones required at school. He may have looked a good deal younger than usual, as a child freshly crawled from his bed, but something about his expression prevented it.

"We didn't have anywhere else to go," said Vincent.

"That doesn't mean you should have come here," Brian shot back.

Vincent didn't make a move to leave. Nor did Jessica.

"We know what's going on with Newsight," said Jessica. "We know everything."

Vincent let out a breath that had been caught somewhere in his throat. Any pretense they had entered with was now gone.

"All the more reason to have let yourselves be taken," said Brian. He had still yet to venture more than a few steps from the door he had just emerged through. He wasn't poised to run, but he was far from relaxed.

"I don't think you believe that," said Vincent.

Even from a distance, Vincent could see Brian's eyebrows twitch upward. "And why is that?"

"What you said," answered Vincent. "After my dream. And the way you looked at me in the simulation." He scanned Brian's face for any betraying sign of recognition. The boy was unreadable. "You know something," Vincent continued. "About Newsight. But we know things too. We know about the bill and the new Lenses and–"

"Stop."

Vincent caught his words mid-sentence and went quiet. Now was the time, he thought. It had been as good as a confession. The men in gray uniforms would be appear at any second.

"Both of you?" asked Brian. They nodded. Brian stayed still, his eyes unblinking, appraising them, then, slowly, he nodded as well. He left the safety of the doorframe and started toward the kitchen table, his footsteps muffled now that they didn't fall on the glass floor above. "I expected Vincent," he said, "But you..." he inspected Jessica, "...I never would have thought, what with your dad. My mom always says how much he loves Newsight."

Jessica snorted under her breath. "He's a good actor."

Brian shrugged. "Apparently not good enough."

Jessica took a step forward, but Vincent held her back. Brian held up his hands as he walked. "Sorry," he said. "It's just habit. We're all in character, after all."

Jessica frowned at this, but Brian didn't explain. He merely kept walking, past the duo of chairs next to the dining table and into the kitchen. He started rummaging around in one of the kitchen cabinets. Its contents were hidden from view. "Sit," he said, motioning to the chairs.

Vincent stayed where he was, braced, still prepared to keep Jessica from launching herself forward.

"Well come on," said Brian, as he poked his head out from behind the cabinet. "If I'm going to risk this for you, the least you can do is show some manners."

"Risk what?" said Vincent. He didn't bother curbing the edge of suspicion in his voice. He had been holding his breath hoping for a scene like this, but now he had it, he wasn't so sure he wanted to play along.

"Everything," said Brian. He emerged from behind the cabinet motioning to the room at large. His fingers were curled around the rims of three small cups. "If my mom happens to bring someone back for a meeting after the raids, they'll turn you in."

"How do we know you haven't already done that?" said Jessica. "Or your mom. My dad always says how under Fatrem's thumb she is."

Brian grinned at this. It was an expression not so unlike the one of his Vincent had seen in the classroom, fleeting, and nearly undecipherable for someone not expecting it.

"Your dad isn't the only one who can act," said Brian.

Jessica shook her head. "That isn't enough."

"Are you really in the position to ask for anything more?"

Jessica opened her mouth to counter him, but she said nothing. Vincent answered for her.

"Just tell us what you know," he said. "Or turn us in. It doesn't make any difference to us."

Brian let his lips curl upward in another grin. They stayed that way for a few seconds this time. "Sit." He motioned to the chairs once again, then turned back toward the kitchen. Reluctantly, but knowing there was nothing else to do, Vincent started for the table. Jessica followed more slowly behind him.

"You should be more careful," said Brian. He was back in the kitchen, filling the first of the three cups under the sink faucet. "If you had walked in any other dome saying what you just said, you would have signed your own death warrants."

"Have we not already?" asked Vincent. He lowered himself into the chair closest to the kitchen as he spoke. Jessica followed suit in the chair closest to the door.

"Maybe you already have somewhere else," said Brian as he started filling the second cup. "But not here. Our dome is protected. The whole management sector of the first ring is. No Lenses in this part of the ring can be connected to the normal network. My mom lobbied for it herself, 'to protect sensitive management conversations'." He flourished the empty cup in the air as he said the last part. "Lucky for you," he continued, lowering the final cup under the faucet, "it protects more than just conversations about management." He shot them what he may have supposed to be a comforting grin, then tilted his head to the left to watch the water level rise in the final cup. Vincent observed him carefully. He seemed relaxed now, unlike he had upon their initial entry. Vincent felt completely opposite. When they had entered the dome, there had been two scenarios: be caught or be saved. Now, the scenarios remained, but Vincent had yet to decipher which one they were in.

Brian crossed over to them and sat the two cups balanced in his right hand in the middle of the table. He kept the third cup for himself. "You're safe here," he said, "but only for a while. They'll have seen you come."

"So they already know," said Vincent. "They *have* been watching. They heard us outside when we were talking about it all." Vincent was almost relieved as the words left his mouth. Their certainty was seductive, but short-lived.

"Maybe," said Brian. The churning in Vincent's stomach resumed. "But the system still has bugs. They won't catch everything at first. Especially during the raids. And it's not like you have to worry about making things worse for yourselves. Running from them already did that." Brian lifted his cup to his lips and took a drink. Vincent and Jessica left theirs untouched.

"So there's a chance we can make it out of this?" asked Vincent. "That we can save our parents?"

"Don't get ahead of yourself," said Brian. "If you've somehow gotten the idea in your head that the Order is some ultra-powerful–"

"The Order?" interrupted Jessica. "What are you talking about?"

Brian stopped, frowning. He looked confused for the first time. "I'm talking about what you asked me to," he said, annoyed.

"We didn't come to talk about the Order," said Vincent. "We're here because we thought you might be a part of some sort of movement against Newsight."

Brian's grin returned. It looked uglier now, for some reason. "That's my fault," he said. "I thought you had worked it all out." He sat his water back on the counter behind him. "The Order is more than just the catalyst Fatrem needed to pass his bill. It's the reason he wanted it passed. Part of it, anyway."

"You're saying the Order still exists?" asked Jessica. "They're still protesting?"

"They're doing more than that," said Brian, "They're resisting. The 'attacks' the Senate has been talking about have all been on Newsight factories. The attacks authorized by the true Order, at least. The ones on civilians, I'm guessing you already know about."

Vincent and Jessica said nothing.

"My mom started telling me about it all when I first started school," said Brian. "Around the time John left."

"John?" said Vincent.

"My brother," said Brian. "He ran off years ago. My mom says he's helping her, but I'm not sure he's even alive."

Jessica squinted, as if concentrating. "I remember John," she said. "Barely, from the Newsight retreats when we were little." She paused, frowning. "What would he be helping your mom with?"

"Something with the Order," said Brian "My mom needs all the help she can get."

"Your mom is in the Order?" joined Vincent.

"She's been on the inside for years," said Brian. "Without her, the Order would stand even less of a chance than we already do."

Jessica raised an eyebrow. "We?" Brian merely stared back. Jessica didn't lower her gaze.

"But the Order has to stand *some* chance right?" said Vincent, breaking the silence. "The attacks must be doing *something*."

Brian held Jessica's gaze a second longer before turning to Vincent. "You're getting ahead of yourself again," he said. "I don't think you understand what Newsight is capable of."

Vincent didn't protest. He had long since given up the pretense of knowing anything for certain.

"Your only sample is what you've seen in the Seclusion," continued Brian. "You have no idea what's going on outside of it, or what *it* even is."

"And you do?" challenged Jessica.

Brian shrugged in his indifferent, secretive way. "I've seen it for myself," he said. "In THE SIM."

"The sim?" repeated Jessica. Her words didn't have the same emphasis. "I don't remember any of our simulations from class having—"

"Not from class," snapped Brian. "From the Order. From Goodwin."

"Goodwin?" said Vincent.

"The leader of the Order," said Brian. "He was one of the first Newsight protestors. He even gouged out his eyes so they could never make him wear Lenses." There was a far off, worshipful look in Brian's eyes as he spoke. "Goodwin made THE SIM himself," he continued. "It's everything, all of Newsight's secrets. It's a hard sim, so it's not stored on the Newsight network. It took him years to..." Brian trailed off. His eyes had drawn close and his head had turned to the side. He was watching something, something in his Lenses. After a few seconds of silence, he looked up.

"My mom is outside," he said. His voice had dropped to a whisper. "There's someone with her."

CHAPTER 6 – THE OFFICE

"What do we do?" asked Jessica. She had grown tense in her seat. She was still as she faced Brian, but she seemed ready to sprint for the door.

Brian stayed where he was, his eyes on the cup in his hand, his cool, presiding demeanor on the verge of panic.

"Brian," said Vincent – he thought he could hear voices outside.

"I'm thinking."

Brian didn't look at him as he said it. He was looking across the Main at the front door, sporadically drawing his eyes close together to focus on his Lenses.

There were definitely voices now.

"Brian," prompted Vincent. "What do we do?"

Brian looked up at them, then at the door across the room. "Hide," he said. He sat his cup down on the counter and started for the stairs. "Hurry!"

"The cups," said Jessica, as she stood. "What should we–"

"Bring them!" hissed Brian.

Jessica snatched up her cup and Vincent did the same. They started after Brian in unison, jogging with lightened footsteps toward the stairs.

"In," said Brian, when they were at the door. "They're almost–"

To their right, there was a soft, familiar beep as the retinal scanner outside prepared to unlock.

"Upstairs!" Brian slammed a palm against the wall next to the door, and the door slid to the side. "Third story."

Behind them, the locks of the main door clicked free. Brian grabbed Jessica by the wrist and pulled her toward the stairs. Vincent lunged after her. The main door slid open behind them–

The dome went black. Vincent froze, held immobile by the darkness. He felt a hand on his arm.

"Go."

It was Brian. Guided by the boy's touch, Vincent found his way through the opening. He nearly tripped over the first stair.

There was a sliding sound behind him – like the seal being closed on a jet of air – then the darkness was lifted. Jessica was standing there with him, her eyes wide, her pupils dilated.

"Brian?"

The voice was muffled – it was coming from the other side of the door.

"What did you just do?"

"Sorry," said Brian. By the relatively clear sound of his voice, he must have been standing just outside. "I just meant to close the door behind me. I didn't mean to get the lights as well."

The other speaker stayed silent for a beat. "Clumsy of you," it said after a pause. Vincent could hear the voice better now. It sounded like a woman's.

"Sorry, Mother," said Brian.

Vincent and Jessica exchanged a look. Neither of them started up the stairs.

"Don't be silly," said Brian's mother. "I don't blame you for trying to hide from Marcus. Everyone hides from him."

The man named Marcus apparently chose to ignore the jibe. "Good to see you again, Brian," he said.

The voice was muffled, but Vincent knew he had heard it before.

"It's quite late, Brian." It was Brian's mother again. "Why aren't you in bed?"

"Couldn't sleep," Brian returned without hesitation. "I...I was thinking about today."

They could hear the sound of Brian's mother clicking her tongue sympathetically. Vincent imagined her head tilting to the side, affectionate. For some reason, though, the image seemed out of place.

"Of course you were," she said. "Why don't you go upstairs and get back in bed. I'll be up there in a little while. Marcus and I have some important things to talk about."

There was a pause, perhaps just long enough for Brian to nod, then more footsteps – Brian was starting for the stairwell door.

Up.

The word appeared on the bottom rim of Vincent's Lenses. And by the way Jessica's eyes darted downward toward the bridge of her nose, it had appeared on hers too.

"We need to move," hissed Vincent. He grabbed Jessica by the hand and started to climb. They had to get out of sight before Brian opened the door. Their legs would remain in view of the Main for several more seconds.

"Mother?"

Brian's voice was right outside; his hand must be hovering over the button.

"Goodnight," he said.

The soft but frantic thuds of Vincent and Jessica's footsteps muffled the reply. The door slid open behind them just as they reached the top of the flight. When Brian stepped through and the door closed after him, he was composed again.

"I thought you'd be eavesdropping," he whispered, seeing the quickened rise and fall of Vincent's shoulders. "They almost saw you."

"Why would it matter?" said Jessica. "I thought you said your mother was part of the Order."

"I already told you," said Brian. "It wouldn't matter if my mom saw you, but she's not alone. You heard Marcus."

Jessica said nothing back, but Vincent could tell she was far from convinced.

"Marcus is Newsight's Head of the Privacy," continued Brian, starting to climb. "If he's here, the Privacy Officers will have finished the raids. It's safer now, but you'll still have to lie low for a while."

Vincent thought back to the men in gray jumpsuits who had stormed through their dome – Privacy Officers, Brian had called them – and to the frail man who had led them there. That same man, Vincent was almost certain, was now only a story below them, with Brian's mother.

"How long is a while?" said Jessica.

Brian shrugged his shoulders. "You'll be safe for a while," he said. He pushed past them and into the open room beyond the mouth of the staircase. It was predictably round, with a handful of doors to line its perimeter. The frosted glass they had seen from the Main served as the room's floor. Vincent took a cautious step onto it.

"Don't follow me," said Brian over his shoulder. He pointed at the glass beneath his feet. "They'll see the shadow. Anyway, you're going to the next story." He flicked a lazy hand toward the bend at Vincent and Jessica's backs where, around the corner, was another flight of stairs.

"Aren't you going to show us where to go?" asked Jessica. She leaned forward and chanced a look through the opaque flooring as she spoke.

"Then they *won't* see the shadow," said Brian. "My shadow." He came to a stop in front of a door on the far side of the room and turned to them. "And I won't be able to talk. I'm not allowed to go to bed with my Lenses turned on."

"You can turn them off?" asked Vincent, surprised.

"It's another perk." Brian grinned at them. "You're looking for the second door on the next floor." He pressed a button next to his own door and the thing slid open. "Mom takes other managers upstairs sometimes, but they never go to that room. I think it's where she hides THE SIM."

"Think?" asked Vincent. "Do you not know?"

Brian shook his head. "She re-hid it after I found it the first time," he said. "But if I had to guess, I would look there. If you're serious about all this, you'll need to watch it." He nodded to them, another indiscernible look, then the door had slid shut once again, this time with Brian on the other side.

"Vincent I don't like this." Jessica had pulled her gaze from the frosted floor just long enough to shoot Brian's closed door a furrowed look of disapproval. "I don't trust him."

Vincent joined her gaze. "I don't think I do either," he said. "But we really don't have a choice."

"Maybe we do," said Jessica. "We could always just—"

The pressurized breath sounded from down the stairs, and Vincent dodged around the corner, pulling Jessica with him. Down the flight behind them, he could hear two sets of footsteps.

"...yes I understand that." It was Brian's mother. "And I completely agree. However, the—"

Let's go! mouthed Vincent. He pulled Jessica up the second set of stairs behind them on instinct. Jessica's mouth remained open from her previous sentence as they began tiptoeing up the steps.

"I see your point," said Marcus. "But their effect has been negated. Fatrem foresaw that long ago."

Vincent stared straight down at the steps as he climbed, gingerly, next to Jessica, but his ears were focused a flight below.

"Let's hope so," said Brian's mother. "If not, none of this will have been worth the trouble."

The man grunted in response, and the pair of them started to climb. Vincent was so intent on listening for the next thread of conversation he nearly ran full-on to the door just ahead.

"Vincent!" Jessica hissed at him as she pulled him back. She reached out and pressed the button. Vincent cringed when the door slid open with its telltale pressurized breath.

"It will be worth it."

The man's voice masked the sound almost perfectly.

"There's no need to worry."

Jessica allowed herself a soft sigh of relief before stepping through the open door. Vincent followed close behind. They were standing in a hallway of sorts, only this one didn't run straight forward and back like those in the school, but at a curve, as if slithering around the outskirts of the two stories below like a constrictor.

"I still think–"

Jessica timed her pressing of the button once again.

"Hurry!" she whispered, and she took the lead this time. The floor was solid here, unlike the frosted glass of the room below. The walls on either side of them were stark white and curved at their tops so they touched together overhead like a smooth-ceilinged tunnel.

"Second door," said Jessica. She was scanning both walls as they walked, but there was scarcely a seam in either. Vincent cast a glance behind them. They were still in view of the staircase.

"There's one!" said Jessica, pointing ahead to an arch-shaped door on their left. "Come on." She tugged on Vincent's arm harder still. Vincent glanced behind them at the door to the stairs. The walls of the hallway seemed to expand in preparation for one final breath. Marcus and Brian's mother had to be getting close.

"There!"

Jessica spotted the second door and started for it, abandoning what little remained of their pretense for silence. Vincent hurried after her. He cast the stairs yet another look as Jessica pressed the second door's button. The panel slid open without hesitation, and Jessica was through. As Vincent started for it, Jessica pressed the button on the door's interior. He was just stepping inside when he saw movement out of the corner of his eye where the staircase was, and the door slid shut behind him.

Jessica leaned back against the wall next to them. Her shoulders were practically vibrating as they rose and fell from her rapid, shallow breaths.

"Can you hear them?" she whispered.

Vincent held a finger to his lips. Struggling to keep his breathing soft, he pressed his right ear against the door.

"How many total were raided?"

By the sound of Brian's mother's voice, they hadn't made it far down the hall – they were still some ways off.

"Almost a dozen," said Marcus. "Some of them were employees but most were Senators."

Vincent tensed at this. And so did Jessica – she had pressed her ear up against the door as well.

"And that's all of them?" said Brian's mother. "All you detected?"

"There are certainly more. But none who can do any damage."

There was nothing but footsteps for a while, the soft thuds of which were growing far too near for Vincent's liking.

"Here?" said Marcus.

Vincent and Jessica leaned away from the door in the same movement. They no longer had to strain to hear the man's voice – it was coming from right outside.

"No," said Brian's mother, and Vincent relaxed. "Keep going."

The footsteps resumed, this time carrying their owners farther away down the hall. When they had faded sufficiently, Vincent let out a breath.

"I thought he set us up," said Jessica.

Vincent thought of Brian's unreadable expression outside the door of his bedroom. "Maybe he still has."

Jessica bit down on the insides of her cheeks, frowning. "Do you think he was telling the truth about THE SIM?"

"Maybe," said Vincent. "Only one way to find out."

He turned around. The room was a small one, and it was unlike anything he had seen before. The walls were curved like those in the Main, but they weren't white, instead a pale crimson. The floor was different as well, wooden panels fitted tightly against their neighbors, grained and patterned in ways Vincent had never seen. Sitting atop this surface in the room's center was a desk as long as Vincent was tall, sturdy-looking and ornate, fashioned from the same rich material of the floor and carved into handle-like curves at its corners. There was a single, equally impressive chair behind it, presiding over the few items on the desk's surface with stoic authority. Behind the desk was a kind of break in the wall where the pale red gave way to ceiling-height shelves of the same bound stacks of paper Vincent had seen on Jessica's dining room table.

"They have books," said Jessica, in awe.

Vincent mouthed the word. *Books.* They had been covered only briefly in the simulations, and, if Vincent remembered correctly, they had appeared only as an accident. The sims hardly ever showed anything outside of the Seclusion.

Jessica stepped forward across the floor, unflinching in spite of the creaking that followed her, and sat her cup of water on a stack of papers. She ran her right index finger across the surface of the desk, dragging a line of dust along behind her, until she had circled to the other side. She stood next to the chair – which came nearly to her shoulders – and stared up at the rows of books.

"What do you think they're all about?" she asked.

Vincent stepped forward as well – sitting his cup down next to hers – but he said nothing. He wasn't sure how to answer the question. He didn't have the faintest idea books were *about* anything.

"I don't know," he said. "But that's not what we're here for. Do you know what a hard sim looks like?"

Begrudgingly, Jessica pulled her gaze from the bookshelf. "My dad used to have some," she said. "They're usually in little discs. They're just bits of film that lie over your Lenses." She watched as Vincent sat down in the oversized chair behind the desk. "You think it's in there?"

Vincent had already started to go through the drawers. "Maybe," he said. "Or if it's small, it could even be in one of those things." He looked up at the books. "But I doubt anyone would–"

"I'll check," said Jessica. "Just in case." Eager, she turned back to the shelf and knelt down. She began pulling the books from their perches and examining each one.

Vincent kept his attention on the ornate sliding drawers in front of him. The desk's surface held nothing of interest, only stray slips of paper and a cup filled with slender sticks with points on one end. He pulled each drawer out with no resistance, no locks, and rifled through the contents. He found much the same as what was on top of the desk, occasionally stabbing himself with one of the pointed sticks. He ran through all eight or so of the drawers without finding anything interesting. He stood from his crouching position and glanced over his shoulder. Jessica was still searching, but she was only on the second shelf – each book she pulled out seemed to fall open at the spine almost immediately, and she would scan the first few lines.

Sighing, Vincent turned back to the desk. It wasn't out of the question that Brian had lied to them, that his mother and Marcus would be in to report them at any moment. It also wasn't out of the question – though perhaps it was much closer to being so – that Brian had been telling the truth.

Sighing a second time, Vincent squatted down so his eyes were level with the surface of the desk. He scanned the underside of it, but his eyes were useless in the dark. Turning to the side, he reached out his arm and felt blindly along the wood. He ran his fingers along the side of the first drawer, over a small protrusion...

There was a flash to the left, and the far wall was no longer a faded crimson. Jessica looked up from her current book, her muscles tense. The wall had transformed into something like the massless screen in the classroom simulation. Its surface had been divided into a series of squares made up of what looked like miniature video feeds.

"What did you just do?" said Jessica. Her most recent book lay forgotten in her lap.

"I don't know," said Vincent. He stood and took a step closer to the wall. He half-expected the video feeds to disappear, but they remained, as clear as ever. "It's...the dome."

Jessica had followed him over. She was staring at the very middle square. The feed there was of the Main. The stripped clean kitchen and frosted glass ceiling were exactly as Vincent remembered.

The other squares contained feeds as well, all different. One above eye level near the upper right showed Brian's bedroom. Brian was in his bed, on his back under the covers, his eyes fixed on the ceiling. Another square showed a room much like the one they were in currently, only without the bookshelf and ornate brown desk. It was a more Seclusion appropriate version of what an office was supposed to look like: undecorated, with a simple desk and single chair, both rounded at the corners, both white. The people inside it, too, Brian's mother in her snow-colored jumpsuit and Marcus in his ashen gray one, matched their surroundings in a way Vincent couldn't quite pinpoint.

"They're talking," said Jessica. "Look."

Vincent leaned closer, and he could see Marcus's mouth moving. There was no sound to accompany it.

"Is there volume?"

"I don't think so," said Vincent. He had felt nothing but the small

59

button he had found on accident.

"Maybe if we…"

Jessica stepped closer and raised her hand toward the feed. Vincent reached out to stop her, but he was too slow. She had already tapped the surface of the wall where Brian's mother and Marcus were pictured. As soon as her fingers made contact, the feed expanded to the full size of the wall, crowding the others around it from view. As it grew, so too did the volume. Marcus was still speaking.

"…and before you say it, yes, they're just children," he said. "But I would prefer not to take any chances, no matter how small."

Brian's mother nodded, slowly, as she lowered herself down into the chair behind the small round desk. Even sitting, she was quite tall. Her hands were interlocked under her pointed chin for support. Her eyes were steady and unrevealing. "I understand," she said. "I just don't want you to lose sight of the larger picture."

"I'm not," said Marcus. "But I'm not going to lose sight of the smaller ones, either."

Brian's mother nodded once again, unreadable.

"What are we watching?" asked Jessica. Her voice was nearly a whisper, as if the people in the feed might overhear them. "Do you think Brian wanted us to find this?"

Vincent shrugged "Maybe. Or maybe he didn't know about it. Whatever *it* even is."

Jessica turned back to the feed, still frowning. Brian's mother was about to speak.

"Were those two the only ones who gave you any trouble?"

"There were some other struggles," said Marcus. "But nothing major. The Senator's and the developer's kids were the only ones to escape."

Vincent and Jessica gave one another a look.

"And *escape* is far from the right word," continued Marcus. "If you would have just let my men–"

"Enough." Brian's mother remained sitting, but her voice had risen. Marcus seemed to shrink slightly. "I've already told you. That order came from above me. I had nothing to do with it." She paused here, ensuring Marcus wasn't going to interrupt. "Besides," she continued, "the order has since been rescinded. You're free to do as you wish."

Marcus perked up at this. Brian's mother noticed.

"But that should not distract you from your other duties."

"No, ma'am," said Marcus. His tone was flat, unconvincing. "My other obligations are few, anyway."

"The detainees?"

"I've delegated."

"Even the priority ones?"

"They require little effort."

"Ah." Brian's mother paused here. A patronizing edge had begun to creep into her tone. "The assignments mandated by Fatrem himself require little effort. I may have guessed."

Marcus shifted where he stood. His discomfort was evident. "I did not say they are not important. I simply mean there is little I can do at the moment."

"And there is no preparation to be done?" prompted Brian's mother. "The first announcement is due to be made in the morning."

"I am aware of the timeline, Lynn." Marcus didn't shrink away from her this time. "Fatrem has trusted me with this matter, and I would expect you to do the same."

If possible, Brian's mother, Lynn, Marcus had called her, grew even straighter in her seat. "I do," she said. "But there can be no mistakes. If Smith is to take the fall for the ID hack, you need to be convincing."

"I will be," snapped Marcus. "But I'll need more leverage eventually. If not for Smith, then for the developer."

"Enough about the children," Lynn shot back. "We have Smith's wife. She's enough leverage for now. And the developer we won't need for long."

Marcus grunted in response. "I had my men check for the children's whereabouts before I met with you," he said. Lynn seemed prepped to interrupt – "Not to pursue them," rushed Marcus. "Just to monitor." He paused for a second, but Lynn remained quiet. "They were off the grid. Do you know what that means?"

Lynn raised her eyebrows, feigning interest. "They're dead?"

"They're in the first ring," said Marcus, ignoring the sarcasm. "In the management sector. They must have been told of the dead zones."

If Vincent wasn't mistaken, he could see a glint of suspicion in Marcus's gaze. Lynn snorted.

"And whoever could have told them that?" she mocked. "It couldn't have been the girl's father. The one who's been digging through the software for years. The one who knows nearly as much as management."

Marcus adjusted his posture so his chin was tilted upward. Vincent got the impression that, beneath the composed exterior, the man was bristling.

"I'm sure that's who it was," he said. They stayed like that for a moment, Marcus with his penetrating, unblinking gaze, Lynn with her own, icy stare back. "Is there anything else?"

Lynn smiled a forced looking grin. "Perhaps not." She stood from her seat and motioned to the door. "I'll walk you out."

They both started out of the frame, and Jessica tapped on the feed once again. It shrank to its previous size, and the volume went mute. Vincent turned to her, a bit annoyed, but when he saw her face, he stayed silent. Her eyes were facing the floor; her jaw hung loosely from its hinge so her lips were just barely apart.

"They have our parents," she said.

"They could have been talking about someone else," said Vincent.

"Don't be stupid," said Jessica. "Your parents are important to them." She looked up at him. Her eyes were beginning to swell with tears. "My dad isn't."

Vincent started to say something back, but he stopped. He couldn't think of a lie that would be convincing enough. Lynn's words had been clear.

Jessica looked away from him once again.

"Jessica you don't know..."

Vincent trailed off mid-sentence when he heard the footsteps outside. He froze where he was; even Jessica went silent. The footsteps were growing louder, closer to the door – but they didn't linger outside as they had the first time. They passed by without hesitation, keeping on down the hall until their sounds began to fade once more.

"We can't think about that," said Vincent. His voice was softer now. "We won't be able to do anything. Not yet. We'll ask Brian's mom after Marcus leaves. She might know where Newsight is keeping them."

"You really trust that woman?" Jessica was looking at the portion of the wall where Lynn had just been pictured. Vincent followed her gaze.

"Yeah," he said. "I do." It wasn't true, of course. He trusted Lynn no more than he trusted Brian, and that was a particularly low threshold.

"I don't know, Vincent," said Jessica. "It doesn't seem right. Marcus already knows we're somewhere in the first ring."

"But we know *exactly* where he is!" Vincent pointed to the checkerboard of video feeds. Marcus and Lynn had just walked into the square of the Main. "We're ahead of them," continued Vincent. "We might not even need to talk to Lynn. Look," he pointed to the feed, "they're talking again. They might be saying something about our parents."

Jessica still looked unconvinced, but the mention of her father seemed to inject some resolve back into her. She tapped the feed before Vincent could.

"It's a pleasure as always," Lynn was saying. They were just outside of the stairwell, about to start for the main door. "Is there anything else I can do for you before you leave?" Something about her tone seemed to push Marcus toward the door, but he stayed where he was, his eyes roaming the Main with deliberate care.

"I won't keep you." He stayed still as he said it, making no move to leave. "Brian seems to need your attention." He glanced at the cup, still half full, sitting on the kitchen counter. "He was up awfully late."

Lynn sighed. Vincent couldn't tell if she was actually concerned. "He had a traumatizing day."

Marcus nodded in agreement. He still didn't start for the door. "You're aware of the Lenses' new capabilities I assume?"

Lynn raised her eyebrows, caught off guard. "I should think so. I helped design them."

Marcus nodded, unfazed. "Then you'll know of their ability to record everything they see. We can't hold the footage indefinitely, but we can go back several hours. Relive conversations."

Lynn crossed her arms. She rose to her full height, which was a centimeter or two taller than Marcus. "I don't recall requesting a lecture on the work of my own department."

Marcus smirked at her. "When I checked on the whereabouts of the children, I rewound their Lenses. They had an interesting conversation about your son. And you."

"Is that so?" said Lynn. She wasn't playing along.

"It is." Marcus was prodding with his words, pushing and poking. He seemed to be in his element. "And before they entered the first ring, they kept looking at this dome." Marcus looked around them, surveying the empty-walled space with scrutinizing eyes.

"What are you implying, Marcus?"

Marcus smirked again. "Nothing at all," he said. "But you'll understand my hesitance to leave without giving your dome a more thorough search."

"A search?" repeated Lynn. "I think you're forgetting where you are."

"Oh no," said Marcus. "My memory is quite good. And it stretches back far enough to know you have a history."

"By association," snapped Lynn. "He ran off on his own. Brian and I have nothing to do with him." She glanced around them, where Marcus's eyes had just been roaming. "You don't have authority here."

Marcus tilted his head and pressed his lips tighter together. "I'm afraid I do," he said. "My job is to monitor privacy. And for some reason, you seem to have quite a lot of it."

"I'm a manager," said Lynn. She pulled her arms tighter around her stomach, as if to hold herself together. "Fatrem trusts me. Why else would he have given me the privacy he has?"

Marcus grinned, mocking. "Perhaps he does trust you. But trust is temporary." His eyes lost focus for a moment, flitting in toward his nose, then to the side. "And so is privacy."

Behind them, the main door of the dome exploded inward. A stream of gray-clad Privacy Officers came pouring through. Lynn didn't blink.

"As you wish." She turned to the men invading her dome. Her voice was steady. "Search," she said. "Everywhere."

CHAPTER 7 – BEYOND THE RINGS

The swarm of men divided into groups of two and spread like a virus around the Main. Lynn and Marcus didn't budge.

"We need to get out of here," said Vincent.

"How?" said Jessica. She was still looking at the screen, eyes wide.

Vincent tapped the wall's surface so the Main shrank back into the checkerboard of its counterparts. The officers had begun to enter the other frames as well.

"I don't know," he said. "But you might be able to find something in the feeds. I want to check something." He turned away and started back for the desk.

"Vincent it's pointless to look for THE SIM if we don't know how to—"

"Just look," snapped Vincent. "And tell me when they're close." He turned from her without another word and sat down once again at the desk. Behind him, Jessica shook her head but stayed where she was, her eyes trained on the screens. Vincent forced himself not to look at them. Instead, he sank down to his knees and felt along the underside of the desk. He paid careful attention to the area around the button that triggered the projection.

"They're starting up the first flight of stairs," said Jessica.

Vincent continued to feel the underside of the desk. There were no buttons but the first.

"Brian is up," she continued. "He must have heard them. It looks like he's activating his Lenses."

For a moment, Vincent felt a spark of hope, but he knew it was foolish. Brian could do nothing for them now. If he was on their side, the best he could do was buy them a little time by not telling Marcus where they were hiding. If he wasn't on their side, he could do much worse.

Vincent abandoned his search under the desk and returned to the drawers, hoping he had missed something.

"They're breaking into Brian's room," said Jessica. "They're saying something to him..."

Vincent kept his attention fixed on the drawer he was searching, but out of the corner of his eye he saw Jessica tap Brian's feed.

"...no, they never came!" It was Brian. "I don't know what you're talking about. Get off me!"

Vincent allowed himself a look. Two officers were holding Brian in an impromptu interrogation, with one man behind him to hold his arms and the second in front, leaned in close.

Jessica tapped the screen again and the checkerboard returned. Two other pairs of men had climbed the stairs. They disappeared into the rooms on either side of Brian's.

"They'll be up here soon, Vincent. We have to do something."

Vincent stood from the desk and pulled the chair around so it faced the bookshelf. He climbed on top of it.

"Vincent we don't have time to—"

"I'm not leaving without it," said Vincent. "Just tell me when they're coming."

Jessica opened her mouth to protest, then said nothing. Vincent had already pulled a book off the shelf at random. He rifled through its pages, ripping the majority as he turned them, scanning every crevice for THE SIM. He tossed the book to the ground when he reached the end and grabbed the next one. He started to flip once again.

"They're almost done searching the other rooms," said Jessica. Panic was beginning to enter her voice. "And there are more of them coming to the second floor now."

Vincent didn't dare look. He forced himself to focus on the pages. He tossed the second book down and pulled out a third, at random yet again. He repeated his method of fanning the pages out wide, all the while trying to ignore the dozen or more books that remained unchecked.

"They're leaving the rooms," said Jessica. The words spilled from her in a rush. "They're starting for the stairs. They're on their way. Vincent we need to get out of here."

Vincent cursed under his breath as he threw the third book to the ground. He would never have time like this. Desperate, he began flinging books from the shelf, not bothering to check their contents, simply hurling them to the ground. There were still almost ten more.

"They're to the top of the stairs," said Jessica, frantic now. "Four of them, and they're through the door. They're coming down the hall. Vincent they're coming."

Vincent flung the books with both arms now. He forced himself to keep his eyes straight ahead. He couldn't afford to look at the wall. There were only a few books left.

"Two of them went to the first room," said Jessica. "The other two are headed this way."

Vincent bit down hard on his lower lip as he pulled the last two books from the shelf. But when they landed behind him, he heard something more than the normal thump. There was a smaller, lighter sound along with it. He jumped down from the chair and spun around to the desk. On its surface, lying amidst the papers and pointed slender sticks, was a thin, paper-width disc the size of an eye: THE SIM.

"Vincent!"

Vincent turned to the screen. Two of the Privacy Officers from the Main were standing right outside. With a lunge, and just before the door could slide open, Vincent grabbed the disc from the desk and forced it into his front pocket.

The next moment, the officers were inside. They saw Jessica first and started for her. On instinct, Vincent surged forward and shoved the foremost man in the chest so the man stumbled backward. He started for the second man as well only for his head to explode with a splitting pain. He fell to the ground, holding the back of his head where the man had just struck him. Through bleary eyes he saw the same man wrap Jessica's arms behind her in a single, fluid movement. A second later, the two officers from the room over were there as well. Vincent watched, blinking rapidly to chase the pain from his head, as they dragged Jessica toward the door, eventually lifting her from her feet entirely to avoid her wild kicks and untrained punches. Vincent could manage little more than a muffled groan as they dragged him along behind. The pain in his head was excruciating. The site where the man's small club had landed had already risen into an unnatural lump. Every step they took was another painful jolt, and by the time they reached the stairs, Vincent's vision had gone foggy with pain.

When he heard the hissing breath of the door, Vincent fought through the fog over his eyes. They were back downstairs. Marcus and Brian's mother, as well as Brian himself (with his own, miniature escort) were there waiting for them. Marcus watched as they exited the stairs. He clicked his tongue in disapproval.

"What a shame," he said, turning to Lynn. "You were the best Head of Product we've ever had. Fatrem will loath to replace you."

"He won't have to," said Lynn. Even through blurred vision, Vincent could see the lack of fear, of anything, really, in the woman's eyes. By her crossed arms and impatient stance, she may have been in a particularly boring meeting.

"I doubt that," said Marcus. "Even *you* won't be able to recover from this. Or Brian."

"Brian and I had nothing to do with this," snapped Lynn. "You can use lie detection if you'd like."

"I think I will," said Marcus. "But later. As you were just lecturing, I have other matters to attend to." He turned to the men holding Vincent and Jessica. "Where did you find them?"

"Third story." It was the man holding Vincent who spoke. "In an office."

Marcus nodded, uninterested. Lynn, on the other hand, looked up at them. Vincent saw something pass across her face that reminded him strikingly of her son.

"Very well," said Marcus. "Take them." Then, with a relishing look at Lynn: "All of them."

Lynn breathed out heavily, more annoyed than troubled. "You'd do better to focus on your own job," she said. "Leave mine to me."

Marcus smirked at her. "I would if I felt safe in doing so."

Lynn shook her head but said nothing back. Marcus nodded to his men. "To the transports." He glanced at Vincent and Jessica. "Get these two out of the management sector."

Jessica stared up at the man with a glare that would have made Mrs. Farring cringe. Vincent knew without asking she was thinking of her father.

"I'll never understand the privacy privilege given to the first ring," continued Marcus, ignoring Jessica. "There's absolutely no excuse for anyone being off the grid."

Through the throbbing pain still beating at the back of his head, Vincent felt his mind clear. Those last three words echoed in his head so loudly they nearly muffled the pain.

Off the grid.

Vincent had heard that expression before. The echoes told him as much. Someone else had said them, someone recent. The only other person in the Seclusion who could have claimed anything to be off the grid.

Simon.

The developer's words came back to Vincent in a flash. He had to get Jessica a message.

The officers began dragging him across the tile, but he didn't resist. He focused on his Lenses. Frantic, and fighting through the pounding in his head with each word he composed, he began to write.

"Would you like me to drive Brian and myself?" asked Lynn. "We have nothing to hide."

Marcus laughed, callous and unpracticed. "We'll be the judges of that," he said. "As for Brian, I had almost forgotten. He can ride with the children." He flicked his head at the officer holding Brian, and the man started forward.

"I didn't do anything wrong," said Brian, struggling against the man. He looked back at Lynn, imploring. "Mother!"

Lynn twitched at the lips, then remained stoic. Brian's face fell, taking its usual composure with it, and he struggled harder than ever. Marcus merely grinned.

Vincent could watch the scene unfold only in his periphery. He was too busy finishing the message. After a few final letters, he sent it with a flick of his pupils and watched Jessica's face as she received it. For a single, betraying second, her eyes grew wide with excitement, then went out of focus, flitting from side to side in their sockets with wild speed. It took Marcus a moment to notice.

"The girl is doing something," he snapped. "Darken her Lenses."

An officer at Marcus's side stepped forward with a short club and placed the tip of it on Jessica's temple. Before she could pull away, he pressed a button on the bottom of the thing, and Jessica's eyes went white. They stayed like that for a few seconds – completely devoid of their usual, rich brown – before returning to normal. When she could see again, she swayed where she stood, disoriented.

"And the boy."

Vincent tried to squirm out of his captor's grip, but it was too late. His vision exploded with a blinding white light, and his Lenses grew hot, burning against his eyes and spurring on the pain already firing in the back of his skull. And then he could see again. He sagged against the officer behind him, lightheaded. Through the blur, he made eye contact with Jessica. Almost imperceptibly, she nodded.

"That will be quite unnecessary with Brian," said Lynn. Her voice was shriller than usual, almost breaking at points. "He's the son of a Department Head." She straightened herself at this. Marcus glanced at her, then at Brian and the man with the club.

"Load them," he said, and Lynn relaxed.

The officers resumed hauling the three of them toward the door. Vincent stole a glance back at Lynn, but her face was once again unreadable. A second later, she was gone altogether, and they were outside. The air seemed suddenly warmer. The edge of the horizon had just begun to shift from pitch black to a dark but revealing gray.

"Put them in here," snapped Marcus. He pointed to a large transport parked in front of the dome. The thing had three wheels and a long, egg-shaped pod in the center. The pod looked large enough to fit half a dozen people.

"I'll follow in a few minutes with Lynn," said Marcus. "Meet in the Center."

Vincent saw the man holding him nod, and they started for the transport. He was released just long enough to be shoved inside, with Jessica close behind. A second later, one of their officers climbed into the seat next them. In the row in front of them, the man with the short club took the left seat and Brian the right. In the rearview mirror, Vincent saw the eyes of Brian's escort go out of focus, then his lips curl downward. The man stayed like that for a moment, then, when the driver's door slid open in the front row, he composed himself once again.

No one spoke. Vincent doubted the gray-suited men were capable of speech at all. He chanced a glimpse at Jessica. Her eyes were fixed out the window to the right. Before Vincent could see what she was looking at, their officer escort shoved him against the seat, forcing his gaze forward once again. Brian was looking back at them. He was wearing the same look Vincent had seen on him during the simulation – the subtle trace of a reassuring grin, the unspoken message perched on his lips – and then he was facing the front again.

When the officer in the driver's seat propelled the transport forward, Brian kept his gaze straight ahead. The man next to him, however, was shifting in his seat. He had let his eyes slide out of focus a second time.

Beside him, Vincent felt Jessica nudge his arm as she fastened her restraints. He made no move for his own. He was still watching the scene in front of him. The man was reaching down into his belt. He was removing his short club. He was raising it up. They were turning toward Ocean. He was about to take aim–

Vincent's head was slammed against the window to his left as the entire pod jerked to the side. They were upside down, weightless for a fraction of a second, rotating in midair. Vincent rose from his seat, unrestrained, his hands searching in vain for a hold. The pod jerked as it landed on its side, sending Vincent hurtling back downward, then jerked again as it came to a stop on the right side window.

There was silence but for the spinning sound of a wheel no longer in contact with the path. Vincent blinked several times, dazed. He tasted the salt of blood smeared across his lips and felt a damp heat on the back of his head. The splitting pain there had tripled, and his vision came in spurts. He was on the ground, where the right window had once been, with his back twisted and stiff, as if cemented down the spine. The officer was next to him, motionless, his lips parted, his forehead gashed all the way across where the side of the pod had caved in against him. Above the officer, Jessica remained in her restraints. Scratches lined her face in grim streaks, and blood matted down the right side of her hair above the ear. She was blinking, slow and lethargic, but she was blinking. In the seat just ahead, however, in the middle right, where the pod had borne the brunt of the impact, there was no such movement. Brian was still. He remained in his seat, fixed there by his restraints, but his entire body was slumped to the side. His neck hung loosely from his shoulders toward the shattered window below. His head was turned at an angle so the blood dripped in a steady stream from his temple. His eyes, still open, faced the ground, as if watching the blood collect there, as if seeing anything at all.

Vincent looked away. His breathing had shallowed. A knot had risen up in his windpipe. He forced his gaze not to return to the middle right seat. Instead, he shifted himself toward the front, but he had barely moved when his entire back erupted in pain. It lit his spine from his tailbone to his temple and parted his lips in a silent scream. It stabbed at him so sharply he grabbed onto the officer's limp body for support.

Catching his breath, and being careful not to move his torso, Vincent turned his eyes toward the windshield. It had completely busted, raining its shattered fragments inward like sharpened hail. The driver showed no sign of movement. The man behind him, however, somehow with his right hand still gripped around the club, was twitching at the eyelids.

Vincent turned his gaze outside. Just visible through the shattered windshield, with its front spun to the left, was Simon's transport. It was unmanned, summoned, just as Vincent had told Jessica in his message. It had taken surprisingly little damage from the collision. Its wheels remained firmly planted on the ground and its front – presumably the point of impact – was badly dented and bent at the frame, but otherwise unharmed. It looked drivable.

Next to him, Jessica began to stir. She opened her eyes, calm at first, then frantic as she looked around them, drinking in the scene all at once. "Vincent?"

It took her a moment to find him. When she did, her expression flashed to fear, but only for a second. She composed herself quickly.

"We have to get out of here," she whispered. "Are you ok?"

Vincent tried to shake his head, but when he moved, he felt the promise of a second wave of pain. He stopped. "No," he said instead. "I can't move. But the transport is here. You can get out."

"So can you," said Jessica. She started to undo her restraints. "We can help you." She glanced at the middle right seat when she spoke. "Brian?"

Vincent bit down on his tongue. "Jessica you don't have time for this," he said. "They'll wake up soon."

"I'm waking Brian up now," she said. "He can help pull you out." She freed herself of the restraints and braced herself on the officer beneath her. "Brian." Her eyes were on the boy by the window. Brian didn't move. "Brian," she said again, louder this time.

"Jessica…" Vincent trailed off. He was shaking his head. "You have to go."

Jessica met his gaze for a moment, then turned back to Brian. She frowned, as if suspicious, as if the two of them were playing a joke on her, but when Brian didn't move, the suspicion faded. Her eyes grew wide, and her bottom jaw fell open, slowly, and tremoring at the lip.

"Jessica," Vincent repeated.

She blinked several times, then turned her head, a bit farther than necessary, to ensure Brian's limp body was completely out of sight. "I can still get you out," she said. The words sounded strained, as if she were forming them around a lump in her throat. "We'll have to go through the front." She crawled over the man in between them and onto the broken window next to Vincent. She reached out for his arm –

"No don't–"

Jessica tugged on him, and the pain erupted yet again. It shot through him in a piercing wave, enveloping him, numbing him to everything but its stabbing embrace. When the world returned, he was gasping for breath, and his eyes were wet with tears.

"I can't. I'm sorry, I can't," he said. "Please just go."

Jessica squinted down at him for a moment, defiant. She glanced out at Simon's transport. "Don't move," she said. "I'll open your door from the outside."

Before Vincent could protest, she started for the opening in the windshield. But as she clambered forward, the officer next to Brian began to move. Jessica froze. The man was coming to. He was looking down at his hands, then around at the pod...then back at them. His face was barely recognizable – it was almost completely covered with blood. His head swayed on his neck as if it would droop forward at any second. Crimson droplets leaked down his cheeks and off his shoulder in a steady stream. He reached up as if to scoop the precious liquid back into his veins, but he didn't touch the blood. He reached instead for the shoulder restraint. Seeing what was happening, Jessica increased her pace. She climbed into the middle row, past Brian, around to the driver's seat and the open windshield...

The man disentangled himself from the remaining coils of the restraints and started after her. She was still within arm's reach. He grabbed her by the overalls of her jumpsuit and yanked backward.

"No!" she struggled against his grip as he pushed her back into the middle row. "Let us go!"

The man crawled past her, then over his companion in the driver's seat, careful to keep his body between Jessica and the windshield.

"Let us go!" she called after him again, punching at his legs, desperate.

"Jessica you have to–" Vincent stopped mid-sentence when his spine threatened to erupt yet again. He could only watch as Jessica, eyes filled with tears, continued her ineffective blows against the officer's back.

"Please!" she shouted at him as he crawled through the broken glass. The man only grunted in response. He held her at bay until he could get through the opening and climb to his feet. He started for the left side door – for Vincent.

Jessica pulled herself through the windshield, and she got to her feet as well, hysterical now as she tugged uselessly at the officer's arms. He batted her away, though not quite as roughly as the others had in the dome.

"Just leave us alone!" Jessica shouted at him again and tried to pull him back. Then, suddenly, Vincent felt a gust of cold rush into the transport, and he turned his neck as far as his back would allow. The officer had pushed the dented transport door three quarters of the way open.

"Stay away from him!" Jessica called out from somewhere outside. "Vincent you have to try and move!"

The officer was about to lower himself into the back row. Vincent wouldn't stand a chance against him now. He wouldn't have stood a chance with a functional back. He had to get out.

Painfully conscious of the man's grunting efforts above, Vincent bit down on his tongue and lifted himself from the broken shards of glass he was resting on. The movement shot another wave of burning pain down his spine. He bit down even harder and shifted another few centimeters, holding the wave at its crest. It forced him to a stop, forced his breath to remain in his lungs, then departed, slowly, and with a threatening echo in its wake.

Vincent felt a set of arms wrap around him from above. The officer was inside the pod, with his arms dropped down into a cradle; he was pulling Vincent out.

Vincent did his best to remain where he was – he had no intention of fighting through the wave once again – but the man was resolute. His arms were steady and unmovable as they pulled upward. Vincent scrambled for something to hold onto, something to stop the inevitable wave of pain, but before he could find anything, he was in the air, glass still sticking to his exposed wrists, and the wave was back. He wasn't sure if he screamed this time, but when he felt the cool breeze of the morning wash over him, his mouth was open, and Jessica was wearing a look of horror.

They were outside. The officer had climbed from the pod with Vincent slung over his shoulders like a large, unimportant sack, and they were sitting atop the transport, both of them panting.

"What are you doing?" said Jessica. Her face was pale except where it was splattered red, and she swayed unsteadily at the hips. "Let him go."

The officer ignored her. He began to move again instead. Vincent braced himself for yet another wave, but as the man twisted around so they were facing the broken door, Vincent's back stayed steady. The man was moving carefully, bracing Vincent the best he could, almost gentle.

"Vincent," said Jessica, her tone calmer, but still afraid. "Are you ok?"

Vincent attempted to say he was but managed only a confirming grunt instead.

The officer began climbing the meter or so down the side of the pod, using the transport's undercarriage as footholds. He lowered them down gradually, cushioning their weight at each step.

When they reached the ground, Jessica made as if to take a step toward them, then thought better of it. She glanced back down the path the way they had come, in the direction of Brian's dome.

"What are you going to do with us?" she asked.

The officer said nothing. Instead, he began staggering forward. Vincent tried to tell Jessica to leave, but his tongue formed only a weak sounding groan.

"What are you..."

Jessica trailed off as she watched them walk. When Vincent looked up, he saw why: they were headed for Simon's transport.

The officer plodded doggedly on without a word. Jessica walked alongside them with her muscles tensed; she seemed ready to catch Vincent if the man decided to drop him. Vincent felt his heart sink as they neared the pod. He knew already what would happen: the officer would load them in the transport and drive them back to Brian's dome. Or he would lock them inside and wait for help to arrive. Either way, Simon's off-the-grid transport would be no use.

Vincent pushed the thought from his mind. They had THE SIM. They hadn't come this far only to be locked in the back of some smoking transport.

Careful not to alert the officer, Vincent dug in his pocket for THE SIM. With some luck, he might be able to gouge out the officer's eyes, or at least do enough damage to buy Jessica some time. He was just pulling out the small disc when something down the path drew his attention. It was a light, bright and fluorescent, and it was getting closer.

"What is that?" said Jessica. She had seen the light too. "Is that...is that a transport?"

Vincent squinted into the light. When he did, he saw the split down the middle – headlights. His stomach sank. No one else would be driving this early. The officer wouldn't have to lock them in Simon's transport after all.

Vincent looked up at the man carrying him. He raised the disc, on the verge of slicing it downward at the man's eyes…then he paused. The man hadn't slowed their pace to greet the transport; he had sped them up. His eyes flitted back and forth between the path and the headlights, with, if Vincent wasn't mistaken, a touch of nervousness.

"That's them isn't it?" asked Jessica, turning to the officer. "Please just let us go." She was pleading now, her voice was cracking, her eyes darting between the officer and the lights. "Tell them we escaped," she said, "anything. Please."

They were only a few meters from Simon's transport. The officer pointed to the driver's side door.

"What?" said Jessica. "In?" The man nodded. He started for the opposite side with Vincent. Jessica didn't move.

"Go," said Vincent. His voice was barely above a whisper. The lights were getting closer – they were moving quickly. "You have to go."

Jessica hesitated, then, looking at the lights, she started for the driver's seat. Vincent clenched his jaw down tight as they rounded the pod for the opposite side. The officer's increase in speed had threatened to reawaken the pain.

In spite of the crash, the door slid open the same as usual when the man pressed the button. He bent at the waist so Vincent's back entered the pod first. The wave rushed through Vincent yet again, sharp and fast, blinding as it passed through him, and then he was in the seat, reclined all the way back. The officer remained outside, panting and glancing over his shoulder. The lights were still several domes away, but they were closing fast.

"West." The man spoke for the first time. It was a low, deep rasp, and it sounded forced, as if each letter had to fight its way out between his lips. "We've disabled the border fence. Leave west for the city." He grimaced on the last word, as if it pained him to say out loud. "Run."

He pushed the button, and the door slid closed. Vincent watched him as he staggered backward, suddenly wobbling. Carrying Vincent to the pod had cost him what little of his strength that had remained.

"What's he doing?" asked Jessica. She hadn't made a move toward the controls. Her eyes were fixed on the officer.

"Go," said Vincent. "He told us to go."

"But he's one of *them*. Maybe it's a trap."

The lights were approaching them now. The officer was pulling the small club from his belt

"We have to go," said Vincent. "Now, Jessica. We need to move."

Jessica's hands shifted toward the controls, but her eyes stayed on the officer. He was pointing his club at the approaching transport. There was something bright shining from the end, though not nearly as bright as the beams rushing toward him. They were seconds away from another collision.

"Jessica go!"

Jessica tore her eyes from the scene and thrust the accelerator forward. The transport shuddered for a moment, then lurched into motion.

The officer was still standing with his short white club held out in front of him. The other transport was headed straight for him, but he didn't move. It was going too fast. It would plow straight through him – Simon's pod would take the brunt of the damage.

"Go!"

Jessica threw the accelerator forward as far as it went. They still wouldn't move in time. The other transport hadn't slowed down. It was meters away from the officer. It was going to hit him. The officer widened his stance. He raised the club with the glowing white tip, now stained with the grim tint of blood, and he plunged it down just as the transport wheels met his legs.

Vincent looked away. He braced himself for the other transport to come hurtling into them. He held his breath...

And he kept holding. The collision never came. He turned back to the window, and he saw the other transport. Only meters from where they had just been, it had skidded to a stop. Its exterior surged with a kind of electric energy, flickering slightly along its surface. The very front, where the tip of the officer's club had made contact, was charred black, and the area just beneath it, near the transport's undercarriage, was breathing smoke. The gray-clad men inside, blurred through the waves of heat, were motionless.

"What happened?" asked Jessica, glancing back for the first time.

"I don't know," said Vincent. "The officer...he stopped them

77

somehow."

Jessica looked over her shoulder again at the site of the crash. Vincent thought she might be looking for the officer. For her sake, he hoped she didn't find him.

"Why would he do that?" she asked.

Vincent shrugged, then winced from the movement – the adrenaline from the accident was wearing off. "The crash wasn't exactly what I had in mind, you know," he said.

"I'm sorry," said Jessica. "I...I didn't mean for any of that to happen." Her voice was shaking, and her eyes kept glancing up in the mirror at the wreck. Vincent followed her gaze. He knew she was thinking of Brian, of his limp form in the middle right seat, of the caved in portion of the pod pressing against his skull.

"It's not your fault," said Vincent. "If it's anyone's, it's mine. I told you to call it."

Jessica was shaking her head. Her bottom lip was quivering. "If we had just waited," she said. "The officer would have helped us. Lynn or Brian must have told him. We should have trusted them."

"We didn't know," said Vincent. "We did the only thing we could."

Jessica nodded, but the tears in the corners of her eyes didn't recede. She kept her gaze fixed forward, along the curved path of the first ring. She was still for several seconds while her breathing returned to normal. "So what now?" she said. She spoke in her usual, calm tone, but it wasn't quite normal. Vincent was getting better at detecting the difference.

"We leave," said Vincent. "He said the fence is disabled."

"What if he's lying?" said Jessica. "And if he's not, where are we supposed to go?"

"You heard him," said Vincent. "To the nearest city."

Jessica raised her eyebrows. "But aren't the cities dangerous?"

Vincent looked at her, and she turned away, blushing.

"I know here is dangerous too," she said. "I just...I've never left the Seclusion before." She turned from the road to look at him. "And our parents are here."

Vincent had thought of that too. He had half a mind to charge headlong into the Center where the Newsight campus was, but he knew it would be pointless. For now, leaving was their only option.

"We can go looking for them," he said. "But not now. We don't know enough yet." He pulled the small round disc of THE SIM from his front pocket. "We need to watch it as soon as possible."

Jessica saw what he was holding, but she didn't seem relieved. "We can't," she said. "You can't watch hard sims with dark Lenses."

Vincent deflated. Of course – the darkeners. Until their Lenses were reactivated, THE SIM was useless. Still, Jessica was staring at it, flitting her eyes between the disc and the road. She sucked her cheeks into her mouth. "Do you really think the Order exists?" she asked.

"I don't know," said Vincent. "But maybe someone in the city will."

Jessica turned back to the path in front of them. They were nearly around the Center. They would reach the other half of Ocean soon.

"So we're really going then?" asked Jessica.

"I think we have to," said Vincent.

Jessica nodded without looking at him. She made the final turn back onto Ocean without lifting her eyes from the road. Behind them, a winding tower of smoke from the crash was still visible, and behind that, the gray line along the horizon had begun to soften into morning. Ahead of them, however, the night was still dark. The path was lit only by the cracked headlights of Simon's transport. The light was weak, but it raced onward, away from the domes, away from the Seclusion, and west

Part II – The City

CHAPTER 8 – THE STAYERS

Vincent blinked, slowly at first – his eyelids felt sticky against his Lenses – then more quickly until his vision returned. He reached his arms up automatically to stretch. Midway through the motion he froze, preparing himself for the wave of pain the movement would surely have triggered, but he felt nothing. Frowning, suspicious of his own body, he completed the stretch as a test, once again braced against the inevitable wave. Still, nothing. That was impossible. If he had tried the same motion in the transport, his eyes would have gone white with agony. In the bed on which he lay now, however, he felt nothing at all.

The room's only door swung inward. Vincent shrank back against the pillow behind him.

"Hello, Vincent."

It was a woman who stepped through the opening. She had a squat, sturdy frame and hands just a bit too large. The skin of her face seemed to be on the verge of wrinkling, and her eyes were partially covered by drooping eyelids.

Vincent shifted toward the wall when the woman crossed over to his bed. When he moved, he felt something tug at his arm. Tracing the pressure down to his wrist, he saw the tube there, protruding from a small hole in his skin. He looked away, suppressing the urge to be sick. "Where am I?" he asked. "Where's Jessica?"

"She's in the next room," the woman said back.

"How did we get here?" asked Vincent.

"In that odd looking car," said the woman. "Jack spotted you when you came racing in. You nearly hit him."

"Jack?"

"My husband."

Vincent nodded, though he was far from understanding.

From the bag over her shoulder, the woman removed a thin book with a slender, pointed stick – like the ones from the office in Brian's dome – clipped onto the binding. She flipped to the closest page that wasn't scrawled with sloppy markings and pressed the stick down onto it. It left more of the same markings as the previous pages behind it as it went.

Vincent looked up once again. He turned to the room's only window, but he could see nothing but wisps of white, vaporous clouds and the open sky behind them. He turned to the door, which had been left ajar. He could see a hallway beyond, but nothing further.

"Where's Jessica?" he repeated.

"Jack is taking care of her," said the woman, patiently. "She refused any treatment until she was convinced you would be ok." The woman made one final scribble with the utensil in her hand, then plunged the book back into her bag. She stood upright. "Let me check a few things." She made as if to lean closer to him, but Vincent recoiled.

"It's ok, Vincent," said the woman. "You're safe." She leaned toward him again. Vincent stretched further away.

"How do you know my name?" he said.

"Jessica told us."

"And where are we?"

"Washing," said the woman. Then, seeing Vincent's confused look, added: "A city."

Vincent looked out the window yet again, hoping perhaps the expanse of blue had been filled instead with dark paned towers and huge, story-height screens. He saw only clouds.

"Who are you?" he asked, turning back to the woman.

"Abigail," she said, as if that answered the question. "Now stay still."

Without waiting for permission, the woman leaned closer to him and inserted a funneled device into his ear. She hunched over to peer through it.

"Other side."

She pulled his left arm so he rolled onto his side, and she repeated the procedure in his other ear.

"What are you doing?" asked Vincent.

"Now on your back." Abigail prodded him, gently, to resume his previous position. When he did, she took hold of his wrist – the one without the tube protruding from it – and pressed down on the largest vein there. She counted something under her breath. "Good," she said, then released his wrist. "Now for your eyes."

She leaned over him, and Vincent backed away once again. "It's ok," she said. "I just want to make sure I didn't miss anything."

Relenting, but keeping his muscles tense and his eyes on the open door opposite the window, Vincent stayed still. Abigail leaned forward so their faces were only centimeters apart, and she peered once again through the funneled device she had inserted into his ears.

"They look different than I remember," she said. Vincent could feel the wind of her words against his cheeks.

"My eyes?" said Vincent.

"Your Lenses," said Abigail. "Is this how they all look now?"

Vincent frowned as Abigail switched her inspection to his other eye. "What do you mean? Mine are just the same as yours."

Abigail leaned backward so her torso no longer hovered over him. She slipped the peering device into the side pocket of her white, smock-like coat. "I don't wear Lenses," she said. "No one in Washing does."

"What do you mean you don't wear Lenses?" said Vincent. "You have to."

Abigail leaned forward once again. This time, though, she was the one with her eyes opened wide. "Not here," she said.

Suspicious, Vincent squinted to inspect the white area just beyond the grayish blue of her irises. There was no trace of the usual thin line, the betraying curved rim. Her eyes were bare, free.

"But…" Vincent struggled to form words. He felt guilty, for some reason, talking to someone who wasn't wearing Lenses. "How do you engage your simulations and—"

Vincent's free hand shot up to his front pocket. He breathed a sigh of relief when he felt a small, hard circle tucked away inside. Whoever this woman was, she hadn't touched THE SIM.

"Pardon?" said Abigail. She glanced down at Vincent's pocket.

"Engaging simulations," said Vincent, lowering his hand. "And sending messages. Accessing the network. Do you not do any of that?"

Abigail smiled once again. "I've heard those questions before," she said. There was a far off, nostalgic quality to her tone. There was pain there, too. "You're from a Seclusion, aren't you?"

Vincent nodded. He was starting to feel less and less of a need to shrink away from the woman.

"We don't watch simulations," she said. "Unlike the other cities. And we don't *send* messages; we carry them ourselves." She glanced out the window, a haze over her gray-blue eyes. "As for the network, I haven't been connected to that for years. The Lenses are the only devices capable of connecting. And other Newsight products, of course."

"But my mother said the cities were being shipped new Lenses," said Vincent. "Why don't you use those?"

Abigail shook her head. "We never received them. Only the people who migrated received the upgrade. Those who stayed, like my husband and I, did not."

"Why would you have to go somewhere else to wear Lenses?" asked Vincent. He thought back to the management sector in the Seclusion. "Is the whole city off the network?"

Abigail squinted, tilting her head in thought. "I suppose you could say that. It was our choice, one not many other cities shared."

"You mean you could choose?" pressed Vincent. "Whether or not to wear Lenses?"

"Whether or not to make them standard," corrected Abigail, "so that everyone would wear them. In the end, we abstained. There were too many protests to do anything but." Abigail's eyes glazed over once again as yet more memories tugged at her mind. Vincent changed the subject to pull her back.

"Where were you and your husband going when you saw us?" he asked. "Were you leaving?"

"Of course not," said Abigail. The focus had returned to her eyes. Her voice was firm. "We were getting supplies. Stocking up for the Order attack."

"So," started Vincent, "you're not *from* the Order?"

Abigail looked appalled. "I most certainly am not," she said. "I'm no terrorist."

Vincent sighed. It had been a ludicrous hope.

"Speaking of the Order," said Abigail. "The attack will be soon. We need to hurry back."

"Back where?"

"The Hole."

Vincent frowned. He looked at Abigail, then out the window. An entire city that didn't wear Lenses – it was a compelling thought. The place called *The Hole*, however, was less compelling.

"You don't have to come with us, of course," said Abigail. "But you should. If you want any chance of surviving the attack."

"How do you know there's going to be an attack?" said Vincent.

"We know," said Abigail. She seemed to think the answer was sufficient. "Now how do you feel?"

At first, Vincent made no response. He had no reason to mistrust the woman – more reason, conversely, to thank her – but he remained far from comfortable. Still, after a pause, and keeping his distance, he sat up in the bed and twisted his back as a test. The shooting, needling pain that had consumed him inside the overturned transport was completely absent. "A lot better," he said, surprised. "What did you do to me?"

"I didn't do much of anything," said Abigail. "It was the injections that did most of it."

Vincent frowned. Newsight's medical injections were the saving grace of the Seclusion. Here, however, he hadn't expected them to be used.

"They're usually saved for the Newsight cities," said Abigail, "but we managed to get our hands on some before they got to be exclusive."

Vincent opened his mouth, but the dozen questions there seemed to dam the flow of his words. He stayed silent.

"Let me take this out for you," said Abigail. Before Vincent could ask what she was talking about, she removed something slender and sharp from his wrist with a flourish. He winced. "All set." She patted the skin of his arm where the needle had just been. "Can you walk?"

Vincent wasn't sure of the answer. He swiveled under the sheets so his legs swung over the edge of the mattress. He stood and took a step forward. His legs wobbled at first from weakness, but they grew steady after another step. "I'm fine," he said.

Abigail nodded, patting him again. "Then come with me." She turned from him and started, rather slowly so he could keep up, for the door. "Your friend is in the next room."

Energized by the thought of seeing Jessica, Vincent forced himself to quicken his walk. Moments later they were in the hallway, a long, dim stretch of empty floor. On either side of them every few meters, doors lined the walls – walls, Vincent noticed, that were completely straight, blocked at the corners with right angles unlike the usual curves of the Seclusion.

"Right here."

Abigail came to a door on the other side of the hall and opened without knocking. Jessica was lying on a bed exactly like Vincent's, in a room almost exactly like the one they had just left. This room's window, however, had a view far different than the last. The sky was the same pale blue, hazed in spots by the translucent wisps of clouds, but it was parted down the middle by dark outlines of distant towers. They joined together to form a single, castle-like unit, shining from the sun's reflection in their tall, dark-paned walls of glass.

A stout, rough-looking man with close-cropped dark hair was knelt over Jessica's bed, talking to her as he checked the machine at her side. When he saw them, he nodded in their direction. Jessica followed his gaze.

"Vincent?" said Jessica. "You're walking!"

"And well, too," said Abigail. She smiled at Vincent, then turned to her husband. "Jack, I think we're ready."

Jack stood from his position next to the machine. "Good," he said. "This one has been trying to get out of bed ever since she woke up."

"I told you I feel fine," said Jessica. She held out her arm, the one still attached to the tube, expectant. Vincent smiled. Shaking his head, but grinning slightly, Jack unhooked her.

Jessica kept her gaze on Vincent. "I think we should go with them," she said. Vincent was taken aback.

"Well we should at least talk about it first," he said.

"What's there to talk about?" said Jessica. "It's a city without Lenses. If anyone knows who we're looking for," she glanced down at Vincent's front pocket, at the small round disc inside, "they'll be here."

Vincent opened his mouth to protest, but Abigail cut him off.

"If you're looking for help that's not medical," she said, "we won't be able to do much. You'll need Kendra."

Jack nodded in agreement. "She's your best bet, whatever you need."

"And she's at this Hole place?" said Jessica. "We can talk to her?"

"She knows us," said Jack. "She'll talk to you if we ask her to."

Jessica got to her feet. She looked to Vincent. Vincent held her gaze for a second before turning to Abigail. He looked at the woman's eyes – actual eyes, not Lenses – and in that moment, in spite of everything, he felt inexplicably safe. He turned back to Jessica. "Ok," he said. "Let's go."

******

The four of them pushed through a thick metal door at the bottom of the stairwell. When they were outside, Vincent drank in great gulps of air – he had never climbed down so many stairs in his life.

"Abigail, you want to take the young lady?" asked Jack. "I can take the boy in the truck."

They were standing on a sidewalk next to two, four-wheeled chunks of metal. The first was rounded and enclosed all the way round. The second was longer and open at the back.

"Why can't we just follow you in our transport?" asked Vincent.

"The transport died on the way here," said Jessica. "They found us a few blocks over."

"But like Jack said," joined Abigail, "we can take you. We have some spare room." She turned to Jessica. "We'll take the van. Jack and Vincent can follow in the truck."

"We'll see you in a minute, then," said Jack. He tried to lead Vincent toward the half open vehicle on the left. Vincent didn't move.

"It's ok, Vincent," said Jessica. "It's not far." She gave him a reassuring look, then started for the other vehicle with Abigail.

"She's right," said Jack. "Come on." He didn't touch Vincent this time as he began walking toward the truck. After a pause, Vincent followed.

Jack rounded the front of the vehicle and pulled open the driver's side door with a jerk. Cautiously, Vincent approached the side opposite. He grabbed the handle of the passenger door and gave it a good yank. When it opened, he had to hike his leg up to climb inside.

"I almost ran into your little Newsight bike when you came flying in," said Jack. "You're lucky I saw you in time."

Vincent nodded absently as he looked around. The inside was far different than that of Simon's transport, darker for one, and more complicated.

Jack pulled a small, jagged strip of metal from his pocket and inserted into the dash. Vincent jumped when the vehicle roared to life.

"The Hole isn't too far," said Jack. "But it *is* in the city."

"You mean toward the towers?" said Vincent.

"The skyscrapers," said Jack. "Yeah."

Vincent looked out the windshield. He could still see the tips of the skyline he had seen from Jessica's room. There was a single, taller building among the others, the top of which climbed upward like a giant staircase.

Vincent's concentration was broken when the vehicle lurched forward. He grabbed onto the side of the door in spite of himself. Simon's transport had been one thing – that ride had been smooth and quiet – Jack's machine was quite another.

"Who were you running from?" asked Jack.

Vincent turned to him, confused, his eyes still darting out the windshield at their now vibrating surroundings.

"What do you mean?"

"Before your transport died," said Jack. He was ignoring the road – his eyes were on Vincent. "Your friend was driving like a bat out of hell. You had to have been running from *some*one."

"We weren't running," said Vincent. He wasn't sure what made him lie. For some reason, though, it seemed the only option.

"Ah," said Jack. He turned to the road. "Of course not." He pressed a button to his left. The window next to him slid down into the door, like a transport door into a pod. He propped his arm against the frame where the glass had just been. Almost instantly, Vincent's nose was filled with a pungent, sticky scent. It seemed to follow them wherever they went.

"Does this not run on a power cell?" asked Vincent.

Jack snorted. "Power cell?" He removed his eyes from the road for several seconds at a time to look at Vincent. "They don't teach you anything in the Seclusion, do they?"

"Yeah they do," said Vincent, indignant. "The simulations teach us all sorts of things."

Jack nodded, the same way he had when Vincent had told him he and Jessica weren't running from anyone.

"I know about injections," pressed Vincent. "My mother works in Incubation back in the Seclusion. She was in charge of giving sick newborns their injections."

Jack breathed out, short and sharp. His mouth hung open. "I think you might be talking about a different kind of injection."

Vincent frowned, confused, but he didn't argue. "Well I know about the cities," he said. "I know about the Order attacks."

Jack lifted his eyebrows at this. "Really? They told you about the warnings?"

Vincent nodded, trying to hide his confusion. Jack wasn't fooled.

"Other cities have been attacked," he said, "but not ours. Not majorly, at least. Our first large scale contact with the Order was just a few days ago. In the outskirts, they dropped enough bombs to wipe a whole continent off the planet. The city itself wasn't hit with a single one. We just got the pamphlets."

"Pamphlets?"

Jack nodded. "The warning pamphlets."

"And what did they say?" asked Vincent.

Jack shrugged, as if it were obvious. "The same thing as always: Leave. All the off-network cities have gotten them."

"Off-network," repeated Vincent. "You mean the cities without Lenses?"

Jack kept his gaze fixed forward as they drove. His eyes were fogged over with the same haze that had covered Abigail's back in the room. "Washing was one of the few," he said. "No one here wanted anything to do with Lenses. Thought they were too much. Too intrusive. But no one has a choice after the Order drops their pamphlets. They have to go to a standard city for protection."

Vincent tilted his head.

"Cities that require Lenses," said Jack.

That sounded more familiar to Vincent, more like a Seclusion. "But why is that where people have to go?" he asked. "If they have to leave, why not go somewhere else?"

Jack laughed, gruff, humorless. "People have tried. Some have tried to travel to a different off-network city, but somehow they never seem to make it. People try staying sometimes, too. The first city the Order dropped the pamphlets on, nearly everyone stayed. That turned out to be a mistake." Jack bit down, hard, clenching his jaw as he stared straight ahead. "But we're different," he continued. "We're prepared."

Vincent was silent for a while. He remembered his father talking about the cities after the first attack on the school. He had said the cities had it worse. Now, that seemed like an understatement.

"So what happens to the others?" asked Vincent. "The ones who leave?"

"They get their Lenses," said Jack. "That's the price of admission to get into a standard city. They won't let you in without Lenses."

"But why?" pressed Vincent. "Why are they mandatory?"

"For protection, mostly," said Jack. "From the Order. They're required for the simulations, too, but people seem to like those."

"Simulations?" said Vincent. "What are people trying to learn about?"

Jack frowned for a second, then, seeming to realize something, he shook his head. "You're thinking of the Seclusions. In the cities..." he turned back to the road, eyes fogging over once again, "...the simulations are different."

Vincent waited for him to continue, but the only sounds that followed were the sputters and kicks of the engine. Sighing, and feeling more lost than before, Vincent turned to the window. He leaned against it so his forehead vibrated against the glass, and he watched the road.

Several minutes later, the towers that had once been silhouettes against the sky now blocked the horizon completely. As the vehicle – the truck, Jack called it – drew closer, Vincent felt like a mouse approaching the edge of some great jungle. His mouth was locked in a perpetual open position as he stared upward. The towers were in denser proximity than he had thought, clustered in blocked-off groves and flanked on all sides by gray-stone paths. Only a little ways down the first of these paths, Abigail rolled the van to a stop in front of them. Jack came to a stop as well.

"Are we here?" asked Vincent.

"Close as we can get in the vehicles," said Jack. He opened his door and jumped out. "We'll walk the rest of the way. The Hole is only a few blocks up."

Pretending like the bulk of the sentence made sense to him, Vincent climbed from the truck. The pungent smell that had hit him when Jack first rolled down his window struck him again, this time stronger than before. In front of them, Abigail and Jessica climbed from the van. Jack took the lead without a sound. There was an eerie silence on the street that didn't seem to want to be broken. It extended indefinitely ahead, no transports, no gray-suited men, no movement. The only noise was the unfailing echo of their own footsteps as they walked.

They continued like that until they had crossed two roads running perpendicular to theirs. Jack brought them to a stop in front of a wide, open air structure with stone ramps lining the inside. He turned around.

"This is it," he said, looking at Vincent and Jessica. His tone seemed far too grave to reference the unimpressive five-story building in front of them. "Let me do the talking."

Vincent nodded, and Jessica followed suit. Satisfied, Jack turned around. He took the lead once again, this time heading for a vehicle-shaped opening in the building's side. The hair on Vincent's arms began to rise. He felt suddenly cold – something about the building's unlit interior and damp stone walls made him uneasy.

"What is this place?" he asked, his voice low, as they approached.

"It *was* a parking garage." said Jack. "Now it's our shelter. We've been working on it for years, fortifying it. It's where all the stayers live. The ones who want to survive, anyway."

Vincent said nothing back. They had entered the opening, and the dark, soil-scented air of the place seemed to hold the words in his throat. The echo of their footsteps was even louder now, but it was distorted, too, altered by the vehicles that scattered up and down the ramps. They faced the walls, pulled in at angles, parked and deserted.

"We're headed down," said Jack, pointing to a stairwell to their left. "The Hole is on the two basement levels."

Vincent noticed that Jack had lowered his voice as well. The usual gruff tone there had been replaced by something more cautious.

Vincent kept his head on a swivel as they started for the stairs. It was all too easy to imagine a swarm of ashen-suited men rushing from the shadows. Jack seemed equally alert, though Vincent wasn't sure what the man was watching for.

They pushed through a solid metal door into the stairwell. Even though it was nearly noon, the space was almost completely devoid of light. They had to pause for a moment on the top step to let their eyes adjust. When the pitch black had turned into more of a murky gray, they started down the first flight. It reminded Vincent of the climb down into Simon's cellar. He was no keener on the idea of going underground now than he had been then. He stayed as close to Jack as he could without kicking the man's heels.

"Stand next to us," said Abigail when they had reached the bottom platform. "So they can see you."

Unquestioning, Vincent and Jessica stepped forward so they stood between their escorts. They were staring at a door exactly like the one they had pushed through above, only this one, instead of having a pane of glass over the knob, was completely solid.

Jack knocked on the door three times, with a slight gap between the second and third knocks. There was a pause, then the darkness gave way to a blinding light. Vincent brought his hands up on instinct, shielding his eyes. He thought the light was coming from above, but he wasn't sure.

"The newcomers?"

A woman's voice, stern and unyielding, called out to them.

"Vincent and Jessica Wright," said Jack. "Our niece and nephew."

There was silence while the lights continued to shine. Vincent managed to open his eyes long enough to see the door. A slit around eye-level had opened to expose a narrow, squinting set of eyes.

The lights above them dimmed, and the door swung inward, instantly filling the stairwell with an inescapable, mechanical racket. Vincent lowered his arms and blinked several times in a row. When he could see again, the outline of the previous image, though fading, was overlain against the open door.

"In," said Jack – he had to raise his voice to be heard over the sound – and he started inside. Vincent followed. The space they stepped into was, in layout, exactly the same as the story above them, but in all other ways completely different. It was much better lit, illuminated in every corner by the white, fluorescent bulbs strung to the reinforced ceiling. The main ramp was lined with cubed structures made of burnt orange metal and covered at the doors with tattered sheets. Left of the structures was an array of tables (most with tents over them to catch the leaks), each with shoes or food or some other necessity on display. It wasn't until Vincent turned to the right side of the ramp that he realized what was making the racket. A pointed, rotating machine was burrowing into the rock of the far wall. It filled the room with the grinding of metal on stone, and provided every other sound – those that could be heard, at least – with a constant backdrop.

"I've paged Kendra!" The woman who had spoken to them through the stairwell door was standing right in front of them, but she had to shout to be heard. "She will have to approve them!" She flicked her head toward Vincent and Jessica. Next, she waved at an idle group of dust-covered men next to the machine burrowing through the wall. When they saw her, they started over. "Stay here!" She yelled once again, then turned away. A plume of dust rose off her tattered brown shirt as she went.

Vincent turned to Jack, but the man wasn't looking at him. His eyes were locked on the half dozen rough-looking men walking in their direction.

"Jack?" shouted the man at the front of the group. He shook Jack's hand. "Who are your friends?" The man turned his gaze on Vincent. Vincent felt the man's eyes roam over the scratches on his face, then the splatters of blood on his clothes.

"This is my nephew, Vincent," said Jack, curling his hand protectively around the back of Vincent's neck. "And this is my niece, Jessica." Then, when he saw the man's gaze lingering on their bloodied clothes, added: "They were in a car crash."

The man snorted. "Lot of traffic out there, that's to be sure." He brushed his dust-covered hands off on his equally dust-covered pants, and he stepped forward. He held out his right hand to Vincent. "Name's Bill," he said. "Nice to meet you, Vincent."

Vincent hesitated for a moment, then stepped forward and took the man's outstretched hand. But they didn't shake. Bill had frozen. A look of horror had begun to spread across his face, prying his mouth open in disbelief.

With surprising speed, Bill thrust his free hand into the waistband of his pants and removed a black, L-shaped strip of metal. It had a hole on its front end and a crescent-like curve at the bend. Bill's index finger hovered just over this crescent.

Jack and Abigail stepped forward, but two of the men behind Bill held them back.

Jack struggled to keep his tone level. "Put the gun down, Bill."

CHAPTER 9 – THE RUNAWAY

Vincent watched, bewildered, as Jack struggled against the man holding him. He watched with equal confusion as Bill readjusted his grip on the thing he was holding – a gun, Jack had called it – so his knuckles went white from effort.

"He's wearing Lenses," said Bill. His voice was shaking. "You can see them."

"The girl has them too," said the man holding Jack. He was close enough to see Jessica's eyes. In a flash, two other men from the circle had drawn objects identical to Bill's from their jackets. They pointed them at Jessica.

"You led them right to us," said Bill. He tightened his hold around the crescent. "They'll see everything."

"They're disabled," said Abigail, trying to calm the man down. "I checked. Twice over."

"You can't turn them off, Abby," said Bill. His eyes were still on Vincent. "You know that."

"They were already off!" said Jack. The words were rushing out now. "They're from the Seclusion to the east. They must know how to turn them off there."

Bill glanced at Jack. "I thought you said they were family."

"I didn't want to cause any trouble," said Jack.

Bill laughed, a desperate, unrestrained sound. "Too late for that. But maybe not too late to stop all this from getting back to them."

Bill breathed in deep as he took a step back, still with the gun pointed at Vincent's head. He curled his finger a millimeter tighter toward the crescent.

"Bill he's just a boy," pleaded Jack, still struggling against the mountain of a man holding him. "The Lenses are off. Please. Please…"

The rest of his words were drowned out by the deafening grind of the machine. Vincent could only watch, staring at the small hole at the end of the gun, at Bill's fingertip as it grew closer and closer to his palm, pulling the thin crescent along with it…

"Stop!"

Vincent followed the voice up the main ramp. A short, round-faced woman was scuttling down toward them as quickly as her undersized legs would allow.

"Put that thing down, Bill," the woman said. "And turn off that damn drill."

Almost instantly, the grinding came to a halt. The sound continued to echo in Vincent's skull for a few seconds before it faded completely.

"They're wearing Lenses!" said Bill.

"Is that true, Jack?" said the woman. She had come to a stop a few meters from the bottom of the ramp. Her hand had begun to stray toward her waistband much like Bill's had.

"Abigail says they're disabled," said Jack.

The woman relaxed slightly. She continued down the ramp. "Then they're disabled." She looked at Bill, whose gun was still pointed at Vincent. "What did I say?"

Bill turned to her, then back to Vincent and Jessica. Scowling at them, he lowered his arm.

The woman came to a stop next to Vincent. She took a second to catch her breath. "Abigail knows better than most," she said. "Jack, bring them up." She gave Vincent a scrutinizing glare before turning around. When she started back up the ramp, Jack and Abigail's captors allowed them to follow. Jessica hurried after them, and Vincent followed as well, but his eyes remained on the "L" of black metal hanging from Bill's white-knuckled hand.

They retraced the woman's footsteps back up the ramp. As they walked, men and women pushed through the hanging sheet doors of their cubed structures to watch. They wore the same, earth-toned, dust-covered attire as the men by the drill, and their eyes showed similar traces of fear.

"Don't mind them," whispered the woman. "They won't try anything with me here."

Vincent looked away, but he continued to feel the heat of a dozen stares on his back. He couldn't breathe normally again until they reached the top of the ramp.

"You should have known better than to bring kids with Lenses here, Jack."

They had stopped in a little nook just out of sight of the ramp. There was a double set of what looked like homemade doors to their left

"I didn't think the lights would be on during the day," said Jack. "No one would have noticed without them." He glanced around the corner back down the ramp. "I'm sorry for the trouble."

The woman glowered at him for a moment, but she softened almost immediately. "Bygones," she said. Then she turned to Vincent and Jessica. "And what of these two? Your niece and nephew, you said?"

Vincent could tell by the woman's tone she could smell the lie. Abigail seemed to sense the same.

"We needed to make sure they got past the door," she said. She paused here, glancing behind them as Jack had. "They're from a Seclusion, Kendra."

Kendra lifted her brow. "The same one as before?"

Abigail hesitated, casting Vincent and Jessica a worried glance, then nodded. "They need help," she said.

"Have you told them?" pressed Kendra. "Do they know about him?"

"Know about who?" cut in Vincent. He was tired of being talked about as if they weren't there. Kendra ignored him.

"It might help them," she said. She seemed to be prompting Abigail, asking for permission of some sort. "I could tell them," she suggested.

Abigail held her gaze for a beat, her face unreadable, then turned to Vincent and Jessica. Vincent saw a sadness in her eyes he didn't understand.

"It's ok, Abby," said Jack. "Kendra's right."

Abigail stared at them for another second, then looked up at Jack. He nodded encouragingly.

"Ok," she said.

Kendra nodded. She placed an arm on Abigail's shoulder. "I can send them down when I'm done," she said. "You don't have to stay."

Abigail smiled in thanks. She cast Vincent and Jessica one last glance, then turned and started for the ramp. Nodding to them, Jack followed close behind.

"Come on," said Kendra, watching them go. "This way." She started for the doors. With a confused look at one another, Vincent and Jessica did the same.

Kendra removed a ring of the same jagged, metal strips Vincent had seen Jack use in the truck. She inserted the largest one into a hole beneath the door's knob, then twisted. Vincent heard the heavy, rusted locks click free in the mechanism's interior. Kendra opened the doors and beckoned them inside.

"Sorry for that," she said, when the doors had closed behind them. She didn't bother explaining. "And sorry for the mess."

Holding back the parade of questions in his mind, Vincent looked around. The floor was the same gray stone as everywhere else, only here it was littered with supplies, some Vincent recognized, some he didn't. A pile of books was strewn across what, somewhere underneath, must be the dining room table. Small, framed pictures dominated the rest of the space, hung with no real order from the sheet metal walls or scattered amidst the supplies on the floor.

"It's been hectic the last few days," said Kendra. "With the drilling."

"I like it," said Jessica.

"Thank you, dear." Kendra motioned to the mound of books on the table. "Why don't you two have a seat?"

Careful not to disturb the precarious looking mound, they lowered themselves into two hard-backed chairs at the table's edge. Kendra took a seat next to them.

"You ran away from the Seclusion," she said. She didn't pose it as a question, as Jack had. "Why? Where are you going?"

"It wasn't a choice," said Vincent, a little defensively. "We *had* to leave. They took our parents."

Kendra didn't seem to need clarification on the *they* Vincent was talking about. "And you want help saving them?" Vincent nodded. Kendra strummed her fingers on the table, appraising them. "Well you're doing better than he was," she said. "*He* didn't even know what he was looking for."

"Who's *he?*" said Jessica. "Who do you keep talking about?"

"The only other Seclusion runaway we've gotten," said Kendra. "His name was John. *Is* John, I hope."

Vincent and Jessica exchanged a look. They had heard that name before, in Brian's dome: the older brother who was never in school, who Brian knew nothing about.

"He knew he was looking for the Order," continued Kendra. "The original Order, I mean – the protestors. But he had no clue how to find them. He may still be here looking had they not come for him."

"The Order came?" asked Vincent. "They found him?"

Kendra shook her head. "Not they," she said. "He. Just one man. He was very old. And tall. Just skin and bones. And his eyes...it looked like they had been gouged out and burnt on the insides." She gave an involuntary shiver, as if to shake the memory from her mind. "John should have been terrified of him. But he was from the Order, and that was enough."

Vincent thought back to their conversation with Brian, to the man without eyes Brian had said to be at the helm of the Order.

"Goodwin," whispered Jessica.

Kendra didn't hear her. Her eyes were still misted over. "Abigail was distraught when they left. She can hardly stand to talk about the Order now."

"Do you know anything about them?" asked Vincent. "Do you know if they can rescue our parents?"

Kendra shrugged. "I couldn't tell you for sure," she said. "But if anyone can help, it's them."

"How long ago did John leave with them?" asked Jessica.

Kendra thought for a second. "Around five years ago," she said. "For Hux. It's the nearest standard city."

"What happened to him?" said Vincent.

Kendra shrugged. "I don't know. Up until about two years ago, I thought he had been caught. We hadn't heard from him since he left."

Jessica scooted forward in her seat. "What happened two years ago?" she asked.

"That's when the packages started," said Kendra. "Hux is protected by Newsight, so I don't know how he got them out, but packages from him started dropping on top of the garage. Some were injections, some were food. And recently, they've been useless, only for people with Lenses. I don't know why he would send them."

Vincent and Jessica looked at one another again. "What did he send?" asked Vincent.

Kendra shook her head, pursing her lips as she thought. "You're probably too young to remember," she said, "but when Newsight first came out with Lenses, there were these devices that came with them called hard sims."

"We've heard of them," said Jessica. The slight weight in Vincent's front pocket seemed to grow a bit heavier.

"Good," said Kendra. "Well anyway, hard sims became obsolete decades ago. But recently, John has been sending them to us. Since he left, we haven't had anyone with Lenses, so we haven't been able to test them." She squinted at Vincent, then at Jessica, sizing them up one last time. "Do you think you could take a look?"

"Definitely," they said at once.

Kendra nodded, grinning. "Then wait here." She stood from the table and pushed through a curtain into the next room. Several seconds later, she returned with a stack of round white cases the size of Vincent's palm. "They come in these," said Kendra. "Look." She handed the top case to Vincent. Cautiously, Vincent unlatched it and looked inside. For a moment, he thought they were looking at dozens of copies of THE SIM, but the tiny black discs inside were much thinner. They were labeled, too, on the outside. A letter, M or F, and a number, usually a range of numbers, 12-15, 30-40, etc.

Kendra rustled around in the other cases she had sat down, and pulled out a sheet of paper. "The first one came with a note. Here's what it says." She cleared her throat to read. Vincent listened as he tried to open one of the discs. Jessica reached into the case to do the same, her ears perked.

"For anyone with Lenses who wishes to enter the city. Without these, people with Lenses will be taken away."

Vincent kept listening, waiting for her to keep going, but she didn't. She was looking up at them.

"That's what I thought," she said, seeing Vincent's confusion. "Here." She handed him the note. "See for yourself."

Abandoning his attempts at the disc, Vincent took the note. The paper was brittle, and the writing on it was barely legible. There were smudges on the edges, and the end of each word slurred into the beginning of the next, rushed.

"Look," said Jessica

Vincent turned to his left. Jessica had opened one of the discs. She emptied the contents into her left palm: miniscule, hair-width slips of film in the shapes of Lenses – they looked almost identical to the contents of THE SIM. The main difference, however, were the barely visible markings on their surface. Tilted at just the right angle, the curved part of the things glinted in complex, intricate patterns.

"Eye prints," said Vincent, in awe. He looked up to Kendra to explain. "Every pair of Lenses has them. It's where Newsight stores personal information. They started out with iris and facial recognition, but it wasn't accurate enough. They've been using prints for the past three or four models."

Jessica nodded in confirmation. "My dad talked about them. He says they're impossible to replicate. These must have come off of real Lenses." She stared down at the things in distaste at the thought. Kendra didn't seem bothered.

"So they're fake IDs," she said. "You must need them to get through the city checkpoints. If you have Lenses and aren't a citizen, you must be reported."

"Does no one travel between cities?" asked Vincent.

Kendra laughed. "Travel hasn't been allowed for years," she said. "Once a city goes standard, it's on lockdown. Newsight says it's for safety. I say it's for control."

Vincent looked down at the thin slips of film in Jessica's hand. "When did you say these got here?" he asked.

"Actually just this morning," said Kendra. "First package in weeks."

Vincent turned to Jessica. He was almost positive she was thinking the same thing he was: Brian's brother, if it were him, seemed to have known they would be coming, and the only way he could have known was through Lynn. It was an electrifying feeling – they weren't as alone as they thought.

"Is there any way we can get to the city?" asked Vincent.

Kendra raised her brow, taken aback. "To the city?" she repeated. "Have you not heard what I've been saying?"

"I have," said Vincent. "But if the city is where the Order is, that's where we need to be." He looked at Jessica, and she nodded in agreement. Kendra peered back at them, eyes misted in memory.

"You're stubborn like he was," she said. A hint of a smile played across her lips, but it faded quickly. "Jack is driving a group to Hux tonight before the attack," she said. "People have been getting cold feet about staying. If you're sure you want to go, there are still a few seats left."

"We'll go," said Jessica without hesitation. She looked down at the eye prints in her hand. "Would you mind if we use these?"

Kendra chuckled. "Take them all," she said, then looked around at her cluttered apartment. "You'd be doing me a favor." She smiled at them, a bit unconvincingly, then stood up. "Jack and Abby will be waiting for you," she said. "They're in spot 14. You'd best not mention any of this to them, though, especially not to Abigail. She doesn't like talking about it."

Nodding, and gathering their cases, Vincent and Jessica stood from their seats. "Thank you," said Vincent. Jessica echoed him close after, and Kendra nodded back. They started for the door.

"Children?" Kendra called out to them. They turned around. "If the Order is real," she said, "and John is a part of it, can you give him a message for me?"

"Of course," said Vincent. "What is it?"

Kendra took a breath, hesitating, as if deciding whether or not to speak. After a pause, she seemed unable to hold the words back any longer. "Tell him to come back for us," she said.

Vincent nodded. "Yes, ma'am."

Kendra dipped her head graciously. She smiled at them, the same afraid-looking grin as before, and watched them leave.

CHAPTER 10 – THE HALO

Vincent's eyelids fluttered open. He reached his arms up to stretch and knocked his fist against the window on accident. Next to him, Jessica awoke from the noise. She raised her head off the glass and rubbed her eyes, blocking the morning light.

They were on the bus, what Jack had called the monstrous vehicle that was transporting them. The previous evening they had spent choosing their identities, settling on an attached pair labeled "M, F: 15-17". Abigail hadn't seen them off.

"How will we know when we're getting close?" asked Vincent. He was looking out the window. The ground was barren for as far as he could see, no life, no color.

Jessica stifled a yawn and nodded toward the front of the bus. "I think we'll be able to tell."

Vincent leaned over and looked down the aisle as well. He knew what Jessica was talking about without having to ask. The entire view out the front window was filled with a vast expanse of skyscrapers, all huddled together in a dense, patternless cluster. But these towers were not quite the same as those around the Hole. These had polished windows that sparkled in the sunlight and designs Vincent had never imagined. There appeared to be things flying between them, as well, tiny black dots soaring from one rooftop to the next, like urban house flies. Below, the city was surrounded by six, enormous white halos. The bottommost was perfectly flat and low to the ground, but the others were tilted at slight angles, their edges rising halfway up the skyscrapers they encircled. They reminded Vincent of rings that had been dropped horizontally on a table and caught mid wobble before they could stop.

"Did the other city have those?" said Vincent. Jessica seemed to know what he was talking about without asking.

"No," she said. "The other city had no reason to keep people out."

"Or in," Vincent added. Jessica said nothing back.

"Ladies and gentlemen." It was Jack's voice, amplified through the bus's speaker system. "We are approaching Hux."

People around them started to wake up, yawning and stretching.

"The lines shouldn't be too bad," continued Jack. "They usually don't pick up until early afternoon, but I would encourage you not to take the chance." He paused for a moment, then looked up in the

102

mirror so he could see them clearly. "Best of luck."

******

When the bus came to a stop, the flying black dots Vincent had seen from afar were in much clearer focus. They were not black, but a dazzling pure white, and they were shaped suspiciously like the pods of transports. The halos, too, looked quite different. They were as wide across as the towers they protected, and their edges were dangerously sharp. On their outermost side, facing away from the city, was written a short phrase in thin, capital letters: THERE IS NO FEAR WITHOUT HOPE.

"This is as close as I can get you," Jack called back to the bus at large. "When you're ready, you're free to get in line."

Vincent and Jessica stood with the rest of the riders. They pushed their way into the aisle to claim their spot in line.

"Good luck. Good luck. Yes, ma'am, best of luck."

They could hear Jack seeing people off from the front of the bus as they approached. The way he spoke, he seemed to be hurrying people out. Vincent didn't blame him; he would need time to get back to the Hole before the attack.

"Good luck to you," said Jack when they reached him. Then, when he realized who they were, he shook their hands. "*Very* good luck to you two." He tipped his hat to them as they climbed the few steps toward the outdoors. "Good luck. Yes, sir, good luck…"

Jack's voice faded as they climbed off the bus. Jessica stopped in her tracks a few steps later

"I guess this is the line?"

Vincent followed her gaze. From the row of kiosks below the giant halos ahead, a line of a few dozen people extended outward. With a sort of nervous sigh, Jessica led the way to the back.

"…no, no we left yesterday morning but the traffic was terrible."

Vincent spotted the owner of the voice instantly as they approached: a tall, round man wearing clothes similar to the ones worn by people in the Hole.

"We ended up just pulling to the side of the road and waiting," the man continued. "Kids are still asleep. Been a long day for them."

Vincent and Jessica settled in behind the man. It wasn't clear who exactly he was talking to. The family in front of him wasn't paying him any mind.

"Hello there," the man said, turning around. "Name's Jim."

Vincent looked up. "Hi," he said. "I'm Vincent."

The man grabbed onto Vincent's hand and shook it without invitation.

"Nice to meet you, Vincent," he said. "And the pretty young lady?"

Jessica smiled curtly. "Jessica", she said, then turned to Vincent. It was a clear signal the conversation was over, but Jim didn't appear to notice.

"Where are you two lovebirds coming from?" he said.

Vincent's cheeks went red. Jessica sighed and turned back around. "Washing," she said.

"Ah," said Jim. "Not too far then. We're from way south. My wife and I had to alternate driving through the night." He turned to his right and craned his neck over the line. Vincent followed his gaze. Some ways off, the road to the south was packed with hundreds of vehicles bumper to bumper. "She's with the kids at the moment," said Jim. "They're all exhausted."

Jessica was still looking at the never-ending line of vehicles. "What are you going to do with your transport?" she asked.

"My what?"

"Your car," corrected Jessica. "Is there not a separate entrance?"

Jim shook his head. "You can only enter with what you can carry." He leaned in close and whispered at a volume Vincent felt sure the front of the line could hear. "I tried to convince the wife to let me carry the car," he said, grinning, "but she wouldn't have it."

Vincent tried his best at a fake laugh. Jim seemed satisfied with it.

"So what are you supposed to do once you get inside?" asked Jessica. "Just start over?"

"Pretty much," said Jim. "But they help you. It's part of Newsight's defense initiative. After you get your Lenses, you get a little startup package: a place to live, clothes, jobs. Even a shiny new car."

Vincent perked up at this. "All from Newsight?" he asked.

Jim nodded, beaming. "Exciting, isn't it? This is the first time we could afford the move. They gouge you for the shuttles, so we saved up for a car instead. Took us a few months, but we're finally here."

"So..." Jessica started, but she seemed to be having trouble processing something. "You actually *wanted* to come here?"

"Of course we did!" said Jim, confused. "Well, Tina took some convincing, but I talked some sense into her." He paused here, frowning. "Aren't you two excited?"

"We are," rushed Vincent. The last thing they needed to do was draw attention to themselves. "Just nervous, that's all."

Jim nodded, knowingly. "Ryan, my youngest, has been that way ever since we left. Only stopped crying long enough to sleep." He shook his head. "He'll realize soon enough how lucky we are."

"I'm sure he will," said Jessica. Her tone was more cautious now. "If you don't mind my asking, why were you so intent on moving?"

"Same reason as everyone else," said Jim, "for the protection. There was an attack a few times a week back home. Here, I've heard they only get one or two a month."

Jessica tried her best to look impressed. "And that's because of Newsight?"

"Yes, ma'am," said Jim. "Fatrem deserves a medal for what he's doing. Tina doesn't think so, of course, no matter how many lives he's saved. She's not a fan of Lenses. Says she doesn't trust them. But you can't argue with the results can you? Two attacks a month!" He gave an impressed whistle. "That's worth it." He pointed up at the giant halos They were only a dozen meters off now. "The Order gets past the halos every now and then. There was a cyberattack just yesterday, I heard – some message from the Order. But even Newsight isn't perfect."

"Those things are Newsight's?" said Vincent, looking up at the halos.

"Of course they are," said Jim. "It's the air defense system. Every standard city has them. Keeps the Order out."

"But they keep people in, too. Don't they?" said Vincent.

"I guess they do," said Jim. "But it's the best thing for us in the end. And it's only temporary. When the Order is finally stopped, things will go back to normal." Jim looked around them, as if he were about to tell some dark secret. "When that *does* happen," he said, his voice low, "I for one hope they let us keep our Lenses." He glanced around them yet again. "Have you heard of the simulations?"

Vincent said they hadn't. He had a feeling Jim would be disappointed if they had.

"They're only possible with Lenses," explained Jim. "It's basically like virtual reality that doesn't look virtual. They're supposed to be amazing. They're expensive – the better versions, at least – but they're worth it. I can't wait to—"

"Dad!"

Jim spun around mid-sentence just in time to brace himself against the small girl hurtling toward him. She wrapped herself around his legs in a bear hug. He patted her on the back.

"Hi, sweetheart," he said. "I was about to come looking for you." He looked up at the woman walking toward them. "Did you see me getting close?"

"We guessed," she said. "Ryan just woke up." She was carrying a young boy who looked a little too large not to be walking on his own. She smiled politely at Vincent and Jessica as she took her spot in line. "Ryan," said the woman. "Do you want to see daddy?"

The little boy glanced at Jim, then nuzzled deeper into his mother's neck. Jim scratched the boy's head.

"Still hasn't perked up?"

The woman shook her head. She looked tired. The skin of her wide, heart-shaped face had sagged so it collected at her cheeks.

Jim sighed, but he didn't seem disheartened. Vincent doubted if the emotion even existed for the man.

"Tina this is Vincent and Jessica," said Jim, turning from his son. "They're from Washing."

Tina smiled politely at them once again, but she seemed as pleased as Jim did timid.

"And now," Jim lifted his daughter with an exaggerated grunt, "we're all from the same place!" He hoisted the girl the rest of the way up onto his shoulders. She grabbed onto his ears, giggling. Jim pulled his wife closer as well. He kissed her on the cheek. "Don't worry, love," he said. "If nothing else, at least we're safe."

Vincent looked away. He was starting to feel sick.

"Good morning, sir."

Jim turned around to face the voice's owner. It was a tall, stone-faced man in the white uniform of the Guard. He was standing inside the kiosk just in front of them.

"Come on," said Jim, turning to his family. "It's our turn!" He shook Vincent's hand. "We'll see you on the other side!"

Vincent watched as they approached the stone-faced man behind the booth. Jim was already whispering something to his wife.

"Next please."

Another man in white called out to them from several kiosks

away. Vincent started forward with Jessica closed behind.

"Good morning," said Vincent when they were at the kiosk.

"Good morning," the man recited back. "Where from?"

"Washing."

"First time in..." The man trailed off. He was peering at Vincent's eyes. "You're in the wrong line. This line is for people without Lenses. You'll want to head over there." He pointed to a separate, empty kiosk to their left.

"Oh, sorry," said Vincent. The man nodded, already scanning the line behind them.

"Next!"

Exchanging a nervous glance, Vincent and Jessica started over to the separate, unpopulated line.

"Good morning," said Vincent, when they reached the new kiosk.

The man behind the counter, reclining in his seat, looked up at them. "Lenses?" he said, sounding uninterested.

In answer, Vincent leaned forward and opened his eyes wide. The man sat up in his seat for a closer look.

"Very good," he said. He stood up. "Come through here." He pressed a button under his desk and a seam next to the kiosk grew into a door. He motioned them inside. After a pause, Vincent stepped in. Jessica followed more reluctantly behind.

"This way," said the man. He led them through the small, plain white space toward a second door. "My colleagues will take care of you." He pressed a button on the door's side, then motioned them forward, this time giving them a little shove so they couldn't hesitate. When they were through, the door slid shut behind them.

The ceiling of the second room was several stories high, and the walls curved straight up, coming to a point at the top like an arrowhead. More men in white patrolled the halls, some carrying small white clubs, others corralling families still stepping through the other kiosks. They were in the bottom halo.

"You have Lenses?" A bored looking man in white stood from his seat when he saw them.

"Yes, sir," said Vincent.

The man picked up a strange looking device from his chair. Its handle was straight like the white clubs, but its end flayed out into a spoon-shaped curve.

"I need to get your IDs," said the man. "Step forward." Vincent obeyed. His heart began to beat a little faster. John's eye prints were about to be put to the test. And judging by the small squadron of Guard members straight ahead who had been watching them ever since they had stepped through the kiosk, it was a test they needed to pass.

"Open your eyes wide."

Vincent did as he was told. He found himself wishing he could silence the pounding in his chest – the man could surely hear it.

"Just a moment here."

The man held the device with the curved end up to Vincent's right eye. The end of the thing glowed white, shining directly into Vincent's unprotected pupil. He forced himself not to lower his gaze.

After a few seconds, the Guard pulled the device away. He looked at a screen on it Vincent couldn't see. "Ben?"

Vincent frowned. "What?"

The Guard checked the screen on the device a second time. "Ben Carlson," he said. "You're from Hux?"

Vincent opened his mouth to correct the man, but he stopped himself. "Uh, yeah, that's right" he said, stammering a little. "Is there a problem?"

The Guard looked down at the screen yet again. "Our records show you disappeared from the city several months ago." The man looked up at Vincent, suspicious. "And your Lenses are dark."

"They are?" Vincent tried to act surprised. The Guard nodded. His companions started forward. "It must have been the Order."

"What order?" said the Guard.

"*The* Order," said Vincent. His mind was racing now. The words came out automatically. "When they took us."

"Is there a problem over here?"

The largest of the other Guards was the one who had spoken. His companions flanked him on either side. They formed a wall between Vincent and the rest of the halo.

"Maybe," said the Guard with the device. He was still staring at Vincent. "You're telling me you were kidnapped by the Order?" He paused, eyes locked on Vincent, skeptical. "That's how you left?"

Vincent chanced a look up at the squadron of men standing in front of him. He was walking a tightrope. "They tried to recruit us," he said. "But we escaped. We just now made it back."

The Guard was shaking his head. "We haven't had an abduction in over a year. That issue was supposed to have been fixed."

"Well apparently the Order hasn't been told that," Vincent shot back. The squadron of men shifted where they stood. Vincent reined in his tone. "We didn't do anything wrong."

He held the man's gaze for several seconds. His muscles were growing tense, preparing to run.

Without a word, the Guard turned back to his device. He tapped a series of buttons there. Vincent expected a stream of security to come pouring in on them any second.

"Your record is spotless," said the Guard. He looked puzzled. "You're listed as priority, as well."

Vincent said nothing. He held his breath.

"Do you want us to take him?" asked the tall Guard.

The Guard who had scanned Vincent's eye said nothing for a beat, then shook his head. "That won't be necessary," he said. Vincent felt a giant weight slide off his shoulders. "But report this to Newsight. Tell them their system has a bug."

The taller Guard straightened, then saluted. "Yes, sir." He cast Vincent a final, suspicious glance before stalking off. The other men followed.

"Wait here," the Guard said to Vincent. "Miss." He motioned to Jessica, and Jessica stepped forward. Vincent held his breath once again as Jessica opened her right eye wide and the man prepared his device. The end of it glowed white once again. Jessica's shoulders rose and fell a bit quicker than usual.

"Lena Carlson?" said the Guard, looking at the screen. Jessica nodded. "The Order took you as well?" Jessica nodded a second time. The Guard looked from her to Vincent, his expression still stony. "This is going on both of your records," he said. "In addition, you will be assigned an escort, and he will organize an investigation. Your re-assimilation will be taken seriously."

"Yes, sir," said Vincent.

The man grunted in response. He held up the stick-shaped device and pressed a series of buttons on its side. He began running the glowing white end up and down Jessica's arms. "If you pass the search," he said, "your escort will be waiting for you outside the halo." He waved the device across the rest of Jessica's body in a few more passes. "You're good." He started on Vincent next. Vincent felt the thumping in his chest grow louder once again. He had to resist the urge to look down at his chest pocket where THE SIM was still tucked neatly inside.

"You as well."

The thumping began to soften.

"Through that door," said the Guard, pointing straight ahead. "And don't go getting yourselves taken again."

Vincent nodded obediently, then started forward with Jessica at his side.

"How did you know to say all that?" whispered Jessica.

Vincent shrugged. "Made it up," he whispered back. "I just hope it worked." He glanced over his shoulder at the Guard to make sure he hadn't come after them — the man had resumed his position in the chair. Relieved, Vincent turned back to the door.

"Now wait a second."

Vincent tensed, but when he tracked the owner of the voice, he relaxed again.

"Is something wrong?"

It was Jim. He and the rest of his family were being processed by a different Guard down the hall. Apparently the scan was not reserved only for entrants with Lenses. The Guard servicing Jim's family was holding the same, white-glowing device Vincent and Jessica had been forced to stare into. Jim had been cleared through the scan, and he stood with his daughter, who had also been cleared, next to a squadron of Guards. His wife and son had been shuffled off to the side.

"Just precautionary," said the Guard. "Our scan may have detected a virus."

"They're not sick!" said Jim. "They've been fine all morning!"

"I'm sorry, sir," said the Guard, obviously trying to quiet Jim down. "It's just protocol. I'm going to have to ask you to follow me." The Guard motioned to one of his colleagues to come take his place, and he ushered Jim and his family the opposite direction down the hall.

"Vincent."

Vincent turned around. Jessica was looking at him.

"Are you ready?" she asked. They were standing in front of the tall, narrow door the Guard had been talking about. Vincent took a deep breath. Jim slipped from his mind.

"Ready if you are," he said. With a nod, Jessica pressed the button on the door's side, and they started forward together into the city.

CHAPTER 11 – HUX

Vincent had never seen so many people before in his life. Crowds of them at a time passed by on the street, jostling against one another as they walked, oblivious to everything around them but some unseen destination straight ahead. Some wore dark pants with matching dark coats that folded in the middle, but most wore the same white, high-collared jumpsuits Vincent was accustomed to. Others, mostly the crowd who were emerging from the kiosks, wore tattered, old-looking shirts like those worn in the Hole. These people – the new entrants – were escorted by men of the Guard, and carried with them an endless number of small white bags. Vincent thought of the "startup" packages Jim had talked about.

"Look," said Jessica.

Vincent turned away from the families and followed Jessica's gaze. She was looking up at the buildings. They seemed larger up close, and there was more space in between them than Vincent had initially thought. At ground level, at least. The streets were wide enough to fit several transports going both directions at once (and there were several racing up and down the street now, some with their drivers fast asleep), but above, the buildings seemed to morph into a single unit. Every few stories, hollow glass arches connected the sides of neighboring towers, like the clinging remnants of a giant spider web. And through this web, the flying transports Vincent had seen from outside zoomed with startling speed.

"Hey! You two!"

Vincent followed the voice to a burly looking man a few meters off. He was starting in their direction.

"Are you the Carlsons?" he questioned. "Ben and Lena?"

Vincent hesitated, then nodded. He was still getting used to their new names.

"I'm your escort," the man said. "They said you need your Lenses activated."

It wasn't a question. Even if it had been, Vincent doubted the man would have taken no for an answer.

"Yes," said Vincent.

"Very good," said the man. He went cross-eyed for a split second as his eyes went out of focus. Vincent turned to Jessica with a questioning look, but she merely shrugged.

"The transport is on its way," said the man. "Stay with me." He motioned for them to come closer, and they obeyed. The man's hulking frame cleared out a decent sized path in the crowd of people still surging around them. "Here it is."

Vincent looked around for the transport, but saw nothing. Jessica tapped his arm. He turned to her, then followed her finger, upward. One of the flying vehicles had swooped down, with its glowing blue underside just a meter above them, and lowering.

"After you, miss." The man took Jessica by the hand as the transport lowered the rest of the way to the ground. He practically lifted her inside when the door slid down into a ramp. "And for the gentleman."

"Do we really have to—"

"Up you go."

Vincent felt his feet lift from the ground, and in a flash, he was in the pod of the transport. The burly man climbed in after him.

"All set." The man pushed the button that closed the door and leaned back in his seat. He took up one and a half of the pod's four, white bucket seats. Vincent and Jessica were in the remaining two. There were no controls.

"Name's Derek," said the man. He shook both of their hands. "Pleasure to meet you both. What happened with your Lenses?"

"Just a malfunction," said Jessica. "We don't really know."

Derek frowned slightly but didn't press. "That's quite rare," he said. "But it happens. You must be rather annoyed."

Vincent nodded in agreement and tried his best to look irritated. He hoped the natural nausea sitting in his stomach would play well into the act.

"How intensive is the process of reactivating?" asked Jessica.

"Oh not too bad," said Derek. "The Newsight operators will take care of you in a few minutes. It'll take more time to actually get there. We still have to cross the city." Derek pointed out the window. Vincent had been avoiding it, but he looked out now, surprised to see almost 100 meters between them and the ground. He leaned back in his seat, stomach churning.

"Is the Newsight facility in the Center?" Jessica asked, out of habit.

"Heavens no," said Derek. "Besides a little HQ in the management sector, the only real estate they have here is the halos. We're going to the highest one. The entry point is on the far side of the city."

"So…" started Vincent, chancing another look out the window – they were level with the shorter of the skyscrapers now. "We couldn't have just driven there?"

"I suppose we could have," said Derek, "but that would have taken an hour or so. Plus, then you wouldn't have gotten this view."

Vincent attempted a grin that turned out more like a grimace. The view was exactly what he had been hoping to avoid.

"It *would* be nice if you could show us around," said Jessica.

Derek looked at her, frowning. "Aren't you from Hux?"

Vincent looked at her as well. The thumping in his chest was starting to return.

"We are," said Jessica – Vincent could see her mind turning as she spoke. "But we've been away for months. And when the Order took us, they tried to brainwash us. We've been having trouble remembering things."

Derek raised his eyebrows. He turned to Vincent. "Is that so?"

Vincent tried his best to look solemn. He nodded.

"I knew you had been taken," continued Derek "but they didn't tell me about that. That sounds awful." He looked at them both, seeming troubled, then glanced out the window. "Maybe I can help bring things back for you."

Vincent let out a breath. Jessica relaxed a little in her seat.

"The city is split into sectors," said Derek. He had shifted so his behind squeezed solely into the seat closest to the window. His nose was pressed up close to the glass. "Right now, we're over the working sector."

Jessica peered out the window, then elbowed Vincent when she saw his gaze fixed on his own feet. Begrudgingly, Vincent looked out. Below them, the buildings were a bit shorter than the others, and less decorative. Their sides were made of an old, soot-darkened stone. From above, they looked no more exciting than a collection of boxes arranged with perfect order on the cement.

"This is the industrial part," said Derek. "It's right next to the entrance, but we do our best to hide it from view. Hard to hide from above though." He winked at them. Vincent managed a nauseated nod back.

"Are there Newsight factories down there?" asked Jessica.

Derek shook his head. "No, ma'am," he said. "Like I mentioned, they only have an HQ here. All their products are produced offsite. They ship them in from the Seclusions. Now, look–" he seemed eager to change the subject "–we're entering the commercial part. Banks, transport services, and the like."

Below them, the buildings had begun to grow, taking on the look of the towers Vincent had seen from outside. Their windows were more polished than those of the plain boxes of the industrial part, and their sides were connected by dozens of the glass arches.

"It's not just right below us, of course," said Derek, seeing Vincent's downward gaze. "It's all along this half of the city, the working sector is."

Vincent turned to the right as they flew. Sure enough, the same forest of polished towers filled the entire line of sight allowed by the window. The difference between those towers and the short, square buildings beyond them was sizable.

"And here we're moving into the management part," said Derek. "Management and political, I should say. The big wigs, the CEOs, all the other C-levels. And the politicians. They all work somewhere here."

Vincent had to resist the urge to scoot back from the window as they passed over these newer, taller buildings. The design of each building was entirely unique. Some were split down the middle and joined at the top like a giant, stretched out "n"; others were twisted together so they resembled a double helix; others still took on the shape of a skinny, four-sided pyramid.

"This is where everyone wants to work," said Derek. "If only for the view." He smiled as Jessica climbed out of her seat so she could get a better look. "Down there is the government's headquarters," he said. "Or...no that's Newsight's. I get them confused."

Vincent saw the buildings Derek was talking about. The first was actually two separate structures, extremely close all the way up but not joining together until the last dozen stories. The second was a single, wider tower, the top of which was curved inward like an enormous glass bowl. Vincent knew without asking this was the Newsight office.

"Now we're moving into the recreation ring," said Derek. "Below us, closest to the management part, is reserved for people who can afford to stay in their sims the entire weekend. They have to be taken care of: fed, watered, cleaned up. That's just for newsims, though.

People will still pay decent money for the knockoffs."

The buildings had begun to lose their flashy designs. They were perfectly round now, polished to a sleek shine and supported, where there wasn't glass, by beams of solid white.

"What are they trying to learn about?" asked Vincent. "With the simulations?" He had asked Jack the same question, but he hadn't gotten a straight answer.

Derek drew back from him, frowning. "Learn?" he said. "The simulations aren't lessons; they're experiences. Fantasies. You can make them whatever you want. Jump out of an air transport for the rush, be a CEO in the management towers." He elbowed Vincent in the side. "Have the girl of your dreams."

Vincent looked away. Jessica blushed. Derek didn't seem to notice.

"But that's all assuming you can afford them," he said.

"What do you mean afford them?" asked Vincent, glad of the subject change. "You mean people have to pay for simulations?"

"Well for the knockoffs," said Derek, "you pay for customization. That's why people go to the recreation ring: to buy the kind of sim they want. For the actual sims though, the newsims, you just pay for access. Newsims predict exactly what you want to experience, even if you don't know it yet yourself, and they create it for you. You can't even tell it's not real. I can't afford them on a regular basis — few people can. Most of us have to settle for the standard sims. They're not as customized, but they're still worth every penny."

Vincent looked again at the perfectly symmetric buildings below them, the ones closet to the management part. He could see their counterparts further in as well, slightly shorter and not as well kept. At the moment, the place looked deserted.

"And here's the main event."

Vincent looked up at Derek, then followed the man's finger straight ahead. Below them, higher than any structure in the management part and higher, even, than the simulation towers, was what looked like the top of a giant, urbanized mushroom. Over a kilometer across, a glimmering all-glass disc was held at cloud height by dozens of symmetrical round towers. Between each neighboring set of these towers, the arches Vincent had seen along the city's outer edge were denser than ever, with two or three joining each tower to its twins every few stories. The thing was a commercially built hive, interconnected and intertwined in its supports below, and presided upon by the saucer-shaped glass disc above.

"The residences," said Derek. Vincent could hear a hint of pride in the man's voice. "If you live in Hux, you have a home here. Most people live in one of the towers, but some, mostly the people who work in the management part, live in the disc."

Vincent continued to stare down at the intricate behemoth below. The disc, as Derek called it, wasn't completely flat as Vincent had thought at first. There was a slight curve to it, bowed up ever so slightly in the center.

"For the most part though, you'll be staying in the dormitories next to the halos," continued Derek. "You can come home to the residences on the weekends if you'd like, but most students choose to stay on campus. And speaking of students..."

They were beginning to pass over structures that, to Vincent, were all too familiar. White, tower-sized domes were stacked up from the ground in clumps, spread across the pavement in all directions like the lumps of a rash.

"The schools," finished Derek. "Newsight sponsored and all. They were built at the same time as the halos as part of Fatrem's initiative."

Vincent looked down at the domes. They reminded him all too clearly of the Seclusion.

Jessica scanned the domes for a moment as well, but she didn't focus there for long. Instead, she turned her gaze to the right, to the very edge of the window's line of sight. "Is all that part of the working sector too?" she asked.

Derek raised his eyebrows, then followed her gaze. It was yet another field of towers, nearly a third of the city. Most of the towers were perfectly round and bleached white, much like those in the recreation ring. "That's the retirement sector," said Derek. "That's what everyone has to look forward to. Work long enough, behave well enough, and that's where you go. Free simulations, even newsim. The government has a contract with Newsight."

Vincent looked over at the field of towers, stricken, without knowing why, by the stillness of them. There were no transports flying between them, nor even any arches to connect them. They merely stood there, stagnant, solitary.

"Why are there so many?" asked Jessica. "Are there that many elderly people in Hux?"

"It's not just the elderly there," said Derek. As he said it, his eyes lingered over the nearest line of towers. "But enough of that. Retirement is the most boring sector." He turned back to the front face of the window. "This is much more exciting," he continued. "The halos."

Vincent turned away from the stoic-looking towers, rather gladly, and followed Derek's gaze. They were passing over the last of the stacks of school domes below and approaching the tower-width halos around the city's perimeter.

"We're going to the activation office," continued Derek. "It's not far from where we'll be entering."

The transport began to decelerate, and as they drew closer to the highest halo, Vincent could see the markings there: words, again, only these formed a different phrase: THERE IS NO LOVE WITHOUT HATRED.

Before Vincent could inspect the words further, the pod had cut off his angle. Their rapid approach had come to a stop just a few meters from the halo's exterior. They stalled there, hovering for a few seconds, until a portion of the white surface slid to the side like a curtain. Vincent grabbed onto the side of the pod as they started forward, but they were through without a hitch.

"Here we are," said Derek. He knocked on the window they had just been looking out, and the door of the pod fell down from the top, forming the fragile looking bridge Vincent had seen from below. Derek stepped down onto the ramp and followed it onto the halo's inside floor. "Come on then," he said. "If your memories still need jogged later, we can go for another ride."

At this last bit, Vincent jumped from his seat a bit faster than he intended. Jessica climbed out at a more measured pace behind him.

"Just a ways off now," said Derek. "Follow me."

He started down the hall without waiting for a response. They followed.

"How long did you say you've been without Lenses?" asked Derek, shooting them a look over his shoulder.

"We didn't say," said Jessica. "But it's only been a few days."

"A few days!" exclaimed Derek. "I can't imagine. I can barely go without my sims for a few hours. Thank heaven I have priority access."

"From Newsight?" asked Jessica. "How long have you been working for them?"

"Oh I don't work for them," said Derek. "I'm not that qualified. I have priority access because I work for the Guard as a Newsight liaison. I deal with Order attacks, mostly, but it's been quiet recently, so I've been getting assignments like these."

"The Order hasn't been trying anything?" pressed Vincent.

"Well there was an incident yesterday. The Order tapped into the network and played a simulation on everyone's Lenses. Some sort of announcement."

Vincent and Jessica exchanged a glance.

"But that was a minor thing," said Derek. "All other major attacks have been stopped by the halos."

Vincent looked around them. This higher halo, like the one they had walked through earlier that morning, looked suspiciously like a normal hallway. "They don't seem like much," said Vincent.

"From the inside," said Derek. "On the outside, they have sensors that can detect a missile from 10 kilometers out. When they detect one, they form this kind of shield over the top of the city to stop anything from getting through."

"Like a dome," said Vincent.

"Exactly."

Vincent and Jessica made eye contact yet again.

"But no system is perfect," continued Derek. "The dome is penetrated occasionally. Or one of the Order ends up finding their way into the city. That's when my job gets ugly."

"How do they get in?" said Jessica. "We had to go through a screening process."

"Everyone does," said Derek. "But apparently it isn't foolproof. We don't know how the Order manages to sneak by so we can't stop them. The best we can do is minimize the damage they cause once they're in." Derek glanced around them, making sure they were alone. "There have been rumblings of letting Newsight take over ground security," he said, his voice low. "The halos have been so effective in the air, the Guard is considering turning ground control over to Newsight as well."

Vincent said nothing back. Jessica seemed to think about responding, but she remained silent as well. They continued down the hall without speaking.

A minute later, Derek came to a stop at a door with a line of white, stiff-backed chairs outside. "This is the office," he said. "They know you're coming, but let me make sure they're ready for you. Go ahead and have a seat."

Derek disappeared through the door, leaving Vincent and Jessica alone in the hall. Neither of them sat.

"We need to figure out what we're going to do," said Jessica. "We don't have much time."

"We will once we get to the dormitories," said Vincent. "Or whatever he called them."

Jessica shook her head. "We're about to be back on the grid, Vincent. As Ben and whatever my name is. They'll be watching us."

Vincent realized what she was saying. Communicating, about anything important, at least, would be impossible after their Lenses were reactivated. Vincent glanced at the door.

"We need to find Brian's brother," he said, his voice low. "He's our only way to the Order."

"But where do we look?" said Jessica. "You saw it from the transport: this place is massive."

Vincent thought for a moment. He kept one eye on the door. "How much older than us is Brian's brother?"

"Three years."

"So he'll be out of school. We know that much."

"That means he'll be in the working sector?"

Vincent shrugged. It wasn't much help. From the transport, the working sector looked like half the city. "What about the residences?" he suggested.

Jessica shook her head again. "You saw that place. It would take years to look through. And I barely remember what he looks like."

Vincent bit the inside of his cheek. They were so close. The Order could be in any one of the buildings they had just flown over, or underneath any of them, and they had no way of knowing.

Vincent paused in his thoughts, suddenly conscious of the slight weight in his front pocket. He was being stupid. Of course they had a way.

"THE SIM," he said. "As soon as they activate our Lenses, we can watch it. It will tell us everything."

"It will tell *them* everything, too," said Jessica. "They see whatever we see. Watching THE SIM would be as good as turning ourselves in."

Vincent slouched at the shoulders. She was right, of course. If Newsight saw them with THE SIM, they would be taken away before they could blink.

"What do you suggest then?" said Vincent.

Jessica started to say something, then stopped. She sighed. "I don't know."

They were silent for a few seconds. Vincent thought he could hear movement on the other side of the door.

"Can we send a message to Lynn?" he asked, lowering his voice.

"Not without Newsight suspecting something."

"So there's no way around it," said Vincent. "We have to find him."

"That's what I've been saying Vincent I just don't know how to—"

"Carlsons?"

Derek had stepped through the door. He was holding it open.

"They're ready for you."

Almost in the same beat, Vincent and Jessica took a breath. Vincent stepped forward first.

"I'll wait for you out here," said Derek. "Shouldn't be long." He nodded at Vincent as he passed him the door. Vincent stepped the rest of the way through with Jessica close behind.

"Hello."

A young woman wearing heels and a short, skintight dress stepped forward to meet them. The room they were in was bare but for a single, reclined chair in the center and a one-sided mirror on the far wall.

"Firstly," continued the woman, "allow me to apologize for this inconvenience. Newsight values our customers a great deal, and we do everything we can to prevent malfunctions, but even *we* aren't perfect."

She said the last part with a smile, as if it were a surprise. She turned from them and crossed over to the reclined chair, her heels clicking against the tile as she went.

"We will diagnose the issue and have you on your way," she said. "Ladies first?"

Jessica glanced at Vincent, looking nervous, then stepped forward.

"Good girl," said the woman. Her voice was sweet, but the aftertaste was artificial, forced. "Sit," she said, and Jessica obeyed.

"Now, all you have to do is put these on over your Lenses."

The woman handed Jessica two dark gray, Lens-shaped devices. Vincent couldn't tell from a distance what the material was made of, but it looked like metal.

With a slight shake in her hands, Jessica dropped the things on top of her Lenses from above. When they were both in, the whites of her eyes, as well as everything else, were no longer visible. She stared out of two sightless circles of dead gray.

"Try to relax, dear," said the woman. Jessica had been sitting stiff as a board. "The diagnosis is already in progress."

Vincent watched, helpless, as Jessica attempted to steady her breathing from the seat. The eyes of the woman standing over her were out of focus.

"Your Lenses were manually disabled," the woman said. "That will have to be reported." Her voice was still sweet, but less so than before. "Now for the reactivation."

Jessica began to shake harder still. Her cheeks were sucked into her mouth so tightly her head looked more like a skull. The empty, ashen-colored coverings on her eyes only added to the image, forcing her eyelids open eerily wide. Her lips were parted without a sound as she writhed in her chair. Her body contorted in odd, unnatural movements everywhere but the head. That remained, as if nailed through the eye sockets into the headrest, as if bolted there by the metallic gray Lenses.

Then she was still. Her body sagged down into the seat, her head suddenly released. She panted, still shaking, as she caught her breath.

"Easy as that," said the woman. She removed the gray Lenses from Jessica's eyes. Beneath them, thick lines of blood spidered out from Jessica's pupils. Some of the precious liquid even leaked from her tear ducts.

The woman leaned forward, barely bending at the hips from the tightness of her dress, and grabbed Jessica by the hand. She pulled her up, and Jessica crossed over to Vincent, her eyes downcast, her arms crossed, wrapping herself tight.

"Now for the gentleman?"

Vincent took a deep breath. He stepped forward, giving Jessica's arm a light squeeze as he passed. Without a word, he slid into the chair. He stared at the observation room window. He could see only his reflection, but he knew without a doubt he was being watched from the other side.

*****

Vincent and Jessica walked out of the room and back into the main hall.

"All set?" said Derek.

Neither of them spoke. Vincent was too busy trying to keep the blood in the corners of his eyes from leaking onto his jacket. The shaking made it impossible.

"I've already called a transport," said Derek. He looked away from them as he talked. He kept a good distance ahead of them, too. "It should meet us at the gate."

The walk was a silent one. Vincent was bent a few degrees forward as they went, focused on his own, trembling hands in front of his face and the quickly widening puddle of blood forming in his palms. Jessica's gaze was downcast as well. Her bleeding wasn't as severe as Vincent's, but her shaking was far worse.

"Here we are," said Derek.

They had reached the opening in the halo they had come through the first time.

"I actually have some work to do here with Newsight to set up your investigation," continued Derek. He still hadn't looked at them. "I'll just catch the next one." He crossed over to the transport, only a meter or so away from the strong winds outside. They were still a few dozen stories up.

Derek pressed a button on the pod's side. "Whenever you're ready," he said. "It will take you to your dormitories, and a different transport will take you to school. You don't have to worry about a thing." He smiled at them, and he forced himself to make eye contact. When he did, his smile disappeared. He looked away again.

"On second thought," he said, "I'm sure I can arrange for you to skip the rest of the day's classes. You must be tired." He paused here, glancing back down the hall the way they had just come. "They gave you free access to a newsim, didn't they?"

Slowly, as if hearing the words at a slight delay, Vincent nodded.

"Then I would enter that," said Derek. "It will help you relax." He glanced down the hall again, then lowered his voice. "Besides," he said, "it looks bad if you don't."

Vincent nodded again, then started up the ramp to the pod. Jessica started up as well, but she swayed dangerously from the shaking as she went. Out of his periphery – he still wouldn't look at them – Derek saw. Something seemed to soften in him.

"You're all right," he said. He stepped forward, forcing himself to look at her, and took her by the hand. "It'll get better." He helped her up the ramp into the pod, not letting go of her until she was seated inside. He took a step back so his feet were on level ground, back in the hall. He looked at them both.

"Stay safe," he said. Vincent nodded, and the ramp folded back up into the door. Derek watched them as the transport lifted off the ground and backed out the way it had come. Vincent didn't return the man's gaze. He looked straight down instead, so the blood from his tear ducts dripped between his shoes.

CHAPTER 12 – THE SIMULATIONS

The transport came to a stop some 10 stories up the side of a cubed stack of dormitories. As it hovered there, it lowered its ramp onto the balcony of its own accord. Vincent started down the ramp, this time glancing back at Jessica to make sure she was steady on her feet. When they were on the balcony, the transport – as if bidding them farewell – waved its ramp upward, then zoomed off through the maze of neighboring dorms.

Vincent turned around so he faced the three doors the balcony was attached to. "I guess two of these are ours," he said. Jessica nodded. The shaking had started to wear off.

As a test, Vincent stepped forward and pressed his eye up against the scanner of the door on the right. The locks clicked free. "This one must be mine," he said. "Try the middle one."

Jessica stepped forward. She had to brace herself against the door to stay steady for the scanner. A second later, the door slid open.

"Good," said Vincent. "You should rest. How do you feel?"

Jessica made no answer as she stepped forward. She paused in the frame just long enough to glance back at Vincent, then she was gone. Sighing, and now with his stomach in more knots than before, Vincent entered through his own door. The dormitory was tiny, low ceilinged and incredibly compact, with only two rooms: one just large enough to fit a twin-sized bed, and another for a toilet and shower. Vincent suddenly found it difficult to breath. The room's size, as well as its stifling white, had made his Lenses feel tighter. Slipping his shoes off at the door, he crossed the room – which amounted only to a few steps –and lay down on the bed. For the most part, the bleeding had stopped, but the throbbing pain had stayed with him. He knew without trying that sleep would be impossible. It wasn't necessarily the pain that kept him awake; it was the memory of the leaden Lenses being slipped over his eyes, of the hair-width wires extending back into his skull, of the raw, relentless intrusion.

Exhaling, Vincent rolled over onto his side. He thought about getting up, going for a walk around the city to explore, but he knew that was out of the question. They were being watched now, and anything they did would be subject to review. They would look for Brian's brother eventually, but to do that, they needed to remain undetected.

Vincent shifted his focus to his Lenses. If there was one thing in the city that everyone seemed to take for granted, that seemed sure not to raise suspicion, it was entering a sim. Vincent navigated to his stored simulations as the woman in the tight dress had instructed them, and was surprised to find an entire library. Well over a hundred thumbnail images scrolled across his vision. All of them were unique; some showed luxurious views of the city, others transports flying at high speeds, others unclothed human flesh. It took Vincent several seconds to reach the bottom of the collection where the most recent ones were. Just as the woman had promised, an unopened simulation had been added to the list. It had no thumbnail image, simply a label: *newsim*. Something about it made Vincent hesitate. He debated again whether he shouldn't get up and walk around. Derek had said school was only halfway through; maybe he could try and find their building. Or maybe he could skip out of school altogether and wander into the working sector, try to find someone who knows a man named John.

Neither of these options moved beyond thought. Vincent stayed where he was. His eyes continued to hover over the black square labeled *newsim*. It was still a Newsight product, but it seemed an exception to the Newsight Vincent had come to know. And besides, he thought, Derek had said it would look bad if they didn't enter the simulations. The things had been a gift, after all.

Closing his eyes, Vincent focused on the black square. A second later, his vision went dark.

"Welcome to newsim."

A female voice, soft and sweet – like the woman's from the office – rang out in Vincent's head. Though it could very well have been coming from somewhere in the room; it sounded so real.

"Your simulation will begin shortly. We hope you enjoy."

Vincent's vision remained black a few seconds longer, then returned all at once. He was no longer in the dormitory. The white walls and low ceilings had been replaced by a more spacious room, cream-colored all the way around and sloped to a point at the top, and with a soft gray floor made of knit, hair-like threads. He was sitting at a table with three other people. The first two he recognized instantly: his parents, though both looked different. Their Seclusion-standard white jumpsuits with high collars had been replaced. Vincent's father wore a shirt with buttons down the front, and his mother wore a light, flowing yellow dress. The third person at the table was a man with wrinkles sewn deep into his face, and with hair as white as the room Vincent had just left.

"That was delicious, Sarah," said Vincent's father. "Thank you."

Vincent's mother nodded in thanks, glowing.

"Just like your mother used to make it," said the old man. "Marvelous."

Sarah – Vincent still hadn't gotten used to the name – glowed brighter still. "I'm glad you liked it," she said, then turned to Vincent. "What did you think?"

Vincent looked up at her, then at his father and the old man. When he turned his head, there was no curtain of black chased away by his gaze, no trace of the rendering pixels. This was real. He felt himself in the chair. He tasted the air from the room. He felt full from whatever meal they had just eaten.

"It was really good," said Vincent, automatically. "Thank you."

Sarah's smile grew even broader; she seemed more thrilled than ever. "I can't believe one of my experiments finally worked!" she said.

"Neither can we," said Vincent's father, grinning.

Sarah rolled her eyes and flung her napkin at him. "Either way," she said, "you still have dishes."

Vincent's father groaned through a smile. "You're a slave driver, woman," he said, standing.

"Gets it from her mother," said the old man. "I've been there, Tom."

The name was as unfamiliar to Vincent as his mother's.

Sarah stood as well. "I think I'll sit on the back porch for a while," she said. "While you're slaving away."

Tom shook his head. "You better join her," he said to Vincent. "She'll put you to work if you don't."

The white-haired man stood as well. "I'm too old for that," he said, "but not for sitting with my favorite daughter."

Sarah smiled at him, then turned to Vincent. "There's an open seat," she said. "Are you done with your homework?"

The answer seemed to have been preloaded in Vincent's mind. "I finished it at school," he said. The words tasted foreign to him as they left his lips, but true.

"Well come on Vince don't keep an old man waiting," said the white-haired man in mock impatience.

Confused, but not really caring, Vincent stood from his seat. The old man draped an arm over his shoulders as they started for the sliding glass door with Sarah. Vincent didn't shy away.

"Tom," said the old man, "why don't you entertain us while we're out here?"

"I can probably think of something," said Vincent's father.

"Oh my," said Sarah. She leaned in and lowered her voice. "Maybe we'll close the door behind us."

"I heard that!" said Tom. He was at the sink now, his hands wet with soap.

Sarah only grinned in response. She led them out the sliding glass door into a wave of warm, natural-smelling air. They were standing next to a small round table, on a wooden platform of boards pushed together at the edges and lifted from the rest of the lawn.

"Tom we need to mow tomorrow," Sarah called back into the house. She was looking at the overgrown grass that covered the fenced in area they had just walked into.

"If by *we* you mean *Vincent*," returned Tom.

Sarah turned to Vincent. "Can you take care of it tomorrow?"

Vincent looked at his mother, then at the lawn. "Sure," he said. The answer seemed only natural.

Sarah squeezed his arm, still smiling, then pulled two chairs out from the table next to them. The old man sat down in the first one and Vincent sat down in the second. Sarah took her seat by the table. From the kitchen, a hummed, light-hearted melody floated out to them, one Vincent knew for certain he had heard before. When the intro was finished, Tom began to sing.

"Here it comes," said Sarah. "You just had to ask didn't you, Dad?"

The old man leaned back and closed his eyes. "Let him go," he said. "The man has to entertain himself somehow."

Sarah laughed and shook her head. She leaned back in her chair like her father had, but she kept her eyes open. She stared straight forward, through the foliage of the trees growing just outside their fence, at the pink-shaded sky beyond. Vincent mimicked her pose. He felt a warmth in him that had nothing to do with the heat of the air. It came from his mother and father and grandfather, from the short brown house with the angled roof, from the sounds of a song sung just out of tune.

Vincent continued to sit.

******

The sharp pulse of a morning alarm pulled Vincent from his daze. When his eyes flashed open, he was back in the dormitory. He had fallen asleep. At least, that's what the time on the clock next to his bed told him. His body told him something entirely different. He didn't feel rested at all. He had fallen asleep within the simulation. Outside of it, his mind had been turning as quickly as ever. Newsim, apparently, was on the same clock as the real world.

Vincent jumped a little when he saw movement near the bottom edge of his vision. He settled when he realized it was just a row of words scrolling across his Lenses. The message was from Derek.

I hope you enjoyed your evening off. I have arranged for a transport to take you to your new school. We tried to place you in your old classroom, but the spots had been filled by the Washing migration. I'm sure you'll fit in with your new classmates just fine... The transport comes at 7:50. It will meet you on the balcony.

Your investigation is scheduled for next week.

Vincent glanced at the clock, then groaned and leaned back against his pillow. Going to school was the last thing they needed to be doing. That was the one place Brian's brother most definitely would *not* be.

Forcing himself up, Vincent stood and crossed over to the narrow door next to the restroom. When it slid open, he was hardly surprised to see a rack of school uniforms. He was more surprised, however, by their uncharacteristic shade of gray.

At 7:48, Vincent stepped out of his room and onto the balcony. Jessica was already there waiting for him, staring out at the expanse of white school domes deeper in the city.

"Good morning," said Vincent.

"Good morning," said Jessica, turning around. She showed no trace of the incident from the day prior. She was steady, and her eyes were clear of blood. They were puffy, though, and the skin directly under them was tinted with the slightest shade of purple.

"Did you try the simulations?" asked Vincent, already knowing the answer.

Jessica nodded, yawning. "I don't think I slept."

Vincent yawned as well. "I don't think I did either," he said. "You got Derek's message, right?"

"As soon as I woke up," said Jessica. "But this isn't what we need to be doing." She caught Vincent's eye on this last part.

"I know," said Vincent. "But we'll have time this weekend. Our investigation – whatever that is – isn't until next week."

Jessica nodded but said nothing back. Vincent knew it wasn't much of a comfort. They would need much longer than a weekend to have any hope of finding a single *building* in Hux, let alone a single person.

"Look," said Jessica, pointing upward. "That's probably ours."

The round pod of a transport was soaring toward them, slowing down as it prepared to deploy its ramp. Vincent and Jessica started toward it.

"Is this ours?"

A lanky, black-haired girl had just stepped through the door on the far left of the balcony.

"It's *ours*," said Jessica, emphasizing the second word, "You might have to–"

"Perfect," said the girl. She pushed past them and up the ramp just as it made contact with the balcony. Jessica turned to Vincent. He merely shrugged.

"I got a message saying you were moving in," said the girl when they followed her inside. "You're the transfers?"

Vincent and Jessica lowered themselves into the bucket seats. Behind them, the ramp folded back up into the side of the transport. They began to rise.

"I guess so," said Jessica. "Does that mean you can just jump in our transport?"

"I don't see why not," said the girl. "We're going to the same place. You're in your final year, aren't you?"

They nodded, and the girl shrugged, as if that settled things. "I'm Annie, by the way," she said. "We'll be in the same class. This is my final year too."

She reached out her hand, to Vincent first.

"Vin–"

"Lena," Jessica broke in, taking Annie's hand mid-shake. "And this is Ben." She shot Vincent a scolding look.

"Ok…" said Annie, laughing a little. "Nice to meet you."

Vincent avoided Jessica's eyes, feeling foolish. He changed the subject. "So how is school?" he asked. "Will we be behind?"

Annie shook her head. "Not really," she said. "We mostly learn about the Order. And the trades, but you'll know all about those."

Vincent and Jessica exchanged a look. They decided to take the girl's word for it.

"I'm just excited for the weekend," continued Annie. "Newsim is free."

"Really?" said Vincent. "I thought you had to pay for it."

"You do during the week," said Annie. "A lot. But on the weekends, Newsight sponsors a discount at the school. If you stay here, you can have all the newsim you want."

"If you stay where?" said Jessica. "The dorms?"

Annie nodded. "Almost the whole school stays. We're here seven days a week."

"What about your family?" asked Jessica. "When do you see them?"

Annie shrugged, indifferent. "I usually don't," she said. "Every few months maybe. They spend most of their weekends in the recreation ring, anyway. The money they don't spend there they give to me as sim allowance for the week." A misty, distant look crossed into her eyes. "But nothing compares to newsim during the weekend."

Vincent thought back to the small brown house in the Newsim. He understood the misty look in Annie's eyes all too well.

The transport was already pulling to a stop over the side of the street. Annie didn't seem to notice.

"It's especially fun when you share," she continued. She was looking at Vincent. There was a raw, hungry look in her eyes Vincent didn't understand. "Are you busy this weekend?" she said.

Jessica pressed the door-button a bit harder than necessary. "Yes," she snapped. "We both are."

The door slid open and Jessica started for the opening, crouching as she pulled herself from the pod. Annie flashed Vincent another smile – one he weakly returned – then stepped out of the pod as well. Vincent followed, feeling confused.

When they were all three out, Jessica pointed to a building up ahead. "Is that it?" she asked.

Vincent followed her gaze. Across the street was a squat, square building some thirty stories high, the flat face of which showed only a handful of windows. It had a dreary, nondescript entrance with an inscription over the archway, the same phrase Vincent had read on the inside of the halo: THERE IS NO LOVE WITHOUT HATRED.

"That's the birthschool," said Annie. "The main building of it, at least. Our school is this way." She started off in the opposite direction without looking to see if they were following.

"Is that like Incubation?" asked Vincent, catching up. "Like from the Seclusions?"

"Maybe," said Annie. "It's just like our school, only for newborns."

Vincent found the answer profoundly unhelpful, but he could tell Annie's mind had already moved on.

"Hurry up," she called back to them. "It's almost eight."

******

The three of them walked into the classroom together just as the bottom of their Lenses began to blink with the time. Most of the other students, all in the same, dreary gray uniforms, were already in their desks.

"Please be seated, children."

The voice had come from the clean-shaven, average-height man at the front of the class.

"That's Mr. Watts," whispered Annie, sitting down. "He's the strictest teacher I've had."

Vincent wasn't surprised; the man's posture was rigidly straight, as if someone had tied a sturdy pole to his back.

Annie tugged at Vincent's sleeve and flicked her head toward the seat directly behind her. Vincent sat down, and Jessica followed suit in an open seat to their right.

"The day will proceed as usual," said Mr. Watts. "The morning sim, then trade work." His eyes scanned the classroom as he spoke, but he seemed bored. "Please accept my invitation."

A string of text appeared on the bottom of Vincent's Lenses. He may have been back in the Seclusion, with Mrs. Farring at the front of the room instead of the rigid, keen-eyed man there now.

Knowing the process all too well, Vincent selected the text and prepared to engage the sim. Before he did, however, he allowed himself a look around. The others had already engaged, but their heads didn't sway this way or that, and no one was facing the wrong direction. Nor even was there the familiar air of nervous excitement as there always had been in the Seclusion. Here, the room was stale.

The necks of the students were straight, their posture stiff, their eyes empty.

Next to him, Vincent felt Jessica kick his foot under the desk. Mr. Watts was looking at him. Turning back to the front of the room like everyone else, Vincent engaged the sim.

He was standing next to a window as large as a wall, staring down at a maze of plain, rectangular skyscrapers. Then the sky blazed red. A streak of white came hurtling toward him. The glass shattered and he went soaring back, knocking into something behind him, pushed there by the force of the explosion. He felt the heat in the air, on his chest. He felt the flames...

The simulation changed. He was running. On a street with cracked pavement, and alongside men and women he didn't recognize. Above them loomed the same skyscrapers he had seen from the window, most of them aflame. The air around them was polluted with smoke. There were sirens coming from all directions, but the sirens couldn't quite mask the constant rumble coming from above. Vincent looked up as he ran – fighter jets, zooming by far too close overhead, some dropping cylindrical loads as they flew, others launching them from their front ends, their aims trained on every building they could reach. Vincent started to cough as the tidal wave of smoke behind him licked at his heels. He increased his pace, but only toward a similar wave of smoke just ahead. The rumbling was louder now. There was a whistle, an explosion...

The simulation changed again. For several seconds, Vincent watched from a bird's eye view as dozens of jets dropped their loads over the towers of the city he had just been inside. He watched as a final, flashing white blaze split the clouds above...

The simulation changed once more. Vincent was on the street again, but he was standing now, and the sirens and jet engines had fallen silent. The smoke had cleared, and the street was still – what was left of it. Chunks of pavement were missing in giant craters, and the cars that had once lined its surface were overturned, their windows shattered, their hoods and side doors bent inward. Through it all, the stench of rotting meat hung in the air like a disease. It wafted up into Vincent's nose from the pavement, where, aside from the overturned cars and jagged craters, the people he had been running alongside now lay. They lined the curbs twisted at odd angles, sometimes piled atop one another, other times completely alone, abandoned in the ash and debris and blood like hunted game too small to collect.

Somewhere, a narrator began to speak.

"The Order has terrorized our cities for far too long."

It was a deep voice, a man's. The tone was angry and harsh.

"The Order is the enemy of the state, the enemy of freedom. Apart, we cannot survive. Together, we cannot fall."

The street disappeared, and the simulation ended. They were back in the classroom. The posture of the students around Vincent was no longer so straight, the eyes of them no longer so empty. A girl to Vincent's left was crying; a boy to his right was shaking all over; Annie seemed prepared to punch someone.

From the front of the room, Mr. Watts began to speak. "Let us not forget who is to blame," he said. His hands were trembling slightly – he no longer looked so bored. "Who are we fighting?"

In unison, as a monotone, obedient choir, the class answered. "The Order."

Vincent looked around him. Everyone but he and Jessica had joined in.

Mr. Watts nodded in approval. "Very good. Now let us begin our–"

Vincent's vision went black. By the gasps and whimpers around the room, he knew the same had happened to everyone else as well. For a fraction of a second, he thought their Lenses had gone dark, just as they had in the Seclusion, but the darkness didn't endure. A room appeared before them, small and cramped, and with a chair in its center lit only by a single lamp. They were in another simulation.

"Stay calm, children," Mr. Watts called out to them. "Remember the first attack. It's just another message from the Order."

This didn't quiet the whimpering.

Vincent tried to turn to Jessica, but instead of seeing her, he saw only the room with the lamp, viewed as if from a camera set on a tripod.

There was a soft rustling – someone had walked in front of the camera, blocking the feed. It was a man, and he was lowering himself down into the seat. His face was pale and his hair was wiry and unkempt. His eyes were bloodshot, with perfect circles of red around where his Lenses ended, and the skin of his cheeks was flat against the bone. He looked different, but Vincent would recognize the man anywhere.

Next to him, Vincent heard Jessica draw in a sharp breath. Vincent merely scooted forward in his seat, and listened. His father was beginning to speak.

CHAPTER 13 – MAINTENANCE

"Hello."

Tom Smith stared directly into the camera as he spoke. His voice was as hollow as his malnourished cheeks.

"Yesterday," he continued, "we launched an attack on Washing. Those who did not heed our warning, were destroyed."

Vincent could feel his heartbeat in a vein in his temple. He felt it as it throbbed, and he fixed his eyes on the blank, vacant stare of his father.

"Our attacks will continue," said Father. "And they will grow in number. We have penetrated Newsight's Department of Identification. We can be anyone. We can be anywhere. Standard cities are no longer safe. The halos will not protect you." He paused, his eyes locked on the camera. "The Order will triumph."

The feed went dark, and the classroom returned. The boy to Vincent's right was shaking even more violently. Annie's knuckles were clenched and white.

"It appears identification has not yet found the source of the hack," said Mr. Watts. "But we will be safe here, children. The halos *will* protect the city, whatever the Order claims. They simply wish to frighten us."

Vincent could tell the man was far from confident. The rest of the class – most of them completely quiet, the others on the verge of tears – seemed to sense the same thing.

"Now," said Mr. Watts, clearing his throat. "For trade-training."

Even in their shaken state, the class rose together with the simultaneity of a single, mechanical unit. Jessica followed suit close behind. Vincent remained seated, his gaze fixed on the desk in front of him.

"To your usual locations," said Mr. Watts, and the classroom unit moved once again, this time starting for the door. Jessica tapped Vincent on the shoulder, but he didn't move.

"Ben," she hissed. "Come on."

They were the only ones still sitting. The rest of the class was filing out. From the front of the room, Mr. Watts seemed to notice them. He started over.

"Ben!" Jessica hissed at Vincent again. She pulled on his arm, but he remained completely still.

"I'm flattered you would like to stay here."

Jessica looked up – it was Mr. Watts. He had come to a stop next to their desks.

"But unfortunately," he said, "I will not be teaching today. You will have to settle for the modules."

Jessica looked down again at Vincent, then back up at Mr. Watts. "Sorry," she said. "We're new."

Mr. Watts cast Vincent's immobile form a suspicious look. "You're the Carlsons?"

Jessica nodded.

"I received notice of your transfer yesterday evening," said Mr. Watts. "I meant to introduce you today, but it slipped my mind." He looked down at Vincent. "The Order's message must have shaken you up especially," he said. "They told me you were taken captive."

"For a while, yes," said Jessica.

"I suppose you saw that twisted excuse for a man in person?"

Vincent looked up for the first time. He locked Mr. Watts with a deadly, reckless stare. Jessica answered before he could speak.

"No," she said. "We escaped."

"So you have," said Mr. Watts. He frowned as he met Vincent's eyes; he saw the anger there. "Well your records say you're from Hux," he continued, turning back to Jessica. "Your trades haven't changed."

"But the locations have." Jessica looked out the door where the rest of the class had just disappeared. "We knew where to go in our old school. Not here."

"Of course," said Mr. Watts. "For the security trade," he looked at Jessica, "your modules are straight down the hall, third door on the left." He turned to Vincent. "For Newsight management, first door on the right."

"Newsight management?" repeated Vincent.

"I was as surprised as you are," said Mr. Watts. "Your file wasn't particularly impressive. But I supposed your lineage helps quite a bit."

"My what?"

"Your father is a Newsight man," said Mr. Watts. "Is he not?"

Vincent opened his mouth to protest, but Jessica cut him off.

"That's right," she said. She grabbed Vincent by the arm, harder this time. "We should get to our modules." She tugged so hard Vincent nearly fell out of his chair. Mr. Watts scoffed at them.

"That one will need all the modules he can get," he said. "Go on then." He turned back to the front of the class. Jessica yanked on Vincent's arm yet again. This time, Vincent let himself be pulled from the room.

"You have to try and get along with him," said Jessica when they were out in the hall.

"Why?" Vincent snapped back. He wasn't in the mood to placate a man like Mr. Watts.

"We'll need him," said Jessica. She held Vincent's gaze when she said it, her eyes wide, as if funneling something else to him she couldn't say aloud. Vincent stared back at her, attempting to absorb whatever message she was trying to communicate. He got nothing.

"Fine," he said. He glanced down the hall where the last of the stragglers were just disappearing into their module rooms. "We should go." He turned away and started for the first door on the right side of the hall, the Newsight management door.

"Ben?"

He turned around, sighing. He didn't feel like talking. He didn't feel like doing anything, really.

"Are you all right?"

Jessica's eyes were shaped in the same, hinting way, at some unspoken message. This time, Vincent had no trouble at all deciphering it.

"I'm fine," he lied, and he turned away once again.

******

The modules lasted for the rest of the day, breaking only for lunch. Vincent had to stave off sleep more times than he could count. The management modules would have been as good as a lullaby *with* a full night's sleep. Without, they were tranquilizers. Still, they had been enough to distract him for a few hours, even if they didn't actually teach him anything. Being a manager at Newsight seemed straightforward: don't share sensitive (or nonsensitive) information with customers, employees, or your family, and do what your superiors tell you to do. Vincent felt better equipped now to keep large quantities of secrets than ever before.

"How were your modules?"

Jessica came up to him in the hall. Their Lenses had begun to blink white only a few minutes ago. The hall was filled with students preparing to leave for the evening.

"Good." He didn't think it would be a good idea to tell the truth.

"How were yours?"

"Good," said Jessica. She didn't hide her lie as well as Vincent had.

"Should we try and get a transport?" asked Vincent.

"Not yet," said Jessica. "We need to do something first."

Vincent started to ask what, then stopped – Jessica had already turned away. He followed her, bewildered, down the hall back toward the classroom.

"Mr. Watts!"

The teacher turned around when Jessica called out. He was just leaving the room, locking the door behind him.

"Ms. Carlson?" he said back, brow raised. "How can I help you?"

"Ben and I were wondering if we could talk to you for a moment."

Mr. Watts titled his head, unsure. "I suppose so," he said. He unlocked the door he had just bolted. "What about?"

"Just a quick question," said Jessica. Mr. Watts grunted at the unhelpful answer but continued to push back through the door nonetheless. He held it open for them as they followed behind, then closed it again. "What is this about?"

Vincent turned to Jessica to listen. He was just as curious as Mr. Watts.

"Well it's actually about Ben," said Jessica. Vincent frowned. "Since the two of you got off on the wrong foot, he wanted me to ask you for him."

Mr. Watts turned to Vincent, wearing a questioning look. Vincent lowered his gaze, if only to hide his own confusion.

"Ok…" said Mr. Watts. "What is your brother's question?"

Jessica glanced at Vincent, hesitant – though Vincent thought he could detect some acting – then back at Mr. Watts. "Well, he's been really enjoying his modules lately," she said. Vincent suppressed a laugh. "And he was wondering if there was any way he could take a kind of field trip. To the Newsight headquarters."

Vincent looked up at her. It was his turn to wear the questioning look. Jessica was unreadable.

"A field trip?" said Mr. Watts. "And why is that?"

"Ben wants to learn from actual managers," said Jessica. "The modules are great, but they don't compare to being taught by real people."

Mr. Watts grunted once again, but he seemed somewhat pleased. "The school corporation does overuse the modules," he said. Then he paused, thinking. "Why can't your father arrange for this?"

Vincent swiveled his head back to Jessica. He felt completely in the dark.

"We thought of that," said Jessica. "Then this morning happened. Our father will be too busy with the hack to set anything up, and Ben was hoping he could do it as soon as possible."

Mr. Watts pursed his lips, thinking once again. He turned to Vincent. "Is this true?"

Vincent looked to Jessica, then back to Mr. Watts. "Yes," he said. He hoped he sounded far more confident than he felt.

"You didn't strike me as so ambitious this morning," said Mr. Watts, probing.

"I was just...shaken up," said Vincent. He didn't have to act now. "I'm sorry."

Mr. Watts held his gaze for a few seconds longer, then began to nod. "It *was* frightening," he said, then paused again. "I do have a connection in the Newsight. No one important, but he might be able to set you up a tour at the very least."

"That would be great!" said Jessica. "If I could tag along, I think a tour would be valuable for me as well. From a security perspective, I mean."

Mr. Watts looked at both of them for another few seconds, but his suspicion was melting. "All right," he said. "I'll see what I can do." He readjusted his stance, facing his torso toward the door. It was their cue to leave.

"Thank you so much," said Jessica. "We really appreciate it." She elbowed Vincent, and he played along, nodding graciously.

"Of course," said Mr. Watts. "I would never prevent you from receiving live instruction. I wish there was more of that, anyway." He frowned, seeming to realize he had said too much. "But never mind that. I need to catch my transport." He motioned for the door. Jessica thanked him once again, then led Vincent out of the room. When they were both in the hall, she started off at a brisk pace.

"Hey!" whispered Vincent. She glanced back at him but didn't stop. "A field trip?" he asked.

"Yeah," said Jessica, impatient. "Like the one you talked about. Now come on." She turned forward once again and continued down the hall. Sighing, Vincent started after her. By the time they had gotten outside, Vincent had caught up.

"Do you know how to call a transport?" asked Jessica.

"No clue," said Vincent. "Can you tell me why you just asked Mr. Watts to—"

"I think that one might be open," said Jessica. She pointed to a pod hovering several meters away over the side of the street. "Let's try it." She took off once again, with Vincent left standing. Annoyed, but with no other option, Vincent followed.

"It says Ben and Lena Carlson," said Jessica. Her eyes were out of focus, pointed at the pod. "Maybe Derek called us another one."

Without waiting, she jumped inside. Vincent stayed out on the sidewalk.

"Come on," she said. Then, seeing his irritated look: "I'll tell you."

Vincent looked around them at their classmates climbing into similar transports. He didn't see how Jessica could tell him anything – assuming all this had something to do with their plan – but he couldn't afford to cause a scene. He climbed up the transport ramp and let the door close behind him. He looked at Jessica expectantly.

"Ok," she said. She paused dramatically. "It was a surprise."

The words were hollow and Jessica's expression was blank. Vincent waited for the punchline, but it didn't come.

"Oh," he said. "Thanks." He looked at her for a moment, at her manufactured smile, but her expression was unreadable. Frustrated, he turned away. It had been naïve to think they could talk about anything important.

They were silent as the pod gained altitude in its typical, stomach-churning fashion. Vincent watched out the window for a while, then, when they started to get too high for his liking, he closed his eyes. He was starting to drift off when he felt something tracing along his spine. He turned around. Jessica was facing the window, but her left hand was closer to him than usual.

"What is it?" he asked.

Jessica turned to him, trying and failing to look innocent. "What's what?" she said. Vincent tilted his head slightly, frowning. She nodded toward the window. "Keep looking."

These words weren't as hollow as the ones before. Frowning deeper still, Vincent turned back to the glass. They were still continuing to rise. Below them, he could see the squat, block-shaped building Annie had called the birthschool.

The tracing started again, and Vincent jumped. He didn't turn around this time though. Something kept his eyes fixed out the window. It was Jessica's finger. He could feel it now. She ran it down the center of his spine, slow and soft. The hairs on his arms started to rise. Then the pattern of the tracing changed: a half curl facing upward, a straight line under his shoulder blades. She paused after that before starting again, this time with a different pattern. Vincent narrowed his eyes, squinting as he looked out the window. He needed to concentrate – Jessica was drawing letters.

They rode like that in silence for almost a minute before Jessica lifted her finger from Vincent's back. Vincent had lost track of some of the symbols, but he could piece the message together well enough: *John. Identification.*

It was the only thing the message could have been, but it was as unhelpful as Jessica's other answers. They both already knew the plan was to find Brian's brother, and the second word seemed completely random.

Vincent turned his gaze from the window and back to Jessica. She saw his confusion.

"What do you think about the hack?" she asked him. He could hear the prompting in her voice. She was trying to tell him something.

"I don't know," he said. "It's scary, I guess."

"Newsight has never been hacked before. How do you think it happened?"

Vincent's frown endured for a moment longer, then began to fade.

John. Identification.

The eye prints. They had to have come straight from Newsight. What if John had infiltrated the HQ? What better way for him to serve the Order than to provide them with false identities? It was the perfect way to smuggle in supporters. He could send the prints to people like Kendra, people who had access to what little resistance that remained in the cities, and Kendra could send in recruits, even on accident. Newsight *had* been hacked. The hacker could only have been John.

Vincent felt the realization wash over him in an instant. Jessica's field trip idea had been brilliant. The Newsight headquarters was the perfect place to begin their search.

"What do you think?" Jessica prompted him.

"I think you're right," he said.

Jessica nodded, smiling. Without another word, she turned back to the window. Vincent did the same. He stared out over the city with his eyes wide open this time. The place no longer seemed so large, so imposing. For the first time in days, they knew exactly where they needed to go.

******

Vincent leaned in close to the scanner with his right eye opened wide. He held it there until the screen blinked its usual shade of green, then pulled away as the door slid open. He was about to step into his room when he saw movement to the left. Beyond where Jessica stood in front of her own scanner, a second transport was approaching the balcony. Jessica noticed it as well, and she cast Annie's door a nervous glance. Suddenly eager to get inside, she tapped impatiently on the screen of her scanner.

"Hello there!"

The voice was much deeper than Annie's, and its owner – the burly man climbing out of the approaching transport – was familiar.

"Derek?" said Vincent.

"How are you, Ben?" Derek climbed the rest of the way out of the transport and brushed himself off. "Lena?"

"Uh...hi," said Jessica. She glanced at Vincent before turning back to the pod. "Is something wrong?"

"No, no, nothing at all," said Derek. As he spoke, a bright-faced woman in a white dress followed him out of the transport. "But you both missed maintenance yesterday at school. I thought I would bring the maintenance to you."

"Maintenance?" said Jessica.

Derek motioned to the woman behind him. Vincent was sure he had never seen her before, but the woman's young features and tight, curve-hugging dress were oddly familiar.

"Hello, children," the woman said, smiling.

"Kara will be ensuring your Lenses are in functioning order," said Derek. "The school reserves Wednesday mornings for this purpose. We wouldn't want you falling behind already, would we?"

The woman in the dress didn't wait for their answer. "Which one of you would like to go first?"

Vincent stepped forward automatically. Jessica, after all, had gone first last time.

"Very good," said the woman. "Step inside please." She motioned Vincent inside, and he obeyed. Jessica, to the woman's annoyance, followed. "Derek tells me your Lenses are newly activated," said the woman. "From a malfunction. Is that right?"

Vincent nodded.

"Then maintenance is even more important," the woman continued. "Especially given the recent hack."

"The hack!" exclaimed Derek. He was forcing his oversized frame through Vincent's small door. "That's what I was going to ask you about on the way here, Kara. Surely Newsight is going to do something about it. It's terribly embarrassing."

The woman smiled, sweetly. "We've received similar feedback," she said. "It will be taken care of." She turned to Vincent and sat the small white case she was carrying on the foot of the bed. "Sit please."

Vincent did as he was told. He watched as the woman unzipped the case and dug inside. She emerged with a silver, needle-tipped device. To Vincent, it looked a bit like the gun that had been pointed at him back in the Hole.

"Open wide," said the woman. She held her finger around the trigger of the device as she raised it up. Vincent glanced at Derek. The man nodded. Taking a deep breath, and bracing himself for the pain, Vincent opened his eyes as wide as they would go. The woman leaned closer to him — he could smell her overpowering, flowery perfume — with the device raised. She lowered the tip down onto the surface of his right eye. It began to water. His reflexes told him to blink—

She pulled the trigger. With a flourish, she shifted to the left eye, then pulled the trigger once again.

"There we are," she said. "Good as new." She turned to Jessica. "Next?"

Frowning, Vincent stood up. The process hadn't hurt in the slightest. The worst of it had been no more than a tickle.

Jessica turned to him before sitting down. He nodded reassuringly. Moments later, the woman had pulled the trigger twice more.

"And we're done," she said, placing the device back in the case. "Quick as that."

Derek clapped his hands together. The noise sounded like an

explosion in Vincent's box-sized dormitory. "Perfect," he said. "Allow me to call you a transport, Kara."

The woman shot Vincent and Jessica one last winning smile, then turned to Derek. He helped her, quite unnecessarily, through the doorway and out onto the balcony. When they were out of earshot, Jessica breathed a sigh of relief.

"I didn't feel anything," she said. "Did you?"

"Nothing," said Vincent. He glanced out the door. A transport was already lowering onto the balcony. "At least it wasn't like the activation."

Jessica shuddered at the thought. "I don't think I could do that again."

Vincent nodded in agreement and started to say something back, then stopped – Derek had reentered the room.

"Well that wasn't so bad, was it?" he said. Neither of them responded. Derek's smile faded.

"I know your hopes for this couldn't have been high," he said, "after last time. It was wrong of me not to warn you about the activation process, and I don't intend to make that mistake again." He glanced out the door to make sure the woman's transport had gone. He lowered his voice. "I came with Kara today because I wanted to warn you about something else." He paused here to make sure they were both looking at him. "Newsight has been monitoring you," he said. "And you've been flagged."

"Flagged?" repeated Vincent. He looked at Jessica – she was wearing the same, puzzled look he was. "What does that mean? Did we do something wrong?"

"No, no, nothing like that," said Derek. "These things usually amount to nothing at all – they're just precautionary – but you should be careful all the same." On these last words, his voice had turned casual, unworried, but his expression didn't seem to match. It was grave, just on the border of afraid. "Do you understand?" he asked.

Vincent and Jessica looked at one another, then back at Derek. Vincent answered for them. "Yes, sir," he said.

Derek nodded, then slapped his knees as he stood up. "Good," he said. His tone had returned to normal. "I didn't expect you to do anything that would raise further alarm, but I wanted to let you know regardless." He glanced out the door. "That will be my transport," he said. Vincent didn't see any coming. "It was good to see you both

145

again." He started for the door, poising his hand over the button as he stepped through. "Also," he said, pausing. "If you wouldn't mind, just keep this between us."

"Of course," said Vincent. Derek nodded back to him, stepped the rest of the way through the door, and closed it after him. Vincent felt a pang of guilt for lying to the man. Their conversation, after all, had been far from private.

"Well," said Jessica, standing. She glanced at the door where Derek had just disappeared. "I should go back to my room." Avoiding the balcony, she started for the door to the hall. She had only taken a few steps when she paused and looked back. "I'm not tired yet," she said. "I think I'll have a sim."

Vincent nodded. He knew what she was thinking. If they had indeed been flagged by Newsight, the simulations would only help them blend in. "I think I will too," he said.

Jessica smiled at him – perhaps relieved – then continued the short distance to the door. She disappeared into the hallway a second later.

When she had gone, Vincent lay back on his bed with his feet still dangling off the end. He let his eyes slide out of focus. It wouldn't have taken Jessica's suggestion about the simulations for him to enter one. Thoughts of the small brown house and grassy backyard had plagued his mind ever since the first sim. If it helped rid them of Newsight's flags, terrific, but that wasn't why he let his eyes lead him to the simulation library; he *wanted* to go back. His Lenses seemed to sense it, too, because he didn't have to scroll to the bottom this time – the black square labeled *newsim* was already at the top. Only now, there was a second label there as well: *1,200*. Vincent sighed, letting his head sink a centimeter deeper into the bed. Derek hadn't given them any spending money, let alone luxury money. Still, on a whim, Vincent selected the sim anyway. To his surprise, it opened the same as it had before, and on the bottom of the screen, a few lines of text appeared as well:

114,000

-1,200

Balance: 112,800

Vincent let out a laugh. It felt odd coming out of him, but he couldn't help it. Apparently, Ben and Lena Carlson had continued to receive an allowance – and a generous one, at that – in spite of their absence. Or, perhaps, their benefactor hadn't noticed their absence at all.

The numbers cleared, and the same narrator as before welcomed Vincent to newsim. Moments later, the black screen began to fade, and he was sitting in the same house as before, only this time, they had traded the hard-backed chairs around the dining table for the soft, sinking chairs in the room over. Vincent and his grandfather both had their own seat, and in between them, Vincent's parents were sharing a single, larger one.

"It would have been a catastrophe." Vincent's grandfather was speaking. "To give any one company that much. I never trusted them, anyway. Not a single one."

"I'm with you, Rick," said Tom. "The last straw for me was when they lobbied against the regulations. We knew then we had let them go too far. Almost all the way."

"Things never quite felt right," joined Sarah. "In the Seclusion..." she shuddered. "It was never home. And the things they tried to make me do in Incubation." She shook her head in disgust. "Terrible."

Tom nodded in agreement. "If only you knew what was going on in the cities," he said. "That was the real reason we stopped things. I just don't know how we let it all get so bad."

"I think the kids saved us," said Rick. "We finally realized the kind of world we were about to pass down to them. And," he continued, smiling, "that simulation was a big part of it."

"THE SIM?" said Tom. "It was *all* of it. And can you believe it was our Vincent who showed us?"

"Of course I can," said Sarah. Tom squeezed her around the shoulders.

"So can I," he said. He was looking at Vincent, eyes beaming with pride. "Why don't we watch it again?" he said. "As a reminder."

"Tom I don't think that's a good idea," said Sarah. "We're safe now. We can forget about all that."

"The hell we can," said Rick. "The second we forget is when it happens again. A different company next time. Maybe a government. I think they should show that thing in schools twice a week."

Vincent's father laughed, but he made no contradiction. "We don't have to if you'd rather not, Sarah," he said. "But it *has* been a while."

Sarah pondered for a second, then relented. "Well all right," she said. "Do you have it, Vincent?"

Vincent reached down to his front pocket on instinct, but there was no pocket there, only a column of buttons and a striped fold of fabric.

"Try your pants, sweetheart," said his mother.

Growing hot at the cheeks, he reached inside both pant pockets. In his left, he felt the hard disc of THE SIM on his fingers. He pulled it out.

"Toss it here," said Tom, standing. "I'll plug it in."

Hesitating as he looked down at the precious disc in his hands, Vincent tossed the thing to his father. He watched as Tom bent down in front of a large, flat screen at the front of the room. Just as he began to insert the disc into its slot, the air in the room went stiff and cold. Everything was still, even the curtains on either side of the backdoor had frozen in their flutter. It stayed like that for a full second before things returned to normal.

"Let's watch a movie instead," said Tom. His voice was cheery and warm, but something about it seemed out of place. He looked back at them. "How does that sound?"

"Great idea," said Rick.

"Perfect," said Sarah.

He looked at Vincent next. "I'll pick your favorite." Smiling, and without waiting for an answer, he turned back to the screen. Unsettled, Vincent grew tense in his chair. But when the screen began to play, and his parents leaned back to watch, Vincent forgot about THE SIM. His parents and grandfather were smiling, and the air was warm again.

CHAPTER 14 – THE HEADQUARTERS

The next day, when Vincent and Jessica climbed into their transport on the balcony, Annie was not with them. The handful of balconies visible to them seemed to be running late as well. It was, however, the end of the week. Newsim was on the horizon.

At school, they walked into a near empty classroom. Still, as soon as they stepped inside, Vincent could sense the difference in mood. It wasn't just lethargy that had taken hold. There was a nervous, excited kind of energy as well. The boys shifted in their seats. Their eyes strayed more often toward the girls. And the girls didn't shy away, as they may have throughout the week. They even sat up a little straighter.

"Good morning, Ben."

Annie had just walked into the room, in a rush. She was standing rather close to Vincent's desk.

"Good morning," said Vincent. Annie flashed him a smile before starting for the seat directly in front of him. She sat down with exaggerated slowness, then leaned all the way back. The scent of her hair should have been overpowering, but this morning, Vincent didn't mind it.

By the time the digits at the bottom of their Lenses had ticked to 8:00, the classroom was full. Mr. Watts hurried in right on time, looking disheveled.

"Good morning, children," he said. They started to call out back to him, but he held up a hand. His eyes were out of focus, already navigating his Lenses. "We're in a rush this morning," he said. "We have an announcement before our Order sim. Please accept."

As he said it, a familiar string of text scrolled across the bottom rim of Vincent's Lenses. Jessica cast him a questioning look. He only shrugged. Glancing down at the invitation, he engaged.

The room disappeared. The simulation was completely black but for a large "Newsight" printed in white down the middle, and their rotating, eye-shaped emblem just below.

"This is a Newsight public announcement."

The narrator's voice rang out in Vincent's head. It was the same, sweet-sounding voice that followed the selection of a newsim.

The black background and plain text changed to an aerial view of a Seclusion. If Vincent wasn't mistaken, he knew that particular Seclusion all too well.

"The suspect in the Seclusion bombing has been apprehended," the voice continued. "The man responsible tapped into the defense system and disabled the network, thus enabling the Order's attack to strike its target."

The feed changed once again. They were in the Center, out front of the Capitol. There was a group of Senators standing on the front steps, all dressed in their usual, high-collared uniforms. Below them, still climbing upward, was a small squadron of white-clad members of the Guard. They appeared to be escorting someone: an average height, unassuming man with a protruding stomach. Vincent couldn't see the man's face.

"We regret to inform you," continued the voice, "that the suspect is one of our own."

The feed changed angles so they could see the face of the man being escorted: the wide nose, the large, beady eyes. Vincent's heart dropped. Next to him, he heard Jessica take in a sharp breath.

"A Newsight developer has been confirmed as the hacker involved," said the narrator. "He is now suspected of having connections to the Order. He is suspected to have played a role in the identification hacking as well. Today, he will face what we expect to be a swift trial."

The feed zoomed out once again so the whole Center was visible from above. The dome of the school, Vincent noticed, had been repaired.

"For our loyal Newsight customers," continued the voice, "there is nothing to worry about. For the inconvenience we may have caused, please accept our gift of a free newsim, and enjoy your weekend."

The feed disappeared, replaced by the simulation home screen where a thumbnail labeled *newsim* had been deposited in the lower right hand corner. That lingered for a few seconds, then the classroom returned. Vincent turned immediately to Jessica. Her lips were parted, and her gaze was fixed on the back of the boy in front of her.

"That's great news," said Mr. Watts, though his tone didn't reflect much excitement. "Now we can begin our day with peace of mind. All of you please hurry to our usual sim."

Vincent stole another look at Jessica. Her mouth was still slightly agape, and her eyes hadn't shifted from the boy's back. Vincent had a feeling she was thinking of the "swift" trial the narrator had mentioned. He had a feeling, also, what the result of that trial would be.

"We won't begin until everyone has accepted."

Vincent turned to the front of the room. Mr. Watts was looking at them. Casting Jessica one last look, Vincent entered the sim. The explosion happened just as it had the day before, then the smoke, the running, the bodies.

******

Vincent exited his module at the end of the day feeling restless. The simulations had been just as boring – if not more so – than the day before, but that wasn't all. The mood of the day was contagious. He felt an odd urge to run and jump, and at the same time, to lie down and do nothing at all. The modules, he felt quite certain, did not provide the outlet for these urges he was looking for.

"Hi, Ben."

Vincent turned around. It was Annie. She was among the first of the crowd exiting their modules for the evening.

"Hi," he said. He looked over her shoulder for Jessica but saw only the crowd.

"Have you thought anymore about my invitation?" she asked. Her voice sounded different. It wasn't as high pitched and rapid. It had grown just a touch deeper, maybe not even that, but warmer, and the pace of it had slowed, much like the way she had sat down in front of him that morning.

"What invitation?" said Vincent.

"About the sims," said Annie. She was standing a few centimeters closer to him than normal. "This weekend," she said. "I asked if you wanted to share one."

"Share?" repeated Vincent. Annie nodded her head, slowly. "Uh…" He glanced over her shoulder once again. "When?" he asked.

"Tomorrow," said Annie. "Night."

A hot, prickly sensation lit the skin of Vincent's face. The restless feeling that had been increasing its hold on him since the morning had been amplified.

"Ok," he said. It didn't feel like his voice that answered, but he let it keep talking. "I'll share with you."

Annie smiled at him. "Good," she said. "I'll message you." She smiled again, then brushed past him, grazing her shoulder against his arm as she went.

"Ben?"

Vincent turned around, expecting – hoping, even – for Annie again.

"Have you finished your modules?"

Vincent sagged at the shoulders. It was Mr. Watts.

"Yes, sir," he said.

"Good," said Mr. Watts. "Because I have good news. My associate at Newsight has agreed to give you a tour."

It took Vincent a moment to realize what the man was talking about. "Of the headquarters?" Mr. Watts nodded. "Oh," said Vincent. "Thank you. I'm sorry yesterday for–"

Mr. Watts held up a hand. "Not at all," he said. "I'm just glad someone else recognizes the value of real learning." He cast the door of the module room a disdainful look. "Where is your sister?"

Vincent turned back around toward Jessica's modules. He scanned the dwindling crowd for a moment before spotting her. She was several doors away, talking to a boy Vincent didn't recognize.

"She just finished her modules as well," said Vincent, turning back to Mr. Watts. "I'll bring her here."

"No need. I've already called a transport. You can meet it out front."

"Oh," said Vincent. "Ok."

Mr. Watts nodded to him, then started to turn away. Vincent did the same.

"Ben."

Vincent turned back to him.

"Try not to let the other students see you."

Vincent nodded. "Yes, sir."

Mr. Watts dipped his head in thanks, then started off down the hall, almost jogging. Vincent started in the direction opposite.

"…but you could make time." The boy Vincent didn't recognize was still talking when Vincent reached them. "*I* can make time."

"Thank you," said Jessica. "But I can't." There was an edge of disappointment to her voice. "I'm sorry."

The boy looked ready to press her further, then he saw Vincent. Casting Jessica one final look, he took off down the hall.

"What was that about?" said Vincent.

Jessica twisted around at the sound of his voice. "Nothing," she said, rather quickly.

Vincent frowned, then turned to watch the other boy walk away from them. He was quite tall, and sturdily built.

"Were you just talking to Mr. Watts?" asked Jessica, changing the subject.

"Yeah," said Vincent, turning back around to face her. Her pupils were wide, as Annie's had been. "He got us the tour."

Jessica's expression changed entirely. "Really? When do we go?"

"Right now," said Vincent. "The transport is out front."

Jessica looked down the hall where Mr. Watts had just disappeared. "I didn't think he would actually do it," she said.

"I didn't either," said Vincent. "I don't think he wants the others to know. Let's wait until they've all gone."

Jessica nodded in agreement as the last few stragglers passed them by toward the main doors. When the hallway was empty, they left the building through the side.

On the street, Vincent spotted a transport with its ramp already lowered onto the pavement. "I guess that's for us," he said. Neither of them hesitated this time. They crossed over to it and climbed inside.

"What all do you think we'll get to see?" said Jessica when the pod started to rise. Vincent could hear the real question. *Will we get to see the identification division?*

"I don't know," he said. "We can ask them when we get there."

Jessica didn't say anything back. Nor did she tell him to look out the window so she could draw on his back again. The plan was simple now. They passed the rest of the ride in silence.

When the pod started to descend along the side of the Newsight tower, Vincent peered out the window. A thin, spectacled man in all white was looking up at them from the street.

"That's probably our guide," said Vincent.

Jessica nodded in agreement as she glanced at the man, then turned her gaze to the front of the building some ways off. There was a transport convoy parked on the street. Four of the large, three-wheeled transports Vincent and Jessica had ridden in back in the Seclusion blocked the better half of the road. A group of white-clad men were climbing out of them and walking inside.

The pod came to a stop just in front of the man with the

spectacles, and the ramp lowered shortly after.

"Hello," said the man. "You are Ben and Lena?"

"Yes, sir," they said in unison.

"Good. Now out you come." He made a beckoning motion, as they climbed down the ramp. "We won't have much time. I'm doing Henry a big enough favor as it is."

When they were fully out, he shook their hands. "Roger," he said. "Pleased to meet you." His tone seemed more rushed than pleased.

"Nice to meet you as well," said Jessica. "We're excited."

Roger grunted noncommittally. "I wouldn't raise your hopes too high," he said. "It's hectic today. You've heard about the hack, no doubt. Terribly embarrassing. That man who claims to be the leader of the Order is public enemy number one at the moment. We're still in the midst of cleaning it up, but we expect a solution to be found quickly. Our Head of Privacy himself is leading the investigation. He just showed up today."

Vincent and Jessica met each other's eyes. The convoy had looked more familiar than they realized.

"But don't worry," said Roger, seeing their looks of concern. "I'll show you everything I can. Henry – Mr. Watts, I should call him – said this was important to you. I couldn't say no, especially to a future manager."

Vincent smiled, gratefully back, but the excitement that had been building in him was turning to something closer to dread.

"How long will the Head of Privacy be here?" asked Jessica.

"For the rest of the day most likely," said Roger. "But he's a whole stratosphere above me, so don't even think about asking for an introduction."

"Wouldn't dream of it," said Vincent.

Roger didn't hear him. He was waving a shooing hand at the transport that had just dropped them off. It started to rise. "Let's get started, shall we?"

Without waiting for an answer, he started for the front of the building where the convoy – and Marcus – had just disappeared. Vincent and Jessica followed close behind.

"Most of this you'll find quite boring I expect," said Roger. "There's a lot of administerial work, especially on the lower levels. Even on the management floors, there's not a whole lot to see."

"That's ok with us," said Vincent as they approached the door.

"We're just here to learn what we can."

The door – big enough for half a dozen people to walk through shoulder to shoulder – slid open to receive them. As soon as they walked inside, Vincent felt as if they had walked back into the Seclusion. The lobby was completely open, as wide as the school dome in diameter, and with a second, narrower tower in its very center. The rest of the room was bare but for the paper-thin front desk.

"This is the main lobby," said Roger. "Nothing interesting happens here. Unless we've had guests, that is." He nodded over to the group of men who were filing into a pod in the enclosed tower.

"We'll work our way up from here," said Roger. "We can start with my level."

He led them across the lobby toward the room where the men had just disappeared.

"Afternoon, Rachel."

The woman at the front desk glanced up at Roger without so much as a grin. Then, when she saw Vincent and Jessica, she beamed. "Welcome to the Hux Headquarters of Newsight," she said. Predictably, Vincent found the voice familiar.

As they neared the tower, the ceiling of the lobby curled back and up, and when it had disappeared altogether, Vincent could see straight above them. Vertical glass columns surrounded the tower's perimeter, each with its own, transport-shaped pod inside. Branching off from the columns, in the dozen or so meters between the central tower and the larger tower that encased it, was empty space.

"There are 186 stories," said Roger when they entered the tower's bottom room. Half a dozen pods were there waiting for them. "We'll be concerned only with the top six."

"But what about all the others?" protested Jessica. "Can we not know what happens there?"

Roger pressed a button on the pod nearest, and the door slid open to let them in. "The first 180 stories are reserved for the Department of Research," he said. Vincent waited for him to say something else, but nothing came. Instead, he motioned them into the pod.

"So what's on the levels we *can* see?" said Jessica when they had stepped inside.

Roger leaned forward and held his eye up to a scanner on the wall. A second later, the pod began to rise.

"The three other departments besides Research," said Roger. "Privacy, Product, and Strategy. Each occupies two floors."

"What about identification?" asked Vincent.

"That's a sub-department," said Roger. "They're under Privacy. I doubt you'll see much of them today. They'll be too occupied with the hack."

Vincent chanced a look at Jessica. Her face was blank.

"Plenty else to see, though," said Roger. "My level is quite interesting. I'm bias, obviously, but the product is the most important part of all this, isn't it?"

Vincent and Jessica nodded simultaneously, as they were expected.

"So that's our first stop," said Roger. "Almost there."

Vincent turned around to face the glass wall at their backs – Roger was right. They had already risen several hundred meters and were slowing to a stop.

"Might want to grab onto something," said Roger.

Just as he said it, the pod jerked outward into open space. It hovered over thin air, just like the transports outdoors, before soaring toward the main, encasing tower. Vincent felt around the pod for some sort of a handhold, but the walls were perfectly smooth. They had come to a stop almost before he had realized what was happening. The pod door slid open.

"Home sweet home," said Roger, stepping out. Vincent gladly followed onto solid ground behind him. When Jessica stepped out of the pod as well, it flew backwards, at a much greater speed, the way it had come. In front of them, the door to the small room they were in slid to the side.

"As I mentioned," said Roger, "this is the Product level."

The room on the other side of the door was curved in time with the skyscraper itself, and filled with a densely packed maze of rounded cubicles. In each one was a desk only slightly larger than those Vincent and Jessica had sat in just an hour prior, and in each desk sat men and women in the standard white uniforms, backs rigid and eyes blank. They appeared to be sharing in a single, widespread simulation.

"The Department of Product is divided into two sub-departments," said Roger. He led them around the perimeter of the room as he spoke. "Lenses and Alternative Products, like transports and injections. Within these sub-departments each employee specializes in either growth: coming up with new features; or maintenance: making sure the existing features function properly. I'm in maintenance. It's a rather new division, but we're growing quickly."

Vincent tried his best to look interested, but the longer he surveyed the sightless men and women in the cubicles, the stronger his urge to vomit.

"In maintenance we assess customer issues ourselves," continued Roger. A hint of pride was beginning to creep into his voice. "In growth, my colleagues determine the direction of the product most favorable to the consumer, but they don't actually do the implementation. They leave that to the developers."

Jessica perked up at this. "Where do *they* work?"

"Research," said Roger. The topic was closed.

Vincent turned to the people in the cubicles. None of them had moved. "So if these people aren't developers, what are they doing?"

"They could be in a meeting," said Roger. "Or at lunch." His tone was that of someone who had just said something obvious. "So," he continued, clapping his hands together. "That's the Product level. Let's keep moving."

"Already?" said Jessica. "We've been here for two minutes."

"And you've already seen it all," said Roger. "It's just like this all the way around – this level and next. Might as well move on to the next department." He took off ahead of them down the path next to the rows of cubicles. Jessica cast Vincent a helpless look, then started after him. Vincent followed, his gaze still trained on the clouded over eyes of the men and women at the desks.

They caught up to Roger and kept pace close behind him. The three of them continued to walk for almost a minute before they reached another transport room. Roger's eyes went out of focus as he stared at the wall, then he turned back to them.

"What did you think of the Product level?" he asked. There was an eager glint in his eye as he said it. The small army of immobile men and women, from his perspective, must have been quite impressive.

"Interesting," said Jessica.

"Really cool," said Vincent. Roger beamed with pride. Vincent felt sure he could have learned more from the modules back at school.

A moment later, an empty pod appeared in the opening next to them. Roger ushered them inside. Almost instantly, the transport moved outward over the empty space between towers. Instead of crossing all the way to the central tower, though, it rose straight up, skipping a floor and re-entering at the one after.

"Now for the Privacy level," said Roger as they came to a stop. "Did you know Newsight had an entire department dedicated to privacy?"

Vincent shot Jessica a look. "We've heard of it," he said.

"Most people *haven't* heard of it," said Roger, "but privacy has always been of the utmost importance to Newsight."

The doors slid open, and they stepped out into an ante-room similar to before.

"We have lobbyists in the Senate, and at the municipal levels to ensure the correct regulations are in place. Not only for our company, but for all others as well."

Roger pressed a button, and the larger doors slid open. As soon as they did, Vincent felt the space open up immensely. The room had just as many desks as the product level, and just as many empty-eyed occupants to fill them, only here, the desks were packed even more tightly together, and there were no cubicles to separate them. In such close proximity, the workers seemed to trade every breath they breathed.

"Marcus runs a tight ship," said Roger. "Very disciplined." He led them through the door and out into the open space. They started once again to their right. "The Department of Privacy essentially audits the rest of Newsight," continued Roger. "Anything Newsight does that is not aligned with our core privacy policies, Marcus jumps on in a second. He's our devil's advocate. Fatrem keeps him around just for that reason."

"Where does Fatrem work?" asked Vincent. "Research?"

Roger didn't hear the edge of sarcasm in Vincent's tone. "Fatrem travels too frequently to work in any one location," said Roger. "When he is here, though, he is said to be on one of the top two levels."

"For Strategy?" asked Jessica. Roger nodded and turned away in his typical, topic-closing way.

"Within the Department of Privacy," said Roger, "there are two more sub-departments: monitoring and identification. Almost everyone you see here is in the monitoring division. If you work in monitoring, you are given access to all company information. Each employee is assigned a set of other employees in the other departments to watch at all times. In this way, we can hold our colleagues accountable."

"When you say watch," said Jessica, "what exactly do you mean?"

"Through their Lenses," said Roger. "Of course, civilian Lenses would never allow such an intrusion. The Lenses worn by Newsight employees are a special model. It's the decision a Newsight employee makes when he first starts: to sacrifice his own privacy for the privacy of our customers."

Vincent looked out at the men and women in their tightly packed desks, at their glazed-over eyes as they watched through the eyes of their colleagues.

"You said *most* of them work in monitoring," said Jessica. She was looking at the employees as well, squinting, concentrating. "So some are in identification?"

"A portion of them, yes," said Roger. "As I mentioned, identification is a comparatively small sub-department, but it remains an extremely important part of – well – you might be in for a treat after all." He was looking straight ahead. Around the bend, the men they had seen from the lobby were on the same path, walking toward them. On instinct, Vincent turned around. He started back for the pod –

Jessica caught his wrist. He turned back to her, to pull her along with him, but she stayed where she was.

"I think I see him," she said.

"Yes I know so do I," said Vincent. "We need to—"

"I'm not talking about Marcus."

Vincent paused, frowning.

"What are you doing?" asked Roger, turning back to them. "The Department Head is coming. Act civilized and you might get to meet him."

Vincent looked down the path at the group of men – they had stopped to talk to someone – then back at Jessica. Jessica flicked her eyes toward the men and women in the desks. She was breathing a bit faster than normal, and she shifted, restless, on her feet. Slowly, as Vincent followed her eyes out to the employees in the desks, he began to realize.

"You think he's here?" he asked.

Jessica opened her mouth to answer, but was cut off.

"Keep walking," Roger shot back at them. He had already started off again down the hall. Marcus and the others had started moving as well. They were still some 20 meters away, but they were closing quickly. Jessica wasn't paying them any attention. Her gaze was focused on the desks.

"We don't have time," hissed Vincent. "Marcus is too close. We can't risk it."

"This will be our only chance," said Jessica. "We have to talk to him."

"Marcus is going to see us. It doesn't matter if it's our only chance or not we need to—"

"Stall," said Jessica. "I just need a minute."

Before he could stop her, she veered off the path and into the field of desks. Vincent opened his mouth to call after her, but held himself back. He cursed under his breath.

"Are you coming or not?" Roger turned around, at first showing only annoyance, then, when he saw Vincent alone, something closer to fear.

"Where did—"

"I couldn't stop her," rushed Vincent, thinking quickly. "I told her to act civilized but she—"

"Where did she go?" hissed Roger. He glanced over his shoulder as he spoke, careful to keep his voice low. Vincent stole a glance down the path as well – Marcus and the others had stopped outside of a glass door, some sort of conference room. Marcus was stepping inside.

"I'm so sorry," said Vincent. He chanced a look over at Jessica. She was still pushing through the crowd of men and women in the desks. They needed more time. "I couldn't do anything she just—"

Roger flung his hand up for silence. He had followed Vincent's gaze into the desks. "What is she doing!" he hissed. He pushed by Vincent, roughly, and cast another glance over his shoulder. Marcus was still in the conference room, but he was at the edge of the doorway, lingering there. He could leave at any moment. Cursing again, Vincent started after Roger. Jessica was far ahead, still jostling past the statuesque employees in the desks, but she appeared to be slowing down.

"Lena!" whispered Roger. "Lena get back here!"

Jessica didn't look at him. She had come to the desk of an employee who only looked a handful of years older than she was. She shook him by the shoulders.

Vincent allowed himself another look behind them as he went. Marcus remained in the doorway. He appeared to be trying to leave, but someone inside continued to talk. He moved a step deeper into the room.

Vincent turned back to the body-width path between the desks, increasing his pace. Ahead, Jessica had shaken the young employee from his daze.

"Lena stop!" Roger hissed at her.

Jessica continued to shake. She was whispering in the employee's ear, trying to rouse him.

"I'm sorry, sir," said Roger. He was almost to Jessica and his colleague. "She got away from me. Incredibly rude of her, so sorry." Roger reached them just after these last words, and he clamped his left hand down on Jessica's shoulder. She winced at his touch.

"We'll let you get back to work," said Roger.

Vincent arrived close behind. He started for the employee as well, but Roger caught him by the arm.

"You've just ruined your chances at a position at Newsight," snapped Roger. "I will personally see to it that any application labeled 'Ben Carlson' is shredded."

The young employee seemed to snap fully from his daze now. Roger jerked on Vincent's arm, back the way they had come.

"I just wanted to ask him about identification," pleaded Jessica, still struggling. "I'm in the security trade. I just wanted to—"

"Excuse me?"

Roger paused, careful not to loosen his grip. He turned around. The young employee had risen from his seat.

"Is there a problem?" he asked.

"No, sir," said Roger. "Sorry to—"

"We're Ben and Lena Carlson," cut in Jessica. There was desperation in her voice. She was speaking loudly enough to make Roger cringe.

"He doesn't care who your father is, now just—"

"Carlson?" said the employee. He tilted his head away from them, squinting slightly, thinking.

"Sir please do not gratify this…" Roger struggled to find the right word, "...attack, with a valid response. I'm sorry to have interrupted your work."

"Not at all," said the employee. "I'm friends with their father."

"For God's sake don't let them—"

"We wanted to ask you about identification," said Jessica. "That's why we came."

For a beat, the employee showed only confusion. But then there was something else, something subtle. It passed so quickly across his face that a well-timed blink would have rendered it invisible.

"Identification?" repeated the employee. "That's far too broad a topic for one question. We would need some time together."

"Trust me," said Roger. "You do *not* want to spend more than a minute with these two." He started to drag them away. "I apologize."

"No need," said his colleague. Then he turned to Vincent and Jessica. "We can talk if you'd like. Tomorrow. I will contact you." He met Jessica's eyes on these last words, then they could see him no longer. Roger had spun them around so they walked in a line, like a dysfunctional little family, down the narrow path.

"You could have lost me my job," hissed Roger. "If Marcus would have seen that, I would have been..."

Vincent ignored the man's rant. On the left, Marcus had exited the conference room just on cue. He was starting down the path again. They were going to intersect.

"...not to mention disrespectful of Henry," continued Roger. "He stuck his neck out for you, and this is how you reward him?"

Marcus paused once more just outside of the room. He was staring back inside, exasperated by whoever was speaking. On the right side of the path, another group, this one with collars a bit higher up their necks than the other employees, was headed for the conference room as well.

"We're going straight back to the lobby," said Roger. "You've earned yourself a one-way ticket out of here."

They were almost out of the desks, but Roger's grip only tightened as they got closer. Vincent's arm was starting to go numb.

"I'm sorry," said Jessica. "I was only curious."

"I don't care what you were," snapped Roger. "We're going."

When they reached the main path, Jessica tried to lead them right, but Roger jerked her back to the left, toward Marcus.

"Sir isn't the transport the other way?" rushed Vincent. "We don't want to cause you any more trouble."

"There's a closer one than the one behind us," said Roger. "I can't afford to give either of you another chance at—"

"Roger?"

Roger froze in his tracks and turned around. Vincent did the same, relieved – Marcus was only meters from them, and his patience was growing thin with the man in the conference room.

"Mr. Morgan," said Roger. "My apologies. We were just on our way out."

"Not at all," said the man who had spoken. He was flanked on either side by men and women in the high collared uniforms typical of Newsight management. Their eyes were all as clouded over as the men and women in the desks. These clouds, however, were quite a bit denser, stickier, like a fog that had never fully cleared.

"Your children?" asked the man called Morgan.

Roger shook his head. "No, sir. Actually..." he turned his gaze on one of the men at Morgan's side, "...they're Mr. Carlson's."

Vincent's lungs stopped mid-breath.

The man Roger had looked at stepped forward. Vincent could hardly tell where the man's irises ended and the white beyond them began. His Lenses seemed blurred, as if smudged, perhaps overused.

"Ben?" he said. "Lena?" He sounded unsure when he said the names. "I..." – Vincent held his breath; his lungs still weren't working – "...I've never seen you before."

A silence hovered between them – even the thumping in Vincent's chest seemed to go quiet.

"Here at the headquarters, I mean," the man continued. "Only in the residences. When you were little."

Mr. Carlson continued to stare at Jessica, a few beats too long. Her eyes were starting to water at the corners – she hadn't blinked for several seconds. "It's been years, hasn't it?" said Mr. Carlson. He looked at Vincent. "Several years."

Vincent hesitated, then nodded his head.

"Come on, William," said Mr. Morgan. "We've more important matters to attend to." He started down the hall, with his colleagues still on either side. Mr. Carlson lagged a little behind.

"This way I suppose," said Roger, impatient. "We'll never get through." He glanced back at the mob assembling outside of the conference room. Marcus had just stepped out of the doorway, waving a dismissive hand at the speaker inside.

"Ben? Lena?"

They stopped once again. Roger allowed them to turn around.

Mr. Morgan and the rest had continued on, but Mr. Carlson had lingered. The haze in his eyes, if only just a layer, had begun to clear.

"Let's spend the weekend together," he said. He was resolved as he said it, his eyes narrowed, as if squinting through the fog there. "In the residences," he continued. "I won't be home until late, but we could have all day tomorrow. Just the three of us."

Behind him, Marcus was walking toward them, still in a fury from the conference room. He seemed prepared to barge straight through the group of managers blocking his path.

"Ok," said Vincent, trying not to appear as rushed as he felt. "We'd like that. But we have to get going."

Mr. Carlson appeared to start to say something, but he stopped himself. He looked confused. "Of course," he said. "Back to your jobs." He began to turn away, then paused again. He looked back at Jessica. "I like your hair, Lena."

Jessica nodded in response. She was hiding behind Roger – her eyes were on Marcus. "Thanks, dad," she said. Mr. Carlson hesitated there for another moment, wearing the faintest hint of a smile, then turned away. Jessica tugged on Roger's arm from the front.

"What are you–"

"He's busy," said Jessica. "We should let him be."

"You *should* have let everyone be," Roger shot back.

"Marcus?"

The voice had come from behind them – it was Mr. Carlson. He sounded in a better mood than he had just a few moments before.

"Would you like to meet my–"

"Not now, William," snapped Marcus. His voice was close, and growing closer. "I'm in the middle of something."

Vincent pushed Roger from behind as they walked. They were almost to the transport room.

"Honestly," snapped Roger, "did your father not teach you any manners?"

Jessica slammed her hand over the button to the transport room door. She slipped through before the thing was even halfway open, pulling Roger and Vincent in after her. She pushed them flush against the wall inside. Roger started to speak, but Jessica held up a hand for silence. Vincent saw the gray jumpsuit of Marcus pass by outside just as the door slid closed.

"Don't you dare try to silence me, young lady," snapped Roger. He slammed a fist against the button to the nearest pod. "No respect. None at all. And Henry." He scoffed, shaking his head. "Ridiculous. This is the last time I ever do him a favor."

The pod zoomed up next to them with its door already open. Roger forced them inside first.

"Last tour I ever give," ranted Roger. "You tell him that."

The door of the pod slid closed, and they started their open-aired journey toward the central tower, and away from Marcus. Vincent had only recently started to breathe.

"Did you hear me?" snapped Roger.

Vincent nodded his head. "Yes, sir."

Roger continued to bristle. He muttered another string of threats under his breath, but Vincent wasn't listening. He was watching Jessica, and she was watching her Lenses.

CHAPTER 15 – THE RESIDENCES

Roger relinquished his hold on them only when they were back on the street. He did so with a final, flourishing shove.

"I'll see to it that Henry devises a punishment for both of you," he said. "And for you," he looked at Ben, "have fun starting over in a new trade." He smirked, then turned away, starting back for the doors of the lobby.

Vincent turned to Jessica. "You're sure it's him?" he said. Then, for the Lenses' sake: "He knows enough about identification to help your trade?"

Jessica frowned for a second, then nodded. "I think so."

Vincent took his first full breath since leaving the headquarters. He looked up at the tower they had just exited. "It would make sense," he said. "Maybe that's how he's been helping. From the inside."

They were silent for a few seconds, both of their gazes trained upward, in awe, on the white-faced tower in front of them.

"So what now?" said Vincent, turning back to the street. "We just wait until tomorrow?"

"I guess," said Jessica. "He said he would contact us."

Vincent nodded. He scanned the air above them. "Should I try and figure out how to call a transport?" he asked.

"We're going to the residences aren't we?"

Vincent was taken aback. "Are we really going to take him up on that?"

"I think we have to," said Jessica. "He might raise the alarm if we don't."

Vincent didn't argue. But even if the man hadn't seen the real Ben and Lena Carlson for over a decade, he would have to suspect something eventually. The fog over his Lenses, whether from the newsims, his work, or something else entirely, wouldn't last forever.

"Ok," said Vincent. "But we need to be in bed before he gets there."

Jessica nodded in agreement. "All the more reason not to call a transport," she said. "I haven't been able to sleep. We haven't walked in days."

Vincent looked up at the transports zooming by in between the tops of the skyscrapers above. He didn't need convincing.

"Walking it is."

166

******

It took them only a quarter of an hour to get through the rest of the working sector, but the progress was slower through the recreation ring. Flashy storefronts lined the streets with blinking, neon signs, just beginning to turn on for the weekend. Even the bottoms of the towers – the circular ones they had seen from above with Derek – sported their own, alluring booths. More of the women in tight white dresses, of which Hux seemed to have an endless supply, stood out front, accosting the passersby as they walked. Most – eager to cash in on their free newsim – stopped, so the streets were clogged. It took Vincent and Jessica over an hour to get through the traffic and arrive at the base of the enormous, flat-topped mushroom structure Derek had called the residences.

"It's bigger up close," said Jessica. Vincent agreed. The towers were full skyscrapers, not just the narrow support beams for the disc they supported above.

"He didn't say where we're supposed to go did he?" asked Jessica.

Vincent shook his head. "He may not even know himself if he didn't know us." He peered through the maze of towers toward the center. A larger tower – almost twice the size of the others – was open all along the bottom story, completely transparent as the Newsight lobby had been. "Let's try there," said Vincent. Jessica followed his gaze, then nodded.

They started forward, and as they entered the shade cast by the saucer above, they could see the towers clearly for the first time. The bases of them were surrounded by what looked like Seclusion domes, only these domes fluttered in the breeze.

"What are those?" said Jessica.

Vincent shrugged. He was less interested in the domes themselves than the people sitting outside them: the men and women with glazed-over eyes in plain, rigid chairs. Their stares were blank and their mouths slightly agape. If not for the occasional rise and fall of the people's stomachs, Vincent may have begun feeling for pulses.

They continued to walk in silence. The only sound came from the flapping of the domes' fabric-like material in the wind.

When the main doors of the lobby slid open to receive them several minutes later, the eerie quiet of the outside was replaced by the soft, echoing cry of infants. The room, nearly double the size of the Newsight lobby, was filled with children, most of whom were accompanied by at least one parent. Some leaned back against the glass perimeter of the space; some simply stretched out in the middle of the tile floor. Judging by the style – and state – of their clothes, Vincent had a decent guess as to where the people were from.

"I guess these are the startup packages everyone was looking forward to," he said. He was looking at the small white bags at the children's feet, the ones the escorts had handed the new families when they first arrived in Hux. Most of the bags had already been torn open so only their wrappers remained. Others, though, still contained the product inside. It was a stack of cards, each with writing at the top and a long, complicated code below. The one nearest – at the feet of a man whose eyes had rolled back into his head, and whose small child lay next to him, sniffling – was close enough to read. At the top of the card, above the code, the thing was labeled *newsim*.

"Vincent," said Jessica.

He had stopped; his eyes were locked on the child. It was exceptionally still.

Jessica pulled at his sleeve. "Look."

He turned to her, then followed her finger. Just a few steps from them, sprawled out among the others with his daughter by his side, was Jim. His eyes were glazed over, but they hadn't rolled back quite as far as those of the man with the infant. They were still present, just barely, and they were looking up at Vincent.

"I remember you," said Jim. His voice wasn't the loud, booming one from outside the halos. It was soft, unsure.

"Hi, Jim," said Vincent. He spoke quietly, just above a whisper. He felt as if too loud a noise would shatter the freshly installed and blood-tinted Lenses in Jim's eyes.

"Have you tried these?" asked Jim. He held up one of the empty wrappers from the newsim access cards.

"I have," said Vincent. He saw how many of the wrappers there were for the first time – the girl was nearly covered with them. "How many did they give you?"

Jim shrugged. The movement seemed to require a great deal of effort for him. "I haven't kept track," he said. "But they pass the time. While the residences find us a place to live."

"This is where they're keeping you?" asked Jessica. "In the lobby?"

168

"For the families with children," said Jim. "Everyone else stays in the tents outside."

Vincent thought of the cloth-made domes surrounding the towers. The only people he had seen there had been adults.

"What about Tina?" asked Jessica. "And your son. Are they in one of the tents?"

Jim shook his head. He jostled his daughter next to him as he moved, but she didn't stir. "They aren't with us," he said. "They're in quarantine. Some sort of virus." He paused to catch his breath. "They'll join us as soon as they're cured."

Vincent bit the inside of his cheek. Jim's wife and son had seemed perfectly healthy at the checkpoint – Jim had said it himself. Newsight, apparently, had diagnosed them anyway. About what the diagnosis was, or what the treatment would be, Vincent did not have a good feeling.

"Now," said Jim, "you'll have to excuse me." He fumbled in a bag propped up against his daughter's head. "I'm going to enter another sim." He paused, holding up the access code he had just retrieved. "It was good to see you."

The man's eyes went out of focus, hesitated there, then rolled back into his head. After he had been still for several seconds, Jessica tugged at Vincent's sleeve. Vincent let himself be pulled away.

They wound through the other motionless families in the lobby until they reached the front desk. After identifying them with the same club-shaped stick the Guard had used, the receptionist told them their suite number and directed them to a room of transports. Neither of them spoke during the ride up. What words they may have said – about Jim, about the simulations – were, under surveillance, better to remain as thoughts.

When the pod came to a stop and slid open, they were staring into a brightly lit hallway. A door with their number on it was directly across from them.

"Wow," said Jessica. "That's service."

Vincent nodded in agreement, but he felt guilty all the same. The service for the families in the lobby, after all, had been nonexistent.

They exited the pod and stepped up to the door in front of them. Vincent leaned in close to the scanner and opened his right eye–

The hall went dark. Vincent froze where he stood. His vision was pitch black but for the white font of *newsim* down the middle and the rotating eye below.

"This is a Newsight public announcement," said the woman with the sweet voice.

The logo and black background disappeared, replaced by a still image of Tom Smith looking directly into the camera.

"After apprehending the Seclusion bomber this morning," said the woman, "Newsight collaborated with the Guard to go after the Order's leader, Senator Tom Smith." The image was replaced by the same room as before – the single chair, the mounted camera – with half a dozen armed members of the Guard rifling around inside. On the floor, there was a body-sized mound, covered by a white sheet and stained on the outside with unmistakable streaks of red.

Vincent's mouth fell open. The saliva there seemed to evaporate all at once.

"With the combined specialties of the Guard and Newsight," the woman continued, "the raid of Smith's headquarters was successful. Smith perished in the crossfire before he could give testimony."

The feed changed once again. It was Marcus. He was standing in front of the Newsight tower, attempting to climb into his convoy of transports, but being blocked by reporters. Relenting, he paused for a comment.

"The hack was extremely embarrassing," he said. "We made the resolution of this matter a priority, and we were rewarded for doing so. Let this serve as a message to the rest of the Order. Thank you."

He broke through the crowd, and climbed into the transport. The image of Tom Smith returned.

"We apologize for any trauma these unwanted appearances have caused," said the woman, "and we promise to do better in the future. Have a great evening."

The hollowed cheeks and pale skin of Tom Smith disappeared, and the hallway returned. Vincent was still staring at the scanner. The door had already opened.

"Ben?"

Vincent kept his gaze straight forward. It took him a moment to produce the words – his mouth was still dry. "They miscalculated," he said. His voice was flat, dead. "He wasn't important after all. He was an embarrassment, and they got rid of him."

Vincent felt the thumping in his chest rise into his throat. They had gotten rid of him. Of them both, more likely. With Tom Smith gone, there was no reason to keep Sarah Smith as leverage.

"Let's go inside," said Jessica. She laid a hand on Vincent's shoulder. "Come on."

Wordlessly, and with his teeth clenched down on his bottom lip to stop it from shaking, Vincent stepped forward. The lights inside were already on. The room was standard: the usual Newsight white and open-concept Seclusion style. The ceiling, however, was far from typical. The entire thing served as an enormous window. There were no beams or supports, only glass, and beyond that, only sky.

"We're in the disc," said Jessica.

Through the glass ceiling, above the lowest layer of clouds, they could see the final pink rays of the sun as it began its descent. In any other circumstances, the sight would have been beautiful.

Jessica went deeper into the room, squeezing Vincent's arm as she went. Vincent followed. He couldn't afford to act out of the ordinary – they were still performing.

"We should have been staying here the whole time," he said.

Jessica glanced into the kitchen. "Maybe it's better we haven't," she said.

Vincent followed her gaze. On the dining table, which was almost exactly like his mother and father's from the Seclusion, was a clear glass bowl filled with newsim access cards.

"Has the identification employee contacted you yet?" said Vincent, changing the subject. The words felt empty coming out of his mouth, meaningless. "The one from the tour?"

Jessica's eyes went out of focus. "We're meeting him in the working sector," she said. "Early tomorrow morning."

Vincent's stomach gave a little lurch. It was sooner than he had thought.

"So I think I'll get some rest," said Jessica. "You should too."

Vincent read the subtext: *Mr. Carlson will be home soon.*

"I will," he said. Jessica nodded. She hesitated for a moment, her eyes locked on his, then wrapped her arms around him.

"Goodnight," she said.

Vincent bit his tongue. "Goodnight," he said back. A second later, she released him, then disappeared through a door on the far side of the room. Vincent stayed where he was. Something swelled up high in his throat, and his eyes grew hot from the moisture in their corners. He didn't cry. That would have been suspicious. Instead, with his tears dammed behind his Lenses, he turned to the container of access cards on the dining room table. He thought of the newsims. He thought of the small brown house with the slanted roof and lush green backyard. He thought of his parents, of seeing them again around the dinner table of their simulated home.

Then he thought of Jim.

******

Vincent's eyes flashed open just in time to see the white stick being pressed up against his temple. His Lenses lit up with a searing heat, then exploded with white light. He was completely blind as a rough pair of hands jerked him from his bed. Blind, still, as a different set of hands closed over his mouth and half his nose.

"Your newsims indicate the presence of a virus," said a voice above him. "You are being quarantined."

Vincent tried to say something back, but the hand over his mouth held the words in his throat. He tried to lash out instead, but his limbs felt as if they had been detached from him, useless and completely immobile in the vice-like grips of his captors. Growing desperate, he was preparing to bite the hand over his mouth when the white light began to fade, and his vision began to clear. Above him, he could start to make out the men dragging him. They were little more than silhouettes in the dark, but he could see the color of their uniforms clearly nonetheless. He could see the gray.

Vincent doubled his struggle, which amounted to little more than a slight inconvenience to the men holding him. By the time they reached the main room, Vincent's captors hadn't broken stride once.

The door across the room slid open, and another huddle of men emerged with Jessica, whose eyes had only just begun to return from their embrace of the pure white. She seemed to be having equally little success in her attempts at escape.

"What are you doing?"

Vincent couldn't see the owner of the voice; his captors were standing in the way.

"Those are my kids!"

Mr. Carlson had emerged from the master bedroom, still in his nightclothes. Before he could utter another word, two of the officers holding Jessica crossed over to him. Vincent's view was blocked once again as his captors towed him closer to the door.

"No!" cried Mr. Carlson. "Don't hurt them! Don't–"

There was a muffled, thudding sound, and Mr. Carlson grew quiet.

The men continued to drag Vincent to the hall. The entire exchange was almost completely silent. What few sounds they *did* make seemed to be absorbed by the night, suppressed and forgotten.

They were almost to the door. They would go to the transport pods. They might even walk right out the front lobby. No one would stop them. It was the weekend – no one would wake up from their simulations.

The men carrying them pressed the button next to the main door and it slid open. They started out into the hall.

The silence of the room split down the middle with a shattering, earsplitting explosion.

Vincent struggled against his captors to look back, but they held fast. Some of them turned, raising their short white clubs, only to crumple where they stood. There was a chorus of more muffled thuds as the officers fell, one by one, and their grips went limp. It took Vincent a moment to realize he was no longer being held. He turned around. The glass ceiling now lay in dagger-shaped shards on the tile below, and at the feet of a half dozen gun-wielding men and women who seemed to have appeared out of thin air. Above the group, were two, militarily-dressed transports with their ramps already extended. A familiar Newsight employee stood at the helm of it all. He looked different outside of his small white desk: taller, broader-shouldered, and suspiciously like Brian.

"John," whispered Jessica.

Before Vincent could inspect him further, John was blocked from view. A large, square-jawed man had rushed forward with a black club shaped exactly like the ones carried by the officers. Vincent recoiled, but the man was too fast. The tip of the club made contact with Vincent's temple, and his vision went black. The same heat fired into his Lenses as before, searing his eyes. The room began to spin, and when his vision returned, he crumpled to the floor. Next to him, he heard Jessica do the same. Arms much gentler than the ones that had just carried him wrapped Vincent under his shoulders and lifted him to his feet. His eyelids drooped down over his eyes as the arms led him toward the transport. He felt his vision slipping into darkness once again.

"What's wrong with them?" asked the man holding Vincent.

John crossed over to them. He pulled back one of Vincent's

eyelids. "The Privacy Officers must have done their disabling before we got here," he said. "The Lenses are reacting against it. We need to get them to the tunnels."

John took hold of Vincent's free arm. Vincent didn't resist as they walked him, supporting nearly all of his weight, to the transport. They had to lift him inside.

"The sim." The words came out of Vincent as a whisper, though he hadn't meant them to. He could manage only a few syllables at a time. "The sim...the...the..."

"You're safe," said John, "you don't need any simulations to—"

"THE SIM." Vincent had to push the words out of his mouth. "We have THE SIM." He patted, weakly, at his front pocket.

"The sim..." John trailed off. Slowly, as if afraid something were going to bite him, he reached into Vincent's pocket. He pulled out the disc. "Oh my god," he said. "Oh my god!" He turned to the other transport. "They have THE SIM! Get us out of here! Go!" He waved his arm at the other transport, and they began to rise.

Vincent let his eyelids fall closed. The voices around him, then the shouts, grew soft and distant, and he was gone.

Part III – The Order

CHAPTER 16 – THE SIM

The place reminded Vincent of Simon's cellar – the walls were dark and damp; the floor was slick and streaked with mud; the air clung to one's skin like a thick sweat. Here, however, the space was not so cramped. It was taller and longer, and curved to the ceiling in the shape of a tunnel.

Vincent looked to his side. Jessica was there next to him, propped, as he was, against a giant metal grate. On the other side of the grate, behind them, the tunnel was dark. Ahead of them the view was equally dull: a rusted table sitting along the left wall, a tattered black curtain hanging from the ceiling.

"Wake her."

Vincent whipped his head in the direction of the voice. Opposite the table, John was leaned up against the wall. Vincent had looked right past him.

"Now, if you can," said John. "We have work to do."

Flustered, Vincent turned to Jessica, but she had already stirred from the voices. She blinked a few times before opening her eyes fully.

"Where are we?" she asked.

"The base of the Order," said John. "In a city 'we' bombed out of existence." He looked around at the curved, grime-stained walls. "Sewers," he said. "But we call them tunnels. It's easier that way"

Jessica was looking up at John now, still seeming confused. "How did we get here?" she asked.

"Transports," said John. "We flew for over an hour. You two were out for most of it."

"But how did we get out of Hux?" said Vincent. "And how do they not know where we are? How did you know they were going to—"

"Easy," said John, grinning. He had a calm, confident way about him that reminded Vincent of Brian. "Our transports are modified," he said. "They're invisible to Newsight satellites. We can go wherever we want."

"Then let's go to the Seclusion," said Jessica. "We can rescue my dad and everyone else they've taken."

"In time," said John, as level as ever. "But you just got here. There are things you need to know."

Vincent remembered in a rush. "THE SIM," he said. "I had it in my…" He trailed off when John raised the small, fragile disc up to the light.

"It's safe," he said. "My mother informed me you may have had it, but I had my doubts. How did you find it?"

"Your brother," said Jessica. "He told us where it was."

John tilted his head back in a silent question. He looked at them both. "Brian told you?"

Vincent and Jessica both nodded. John looked away from them. His gaze was locked on a puddle that appeared to be leaking from under the grate.

"Were you with him in any of your newsims?" he said, looking up. "Or my mother?" His tone was wavering now – he sounded concerned.

They shook their heads. "No," said Vincent. "Why?"

John took a breath. He held up the small round disc in his hand. "These are the kind of sims you know," he said. "You're more familiar with the digital format, but the idea is the same: they're instructional, simple. Newsims aren't so straightforward. You'll have been told how they work – they detect what the user wants to experience – but you won't have been told why. It's not for the user's benefit, it's for Newsight's. They monitor each newsim closely, and any suspicious activity is reported and tracked."

"And flagged," said Jessica.

John nodded. "That's why I asked about Brian and my mother," he said. "If either of you were with them in your newsim, and you spoke about the Order, they could be in danger."

Vincent cocked his head, frowning. "They?" he repeated. "Did…Lynn not tell you what–"

"I never saw them," cut in Jessica. Vincent turned to her, confused, but she didn't look at him. "I was with my dad," she continued. "My mom was still alive, too. We were working on our transport to take it off the grid."

John nodded, relaxing a little. He turned to Vincent, expectant. Vincent was still looking at Jessica. Her cheeks were sucked into her mouth.

"Vincent?" prompted John.

Vincent watched Jessica for a moment longer, frowning. "I was with my parents, too," he said after a pause. He turned back to John. "We were just talking. Maybe about things we shouldn't have been."

"It's all right," said John. "That doesn't matter now. My family is safe, and so are you two." He smiled as he looked down at them. Vincent turned once again to Jessica. She refused to look at him. "You cut it close, though," said John. "Had we not been watching you after the HQ run in, you may have been taken away."

Jessica frowned. "To where?" she said.

"Save your questions," said John. "This will answer them far better than I can." He held up THE SIM once again.

"Have you seen it?" asked Jessica. "Has all of the Order seen it?"

"I have," said John. "But most haven't, no. This is the only copy." He tossed it to them. Vincent caught it, a bit clumsily, in his palms.

"There's only one?" he asked.

"Only one container," said John. "There are about a dozen copies inside, but they're always kept together."

"So what happens if they're destroyed?" asked Vincent.

John grinned. "Better to risk having them destroyed than to have copies floating around in the wrong hands. Anyone who wants to watch will have to sit where you're sitting."

Vincent looked down at the ordinary, dirt-covered mat that had been spread out beneath them.

"Do *we* get to watch it?" asked Jessica. John smiled.

"Of course you do," he said. "You're in the Order now. And you're heroes for bringing that with you. Goodwin will be pleased."

"So he *is* real," said Vincent. "Goodwin?"

John smiled once again. He pointed to THE SIM. "It's all in there," he said. He started for the curtain. "You'll see."

"But how can we watch it?" asked Vincent. "They darkened our Lenses."

"And so did we," said John. "You're on *our* network now. You can communicate with other members of the Order, and you can watch whatever sim you like. Newsight is blind." He started once again for the curtain. "We can talk more when you've finished." He shot them one last smile, and he was gone.

Before the curtain had settled, Jessica was reaching for the disc. Vincent closed his fist around it before she could take it.

"What are you doing?" he said.

"He said we could watch it. I'm just—"

"Not that," said Vincent. He motioned to the curtain. "With John. Why didn't you let me tell him?"

Jessica looked up at him for the first time. Her face was lined with guilt. "We just got here," she said. "I didn't want to ruin it before we learned anything. Besides, what happened to Brian was my fault and John would—"

"It wasn't your fault," said Vincent.

Jessica said nothing. She merely stared, weakly, back at him. Her teeth were clenched down on the inside of her cheeks. Her eyes were wide, glistening at the corners. In the dim, yellow glow of the bulbs above, Vincent could see the hurt hiding beneath her Lenses. The guilt.

"Jessica it wasn't your fault," he said. His voice was softer now. His words faded as quickly as the faint dripping behind the grate. "It wasn't," he repeated. "John will understand that."

Jessica looked up at the curtain where John had just disappeared. She didn't seem convinced.

"I can be the one to tell him," said Vincent.

"No," said Jessica. "I'll tell him." She turned away from the curtain, back to Vincent's closed fist. "But after this."

As if by a switch, she seemed composed again, but Vincent wasn't fooled. He could read the emotion in her face just as he had learned to detect the slight shake in her voice.

"There will be a better time," pressed Jessica. "Just not now."

Vincent watched her for a second longer, then glanced at the curtain. He bit his bottom lip.

"Here," said Jessica. She placed her hands on his, gently, and pulled his fingers open. Before he had turned back to her, she had lifted the disc from his palm and flipped open the top.

"We'll watch it for Brian," she said.

Vincent looked down at the thin, miniature Lenses in the container. "And we'll tell John?" he said.

"We will," said Jessica. "Soon."

Vincent watched her for a moment longer, then took a breath. He nodded.

Moments later they had laid the thin prints over their eyes. The dimly lit tunnel had turned completely dark, no outline, no silhouette, just black; and a deep, hoarse-sounding voice was beginning to speak

"THE SIMULATION OF THE ORDER"
"Control by Lenses"

"Newsight is three different companies to three different types of consumers. To understand Newsight's various methods of control, we must first understand the types of consumers being controlled.

"The first type, the majority, prioritizes happiness over freedom, and is by far the largest of the three. People of this type have only two needs: safety and entertainment.

"The second type, the minority, prioritizes freedom over happiness, and is significantly fewer than the majority. People of this type require careful cultivation of two main qualities: their intellect, and their desire for fulfillment.

"The third type, the few, has no priority between freedom and happiness. They are indifferent. These people are the easiest to control. In the eyes of Newsight, however, they are also the most detestable.

"With these three types in mind, let us consider Newsight's most prominent method of control: Lenses. Lenses have an uncountable many features, but we will concern ourselves only with the most important: the simulations and the collection of data.

"Newsight uses simulations to control its individual consumers. The method of this control, of course, varies by type. For the majority, simulations provide a customizable, virtual experience with no effort on the part of the user – called newsim. Newsim is designed to satisfy every impulse imaginable: the violent, the vain, the gluttonous, the adventurous, the cruel. Each experience is tailored to the specific tendencies and desires of the participant. One newsim might depict an entire fabricated world in which the participant lives long term and in real time. Another might depict nothing but a single room for a single moment. Others still might be limited to singular sensations or emotions. These capabilities alone would combine for near perfect entertainment, but the activity would still require some sort of effort by the user, which, for the majority, is like repellant. Newsim, however, requires no such effort. The nature of the sim, the creation of it, the context – everything is handled by Newsight. The only action required of the participant is the decision to begin the simulation. Newsight, with their near omniscient collection of data, knows without asking what the user wants to experience, even if, in the user himself, that desire is unclear. For the majority, newsim is the perfect form of entertainment, and, often, their only reason for existence. The simulations are, after all, much more favorable than real life.

"For the minority, instructional simulations provide ample opportunity to gain knowledge. Long term, these simulations fall short in satisfying the minority's need for fulfilment, but, as we will see, Newsight has devised a solution to this shortcoming.

"For the few, simulations are irrelevant. Newsight has no desire to control the few.

"Simulations provide Newsight with a mechanism to control individuals on a day-to-day basis. The collection of data, conversely, provides Newsight a method of control on a larger scale. Once again, this method, this harvest of data, is reliant upon Lenses. Lenses have access to everything about their user: where he goes, who he sees, what products he looks at in the store window, what jokes he laughs at, what women he looks at longer than others, what he spends his currency on, what currency he has, what mistakes he makes, what laws he breaks, what food he shoves down his throat. The technology of the Lenses allows for a near seamless interface between human brain and computer; in fact, a near upload of the former to the latter. For years, the government restricted the kind of information Newsight collected. Eventually, however, some politicians wanted the information just as badly as Newsight. What did the voters want them to say? To look like? They were prepared to lift whatever regulations necessary to answer those questions. But this readiness to repeal the regulations was not universal. There still existed a surprising number of politicians whose value of privacy exceeded their desire for re-election. As long as these men and women held firm, the privacy regulations could not be repealed on a large scale. To counter this resistance, Newsight shifted from the collection of data, to the manipulation of it.

"For anything less than an omnipotent organization, to censor is to risk revolution. The producer of the original content, unless censored himself, will tell of the fabrication, and the consumer of the content, if not sufficiently surrounded by other fabrications, will sense the lie. Newsight recognized this early on, so in its counterattack of the politicians in its way, it did not use the Lenses to alter existing news. Instead, it made news of its own. Thus, Newsight began acting in the name of the Order.

"We will discuss the implications of this strategy, but first, some history.

"Geographic Alteration by Terror"

"Newsight was founded some 40 years ago by a young entrepreneur named Alduss Fatrem. The company began with only one product. Though technologically revolutionary, Lenses were incredibly simple. The small slips of glass did only what cell phones did previously: communicate, browse the web, and service applications. It was the first time humans had interacted so intimately with technology, and there was a ripple of panic. Fatrem had anticipated this, and before the ripple could turn into a wave, he lobbied for privacy regulations against his own company. He chained his own hands and gave the government the key. They would do quarterly audits on the information collected by Newsight, and neither the politicians nor Fatrem would have access to it. To the public, it was a dream come true. They traded none of their privacy for all of the convenience they could imagine. But it turned out they weren't imagining large enough. By the time Lenses had been adopted on a large scale, Newsight's product line had sprawled into every industry imaginable. They focused on projects for the social good: defense, space exploration, energy. But their forays included the everyday, as well. They made vehicles, called transports. They made houses, called domes. They made medicine, called injections. They did everything. Their products had created an entire cohesive network. Daily life had become intertwined with it, in some cases held captive by it. The market had been penetrated, but Fatrem was far from content. His plan had only just begun.

"It is commonly known Newsight produces defense systems for cities, and, in some cases, entire nations. It is also commonly known that Newsight's satellite and global positioning technology dominates the western hemisphere. What is far from common knowledge, and what has yet to be confirmed by actual evidence, is Newsight's production of weaponry. This theory, that Newsight is capable of producing arms, in conjunction with Fatrem's fondness of buying large, isolated tracts of land, points to one undeniable truth:

"Newsight, with its vast, privatized territories, and with its near monopoly on satellite surveillance, has established factories to produce an arsenal. It has stockpiled enough missiles, launch facilities, and fighter jets to furnish a large scale terrorist organization. Only it has not just furnished such an organization; it has become one.

"By acting as terrorists in the name of the Order, Newsight solved three problems in one admittedly genius stroke. The first of these problems was the existence of the actual Order. For years, the Order had been Newsight's main opponent, lobbying for stricter regulations on privacy, and campaigning against the latest products. The Order was a constant thorn in Fatrem's side.

"The second problem, and the one already mentioned, was Newsight's lack of data access. Fatrem had built an empire, but his subjects had been sealed from him by the politicians still in resistance.

"The third and final problem was the inherent differences between how the majority and the minority used and reacted to Lenses. As we have mentioned, the setting of interaction for these two groups is vitally important to their control.

"Three problems, one solution. Let us proceed with each problem in more detail.

"Newsight's first terrorist attacks came, fittingly, against its own factories. There was real damage, with real casualties, from real bombs. It didn't take much investigation for the public to decide the attack had been launched by the Order. The known leaders of the Order's protest at the time were imprisoned, and things were silent for a while – people thought the Order was dead. When the attacks continued, some against more Newsight locations, others against areas high in Newsight support, the media latched onto the only feasible explanation: the Order lived on, and they were determined to wreak as much havoc on Newsight as possible. The identity earned by the earliest members of the Order as nonviolent protestors had taken a murderous turn.

"By undermining the name of the Order, Newsight solved their first problem: the presence of protestors. The solution to the second problem, the one pertaining to data access, follows close behind.

"Slowly, the attacks began to expand from Newsight related targets to civilian settlements, then to government buildings. The true Order began to disappear, and Newsight's Order began to grow. The public came to view the Order as the world's menace. Every government west of the Atlantic declared open war on terrorism, and they expended innumerable resources in pursuit of the Order's defeat. After years of these ineffectual efforts, the public grew restless. They wanted justice; they wanted blood. And who else should offer their help? Newsight began approaching municipalities, insisting that, with the right data, and with total participation in the Lens standard, it could find the secret members of the Order and put a stop to the attacks. The pressure on governments to mandate the wearing of Lenses increased with every attack, and eventually, at the urging of the public, it grew to be too much. City after city gave in – they required their citizens to wear Lenses; they gave Newsight access to the data – and each was rewarded with relative peace. The cities that repeal the regulations, however, never quite see an end to the violence. Newsight makes sure of it. A complete stop would mean the cities have no reason to continue to allow Newsight access to their data. A complete stop, also, would invalidate Newsight's meticulously executed strategy of discovering politicians to be shadow agents for the Order. Without a continued stream of minor attacks, Newsight's undermining of the government they aim to overthrow would crumble.

"This solves Newsight's second problem. In exchange for catching the perpetrators of the violence it itself manufactures, Newsight receives more data than any one man could possibly conceive. The remaining hope in this arena is that, in spite of the cities' individual weaknesses, the national government stands strong. To date, the Senate has abstained from widespread privacy regulation repeals. This fragile and rather surprising show of strength is the only obstacle between Newsight and total control of public information.

"The third and final main problem faced by Newsight was mentioned at the very beginning of this simulation: the inherent difference between the majority and the minority, and the need to separate them.

"Newsight's attacks were not intended solely to instill fear – they served a clear purpose. They began on the outskirts of society, in rural areas, in the sparsely populated countryside, herding people to the cities. The cities that have made a deal with Newsight – standard cities – serve as a trap for the immigrants unlucky enough to enter their gates. The cities that resist, are only temporary. One by one, they have received their warnings: join our fight against Newsight or die (there is, of course, no way of joining the fight), and one by one their inhabitants have either fled to standard cities, or they have perished. What results is a population concentrated in large, easily surveilled settlements. This provides the perfect opportunity for sorting.

"The majority, with their systemic lack of motivation and craving of leisure, are most easily controlled by Newsight if they are kept in a state of perpetual bliss. The minority, with their longing for fulfillment and knowledge, are deeply unsatisfied by meaningless leisure, and on it they catch the scent of manipulation. The most reasonable course of action for Newsight, then, assuming their ultimate aim is ultimate control, is to segregate these two groups. Cities are reserved for the chains of mind-numbing entertainment, and Seclusions for those of metal. Therefore, when driven into a Newsight stronghold by the Order's warnings, every man woman and child is subjected to review upon the reception of his or her Lenses. Those judged to be in the majority are allowed to stay in the city; those judged to be in the minority are sent to a Seclusion; and those judged to be in the few are taken away.

"Residents of the cities, largely because of newsim, grow enamored with Newsight. This love is how Newsight maintains control in the cities, but that is only half of their effort. Their mantra: THERE IS NO LOVE WITHOUT HATRED, requires a second part as well. Newsight believes that for any individual to offer love, he must also offer hate. For this reason, Newsight ensures citizens of the cities maintain a healthy hatred of the Order. If the residents for some reason begin to forget this hatred, they are reminded of it through another attack. Thus, Newsight can continue to be loved, and the cities can continue to be controlled.

"Residents of the Seclusions, besides those inhabitants of Newsight's own Seclusion, are essentially workers in a labor camp. They are underfed, mistreated, tortured, and filled with terror. This fear is how Newsight maintains its control in the Seclusions, but, like in the cities, Newsight requires something else as well. Listen to their mantra: THERE IS NO FEAR WITHOUT HOPE. Newsight believes that no man can be afraid of his captors without first having some small hope of deceiving them. For this reason, Newsight encourages the slim but ever present promise of escape. If Seclusion residents begin to lose their hope for this escape, they are renewed of it by watching one of their fellows find his freedom. Thus, Newsight can continue to be feared, and the Seclusions can continue to be controlled.

"Newsight's three main problems – the presence of protestors, access to data, and separation of the types – have been comprehensively solved by the conversion of the Order to a terrorist group. Newsight's Order, however, is only a mask. The face beneath is far different.

"The True Order"

"The Order *does* exist, and it *is* resolved against the aims of Newsight. However, this does not make the prospects of its victory any less daunting. The situation just outlined is on the brink of uncorrectable. Perhaps it has already crossed this threshold. Either way, we cannot stand by and watch our world fall to men who would destroy it only to sit atop the rubble. What follows is what we know.

"Newsight is not the only producer of Lenses. The technology has been successfully replicated by two other corporations: WeSee, which manufactures for a large portion of the Asian continent; and Allwatch, which manufactures for the European and African continents. The trajectories of these other companies are eerily aligned with Newsight's own. We must operate under the assumption, then, that we will receive no outside help.

"If you are watching this simulation, you are now one of the Order. You have joined the fight against the corporation called Newsight. Believe as we do: the Lenses will be removed, and the world will see once again."

The voice ended with an echo, and the blackness of the sim was filled with the rotating eye of Newsight. Only now, the eye lacked its central part – it was only the outline that remained. It continued to rotate, in complete silence, as the blackness faded, and the tunnel returned.

"The Lenses will be removed, and the world will see once again."

The last line of THE SIM was recited again by the same, deep voice that had said it inside their heads. Vincent blinked several times to make sure the simulation had ended. He blinked several more times when the curtain they were facing split down the middle, and a tall, wrinkled man with hollowed out pits for eyes walked through the center. Vincent knew without question this was the owner of the deep voice.

"My name is George Goodwin," the man said. "Welcome to the Order."

CHAPTER 17 – THE ORDER

Vincent and Jessica said nothing back. Vincent was transfixed by the sightless craters in the man's head. They were charred and black on the insides, never ending.

Goodwin took a step forward. He ran his long fingers across the tunnel wall next to him for support. "You are finished," he said, "yes?"

Vincent nodded. Then, feeling foolish, spoke aloud. "Yes, sir."

Goodwin grinned. "Very good," he said. "Leave the prints here. You will come with me."

It wasn't a request, not even a command. It was a fact, unalterable, irresistible.

Vincent plucked the prints from his Lenses and inserted them back into the disc. Jessica did the same. By the time they stood from the mat, Goodwin had already disappeared through the curtain. They followed through after him, having to glance in either direction before seeing him, on the left, continuing to trace the wall down the tunnel.

"You would do well to thank Johnathon," said Goodwin when he heard them approaching. "His actions led you here."

Vincent looked around them. *Here* was still an indefinite word in his mind. This tunnel was as nondescript as the last: dark but for the yellow bulbs above, and damp with a scent that could never quite be erased.

"You mean with the eye prints?" asked Jessica. She was talking to Goodwin.

"Yes," said Goodwin. "It took him years to become a Newsight employee, but the reward was well worth it. With his knowledge, every convert we made could have their prints removed. They became ghosts to Newsight, unidentifiable. And their identities could be recycled."

"So what about Ben and Lena Carlson," said Vincent. His voice sounded exceptionally small when preceded by the powerful, deep voice of Goodwin. "Are they members of the Order?"

"They were," said Goodwin. Vincent waited for him to explain, but he changed the subject instead. "There are certain items in THE SIMULATION that were not covered," he continued. "We manufactured the hard sims over a decade ago. Since then, much has happened."

Neither Vincent nor Jessica dared to speak. Goodwin had paused, but the echo of his voice seemed to linger longer than usual. Any words spoken on top of it would have been an interruption.

"You spent time in Hux," continued Goodwin. "Much of the information in THE SIMULATION regarding the cities, hopefully, was redundant. You have experienced the halos and threats of attacks and newsim firsthand. The existence of those things, as well as their purposes, are apparent."

Goodwin paused. The echo of his voice hung over them once again, following them as they walked.

"What has become clear to us only in the years since the production of THE SIMULATION, however," he continued, "is the mechanism by which these factors of control have grown so effective. In our earliest days, we anticipated that even the majority would pose some form of resistance to the sprawling power of Newsight. We were disappointed by the measure of resistance there grew to be, but this shortcoming was not entirely unexpected. We were not truly shocked until what little of this resistance remained was converted into unquestioning compliance."

Goodwin let the last words reverberate off the stone walls of the tunnel. He seemed to need to catch his breath every few sentences.

"Hatred of the Order grew to an unprecedented magnitude," he continued. "Love of Newsight grew by the same amount. The morning simulations in the schools and in the working sector were having a devastating impact. Even our own recruits, those still in the cities, began to defect."

Goodwin's fingers ran off the end of the tunnel wall – they had come to an intersection. Goodwin stopped in the center, breathed in deeply through his nose, then continued forward. He found the wall of the next tunnel without seam.

"Newsim became irresistible," he continued. "Adults began spending more and more of their time in the recreation ring, and children in their dormitories. The children are hardly ever alone. Even the very young." His wrinkled lips curled into a disgusted scowl. "It all coincided, I determined, with the founding of Newsight's newest sub-department: maintenance. For years, they offered no maintenance because Lenses required none. But a few models ago, the upkeep suddenly jumped. Newsight claimed that, from then on, Lenses would require weekly maintenance. Terrified of losing access to their simulations, the people complied. But the Lenses themselves needed no attending; they were made to be resilient. The 'maintenance' that occurs has to do with the injections. You have heard of injections, yes?"

Vincent waited for the echo to soften before he spoke. "We know of them," he said. Goodwin turned to him, his eyeless sockets pointed directly at Vincent. Vincent looked away.

"Then you are familiar with Newsight's medicinal capabilities," said Goodwin. "Until recently, we believed these capabilities to be inconsequential. But after maintenance was introduced, we had other suspicions."

They came to another fork. Goodwin turned into the left path without breaking stride.

"Johnathon tells me you found him in the Newsight headquarters in Hux," continued Goodwin. "Is that correct."

"Yes, sir," said Jessica.

"During your tour," said Goodwin, "you will have learned of a department in Newsight called 'Research'. I think I am safe in assuming the purpose of this department was not explained to you." He waited a beat for them to correct him. They stayed silent. "Its true function is almost entirely data management, merely a warehouse for Newsight's computers that comb through the data they take in. But a portion of the department is dedicated to actual research. In this portion lies the true nature of maintenance. Here, Newsight develops, tests, and produces various chemicals that are administered directly to the brain. Some are designed to trigger fear, others anger or happiness, others lust. They come in minute doses, as serums, but in such direct administration, the quantity is not important. These drugs are cerebral puppet strings. Release one, so moves the arm. Release another, so moves the leg."

Goodwin paused here for a breath. The topic, as well as the words themselves, seemed to be taking a toll on him.

"Before she could learn anything else," Goodwin started again, "our informant was 'taken away'. That is what they call it." He paused again, gnashing his teeth. "But the rest is unfortunately clear," he continued. "These serums are being injected into the Lenses during maintenance. The newest models have the capability to release the serums whenever Newsight deems fit. During the morning simulation against the Order, a drop of adrenaline; during a newsim, a drop of dopamine; during a Friday afternoon in an adolescent, a mix of aphrodisiacs. In the birthschool, these drops are even more abundant. It is easy to see how dramatically Newsight's control can be amplified."

Vincent thought back to that previous afternoon in the school, to his conversation with Annie. The feeling had hit him almost instantly: the warmth in his face, the restlessness in his legs. So too had the satisfaction with the newsims. Part of it had been real, the bulk of it, even, but the remaining portion had been manufactured in the bottom 180 floors of the Newsight headquarters.

"That is the first development," said Goodwin, "and a large reason we decided to mobilize as we have. The second development is somewhat of a formality, but it is an important one. The Senate has repealed all litigations that previously bound Newsight. Data management and transparency, trust and monopoly prevention, every last restriction has been lifted to aid Newsight's pursuit of what the public imagines to be the Order. The individual municipalities have been tending in this direction for years, but a mandate by the Senate has solidified the trajectory. The beast that is Newsight has been freed from its cage."

The tunnel was beginning to tilt downward. They were entering the bowels of the place. At the end of the hall, Vincent thought he could make out a door.

"The Senate was given the new model before everyone else," said Vincent. "Newsight must have needed the maintenance to make sure the Senators would comply."

Goodwin nodded his head. "I think so as well. The Senators were powerless against the combination of the serums and the attack. Even the noblest of them." He turned his sightless gaze on Vincent once again. Vincent didn't look away this time. "I was sorry to hear of your parents," he said, then turned to Jessica. "Your father, I think, remains well. As well as one can be when in the grip of Newsight."

"When can we rescue him?" asked Jessica. "We can take your transports. The ones they can't see."

"In time," said Goodwin. "It is in the blueprint of our plan. All will be revealed shortly."

They had come to the end of the tunnel. A thick, wooden door blocked their path.

"I will inform the whole Order of our course of action," said Goodwin. "In our congregation. Until then, you will have to excuse me. Johnathon will see you are tended to."

With a final dip of his head, Goodwin spun the knob of the door with the grip of his long, slender, fingers, and he passed through it. The sound of the door closing behind him seemed to carry the same weight his voice had, leaving an echo in its wake. It may have filled the tunnel for several seconds longer, had the door not swung open once again.

"What do you think?"

It was John. He had stepped out into the tunnel to meet them.

"How do you feel?" he asked them.

Vincent wasn't sure how to answer the question. "Real," he said. "But that doesn't make sense."

John smiled. "It makes all the sense in the world. It's why I've risked everything for the Order. It makes all the time I spent blending into Newsight, and nearly losing myself in the process, worth it. The raid at the residences, the prints I sent to you, it's all been worth it."

"So you did send us the prints," said Vincent.

John nodded. "Through Kendra," he said. "I knew you were–"

"Wait," said Jessica. "Kendra. We were supposed to give you a message from her."

John turned to her, brow raised. "What is it?"

"She..." Jessica hesitated, unsure for some reason – she seemed worried. "She said to come back for them."

John's eyes grew wide. "To the Hole?" Jessica nodded. "And Jack and Abigail," said John, "they're there as well?" Jessica nodded again.

John hesitated for a moment, his gaze cast downward into the shallow puddle at their feet, then turned away. He started down the tunnel in the opposite direction.

"What are you doing?" said Vincent, following.

"Going to the Hole," said John. "Kendra wouldn't say something like that if they didn't need help."

"But isn't Goodwin speaking soon?" said Jessica.

"I'll be back in time."

"Well can we come with you?" asked Vincent.

"Newsight will be monitoring the area," said John. "They always do after an attack, to look for stragglers. You should stay here."

"But you haven't been there in years," said Jessica. "Will you know where to go?"

"I'll figure it out."

"Under Newsight surveillance?"

Vincent had to dodge to the side to avoid a collision – John had stopped in the middle of the tunnel. He had turned around, fixing them both with a stern, parental kind of glare. "I suppose you don't plan on jogging my memory," he said.

Vincent took a step back so they were level again. "Not from here," he said.

John turned to Jessica – she merely shrugged. Sighing, he cast a glance back the way they had come. He hesitated like that for a second, then, without another word, he took off once again down the tunnel. Vincent and Jessica followed close behind.

******

They had reached a vertical, cement-walled tube just wide enough for one person at a time to squeeze inside. The front wall of the tube was furnished with a rusted metal ladder.

"The transports are just outside," said John. He glanced at the ladder. "I'll go first."

Without another word, he started up the ladder, scaling the thing with practiced ease. Jessica and Vincent followed more slowly behind him. When they breached the tube and emerged into the sunlight, they were in the middle of a street. It reminded Vincent of the scene from Mr. Watts's morning sim – barren and dusted over with the remnants of crumbled buildings, vehicles overturned and deserted.

"Right over here," said John. He stared toward a pile of rubble at the curb. "Washing isn't far, but we'll have to hurry."

Vincent pulled his gaze from the wreckage. He took off after John with Jessica at his side.

When they got to the rubble, John reached over the nearest boulder, like he was trying to flip it. Instead, he stripped the thing of its fabric disguise and exposed one of the military looking transports beneath. He pressed a button on the door and the ramp extended.

"After you," he said, and they climbed in.

Seconds later, they were flying. They went much faster than any of the transports Vincent had seen in Hux. The outside was a blur of gray and black as they left the outskirts of the city, then gold and green as they zoomed past the fields outside the city limits. It took them well over a minute to reach what seemed like their top speed, and only then did Vincent's back come unglued from the seat behind him. He stared out the window in awe. John grinned.

"Newsight doesn't have *all* the engineers," he said proudly. "Just most."

They continued like that for a few seconds, the blur out the windows, the thundering of the wind on the glass.

"Your mother is an engineer," said Jessica. "Isn't she?"

John propped his head up from its position against the glass. "She was the last time I talked to her," he said.

"When was that?" asked Vincent.

"Recently, but we only talk about the Order. She doesn't tell me anything else. Not even about Brian."

Vincent bit down on his tongue, nodding. Lynn, apparently, had been avoiding the news as well.

"So she *is* in the Order?" said Jessica, shifting the subject.

"Of course she is. She helped build it."

"And what about your father?"

"I wouldn't know," said John. He turned back to the window. "He started travelling before I was born. He's a lobbyist. Or was – I don't know if he's still alive. But Newsight consumed him, like they do everyone. I've always thought that's why my mom sought out the Order. To get back at him for leaving. But then *she* started leaving more, too. Even when she was home, she wasn't really there, not for Brian. She stayed away from him. I was the one who took care of him." He shook his head at the thought. "I was barely old enough to take care of myself."

"How old were you?" asked Jessica.

John thought for a moment. He watched the blurred landscape outside. "Eight," he said. "That's when she started coming home late. Later and later. Then not at all, sometimes for days. I was the one who got Brian ready for school in the mornings. Made him dinner at night. I was so angry. At her, some, but mostly at him. Like it was his fault. I couldn't stand to be around him. There was always something he needed, something I had to give him."

Jessica was watching John closely. Her posture was so delicate, so careful she may have been floating a centimeter off her seat. "So you left," she said, her voice soft. John nodded.

"I was 11," he said. "But I already knew how to drive a transport. So I took off. It was easier, back then. The Lenses came out. The transports could be taken off the network. You could still disappear, so that's what I did. I ended up in Washing with Jack and Abigail before they lived in the garage." He smiled at the thought, in a way he never had when talking about his mother. "They introduced me to Kendra and the rest of the protestors, the people who refused to wear Lenses, and I became a part of the movement. I might still be with them had Goodwin not found me."

"How did he find you?" asked Vincent. "Did he make you part of the Order?"

John lifted his head from the window, blinking, as if pulled from a dream. "He did, just like that," he said. "I expect my mother was the one who told him. She knew where I was, somehow. It was just like her to send someone else after her own kid." He let out a puff of air, shaking his head again. "But it was better that way. Goodwin showed me THE SIM. He told me the truth about the world. And he let me do something about it. He told me about his idea to infiltrate Newsight, to go after the prints. I felt guilty leaving Jack and Abigail, but I knew I had to go to the city. I think even then I knew the Lenses wouldn't always be temporary. I think I was still looking out for Brian. I knew he would need a way out someday, when he was old enough. Now it's finally time to go back for him."

Vincent turned to Jessica. She was looking out the window. Her cheeks were sucked into her mouth; her hands were fidgeting in her lap. "So we *are* going back," she said "To the Seclusion."

Vincent shot her a look, but he said nothing. He knew what she had been thinking about with her gaze fixed out the window – not about the Seclusion, but about the Hole, about John's reunion that news of Brian would only ruin.

John straightened in his seat, suddenly unreadable. "That is for Goodwin to tell you," he said, and he turned back to the window. Vincent didn't attempt to restart the conversation, and nor did Jessica – she seemed more than content with the silence.

It was several minutes before the transport began to slow. By that time, the green and gold blur had begun to morph back into a familiar gray and black.

"When were the pamphlets dropped?" asked John, breaking the silence.

"About a week ago they said," said Jessica. "The attack happened the day we left."

Vincent remembered the way Jack had hurried back in the bus. They had all known the attack would come, but it was an odd feeling all the same as the transport slowed, and the blur out the windows became the shattered remains of fallen skyscrapers. The city that had stood as the final reminder of everything untouched by Newsight, now lay in ruins.

Slowly, they began to decrease altitude. Vincent could see the parking garage not far ahead. Only the far half of it seemed seriously damaged. The upper stories had been completely torn off, but the base – the important part – seemed intact.

"That's it?" said John. Vincent and Jessica both nodded. John's eyes went out of focus as he assumed manual control of the transport. Vincent looked around at the six-man pod they were seated in. Somehow, he doubted everyone in the Hole would fit.

"Setting down," said John. "Hold on."

The pod tipped forward as they started for the street next to the garage. Vincent didn't bother looking for a handhold – the transports never afforded any. Instead, he closed his eyes until he heard the ramp fall onto the pavement outside.

"Here we are," said John. Vincent could hear the excitement in his voice.

John's eyes flashed out of focus yet again, and the pod fell the last few centimeters to the ground with a thud. Vincent jumped. Grinning, John climbed from his seat and out the sliding door to the ramp.

"Through there?" asked John when they had both followed him. He was pointing to the vehicle-sized opening in the garage's side.

"I think so," said Vincent.

John started forward without another word. There was a spring in his step now Vincent hadn't seen back in the tunnels.

"Do you think we'll be able to get in?" whispered Jessica. "The entrance may have collapsed."

Vincent looked up at the corner of the garage that housed the stairwell. It looked as sturdy as ever. "It looks fine to me," he said. Jessica followed his gaze. She still looked skeptical, but she stayed silent as they followed John across the debris-strewn street. They didn't speak again until they were inside.

"They had only just started to work on it before I left," said John, slowing his pace. "But Kendra said they were building supports. I'm not surprised the thing is still standing."

He looked around them as they walked. The echoes of their footsteps followed him like a shadow, consuming his voice, muting it as soon as it left his lips.

"Which way?" he asked.

Vincent pointed to the stairwell. Nodding, John started for it. Jessica drew a bit closer to Vincent as they followed. Vincent could hear her breathing: shallow, quiet, as if not wanting to disturb the fragile air around them. By the time they had gone down the first few steps, the breathing was all Vincent could hear. It was growing shallower.

"This is where you entered?"

John had reached the bottom landing a flight ahead of them. When they rounded the final corner to catch up, the breathing stopped — the door to the Hole was ajar. There were no piercing bright lights to greet their entry this time. No warning voice calling out from inside.

"Is this it?" pressed John. He was pointing at the door.

"Yes," said Vincent.

John must have heard the quiver in Vincent's voice, because he didn't step forward right away. Instead, he hesitated, there at the knob, eyes locked on the sliding metal slit at eye level. After a pause, with both hands laid on the door's surface, and with his shoulders rising and falling a bit quicker than usual, he pushed. The scent of the air that blew in to meet them was one Vincent had smelled before. Though he hadn't tasted the stench in real life, the simulation had provided him more than enough experience to know its source. John seemed to know it too, but he kept forward all the same. Vincent and Jessica followed at a distance. The breathing resumed, but with even longer pauses between inhales now, longer pauses between each drink of the foul-tasting air that surrounded them.

Most of the fluorescent lights from the ceiling lay shattered on the ground. The rest provided the place with weak rays of white light. They cast their feeble beams on utter stillness. They detected no movement through the perpetual, underground shadow but that of John and Vincent and Jessica, and even that had been stalled. The three of them stood at the mouth of the stairwell, unmoving, gripped by the total silence of the place, transfixed by the half-shadowed mounds in the shapes of bodies, filled with the odd hope that some would rise up and greet them, shocked into numb observation by the crimson streaks on the pavement where the inconvenient bodies had been dragged away to clear a path to the stairs.

The breathing began to quicken once more, coming in short, sharp bursts – the stunned, realizing breaths that preceded tears. Vincent felt his shoulders shake in time with the ragged inhales; the breaths were coming from his own lips now.

Next to him, Jessica turned away. Her face was pulled into a look of sour disgust, her eyes glassy. Ahead, John remained where he stood, not turning at the neck, but seeming to take in the entire scene all the same. After several seconds, he spoke.

"Let's go," he said.

His words cut through the fragile blanket of silence like razors. He didn't seem to care. He had turned around and was already starting for the stairs. He bumped into Vincent's shoulder as he passed, but said nothing in apology. Slowly, and with Jessica close beside him, Vincent followed.

******

On the flight back, John kept his eyes fixed on the blurred landscape out the window, and Vincent and Jessica looked straight down, completely still. The slightest sound seemed to bring them back. The silence was their only hint of escape.

The transport descended to its previous spot in the disguised rubble, and John was out of it before the ramp had extended. Vincent and Jessica followed, having to track John's footsteps at times through the dark – the sun had set long before their landing. Goodwin's meeting would have started without them.

They scaled down the ladder and back into the tunnel before any of them spoke again.

"If we hurry we can still make the bulk of the meeting," said John. His voice sounded detached. His eyes were still glazed over, his posture slumped – it was impossible for such normal words to have come from him.

"John maybe you should rest," said Jessica. "If you show us where to go, we can fill you in tomorrow."

John shook his head. "I'm going." He started off down the tunnel. Jessica sighed, then started after him with Vincent. They kept walking until they were back at the solid wooden door Goodwin had disappeared through. John pushed inside without hesitation.

Immediately, the space opened up, and the silence erupted. The low-ceilinged tunnel became an enormous cavern, lined along the perimeter with giant, pitch black holes for the other sewer lines. Outside each of these holes was a steel platform, each packed to the edges with its own, wildly cheering crowd. Below, a round slab of pavement three men long had been raised up like a stage from the ground around it. On the slab, stood Goodwin, his arms raised, his eyeless face lit yellow from the wire-strung bulbs overhead. He was preaching to a crowd much bigger than Vincent had expected: several hundred strong, bunched together on the metal platforms to watch from above, or huddled into a single, writhing mass next to the slab of stone below. The door John had led them through was on the bottom story. Vincent had to rise to the tips of his toes to see Goodwin's face. When he did so, he noticed the men around him, as well: three at his front and three at his back, staring out at the crowd with steely eyes.

"Who are they?" Vincent had to shout to be heard.

"Goodwin's Officers," John shouted back.

Vincent looked again at the circle of men surrounding Goodwin. The man had replaced his own eyes with a dozen others.

"Quiet! Quiet!" Goodwin called out to them, motioning for silence. Vincent had to read the man's lips to discern the words – the cheering was deafening.

"Quiet!" he called again, and his voice was actually audible this time. "Please, quiet."

He waited for the remaining applause and whistles to die down before continuing.

"We have been waiting," he said. His voice carried through the entire cavern with unamplified power. "But we will wait no more."

More applause, more whistles – the place seemed already prepared to erupt again, and the feeling was contagious. A needling heat was beginning to itch beneath the skin of Vincent's face. Goodwin raised his hands once more.

"You would charge headlong into every city and every Seclusion armed with only your bare fists," said Goodwin. More cheers. "But I will not ask that of you." A moan of disappointment rose up from the crowd. Most of them looked frenzied, their muscles tensed, their eyes wild and bloodshot, and they swayed together, pushed and pulled by the sound of Goodwin's words.

"We must be calculating," continued Goodwin. "Our chance to strike will come only once. We cannot waste it on ill-timed acts of blind rage and carnage."

The words may have calmed a normal crowd, but this one had already been pushed to the brink of a mob. Goodwin's calm demeanor only seemed to inflame them.

"There is no giant switch," he continued. "No trigger that kills the Newsight network. But there *are* switches. There are triggers that if pulled will fire fatal bullets at their small portion of the Newsight beast."

Goodwin paused. Even in the cavern, even over the constant seething shouts of the crowd, the echo of his words seemed to hang in the air.

"For each city," he continued, "there is one such switch. One such trigger. And one by one, we will pull them all."

The crowd erupted once again. The young and wrinkle-lined called out as one, shouting words so indiscernible they blended together into a single, resounding roar. The needle pricks under the skin of Vincent's face grew hotter.

Goodwin held up his hands. Slowly, the crowd quieted.

"Before this, however," he called out, "we must arm ourselves. We must strengthen our numbers with the oppressed. We must cripple the Newsight Seclusion to render a counterattack impossible."

The crowd cheered again, and Vincent found himself joining in this time.

"We begin with arms," called Goodwin. He made a flourish with his hand, a signal of sorts, and the wall at his back lit up with a giant projection. It was a map. On it, Hux was near the center; to the northwest, Washing; to the east, a dome-shaped structure Vincent didn't recognize; to the south, the labels of other cities equally unfamiliar; and finally, to the north, the Newsight Seclusion.

"Our first mark is northeast," continued Goodwin. With surprising accuracy, he pointed to the domed structure on the map. "The Newsight defense factory. We will overtake the facility and its stockpile of weapons to increase our arsenal by tenfold."

Another roar. A man in front of Vincent yelled his appreciation so loudly his face turned beat red, and a vein in his neck throbbed from the effort. Even so, the man's yell was drowned out by Vincent's own.

"With these arms," continued Goodwin, "we will launch a direct attack on the Newsight Seclusion." He pointed, flawlessly, once again. The cheering began to rise. "We will rescue their prisoners, we will destroy their factories–" he had to shout to be heard, "-we will bring Fatrem to his knees!"

Vincent roared his approval with the rest of the crowd. The man in front of him beat his own chest as he yelled out. Spittle flew from his lips. His teeth seemed suddenly sharp and animal-like. To the side, Vincent could hear the growling, crazed yells of John, and the higher pitched but no less murderous ones of Jessica. Their voices faded seamlessly into the rest of the mob.

"We attack at first light!" shouted Goodwin. His voice was barely intelligible over the roar. "We attack at first light!"

The man in front of Vincent shook his head so violently Vincent thought his neck would snap.

"Now!" he called out. "Do it now!"

The rest of the crowd took up similar calls, more aggressive than ever. They seemed to surge in on Goodwin, flinging their fists in protest, wide-eyed and red-faced, not chanting, not having the presence of mind to chant, nor any presence of mind at all, merely screaming their discontent, no longer voices but noise, guttural, uncontained noise. Vincent screamed along with them, pressed deeper into the crowd by those around him, pressed into the mob as another suit of flesh, swaying and flailing his arms in time with his neighbors.

"Quiet! Quiet!" Goodwin mouthed the words, though he may have shouted them – Vincent couldn't tell. "Quiet!"

It was several seconds before the noise lowered to a level over which Goodwin could speak. The crowd had collectively leaned forward, their jaws jutted out, primal, daring Goodwin to deny them. The man with no eyes merely grinned.

"If you cannot wait," he said to them – there were shouts and curses of affirmation. Goodwin paused. "Then we attack tonight."

Vincent's eardrums might have gone mute for the explosion of sound that followed. More beating of chests, beating of one's neighbor's chest, clawing of skin in grim satisfaction. The man in front of Vincent staggered where he stood, leaning on those around him for support, near the brink of passing out from exertion. And still, he yelled.

"Captains!" Goodwin called. "My Captains! Gather your men! Tell them our plan!" The crowd surged this way and that. They anticipated his words. They could feel them. "We will attack!"

Another eruption. Vincent joined in. He felt the veins in his neck starting to protrude, felt his head growing light and dazed from the effort, saw the crowd as if through a red haze. Then he was moving backward, away from the slab as the crowd expanded. John turned to him – he too was being pushed back – and cleaved through the crowd toward the door, the flesh of his face still inflamed and hot. Vincent knew without a doubt the young, exiled Newsight employee was thinking about the Hole.

CHAPTER 18 – THE DOME

In the same six-seat transport they had travelled in to the Hole, they were flying. John sat at the window across from Vincent and Jessica, and three others – two men and one woman, none of whom Vincent had seen before – filled the remaining seats. It had been several minutes since Goodwin's fiery speech in the tunnels, but their faces remained red, their hearts beating just a little faster than normal.

"Do we have a plan?" asked Jessica. Out of them all, she seemed to have recovered the most fully. She was looking at John. He was one of Goodwin's captains.

"We do," said John. "This isn't on impulse. Goodwin knew they would be worked up after his speech. They always are. He never planned to attack in the morning."

"So what are we supposed to do?" asked Vincent. "Are we bombing them?"

John shook his head. "The factory is too valuable to damage," he said. "We'll go in on foot. Take the place by force."

Vincent glanced at the three others with them in the pod. None of them were armed. "Will we be given weapons?" he asked.

"Some will," said John. "But most won't need them. The factory isn't heavily armed once we get inside. It's getting in that required planning."

"Is that our job?" asked Jessica.

"Goodwin's," said John. "His officers have been watching the patterns of the place for weeks. Every night, the dome receives a truckload of supplies. Goodwin will be on that truck with the rest of his officers, and once they're in, they can open the gate for the rest of us."

Vincent looked out the window at the fleet of transports flying close by, all tightly packed together, all very close to the ground. "How will they do that?" he asked.

"Leave that to them," said John. "Our job is to secure the facility once a path has been cleared for entry. Afterward, we can begin assembling our force for the Seclusion raid."

"So we aren't going back to the tunnels?" asked Jessica, sounding hopeful.

"Not right away," said John. "We'll have to move quickly once we take the factory. Word will reach Newsight whether we want it to or not, and our window to attack the Seclusion will be slim. We can't afford a return trip."

Vincent nodded. He was sure he didn't understand the larger plan at play, but he *did* understand the nearness of their return to the Seclusion. This return, though, no longer seemed so important to him. After all, there was no one there waiting for him.

John didn't explain any more of the plan, and Vincent and Jessica didn't ask any more questions. The three others with them seemed already to know, or simply not to care.

After several minutes, the transport began to slow, in time with its counterparts alongside, ahead, and behind. In the distance, through the front window, Vincent could see an enormous lump rising up out of the darkness, a blemish on an otherwise smooth, barren plain, lit with sterling white light from the base upward.

"The factory dome is straight ahead," said John. He was looking out the window, with an attached pair of glass-ended tubes held up to his eyes. "Goodwin and his team are already in place." He lowered the thing he was holding, then handed it to Vincent. "Have a look." He motioned to the window. Hesitant, Vincent lifted the device up to his eyes as John had done, and he peered through the glass. As soon as he did so, the dome ahead grew 10 times larger, magnified. Taking a second to regain his bearings, Vincent detected movement at the dome's base. At the front gate – what appeared to be the only entrance – was a large, box-shaped truck the size of Tom's bus. In the light, Vincent could see uniform-clad men walking up to it.

"Let me see," said Jessica.

John took the device from Vincent's hands, and the dome returned to normal size. "Everyone can look," said John. He handed the things to Jessica. "But stay ready. We'll be inside soon."

Jessica lifted the device to her own eyes, apparently settling on the same scene Vincent had. "They're talking to the driver," she said. "They're...they're waving him in."

John's eyes were out of focus. He was staring at a patch of ground between Vincent's feet.

"It looks like the gate is opening," said Jessica. "The truck is driving through. But...it's closing. The gate is closing after it." She dropped the device from her eyes and turned to John. "Is it supposed to do that?"

"For now," said John. His eyes had returned to normal. "Goodwin is inside. All we have to do is wait for his signal."

Nodding, and this time without the aid of the magnifying tubes, Jessica turned back to the dome. Vincent followed suit. Even from a distance, he could tell the thing was giant. The school dome from the Seclusion would have fit inside several times over.

"Get ready," said John. His eyes were absent again. "They're on their way to the gate."

The woman and two men next to them writhed in their seats. Vincent felt himself growing restless as well. As if from a switch, the energy that had filled him during Goodwin's speech in the cavern began to fill him once again, just trickling now, but with a force of an entire current behind it, waiting.

"Almost," said John, his eyes still unfocused. "Almost..."

There was silence in the pod. The others had shifted forward to the front of their seats...

"Now."

The pod shot forward, throwing Vincent back against the wall. The men next to John caught themselves on the glass just before they went hurtling into the woman across from them. Not one of the three flinched – they seemed gripped with the same, grim concentration as Vincent.

"Give me the binoculars," said John. Without waiting, he took the set of tubes from Jessica's hand. He twisted in his seat to see the dome, now racing toward them at breakneck speed. "It's opening," he said, excitement beginning to enter his voice. "We're going in."

As John lowered the binoculars, Vincent could already see the entrance opening up to receive them. The transport careened toward it at a pace faster than Vincent thought possible, still in perfect form with the others around it.

"Prepare to de-board," said John. He pulled an L-shaped piece of metal from inside his jacket, the same shape Vincent had stared down the barrel of in the Hole.

The thought of the Hole called back to him the image of the body strewn garage, the sheet metal houses peppered with small round holes the same as the bodies, the blood and dust on the cement.

His face began to tingle with heat. He felt the trickle begin to grow, gushing now, filling him, heating his whole body and clenching his hands into fists.

"Slowing!" John shouted, even though the pod was mostly silent. He seemed ready to throw himself out the window just to get there faster.

The dome was racing toward them less rapidly now, but it was larger than ever. Untarnished all the way around, it reflected in the fluorescent beams of the lights below, the perfect, detestable hue of Newsight.

"Go!"

John shouted as soon as the pod touched the ground. He sprang from his seat, and Vincent was up with him, out of the pod, running, the crowd of others at his shoulders, the same crowd from the cavern, more inflamed than ever as they sprinted for the entrance. Vincent lost track of Jessica in the mob when they funneled inside, pushing and shoving at each other to get in. Then they were through. On white tile, they ran. On open ground lined with wire-topped fences, along gray stone buildings with steel vents and smokestacks, they ran. Vincent let himself be washed onward by the wave, feeling for a fraction of a second he was back in the working sector of Hux, in the industrial part, swimming through smog. He was swept forward by the pounding legs around him to the first of the dome's fenced-in buildings. He was sprinting at gray-clad men on the shop floor, tearing at their clothes, dragging them across the tile. Somewhere behind him, he heard a loud popping sound. Some of the red-faced men and women around him were carrying the L-shaped strips of metal that John had carried. Vincent needed only his hands. They were clubs now, swinging at every patch of gray cloth they could find, urged on by a wild, insatiable current that had been only a trickle back in the transport. He was still running, swinging, clawing as he went, when the men and women in gray started to flee. He narrowed his gaze, still fogged and blurred, on the woman closest. Her stride was laden with a slight limp, almost comical the way her left side drooped and dragged in vain effort to keep up with her right. Vincent tore after her, spurred faster by the geyser of hot energy gushing inside him. He spun the woman around. He raised his fist. He flexed his chest with his knuckles pulled tight—

He stopped where he was. The blur in his vision had cleared just enough to see the woman up close. Her gray Privacy Officer jumpsuit was unmistakable, but so too was her wide, heart-shaped face. Vincent had seen that face before, had talked to it. It wasn't a gray blur like the rest. It was real, here, and afraid.

Vincent dropped his hand to his side, and the woman took off running once again. He started back the way he had come, his fists still clenched, his vision fading in and out of focus. He staggered through the mauling herd still in pursuit of their ashen gray prize, until he was to the wall, then to a door. He pushed inside and closed it behind him, bolting the lock. With the screams outside now muffled, he could hear the rasp of his own breaths, heavy and strained. He began to shake as he crossed over to the sink. His eyes were lined and red, wet not with tears but with something else. The rims of his Lenses had grown darker than normal. They seemed to throb in the light, in time with his pulse, the beat of which refused to slow.

Vincent leaned forward at the waist, bracing his weight on the sink, gripping its sides with white knuckles. He wanted to go back out. He wanted to swing madly at everything that moved, to hunt the gray-clad men with the rest, to find his revenge for the stayers who lived in the Hole. The desire was overpowering, irrational with the force it urged him out the door, almost irresistible. But then he thought of the woman's face, the face he had seen before. With its image seared into his mind, and with his fingers still curled to the bone around the sink, Vincent stayed where he was, blood still beating through him like a drum, face still ablaze, and he listened to the screams.

******

Vincent awoke under the sheets of a body-width mattress. His pulse had steadied. The screams had long since faded. There was silence, and the trickle in him that had risen to a torrent was now dry.

Vincent sat up. On either side of him, beds were stacked in bunks, filling the room from end to end. The men and women in them, in their freshly cleaned white jumpsuits, were beginning to stir. Vincent looked down at himself. His clothes had been changed and cleaned as well, wiped of their previous red stains. But for the stubborn memory of the woman with the familiar face, he may have thought the previous night to have been a dream.

Vincent rose from the bed and started for the exit, surprised to feel his legs rather steady beneath him. When he was outside, he found himself sandwiched in between two buildings, and nearly at the dome's edge. Deeper into the dome was his only option. He walked until the buildings on either side of him opened up into a space more familiar: the outer edge of a wide circle of dark, block-shaped factories. He turned around. Behind him was a series of long, rectangular buildings only one story high, none with windows, all with their shorter ends facing the center of the dome. For as far as Vincent could see, the buildings continued one after another around the dome's perimeter, each, presumably, housing the same sort of barracks he had awoken in.

He continued forward, down the middle of the factories straight ahead. The air was cooler here, shaded and acting like a tunnel for the wind. As he walked, he shrank into the clothes that had been given to him, his head bent against the chill. He looked up only when the tunnel had opened and the barracks were barely visible at his back. He had walked into something of a courtyard, a wide circular region in the dome's very center, around which the factories – four others in addition to the two he was between – stood as sentries. The circle was oddly empty, no structure or markings to indicate it, only empty ground.

Vincent started around the edge of the space to the mouth of the factory next to him. It looked identical to the all the others: several stories high, square and plain, and with only a handful of windows to let in the artificial light. It was too dim to make out, but atop the building's entrance, there seemed to be an inscription. Even in clear light, Vincent doubted he could have read it – the words appeared to have been painted over.

"Good morning, Vincent."

John and what looked like a group of Goodwin's officers came into view as Vincent rounded the corner. John excused himself and broke off, crossing over to him.

"Did you just wake up?"

Vincent nodded. "But I don't remember going to bed." He glanced up at the factory. "What happened last night?"

John motioned to the dome at large, as if that explained things. "We did it," he said. "We overran them. The whole place is ours."

He said it proudly, but Vincent could hear a bit of confusion in his voice as well.

"What about this?" said Vincent, looking down at his jumpsuit. "I don't remember changing."

John shrugged, wearing a slight frown. "I'm not really sure," he said. "Goodwin must have had one of the other captains organize a cleaning effort." He flicked his head in the direction of the group of men next to the factory entrance. "We're preparing the plans for the Seclusion attack," he said. "Care to sit in?"

Vincent looked over at the group. They had stopped their conversation – their gazes were trained on him. "I'm all right," he said. He turned back to John. "Where's Jessica?"

John looked around, as if scanning for her. "I just saw her," he said. "She slept in the factory with some of the others."

Vincent raised an eyebrow. "She slept in the factory?"

John shrugged. "She's fine," he said. He glanced back at Goodwin's officers. "I should get back. Try this factory first." He patted Vincent on the arm, then returned to the group. Pausing for a moment, Vincent followed at a slight diagonal, starting for the doors they had crammed through the night before. He passed through them without the jostling of shoulders this time, and into the factory. The space was larger than he remembered. Immense, industrial-grade conveyers split the factory in half, with different stations along its edges. Perched on its surface were man-sized, cylindrical chunks of metal with rounded, cone-shaped tips and triangular fins on the opposite end. The factory floor was as clean as Vincent's white jumpsuit. Not a trace remained of what had transpired the evening before.

"Vincent?"

He turned around. Jessica was seated against the wall, with several others, some ways off. She looked like she had just woken up.

"I was about to come looking for you," she said.

Vincent walked over to her. She didn't stand to greet him. Instead, she laid her head back against the wall behind her.

"Are you ok?" asked Vincent.

Jessica nodded. But as she looked around, she wore the same, troubled expression John had. "I don't remember what happened last night."

When she said it, a feeling of unease began to settle deep in Vincent's stomach.

"Do you?" she asked.

"I remember enough of it," said Vincent. He scanned the people next to Jessica along the wall. Several of them were beginning to awaken. "Let's go somewhere." He reached down and took her by the hand. She felt like deadweight as he pulled her up.

"I'm tired," she said. "Why can't we stay here?"

"Just trust me," he said back. He pulled her to her feet. She didn't resist – or couldn't resist, from fatigue – and allowed him to pull her farther away down the wall. When they came upon a sturdy looking door, Vincent pulled it open and ushered them inside.

"Vincent what's wrong?" said Jessica. Her grogginess was starting to clear now. "Did something happen?"

"I think so," said Vincent. "I don't know." He stopped, glancing at the door they had just come through to make sure it was closed. "Do you remember any of last night at all?" he asked.

Jessica frowned. "I remember the transport," she said. "I remember running in with everyone else. The gunshots. The rest is blurry. I just remember being so angry." She paused, looking down. "I don't remember going to sleep."

"Neither do I," said Vincent. He looked around to make sure they were alone. "I remember some things, though. I remember attacking the privacy officers. With the rest." He hesitated, focusing on the memory, determined not to let it slip away. "But some of the people from last night," he continued, "some of the privacy officers…they seemed different. They seemed afraid."

Jessica was squinting at him. Her cheeks were sucked into her mouth. "I don't remember that," she said. Vincent took a deep breath. He hadn't wanted to say anything about this – he knew what she would say back to him – but he didn't have a choice now.

"I recognized one of them," said Vincent. He thought back to the woman with the heart-shaped face. "It was a woman. She looked like Jim's wife, from Hux. I can't remember her name."

"Tina?" asked Jessica.

Vincent nodded. The name hit him with the force of memory. Real, concrete memory.

"But why would she be in a Newsight factory?" said Jessica. "Jim said she was in quarantine."

"I know," said Vincent. "I don't know why she would be here, but she was. I'm sure of it." He said it firmly, as if to convince himself as well as Jessica.

Jessica was frowning. She looked unconvinced. "If there were people here that weren't Privacy Officers," she said, "then why would we have attacked? Why would we not have rescued them?"

Vincent started to speak, then breathed out instead. "I don't know," he said. "I just think we should be careful. Something about this just..."

He trailed off when a hoarse, measured breathing rose up inside of him. The breathing wasn't his own – it was coming from his Lenses.

"Fellow brothers and sisters of the Order."

It was Goodwin's voice, and it was inside Vincent's head. By the look of confusion on Jessica's face, it was inside hers as well.

"You will assemble in the center of the dome," said Goodwin. "Now."

With that, the voice went silent. It was the same, undeniable, irresistible command as usual.

Next to them, the door slid open.

"Hello." A man – Vincent recognized him to be one of Goodwin's officers – had stepped through. "We are rounding people up," he said, in a hard, iron voice. "Everyone is meeting in the center."

Jessica nodded and started forward, but Vincent stayed where he was.

"Is there a problem?" the man asked.

"How did you know we were here?" asked Vincent.

"Vincent come on," said Jessica. "He's just trying to help."

"How did you know?" repeated Vincent. He was looking up at the man.

"Someone saw you go this way," the man replied. His tone was level, just shy of robotic. "Is there something wrong?"

Vincent held the man's gaze. Jessica watched them both, looking nervous.

"No, sir," said Vincent. He emphasized the second word. The man didn't seem to notice, or care. He motioned them to the door.

Vincent followed Jessica back onto the factory floor and next to the conveyer belt. Behind them, the man peeled off, presumably to round up the rest of the stragglers.

"What are you doing?" hissed Jessica when the man was out of earshot. "Are you trying to get us in trouble?"

Vincent glanced back at the man. "He wasn't here when we went into the hall. And no one else saw us."

Jessica shook her head, exasperated. "You're being ridiculous, Vincent. Come on." She took off for the exit. Vincent followed, more slowly, behind.

By the time they reached the eerily open space in the dome's center, most of the others were already there. Vincent walked up behind Jessica, who had arrived several steps before him. They had passed the walk in silence.

"Brothers and sisters!"

Goodwin's voice rang out from somewhere in the circle's center. Vincent craned his neck, and he saw the man climbing up on some sort of stool, to be higher.

"Brothers and sisters," he repeated. "We have claimed the Newsight factory."

There was a cheer of approval, but the rigor of the night before was nowhere present.

"As we speak," Goodwin continued, "our engineers are preparing the fighters for attack. We will fly on the Seclusion at dusk."

Another cheer. This one was a bit louder, but there was no beating of chests, no veins protruding from necks.

"However," said Goodwin. "There is first the issue of last night's attack."

Vincent's ears perked up at this.

"It has been reported," continued Goodwin, "that many of you are having trouble remembering it."

Around them, various heads began to nod.

"This is no cause for alarm," said Goodwin. "I have consulted our brothers and sisters who spent time in the enemy camp, in the Newsight Corporation, and it is their belief that this memory obstruction was caused by the Lenses."

A murmur coursed through the crowd, an affirming one, as if they had already known. Vincent continued to stare forward, frowning.

"It was a reaction to our darkeners," said Goodwin. "Trauma, it seems, is the triggering action. And last night, though victorious, was surely traumatic."

Goodwin's tone was somber and his head was tilted downward, as if looking out at them through imaginary eyes, overtop imaginary spectacles.

"There will be more of this trauma at dusk," he continued, "in the Seclusion. It is imperative, however, that you remember this attack, for it is one you will tell your children about, and they their children."

Another murmur of approval – still no wild yells and applause.

"For this reason, our Newsight knowledgeable colleagues have been working without rest to determine a fix for this problem, and that is exactly what they have done. For those of you who experienced an impairment to your memory, please follow my officers to the facility we have erected in factory six. There, your Lenses can receive what little maintenance they require."

He nodded to them, then stepped down off his riser. The crowd began to funnel itself in the direction he had pointed. Vincent stayed where he was.

"Jessica."

She looked over her shoulder. She had already started forward with the crowd. "Aren't you coming?" she asked.

"No," said Vincent. "And I don't think you should either."

Jessica stopped. People jostled by her to get around. "Why not?" she said. "You were just talking about this."

"I know," said Vincent. "But didn't you hear him? He said they're going to do maintenance."

Jessica rolled her eyes, sighing. "He obviously didn't mean that kind," she said. "Just come on. Don't you want to remember tonight?"

Vincent looked toward the center, where Goodwin had just disappeared. "I'm going to stay," he said, suddenly sure. "I can't make you, but I really think you should do the same."

Jessica hesitated there, her eyes scanning the crowd of men and women walking by them. "I can't," she said after a pause. "I want to remember seeing my dad again." She gave a weak, sympathizing look, then let herself be swept away by the mob.

Vincent breathed out as he watched the last of them start off in the same direction. Near the center, where Goodwin had just been, the man who had found them in the hallway was standing with the rest of Goodwin's officers. His eyes were on Vincent. Vincent felt a chill shoot down his spine for no real reason. He looked away from the man, then started, after the crowd, toward factory six.

******

When he judged he had waited long enough, Vincent stepped out of the restroom. The factory floor, which earlier had been lined with tables set up for maintenance, was now empty.

"You there."

It was the same, iron voice they had heard in the hallway.

"Have your Lenses been fixed?"

212

Vincent turned around, unsurprised to see the same man as before.

"Yes, sir," he said. They hadn't, of course – he had come to the factory only to avoid any unwanted attention.

"Are you certain?" the man pressed.

"If I'm remembering correctly," said Vincent.

The man scowled at him. He was beginning to speak again when a second voice sounded behind them.

"Vincent!"

Vincent turned around. It was John.

"We've been looking for you," he said. "Goodwin needs us. It's about the Seclusion attack."

"He needs to have his Lenses fixed first," said the man with the iron voice.

"I already have," said Vincent, firmer this time. He turned to John. "Let's go."

Before the man could stop them, Vincent led them back the way John had come. He didn't look back.

"Everything ok?" asked John, catching up.

"I don't think so," said Vincent, but he could say nothing more. They had reached the other side of the factory's enormous machine, and Goodwin was there, standing with Jessica. He was leaned down, talking to her, his tone soft.

"What do you mean?" said John, still looking at Vincent.

Goodwin heard them. He straightened his posture. Jessica was nodding.

"There you are, Vincent," he said. "Now we can begin. John, can you find us a room?"

John turned his gaze from Vincent, and his frown was gone in an instant. "Of course." He scanned the perimeter of the factory, and spotted a promising, large-windowed room not far off. He led them to it, then inside. They settled into rigid-backed chairs around a long, rectangular table.

"You will have to excuse my secrecy," said Goodwin, "but a certain amount of it is necessary."

Vincent looked out the room's giant window. Apparently, they needed very little secrecy indeed.

"The three of you will play a pivotal role in the attack," continued Goodwin. "Of all our other brothers and sisters, you are the only to have set foot in the Newsight Seclusion. For the attack, this knowledge will be invaluable. Are you willing to share it?"

"Yes." John and Jessica echoed the word at the same time.

"Yes." Vincent said it a beat behind.

"Very good," said Goodwin. "The Seclusion is protected by Newsight's most advanced air defense network. Our transports, nor even our fighter planes, are capable of penetrating it. The attack will succeed only if the defense network is shut off. This will be your job."

Vincent looked at John and Jessica. They were nodding, unflinching.

"You will be smuggled into the Seclusion," continued Goodwin. "From there, it will be your task to infiltrate the Newsight campus and disable the network."

Jessica leaned forward in her seat. "Will my dad be in the Newsight campus?" she asked.

"I believe all the prisoners will be," said Goodwin. "And if you can do only one: save the prisoners or disable the network, choose the prisoners."

Vincent felt a hollow, empty sound to these words, but he said nothing.

"But this decision will not be necessary," continued Goodwin. "You will be able to do both. I believe in all three of you." His sightless gaze lingered on Vincent here. Vincent stared steadily back.

"When do we leave?" asked John.

"This evening," said Goodwin, turning to him. "You will arrive by ground transport to avoid being detected by the Newsight satellites."

John nodded. He shifted slightly in his seat, seeming anxious. Vincent got the feeling he may have run to the Seclusion if given the chance.

"You will not be alone," said Goodwin. "We will be with you. From above. From our few sources within the Seclusion." He turned the charred, cratered holes in his head once again onto Vincent. "We will be watching."

CHAPTER 19 – HOLDING

The three of them had been in the transport for the past several hours, trapped beneath the concealing sheet overtop of them. They had scarcely spoken to each other the whole trip. Since that morning, Vincent had uttered only a handful of words to Jessica, and she even fewer back to him. Now, nearly sundown, as they neared the outer bounds of the Seclusion, talking seemed impossible. There were too many thoughts that needed attending. Goodwin's officers had relayed the plan to them several times over, and it was a simple plan, but it wasn't a thing one could avoid thinking about.

The transport began to slow.

Approaching.

The word scrolled across Vincent's Lenses, and he went still. Next to him, John and Jessica did the same.

They were being towed. Goodwin's officers were in the lead transport and, for now, would be doing most of the work. Vincent and the others were to do nothing but remain under the sheet and avoid detection.

The transport had eased to a stop. There was silence for a beat, then footsteps. Someone outside started to speak.

"Good evening, gentlemen. May I see your permit?"

Goodwin's officers offered no response. Now was the time to hand over the fabricated paperwork.

"That looks in order," said the Guard. "What is your delivery?"

Vincent thought certain he could feel the man's gaze turning toward them through the window.

"A transport," said their driver. "For Newsight."

There was another pause. Vincent's feeling of being watched only intensified.

"Of course," said the Guard. "Please allow me a few minutes to search your vehicle."

Next to Vincent, Jessica drew in a sharp breath. Goodwin had said they wouldn't be searched.

"Yes, sir," said their driver. "But would you mind waiting for my escort? That should be her just ahead."

Vincent turned to John, frowning. This wasn't part of the plan. They hadn't been told about an escort.

Vincent mouthed a question, but John only shrugged in response

"I suppose so," said the Guard. "Who is your–"

"Excuse me?"

A sharp, familiar voice sounded from outside. It seemed to shoot through John like an electric current. His whole body tensed in a single movement; his ears were perked.

"Is there a particular reason you are detaining my transport?" the woman asked.

"Just protocol, ma'am," said the Guard. Vincent could hear the tightness in every syllable. The man had snapped to attention.

"Well I don't have time for protocol," said the woman. "Do you have any idea how much I paid for this?"

The Guard was silent.

"I didn't think so," she said. "Now are you going to let them through or not?"

There was another pause. Vincent felt the Guard's gaze on them through the window.

"Yes, ma'am," he said. "My apologies."

Outside, the woman gave the Guard a curt thanks, then walked back to the transport she had arrived in. Their own transport began to move once again.

"Did you know she was coming?" hissed John.

Vincent shook his head. "No idea," he said, truthfully. Jessica said the same.

John sighed, looking down. "Goodwin didn't want me to back out," he said. "I should have known we would need someone on the inside to let us in."

Vincent hadn't given it any thought. The only other time he had come near the boundary of the Seclusion had been with Jessica on their way out. Then, the way had been prepared for them.

"Did you hear anyone else?" asked John. "Anyone with her?"

Vincent knew he was thinking of Brian. Jessica seemed to sense the same. She took a deep breath.

"John," she started, "we should have told you this a long—"

John held up a hand for quiet. His eyes were out of focus. Vincent could see it too. On the bottom of their Lenses, one of Goodwin's officers had sent them a message.

Stay quiet. We are being followed.

Jessica was persistent. "John you need to hear what—"

"You saw the message," said John. "Not now."

"But it's important it's about—"

"I said not now."

John glowered at her for a few seconds, then perked his ears for any sign they had been heard. When he was satisfied, he turned back to the front. Jessica looked to Vincent, but Vincent only shrugged back, as helpless as she was. They continued on like that, silent, for over a minute. John refused to look at either of them. No one budged until the transport came to a stop, and the man with the iron voice threw off their sheet.

"We are in the first ring," he said. "Management sector."

Vincent had a feeling he knew exactly where they were.

"John?"

It was Lynn, their escort. She was standing just outside, in the driveway of her dome, looking in at them.

"You've grown." Her voice wavered slightly. It no longer seemed as detached as it had been with Brian. Although, Vincent reminded himself, that exchange had taken place under the careful watch of Marcus.

John rose from his cramped position and climbed from the pod. His mother reached out to embrace him, but he made no move toward her. He looked around instead. "Where's Brian?" he asked.

The air around them grew suddenly tense. No one spoke. Even the officers grew still. John looked around at them, frowning.

"Is he inside?" he asked, turning to the dome. "I want to see him." He started for the front door, but Lynn caught his wrist. John looked back at her. His shoulders were rising and falling a bit quicker now.

"He's not here, John," said Lynn.

John looked at the officers, then back at the door, as if expecting Brian to come bursting through at any second. "Where is he then?" he said.

Lynn started to speak, then stopped. She looked down.

"Where is he?" repeated John. His voice was firmer this time. His eyes were on his mother.

"I thought you would know," she said. She turned her gaze on Vincent and Jessica. They looked away from her.

John didn't seem to notice. He was growing restless, shifting on his feet. "Know what?" he snapped.

Lynn turned back to him. Her head was tilted to the side, sympathetic, genuine. Her usual cold mask was nowhere present.

"There was an accident," she said. John grew still. "When Marcus searched our dome, Brian was taken away in a transport, and there was a collision."

John continued to stare at his mother. His gaze flitted between her eyes, searching.

"The other transport hit his side head on," continued Lynn. Her voice was tighter now. She had to squeeze the words out one by one. "He didn't make it."

John started to shake his head. He pulled his wrist out of his mother's grip. "What do you mean he didn't make it?" he said.

"I'm sorry," said Lynn. She turned to Vincent and Jessica. "I thought they would have told you."

John turned to face them as well. He no longer appeared so much older than they were. His face had a childish look about it now, vulnerable, confused. His mask had fallen away the same as his mother's.

"You knew?" he said.

Jessica looked down, biting her lip. Vincent forced himself to hold John's gaze.

"You knew?" John repeated. He stepped forward as he said it this time, but the man with the iron voice moved in front of him before he could go any closer.

"Enough of this," the man said. "We are on a schedule." He turned to Lynn. "We need to move."

Lynn kept her gaze on John for a moment before turning to the man. "Of course," she said. "John, we can speak about this at another time."

John said nothing back. His breathing had yet to ease. His eyes had yet to leave Vincent.

"There has been a change of plans," continued Lynn. "I will infiltrate the heart of the Newsight campus to disable the defense network. The three of you will handle the prisoners. You will be joining them shortly."

"Joining them?" said John. He turned from Vincent to look at his mother. Vincent felt the burning sensation in his face begin to subside. "What does that mean?"

"I have to take you in," said Lynn. She moved a step closer to John, cautiously. "It's the only way you'll be able to free them. And it's the only way I'll be allowed into the defense portion of campus.

Marcus has been keeping a close watch on me."

"So you're just going to hand us over?" asked John.

"With protection," said Lynn. "The officers will be accompanying you." She motioned to Goodwin's men. "When I give them the signal, they will help you escape."

John continued to stare at his mother. He looked prepared to argue when the officer holding him interjected.

"We should leave, ma'am," he said. "The attack cannot start until the system is down. Goodwin is waiting."

Lynn's posture straightened at the mention of the name. "Very well," she said. She turned to Vincent and Jessica. "You two stay where you are. You'll be with me in the first transport." She started forward to their pod. "John," she continued, "you'll be in the second."

John didn't move. As his mother and the officers started for the transports, he stayed where he was. He didn't seem to notice them. He had eyes only for his old dome, and for the stubbornly still surface of its front door.

******

Vincent was sitting on the far left side of the back row, Jessica on the far right. One of Goodwin's officers was in between them, and Lynn was directly in front. The man with the iron voice had gone in John's pod.

They were in the center, and straight ahead was the Newsight campus. In the usual dome shape, the building was completely circular but for the hallway-width offshoots around its perimeter. The offshoots snaked outward in enormous s-curves, sprawling from the body of the place like the arms of an octopus.

"We'll go through the front," said Lynn. She turned back to them. "Remember your place."

Vincent knew exactly what she meant, though she couldn't say it aloud for fear of being watched: they were to act like prisoners.

Jessica nodded, and Vincent followed suit, more hesitantly.

"Good," said Lynn. "Let's go."

She opened her door and climbed out of the pod. Seconds later, Vincent was outside as well, with the hands of two officers forcing his arms up behind his back. He got the feeling there would be no need at all to *act* like prisoners.

They started for the main entrance – an arched, open-aired space just ahead – at a pace that nearly forced Vincent into a jog. When he lagged, the men holding him wrenched his arms up higher still. They, apparently, had embraced their roles wholeheartedly.

They came to a stop in a high ceilinged lobby, around which were well over a dozen hallway offshoots. Instead of any of these, they approached the front desk in the room's center, and were greeted with the usual, tight-dress receptionist.

"Ms. Department Head," said the woman, seeming surprised. "I thought you had gone for the day."

"I had," said Lynn. "I would have preferred to stay that way also." She glanced back at the group of them. The woman seemed to see the strange party for the first time. "I need, Marcus," said Lynn.

"Of course," said the woman. "He's still in. I'll page him."

The woman's eyes went out of focus for a beat. No one spoke.

"He has requested you meet him in holding," she said after a pause. Her eyes were still trained on nothing in particular. They were starting to roll backward. "I've given you access."

Lynn nodded her thanks, then motioned them forward. Vincent felt a twinge in his shoulder as his overzealous captors urged him into motion. They started for the door of one of the larger halls, deeper into the place. When the door slid open to receive them, they could see Marcus emerging from a door several meters ahead.

"You're not usually here so late," said Marcus.

"I'm not usually doing your job," said Lynn. She motioned to Vincent and Jessica and John behind her. When Marcus followed her gaze, his eyes grew wide.

"How…" He looked first at Vincent, then at Jessica. John didn't seem to peak his interest. "Where were they?"

"Outside of Hux," said Lynn. "As I understand it, you were just there. Pity you couldn't have brought them in yourself."

Marcus was still staring at them, as if suspicious they might disappear at any second. "I was only there for a day," he said. He looked up at Lynn. "How did you find them?"

"They were trying to buy prints," said Lynn. "The ones you lost in the hack."

"That was a fluke," snapped Marcus. "Our security was flawless. They must have had someone with knowledge of the system." He glanced at Jessica. "Someone far more capable than the developer."

Jessica jerked against the arms of the men holding her. She only moved a few centimeters.

"Whoever it was," said Lynn, "just be glad your mess was cleaned up for you. Consider these two a reward for poor performance."

Marcus looked at them again, this time lingering on John. "Correct me if I'm wrong, but it appears as if you've miscounted."

"The third is a print scalper," said Lynn. "He's a nobody, but he might assist in your investigation of the hack."

John shifted against his captors, scowling back at his mother. He, like Jessica, didn't seem to be doing much acting.

Marcus gave John a doubtful look. "I suppose you want me to hold them for you?" he asked.

"I don't care what you do with them," said Lynn. "Take them away. Ship them to a Seclusion. Whatever you want." She paused. "Or if you'd rather I take them I'm sure I can–"

"No," said Marcus. "I can find a place for them. You can leave your men with me." He motioned for the officers to follow him as he turned away, back toward the door from which he had just exited.

"Actually," said Lynn. Marcus turned to face her. "I'm here about the defense network as well. The alternative products sub-department notified me of an issue just today. And because the network inexplicably falls under your department, I was hoping to have a word."

Marcus raised his brow, expectant.

"A *private* word," said Lynn. "Surely you of all people can arrange for that."

Marcus smirked at her, then flicked his head at the men holding Vincent and Jessica. "What would you have them do?" he asked.

"Do you know where holding is?" asked Lynn, looking at the officers. As one, they nodded. "There," she said. "They can escort themselves."

Marcus grunted in response, unconvinced. He took a step closer to survey the men more carefully.

"Of course, you can always summon others," said Lynn. She had stepped forward as well. She didn't seem keen on Marcus's having a closer look. "Have someone hold their hands from here, if you must."

Marcus cast the men another look. "That could be arranged," he said. His eyes flashed out of focus so quickly it looked like a kind of open-eyed blink. "I've summoned a man," he said. "We can talk in my office."

"Perhaps in network management would be better?" suggested Lynn. Marcus seemed hesitant. Lynn rolled her eyes. "I bring you gifts and you won't even show me my own products?"

Marcus snorted. "Fine. With me." He started off deeper down the hall. Lynn followed without so much as a glance back. They were still in sight when the door Marcus had emerged through slid open once again. A crisply dressed, prim-looking man stepped out to meet them. His uniform was not as elaborate as the high-collared jumpsuits of Marcus and Lynn, and nor as plain as the gray uniform of the officers.

"Step inside," he said. He backed away from the doorframe and motioned them in. The man with the iron voice, still with John as his captive, led them inside. The room was plain and miniature, only just big enough for all of them at once, and bare but for two separate doors on the wall they were facing. The first looked no different than the one they had just passed through. The second was made entirely of glass, and curved outward like the side of a fishbowl.

"You will deposit your guest through this door on the right," the prim-looking man said. He pointed at the fishbowl door. "The boys together, the girl separate."

The man with the iron voice inspected the door, skeptical. "And we will accompany you to the observation deck?" he asked.

"That hardly seems necessary. Watching the guests is a one-man job." The prim-looking man surveyed the officers with more than a hint of distaste "You can return to the quarters." He turned to the door. "Now, if you would. The girl first."

Vincent felt the air grow thick with tension. This was not part of the plan.

"Wait just a moment," said iron-voice. "We went through a great deal in order to secure these guests. We want to see they are properly detained."

The prim-looking man sighed in exasperation. He seemed bored. "Marcus designed this system himself. You have no need to worry. There's no room for all of you, anyway."

"Just me then," said iron-voice. Had Vincent not known the direness of things, he would have thought the man was at the dinner table — his tone was perfectly composed. "It would give us all peace of mind." He glanced at his companions, and they nodded, in sync as usual. "And I know Lynn would appreciate it."

The prim-looking man's brow was furrowed comically low as he considered them. "If you're so insistent," he said, "I'll let one of you accompany me. The others will have to leave."

"I will go with you." Predictably, the man with the iron voice stepped forward.

"Good," said the prim-looking man, puffing up slightly. "Let's load the guests, shall we?"

Iron-voice nodded, and he motioned forward to the officers holding Jessica. The prim-looking man stood over them wearing his best impression of a commanding look.

The fishbowl door slid open when they approached it. Without hesitation, they hauled Jessica inside. Jessica looked out at Vincent as the door slid shut. Vincent watched, horrified and intrigued, as the glass pod receded back into the wall, then began to the right, taking Jessica with it. A moment later, Jessica had gone, and a second, empty pod moved into place.

"The gentlemen now," said the prim-looking man. John and Vincent were shoved in the new pod simultaneously. John had to hunch at the neck so his head didn't brush against the ceiling.

"Easy as that," said the prim-looking man. "Now your men can—"

The glass door slid shut, and the prim-looking man went mute. The pod was filled with silence, and Vincent could feel the tension in it. He kept his focus on the scene outside: the prim-looking man finishing his rant, iron-voice waving his men out into the hallway.

The pod began to recede back into the wall, and the loading room disappeared. They were cast into shadow, then into darkness completely as they continued deeper along whatever track was carrying them. It was pitch black but for a faint light above.

"We should have told you," said Vincent.

John continued to stare at the glass wall in front of them. His expression remained unrevealing, cold – his usual mask had been reaffixed.

"There never seemed to be a good time and…" Vincent trailed off when he heard how insufficient his words sounded. He looked out into the pitch black of the tunnel, searching for something to say that would even come close to making a difference, but he found nothing. Instead, his mind settled again and again on the same thoughts, the same images: Brian's limp body hanging from its restraints, the open, sightless eyes staring down at a puddle of blood...

Vincent turned his gaze back to the interior of the pod, back to John, to shake the images from his mind, but they didn't fade. They only grew more persistent, as if to pry their way outward, toward the person they would hurt the most.

"I'm sorry," said Vincent. The words sounded tiny, even in the miniature pod, and weak, disappearing into the silence the second they sounded. Vincent forced them out again. "I'm sorry," he said.

John turned from the wall this time. He met Vincent's eyes.

"For not telling you," said Vincent. "And for forcing you to find out the way you did." He paused – the air between them seemed to tighten, as if anticipating the next few words. "And for your brother," he said. "I know it doesn't matter now, but I'm sorry."

John bit down, hard, at the mention of Brian. He said nothing in response. He only continued the same, accusing glare he had worn back in the driveway. Vincent struggled to stare back, and just when he was about to look away, John turned back to the glass. With his eyes unfocused, fixed out into the tunnel on nothing in particular, he breathed out, slow and heavy. He opened his mouth to speak–

The pod jerked to a stop. Vincent turned to the pitch black beyond the glass. Below them, the darkness split down the middle with white light. The floor of the tunnel was spiraling outward, forming a hole just large enough to receive them. There was a lurch, a brief second of decreased gravity, and they began to sink. The pod was dropping through the opening, supported below by nothing but thin air. As they descended, Vincent had to hold a hand up to shield his eyes from the light. He blinked so his eyes could adjust...

The floor of the pod slid out from under them, and they were falling. They landed only a fraction of a second later on the surface of thick glass. Brushing himself off, and still trying to blink away the light, Vincent got to his feet. They were in a much larger pod now, maybe ten times the size as their miniature one, and the walls were made entirely of mirrors. A dozen other prisoners, all men, were in the pod as well. Most kept their gazes on their own feet, but the rest were looking straight up at the fishbowl shape transport Vincent and John had just arrived in. They wore looks of utter indifference as they watched the thing rise, then looks quite the same after it had gone.

"No."

Vincent turned toward the voice, and when he did, he found himself facing a round man with an unmistakably wide nose and large, beady eyes – the eyes of a developer.

"No," Simon said again. His voice cracked as he spoke. He shook his head, lips quivering, eyes shining. "No."

He repeated the word over and over again as he sank to the floor. He stared up at Vincent, accusation in his eyes, a tremor set in his lower jaw.

"She was with you," he said. "She's here, isn't she? They have her."

Vincent opened his mouth to speak, but the words seemed to be caught in his throat.

It was all the answer Simon needed. He began rocking silently where he sat, with his hands shaped like a cage around his face, not quite touching it, but flexing all the same, as if prepared to claw at his own skin.

"Simon…" Vincent started, then stopped again. There was no way to communicate anything important. The inside walls of the giant, bowl-shaped pod were mirrored, but Vincent had a strong feeling the outside ones were completely see-through.

"She's ok," said Vincent. Simon looked up at this. "She's safe."

"Safe?" repeated Simon. "Is that what you call this?" he held up his hands, motioning to nothing in particular.

"No," said Vincent, "but…but she's not hurt." It was the best he could do. Simon was unappeased.

"That's just temporary," he said. "When they don't need her, they'll take her away. They always take you away." He pulled his knees into his chest as he scooted backward, pressing himself up against the mirror there, still rocking, still shaking his head.

Vincent looked over his shoulder for help. John was still standing in the center of the pod, making no move forward. He looked confused. Sighing, Vincent crossed over to Simon and sat down against the mirror next to him. The developer was wiping his tears with his shirt, which, Vincent noticed, seemed to have gone unchanged since their first meeting.

"I'm sorry," said Vincent. "I tried to look after her."

Simon sniffled, clearing his throat, trying to compose himself. "She doesn't need looking after," he said. "Never has." He smiled for a moment, then sniffled again. He looked up at Vincent. "You said she's not hurt?" he asked.

"Nothing major," said Vincent. "Just some scratches."

Simon nodded. He seemed to be regaining control of his breathing. "Were you in the city?" he asked.

"Yes," said Vincent. "Hux."

Simon allowed himself a hollow grin. "You got that far?"

"It was mostly Jessica," said Vincent. "She would have gone even farther if she thought it would help you."

Simon's grin grew wider, his eyes a bit glassier. "It must have been difficult for you, as well," he said. "With them using your father."

Vincent nodded. "Yeah," he said. He didn't think he could manage anything else.

"At least he's important," said Simon, with only a trace of bitterness. "That will keep him safe. Your mother, too."

Vincent didn't bother to correct him. They sat in silence for a while.

"How was the city?" asked Simon.

"Worse," said Vincent. "Different, but worse."

Simon nodded, unsurprised. "Have the 'attacks' stopped?"

"They've decreased," said Vincent.

"Everywhere or just in the standards?"

"Just in the standards *is* everywhere."

Simon lifted his eyebrows, for a fraction of a second surprised, then lowered them again, sighing. "It was just a matter of time," he said. "Sometimes I think Newsight is better at being the Order than they are at being themselves. I don't know why they bother with two names."

John looked over at them from the center of the bowl. "Newsight can call themselves whatever they want," he said, "but the true Order will always go by their rightful name."

Vincent went stiff. His eyes strayed to the mirrored surface over John's head.

"The true Order?" said Simon. He laughed. "You mean a resistance?"

John seemed prepared to shoot something back, but Vincent caught his eye. He held the words in.

"Of course there's a resistance," said Simon. "But that doesn't mean it's real."

"I know for a fact you're wrong," snapped John. Vincent cast the mirror another nervous look.

"Do you?" said Simon. "You've seen it?"

"I'm a part of it."

"John we shouldn't be talking about—"

"It doesn't matter Vincent," snapped John. He followed Vincent's gaze up to the mirror. "They know. It's why we're here."

Simon frowned at these last few words. He turned to Vincent. "What does he mean that's why you're here?" His tone had grown serious, no longer the mocking, depressed one of before.

"He's just upset," said Vincent. "We were caught when our fake prints stopped working."

Simon seemed to smell the lie. "Vincent this is important," he said. "Tell me you and Jessica haven't gotten wrapped up in this."

"We haven't," said Vincent. He looked at the mirror over Simon's shoulder. He could feel them watching – he just didn't know where from.

"Vincent," said Simon. "Look at me when you say it."

Vincent turned to the man, to his large, beady eyes with the telltale curve of the Lenses just beyond the irises. "Simon we shouldn't be talking about this here," he said.

Simon looked at the mirror behind him as well, then turned back to Vincent. "Here is the same as anywhere else," he said. "In holding, in the middle of the Center, in whatever 'secret' base the Order has constructed. They still hear."

Vincent shook his head. Simon was drawing him in, just as before. "Not everywhere," he said. "The Lenses can be turned off. Newsight has devices for it. The Privacy Officers used them on Jessica and me so we couldn't communicate. The Order has them, too."

Simon stared at him a moment longer. He seemed to sense the spark in Vincent's eyes, the hope.

"You believed them, didn't you?" he said. "You joined them?"

Vincent said nothing. He merely stared, defiantly, back.

"Vincent the Lenses can't be turned off," said Simon. "They can't be taken out or disabled. They're permanent."

"But the devices can—"

"The devices are a hoax," said Simon. "They shut the Lenses off for the user, not the producer. Dark Lenses are just like this glass." He looked up at the mirrored bowl that encased them. "One-way. Just because we can't see, doesn't mean Newsight can't."

"You're delirious," said John. Some of the other captives were beginning to look up. "You don't know what you're talking about."

"I programmed for Newsight my whole life, son," said Simon. "I've seen the code."

"But that doesn't make sense," said Vincent. "Those devices are the only reason Jessica and I were able to escape from the Seclusion." He thought back to the night of the crash, then to the officer carrying him to the transport. "And there are people in Newsight who are part of the Order," said Vincent, piecing it together all at once. "One of the officers helped us escape."

"He may have," said Simon. "But only because those were his orders."

Vincent opened his mouth to shoot back some protest, but he was brought back to that night once again. He was in the back, and the officer was right in front of him. The man's eyes were out of focus. He was receiving some sort of message...

"He could have been communicating with the Order," said Vincent. He wasn't sure if he was talking to Simon or himself. "They could have told him to help us."

"Then Newsight would have seen the message," said Simon. He sounded almost sympathetic. "And they would have stopped you. At any point they wanted, they could have stopped you."

"But they didn't!" said Vincent. "Because they couldn't. Our Lenses were dark."

"I already told you," said Simon. "They're never dark, not for Newsight. Whatever you were seeing was valuable to them, so they let you go. For a while, at least."

Vincent looked up to John for help, but John had gone quiet. He was looking at Simon.

"That still doesn't make sense," said Vincent. "We weren't seeing anything important."

"Maybe you weren't," conceded Simon. "Or maybe you just didn't realize the importance of what you *were* seeing."

Vincent frowned at this, confused. Simon looked back at him, his expression still tilted in the same, sympathetic look as before.

"You did see something," said John. He hadn't moved from his position in the center of the place. "You saw some of the last people alive without Lenses. In the Hole." His gaze was fixed on Vincent. It was a fact, a simple statement, but there was an accusation there as well. Vincent thought back to their return to the parking garage just a day prior. The structure had remained intact. The inside, however, had been far from that. It had been the aftermath of a raid, not a bombing. Newsight hadn't bothered bombing the building – they knew the garage had been reinforced. They knew, as well, there were people inside without Lenses. They knew the exact stairwell to send their men to get inside. Somehow, they had known it all.

Vincent looked away. He could feel the heat of John's gaze on the back of his neck.

Vincent turned back to Simon. The thumping in his chest had returned. "But how would they have known we would see anything?" he said. He was still looking for a way out. "Why wouldn't they have just tracked us down and taken us back?"

"Because that would have spoiled the charade," said Simon. The gloating edge he had begun with had faded completely now. He spoke with something closer to regret. "If they had tracked you down, you would have known the darkeners didn't work, you would have *known* there was no way to escape, you would have *known* there was no use trying." Simon paused, looking at John, then back at Vincent. "But they don't want you to know that," he said. "The second you know is the second they lose you."

Vincent didn't shake his head. He didn't shoot something back in protest. He merely held the developer's gaze, feeling even more ensnared now than he had that night in the transport.

"What about the hack?" said John. His brow was still furrowed, his mind still turning. "That was real. I did it myself. We unlocked the code we needed to produce the prints."

"You can't unlock doors that are already open," said Simon. "There's been a hole in the print encryption for years. I tried to fix it myself once, but I was denied."

John continued to stare at the man, defiant. He was still searching for a way out of the net cast by Simon's words, and he was squirming.

A sharp thump sounded just outside the mirror. Vincent turned around. It had come from directly behind him. Simon didn't flinch.

"Whoever brought you here," said Simon, "whether by force or by plan is playing you. You're on the wrong end of a set of puppet strings. The Order the terrorist organization and the Order the resistance are just two masks for the same face. No matter which one it wears, Newsight has the same eyes as always."

Vincent felt his breaths come a bit sharper, a bit shallower. He could say nothing back. John, too, remained silent, merely staring at Simon, accusing, resentful, as if Simon had spoken the truth into existence, not merely reported it.

Simon was opening his mouth yet again when the mirror at his back disappeared. It slid to the side so quickly he fell backward, into a brightly lit, sterile-looking room beyond. Before he could right himself, his arms were grabbed from behind, and he was dragged out. Vincent jumped to his feet. Out the opening, he could see the prim-looking man from the hallway, bloodied at the temple and hunched at the waist, his body slung over a railing just outside. Next to him, Goodwin's officers were still dragging Simon across the floor. The developer didn't struggle.

"Don't tell Jessica," he called back to Vincent. His expression was calm, his tone level. "Don't tell Jessica."

Vincent stared after him, but his vision was soon blocked. A man had stepped into the doorway, the man with the iron voice. The iron eyes. They reminded Vincent of the slips of metal the sweet-voiced woman had used to activate their Lenses.

In that moment, what little doubt of Simon's theory that remained in Vincent's mind was extinguished. The man with the iron voice seemed to sense it, and before Vincent could move, the man's club was swinging against his temple.

CHAPTER 20 – THE TRINITY

The pain pulled Vincent from his sleep. It was in his head, throbbing, beating against the inside of his skull. It sat behind his Lenses like an infection when he opened his eyes, but he could see the room's wood panel floor and pale crimson paint just the same. Even the square video feeds on the rightmost wall were sharp and in focus.

"Welcome back, Vincent."

The deep voice. The slight rasp. The echo that lingered longer than normal.

Goodwin leaned forward in the chair of the ornate desk and interlocked his fingers. "You've been here before," he said. He may have posed it as a question, but he didn't. "It was quite out of order when I returned," he continued. "You seemed to take quite an interest in my books."

Vincent looked up at the bookshelf, at the colorful spectrum of titles there. He thought of Jessica.

"She's safe," said Goodwin. The craters in the man's head seemed to move when he spoke, flexing muscles to move eyes that weren't there. "Much more so than you," he said. "You have presented a problem, but not one that lacks a solution."

For a moment, Vincent expected the man with the iron voice to come bursting through the door. To apprehend him, to take him away. But the room was still. The hallway beyond, too, was silent. There was nothing keeping him in the room. It was indubitable he could outrun the blind man at the desk. What was in much higher doubt, however, was the location of his running, and the purpose.

"Wise of you," said Goodwin. "You've nowhere to go."

Vincent got to his feet. Goodwin remained where he was.

"The developer has complicated things," he continued. "He has always had an appetite for knowledge that does not belong to him, and for sharing that knowledge with others."

Vincent was looking at the feeds. They no longer pictured different rooms of the dome; they showed the Seclusion, not from steady, tripod-like views, but from bouncing, uneven ones, running ones, blinking ones. Goodwin seemed to notice his gaze.

"Even the Order needs monitoring," he said. "For their own protection."

Vincent watched through the eyes of the Order as the domes around them were razed by the bombs of fighter planes above. There was no volume, but if there were, Vincent was certain he would be able to hear the screams.

"Do you know why you're here, Vincent?" asked Goodwin.

Vincent turned from the feeds. "To be taken away?" he said.

"If that were the case," said Goodwin, "I would never have requested you be brought to my home."

"*Your* home?" said Vincent. Goodwin grinned. Vincent felt an urge to be sick, not so much from repulsion as from realization. The loyalties of Brian and John and Lynn no longer seemed so certain. The bedrock on which Vincent had built his faith was turning to sand.

"Why are you here, Vincent?"

Vincent looked again at the feeds, then at the books. "I don't know," he said.

Goodwin breathed out, disappointed. "You brought us THE SIM, did you not?" Vincent nodded. "And you watched it in its entirety, correct?" He nodded again. "Then you know the nature of Newsight," said Goodwin. "Control. And how is someone of your type controlled, Vincent? Someone of the minority. How do we control you?"

We. Goodwin had said it himself. *We:* the Order. *We:* Newsight. *We:* one and the same.

"Vincent?" prompted Goodwin.

"With fear," he said.

"Very good. Your type prioritizes freedom over happiness. Is that your choice?"

"Yes." Vincent didn't have to think.

"And do you feel you can ever be free?"

Vincent said nothing. There was something at war in him. The answer he wanted to give was being smothered by the one he knew to be true.

"Allow me to remind you," said Goodwin. He turned in his seat toward the feeds, and they morphed into just one, larger image. It was of a girl, one Vincent recognized: Annie. She was in a hallway, staring directly at whatever was capturing the video.

"Have you thought anymore about my invitation?" she said.

The feed went black for a fraction of a second as it fast forwarded.

"Ok," said a second voice. It took Vincent a moment to recognize it as his own. "I'll share with you."

Goodwin paused the feed. "Did you want to share a simulation with this girl?" he asked.

Vincent thought of Jessica. The answer was obvious. "No," he said.

"Would you have, anyway?"

He hesitated, then thought of the restless feeling in his legs, the prickling heat under his skin. "Yes," he said. He hated the taste of the word as it left his lips.

"And here," said Goodwin. The feed had changed. They were in the Hole, looking out of Vincent's eyes. John was standing just ahead. Bodies of the stayers littered the garage floor. "Did you intend to inform Newsight of the resistance in Washing?"

"No," said Vincent.

"Did you regardless?"

Vincent forced himself to look at the image, at the bodies. John had known it in holding, and Vincent knew it now.

"Yes," he said.

The feed changed again. They were in the tunnels, in the cavernous room with the crowd, with Goodwin speaking in its center. This time, they weren't looking through Vincent's Lenses but at them, from across the cavern. Next to Jessica and John, Vincent was in frame. His face was red, his eyes bloodshot. He was screaming with the rest of the crowd, his lips forming obscene words, his hands the same gestures.

"Did you mean to be moved to anger?" asked Goodwin.

"No," said Vincent.

"Were you so moved regardless?"

"Yes.

Again, the feed changed. They were in the factory. Vincent was running with the crowd of ragged-clothed Order members. Men and women in gray were fleeing from them, faces pulled into looks of terror.

"Did you intend to harm these people?" asked Goodwin.

"No," said Vincent.

"Did you beat and claw their skin?"

Vincent hesitated. He thought of Jim's wife, of Tina. He hadn't touched her. He was sure of it.

"You didn't harm her," said Goodwin. "But you *were* powerless to stop harm from befalling her. Correct?"

"Yes," said Vincent.

The feed changed yet again, but it remained in the factory. The same men and women that, before, had been wearing gray, were now dressed in a blinding white. They stood as dead tree stumps along the conveyor belt down the center of the room, twisting a bolt onto a part here, rinsing the threads of a screw there. Vincent could see their fragile frames, their sallow, sunken skin. Around them walked dozens of officers, lean and brawny, eyes cold, and above them all, over the main entrance, the inscription that had been painted over was now clearly visible: THERE IS NO FEAR WITHOUT HOPE.

"Were you aware the dome we attacked was not a Newsight factory?" asked Goodwin.

"No," said Vincent.

"Do you see now it was a labor Seclusion?"

Vincent scrutinized the feed, willing its projection to change, to shift back to the gray-clad men and women of before, to show them beating *real* officers, not the frail, white-suited captives.

"Do you see?" repeated Goodwin

"Yes," said Vincent.

The feed went dark.

"And do you wish me to know your thoughts at this moment?" asked Goodwin.

"No," said Vincent.

"And are you certain that I do?"

"Yes."

Goodwin breathed a sigh of relief. "You see now that our power is absolute. So tell me again, Vincent," he said, "do you feel you can ever be free?"

Vincent attempted to hesitate, to doubt, but it was impossible. "No," he said.

"You are correct in this belief," said Goodwin. "Do you see why this poses a problem to us?"

"No."

"The developer has already told you." Goodwin's tone was paternal: prompting and patient, oddly warm. "There is no fear without hope. You have no hope of freedom. Therefore you have no fear of your captors. You have nothing to lose."

"I have Jessica," he said. It was his last rock. "And Simon and John."

"Simon has transitioned into the few," said Goodwin. "He will be taken away. And John has already spared us the trouble. The realization of his true allegiance proved too disturbing for him. He was taken away by his own hand. As for Jessica..." Goodwin's lips twitched upward, "she will remain in the Order."

"So she'll live?" said Vincent. "You won't hurt her?"

"I will not," said Goodwin. "Whether or not she lives, however, is a separate question." He paused at this, seeming, somehow, to inspect Vincent. "Do you believe there is any chance Jessica will ever be free?" he asked.

Vincent started to speak, then stopped again. He turned to the wall where the feeds had just disappeared. He thought of Simon being dragged away, limp and unresisting.

"No," he said.

"And as the minority type," said Goodwin, "do you feel there is any true life without freedom?"

"No," said Vincent.

"So if you still care for Jessica," pressed Goodwin, "and her life is without meaning because she will never have freedom, is it true you have no reason to fear her loss?"

Vincent felt as if a knot were being tied with his intestines and pulled tighter with every question. He had sealed his only way out. "Yes," he said.

"You have nothing," said Goodwin. "You will never fear us. This is important, Vincent, you must understand this. Understand everything."

"I understand," said Vincent.

"You understand the Order never existed," said Goodwin, "never will exist, and was, itself, created by Newsight?"

"Yes."

"You understand Alduss Fatrem is whomever I declare?" said Goodwin. "That he will forever exist and forever rule?"

"Yes."

"You understand that every fraction of every second of every thought, sight, and sound is monitored by the software and developers of Newsight, and that every member of the Order has been allowed to be so only because Newsight allowed it?"

"Yes," said Vincent.

"You further understand that every attack of the Order was

orchestrated by Newsight management for the advancement of our own ends?"

"Yes."

"And you lastly understand," said Goodwin, "that the new Lenses are incapable of being removed, impaired, or otherwise harmed without the resultant death of their owner?"

He looked into Goodwin's deep black craters, the never-ending Lenseless pits. Goodwin grinned.

"I have never worn Lenses," he said. "I am the only one."

A wild, fanciful hope surged through Vincent. "You could leave," he said. "You could escape."

Goodwin grinned wider still. "From my own kingdom?"

The hope left Vincent like the flame of a candle snuffed by an ocean.

"You understand," said Goodwin. "You have broken the mold of control we have so carefully crafted for you, for all the minority. And now we are left with only one option. Can you think what that is, Vincent?"

Vincent ventured a guess, knowing, in advance, he would be wrong. "To take me away?"

"No!" thundered Goodwin. "You will not be taken away. Only the few are taken away, only those completely indifferent to our rule. They are not worth controlling. There is nothing in them to control. They are puppets without strings, hollow, useless." Goodwin's face had grown animated. His black-scarred sockets were fixing Vincent with an unbreakable stare. "You have far more to give than they do, and we will not waste a drop of it by taking you away." He paused, gaining his breath, returning to himself. "Answer this first, Vincent," he said, "and you will be able to answer the other. Why should we want control? Why should we want power?"

The man's mouth – cracked and white at the lips – was parted, an answer to his own question already perched on his tongue. Vincent knew what it would be. For the majority: a protector from evil and a source of senseless pleasure. For the minority: a fuel to be burned by the churning engines of freedom, a fight, a passion. And for the few: a swift kiss of the guillotine, an angel of death in the face of a complacent life not worth living. For the benefit of all, for the greater good of–

"Incorrect," snapped Goodwin. "Vastly incorrect. We are no

one's messiah. No more than the farmer is to the pig he butchers. Power is its own end. It is taken because it is desired and clung to because it satisfies. But satisfaction is not constant. Rule over a million of the few, those who care not either way whether or not they are ruled, and power is pointless. But rule over just one of the minority or the majority, and you are a god. Power is had only over those who would rather be free. Who feel. If you feel nothing, we take you away. We desire to preside over only those whose full spectrum of existence we can satisfy at once. He who would be free, we oppress him only so we can provide him an escape. He who would be happy and secure, we terrorize only so we can provide protection. We are fear and hope, love and hatred, all at once. To have power is to be everything, to be real. We cling to power for this reason and this reason alone. Do you see now why your situation is problematic?"

Vincent was beginning to understand, as much as one could understand the man without eyes. He frowned as he spoke. "Your purpose of power is to be two opposites at once," he said. "If you achieve that, you have done the impossible. You are god."

Goodwin nodded to him, encouragingly, prompting, like a father.

"As my type in the minority," continued Vincent, "my fear of Newsight is motivated by my hope of escape." Goodwin nodded again. "But I have no such hope," said Vincent. "And so I cannot have the fear to accompany it. I am not worth having power over."

"Close, Vincent," said Goodwin, "very close. It is true you have broken the mold of your type, but that you are not worth having power over is entirely false. You are not hollow, like the few. You contain the capacity to feel and to be driven. Though no longer does this capacity support fear and hope, it does support love and hatred." He paused, considering something. "You remember well your time in Hux, Vincent?"

"Well enough," he said.

"Then you will understand our method of maintaining power there," said Goodwin. "You saw in THE SIM that upon sorting, the few are taken away, the minority are sent to the Seclusions, and the majority are sent to the cities. Once in the cities, the majority wish only to be happy. They wish to be entertained, to be safe, to love. The Order threatens them, ravages their families and colleagues, and for the Order, they are filled with hatred. Newsight protects them, entertains them, and offers them joy, and for Newsight, they are filled with love. We are two opposites of the same whole. Power in the cities is just as valuable as it is in the Seclusions, only of a different taste." He stopped here. His eyes – Vincent had begun to see the craters as giant pupils – were fixed on Vincent. "This is the power we wish to hold over you."

Vincent leaned back, stunned. "That's impossible," he said. "I hate Newsight."

Goodwin began to laugh, deep and hoarse. His sunken and unseeing pupils writhed inside their hollow cavities, mocking Vincent, taunting him.

"I hate Newsight," repeated Vincent. This was one thing, one of the last, of which he felt absolutely certain. "I hate Newsight." The prickling heat began to rise up under the skin of his face, the same as it had in the cavern and in the factory, only this time, there was no maintenance to stir it in him, no serums.

"I believe you, Vincent," said Goodwin. "I do."

Vincent said nothing back. He let the heat continue to rise under his skin.

"But your hatred of Newsight," continued Goodwin, "only increases your capacity to love. It will only provide us more satisfaction from having power over you." He smiled – too broadly now to be just a grin – and leaned back in his chair, confident. Vincent was but a trifle. "Cling to your hatred, Vincent," he said. "We need it."

CHAPTER 21 – 2098

Vincent was standing at the sink holding a plate that had been spotless for several minutes. He let the warm water continue to run over his hands, losing himself in the slow, circular rhythm of his cleansing strokes.

He was taller now, though not by much. He had gained weight, too, as the time had passed. He had a man's brawn to him. His skin had lost some of its youthful glow, but the difference was barely perceptible. He bore no sign of wrinkles, except where the water from the faucet had been streaming down onto his fingers.

"I'm home!"

A voice called out over the creaking of the front door. Vincent looked up. Jessica stepped into the living room and shed her coat on the nearest chair.

"Did you eat without me?" she asked.

She had changed very little. Her eyes shone with the same, wide curiosity as they always had. Her hair, still dark, was pulled back. And her face, still somewhat flat, wore the same, constant hint of a smile.

"I have a group to get settled in tonight," said Vincent. "I tried to wait for you."

Jessica dropped her bag and lowered herself into the chair across the counter. It was a process – she had gained much more weight than Vincent. Of course much of it, especially in the large, rounded part of her stomach, was not her own. "You're working late again?" she asked.

Vincent raised his brow, then looked down at his watch. "I'm the one working late?"

Jessica waved a dismissive hand. "You know how crazy it is when we're in session," she said. "I have to be there."

"Not in your current state you don't!" said Vincent. Jessica looked down at the bulge in her stomach, rolling her eyes.

"You do know you're the one who put me in this 'state'," she said, with a grin. "Don't you?"

Vincent smiled back at her. He shook his head and shut the water off. The plate – now sparkling – he set in the drying rack. "Well you only have one more night," he said. He circled the counter over to her and she spun around in her chair to receive him. He placed a hand on the upper part of her stomach. "So I thought just maybe you would be home on time."

Jessica looked down at Vincent's hand, smiling, and placed her own hand there as well. "She only makes me want to work later."

Vincent sighed, but he didn't argue. He didn't disagree. "How is the legislation coming?" he asked. "Are the trade blocks finalized?"

"Nearly," said Jessica. "We're getting close."

Vincent nodded back, and gave her stomach one final, gentle pat before turning away. He pulled his coat from the rack.

"Refugees?" asked Jessica.

"A family of them," said Vincent. He threw his coat around his shoulders. "They're getting here at 8:00."

"8:00?" repeated Jessica. She cast a look down at her watch. "You're leaving awfully early."

"I don't want to be late," said Vincent. Jessica grinned.

"You're taking a ground transport, aren't you?"

Vincent bent down to retrieve his briefcase, careful to keep his back turned. He could feel Jessica smiling behind him.

"You'd save so much time if you flew," she said.

Vincent pulled the case up to his hip by the handle. "Food's in the oven," he said. She rolled her eyes, and he smiled back. He crossed over to her once again and kissed her on the forehead.

"Hurry back to us," she said.

"I will," said Vincent, and he started for the door, still smiling.

******

Vincent sat down in one of the black leather chairs outside the usual door. It was nearly 8:00. The ground transport had eaten up much of his time, as Jessica had warned him it would. The traffic in the city, though working hours had long since ended, never seemed to thin. With the refugees coming through the halos and the activists protesting outside the Capitol, the streets were nearly overrun. Vincent wasn't bothered, though. The energy in the air was infectious. There was a shared, crusading kind of spirit, and it filled him to the brim. He didn't mind working after hours any more than Jessica did.

"Just through here."

Vincent stood when he heard the voice. The door across from him had opened.

"Allow me to introduce you to your guide."

A hulking, red-haired man in a black suit stepped into the hall first. He was pointing to Vincent with his left hand, and ushering three people through the door with his right.

"Vincent Smith," the man continued. "Vincent, meet the Lees."

Vincent stepped forward with a bow. The father, a lean, small-framed man with narrow eyes and olive-colored skin, bowed back.

"They are in your charge now," said the red-haired man. He turned to the family. "You're in the best of hands." He smiled at them, then disappeared back through the door.

"Nice to meet you," said Vincent. "We're happy to have you here."

The father bowed once again. "We are very grateful," he said. His English was a bit broken in parts. "You can call me Steven. This is my wife, Zoey and my son, David."

The woman behind Steven bowed but said nothing. Vincent bowed in turn. The boy, not yet in his teens and almost identical to his father, did not bow but reached out his hand instead. Smiling, Vincent shook it.

"It's nice to meet all of you," he said. "Where are you from?"

"East," said Steven. Vincent nodded — that was description enough.

"I assume you've already spoken with someone about other potential refugees?" asked Vincent. "Any family you might have?"

"Yes," said Steven. "My parents were not able to escape. The man we spoke to seems to think they can be rescued. Is that true?"

Vincent nodded. "We'll do everything we can," he said. "The Senate is enforcing the necessary trade blocks and organizing search and rescue as we speak."

Steven nodded in approval. "We were lucky to make it out. Your spies assisted us."

"Well we're glad you made it," said Vincent. He smiled at them. "Would you like me to show you where you'll be staying?"

Steven nodded, graciously. "Yes please."

Vincent motioned forward down the hall. They started to walk. "It's not too far," he said. "The refugee homes are actually attached to the halos."

"The halos," said Steven, "that is what you call your air defense system?"

Vincent nodded. "We kept Newsight's original name for them," he said. "But they're completely under Senate control now."

Steven looked around, seeming unimpressed. "They are different than ours," he said. "Not as much security."

"We don't need much," said Vincent. "The air defense network hasn't been activated in years, and the identity checkpoints are no longer in use."

Steven frowned. He glanced back at his family – David was listening intently. "So we will not be identified?" he said. "To be monitored?"

"You'll be ID'ed," said Vincent. "But only with paperwork for census purposes. For school, as well."

"How are the schools?" joined David. "Are there simulations?" He said this last part a bit nervously. Vincent shook his head.

"No simulations," he said. "Just teachers."

David nodded, but he still seemed skeptical.

"What information does the government request during the identification process?" asked Steven. There was suspicion in his voice. His eyelids were pulled close.

"Just standard things," assured Vincent. "Name, family ties, region of birth – details like those. You'll be assigned an ID number as well."

"And they track you?" said Steven. "With this number?"

Vincent shook his head once again. "No tracking. Your information will go into a database with your picture and your fingerprints. That's it."

Zoey, the man's wife, tugged at his sleeve. He turned to her and said something, rapidly, in another language. She returned something in the same tongue, with several nervous glances at Vincent. Vincent watched, patient.

"My wife is doubtful," said Steven, turning back to Vincent. "She does not trust the government. Ours worked very closely with WeSee. At first they did not collect much, but that changed very quickly. How do we know that will not happen here?"

Vincent could have predicted the question. He fielded the same one day in and day out. The refugees they received from WeSee in the East and Allwatch in the North all had the same suspicions.

"Public officials are vetted now more closely than ever," said Vincent. "The government's and anyone else's collection of personal data is limited, and we've gone to great lengths to make sure it stays that way."

"With regulations?" pressed Steven. "That is what *our* government

242

tried. It did not last."

"No, not with regulations," said Vincent. "The Senate actually regulates our businesses very little. It's the people who regulate them. If a company comes close to overstepping its bounds, the people take action. They boycott; they protest; they do whatever they have to. No one wants another Newsight. We're protected by memory now. We don't need litigation."

Steven didn't look convinced. Still, he turned to his wife to translate. When he turned back to Vincent, he pressed no further. They walked in silence for a while.

"What about the attacks?" David spoke up. "You said there haven't been any?" The boy was trying to hide it, but the fear in his voice came through regardless.

"Not recently," said Vincent. "The last prominent terrorist organization we had to deal with was Newsight, and they're long gone now."

Vincent slowed them to a stop outside of a second door, the one that led to the refugee residences.

"Is there anyone else?" asked David, when they had come to a stop. "Does anyone else have missiles?"

Vincent froze with his hand on the knob. The rawness of the question raised a lump in his throat. It was questions like those that drove him time and time again to the halos, to the refugees.

"Yes," said Vincent. "There are people with missiles."

David's face fell.

"But the halos have stopped every attack so far," said Vincent. "You don't have to worry."

Vincent smiled at him, then at his parents. "All right," he said, turning back to the door, "this is where all refugees begin their stay. The residences are…" He trailed off when he saw David out of the corner of his eye. The boy kept casting nervous glances at the ceiling, as if he expected it to come crashing down at any minute. Vincent felt the lump rise up in his throat once again. Taking a step back from the door, he crouched down so he and the boy were on the same level.

"I won't lie to you, David," he said. "You might not be completely safe here."

David looked up at the ceiling once again. His lower lip was starting to tremble.

"But even if you're not safe," said Vincent, "you'll be something even better." He took the boy by the wrist, and David pulled his eyes from the ceiling. Vincent smiled at him. "You'll be free."

******

In the dark, Vincent eased the front door back into the closed position as quietly as he could. He hung his coat on the free hook in the closet and slipped his shoes off. It was well past 11:00. After getting the Lees settled, he had opted once again for a ground transport.

Tiptoeing, he made his way into the living room. As he had expected, the television was still playing with the volume turned all the way up, and Jessica was fast asleep on the couch. Smiling, Vincent crossed over to her and pulled the blanket at her feet up to her shoulders. The bulge of Jessica's stomach rose the blanket up in the middle like a miniature tent. Vincent smiled again, then found his mouth opening in a long, deep yawn. He would need rest for tomorrow, real rest. The allure of sleeping here was almost undeniable, *was* undeniable most of the time. If he stayed, he would likely awaken rested as normal – he was being given the most advanced treatment available, after all. But he didn't want to take any chances. He had to be refreshed, completely present tomorrow morning. He would go back, just for a little while.

Vincent kissed his hand and rested it on Jessica's stomach over the blanket. Then, with a double glance up and to the right, the couch and television and entire house disappeared. He was back in his room. Yawning once again, he lay down on his plain white mattress, in his plain white nightclothes, and he slept.

CHAPTER 22 – THE HIGH TOWER

It was the next morning, and Vincent was at the window. He stared through the thick glass at the neighboring tower. It, too, was a dashing, pure white, and circular. All the towers in the retirement sector of Hux were. He assumed the insides of the other towers were the same as his, also, sectioned off and isolated, completely solitary but for the Newsight nurses that stopped in as monitors. He had not left the tower, not even left his own small portion of it since he had first arrived. Retirement, they called it. It always seemed to Vincent like a funny word to describe his current state. He had done no real work, and yet he was treated like an irreplaceable asset. The windows were too thick to throw oneself through. The dinnerware was not sharp enough to cut oneself with. The sheets were not long enough to enable a sturdy knot to be tied in them. The food was pumped into one's body intravenously if one refused to eat it the normal way. And biting one's tongue or bludgeoning oneself against the wall was impossible to do to completion without being halted by the nurses. None of it ever worked. Couldn't work. Vincent had been deprived of the escape of death. He had been afforded no activity outside of mere existence save for the newsims. For quite a long time – he prided himself on the length of it – he had abstained from the simulations altogether. He had begun by passing his days in silent compliance. That had gone on for as long as he could manage. He had no way of knowing how long exactly that was, of course. His Lenses no longer told time and his manual count of days had long since been abandoned. He had been given no point of reference, no news of the outside world, nothing of the Newsight Seclusion, of the other cities, not even of Hux itself. He was stranded in time and place. His only semblance of an escape was the newsims, and those were as much an anchor as they were a raft. After a time, though, he had used them just the same.

Vincent did not know what had befallen Jessica: whether she had perished in the attack, been taken away, or continued on with the Order as Goodwin had said. Any of the three would have been the same to Vincent. The results were equivalent. He understood now why Simon had lain so still as they dragged him from holding. Resistance was resignation. It was what Goodwin had taught him. The one thing he knew for certain. To resist Newsight, you were in the Order. To be in the Order, you were part of Newsight. To flee from the bombing, you fled from the Order and into the cities. The cities were protected by Newsight, so in fleeing from the Order, you fled to Newsight, who was the Order. It made his brain hurt trying to keep it all straight.

Sighing, Vincent turned from the window and walked the short distance back to his room. That was his space: the hall with his window, the room with his bed, and the bathroom with his shower and sink (the nurses always came long before the water reached a level into which one might lower one's face). He walked past the bathroom and went to his bed. With his eyes trained on the ceiling, he could have dozed easily off into a restless, dream-filled sleep. In the days when he did not engage his simulations, that had been his only option. He had felt like a captive then, riddled with thoughts of his parents, of Jessica, of Simon. When he had finally made the decision to give up, to allow himself to escape with newsim, however, he had begun to feel less like a captive. The walls, of course, were just as claustrophobic, and the windows just as impenetrable, but the experience was far different. He had stopped being a captive, and begun being a guest.

"Vincent?"

His head nurse had poked her head through the door. Vincent nurtured a stronger hatred for her than any of the other nurses. She was always the first one to shut off the running water in the sink, or staunch the bleeding of his tongue. But of course, she was quite closely endeared to Vincent, as well. He was fond of her just as equally as he was abhorrent. She always delivered the newsims.

"I have more access cards for you," she said, stepping deeper into the room. "You should return to your treatment. I don't know how many times I need to tell you: there's no need to exit the simulation. You will be taken care of." She set a bowl of access cards on the table next to his bed. He smiled at her. He also felt a lurking desire to reach for her throat.

When the nurse had left, Vincent reached over to the bowl and withdrew a card. Nearly shaking with excitement, he let his eyes slide out of focus, and he scanned the code. The usual, sweet-sounding voice rang out inside him. He oftentimes found himself wondering if the woman whose voice played in his head was an actual woman. He would like very much to share a simulation with her. Although, her voice was also the one he heard when ramming his forehead into the wall above his bed, and the one that never quite seemed to be all the way silenced.

Vincent's usual newsim began to load. He had been living inside the same one ever since coming to the retirement tower. He had grown up in the small brown house with his mother and father and grandfather. He had met a girl with a short black ponytail who sat next to him at school. They had gotten their own small house. Nothing in it had been painted white.

The eye on the loading screen came to a stop as it finished its final rotation, and the pitch black began to fade. Vincent began the newsim where he had left off the night before. He was pulling his coat off the hook in the closet. He was walking into a hospital room. He was holding the hand of the woman in the bed. He was listening to the thumping in his chest, to the woman screaming, to the doctor talking in a soothing tone. He was staggering backward and sitting in the chair at the foot of the bed. He was reaching out for a bundle of brown blankets. He was staring down at the tiny wet face of a baby girl, at her button nose, at her clear, unobstructed eyes.

In that moment, the two camps in Vincent's mind, the irreconcilable passions directly at war with one another, the resolutions both for and against the creators of the Lenses, were joined. There was no force needed to keep them intertwined. They were inseparable, had *been* inseparable all along. He felt foolish now for having denied himself the peace of their union all this time, foolish for staving off the clarity with which he now saw.

"Vincent?"

He was pulled from the newsim. The nurse had returned. She was beaming from ear to ear.

"Your treatment is complete," she said. "Would you like me to call you a transport?"

Vincent stood from his bed, in a daze. He felt the thumping in his chest, the slight stiffness in his aged joints, the warmth of the child he had just been holding...

"Vincent." The woman prompted him again. "Would you like a transport?"

Vincent didn't respond. Instead, he sat back down on his bed and selected a second access card. Smiling, the nurse left him. Vincent didn't follow. There was no transport that could take him to the hospital he had just left. Only the slips of glass over his eyes could do that. It's why he prized them, why he trusted them. Sure, they had distorted and stolen his sight and his sound and his thought. But they had given it all back. They had given him everything. Now in his resentment, there was obligation. In his desire to rip the things from his eyes, there was an insatiable lust to disappear behind them. The reconciliation was his. He loved his Lenses.

THANKS FOR READING!

Thanks for reading! I hope you enjoyed the story. If you did, I have good news: there's a whole world left to be explored. I have two more books in the works: the story of how John infiltrated the Newsight HQ, and the Newsight origin story. You can check out sample chapters of each at masonengel.com/next.

Thanks again!

-Mason

ABOUT THE AUTHOR

Mason Engel is a 22 year old science-fiction writer from Columbus, Indiana. Though he graduated from Purdue University with a degree in mathematics, Mason is obsessed with the power of words and the stories they tell. No matter what he writes, the end product always seems to tie into one of two themes: the omnipresence of technology, or our perception of reality. It sounds philosophical, and at its core, it is. On the page though, in the prose of the plot itself, for Mason, philosophy takes backseat to story. In every novel he writes, his first and foremost goal is to entertain YOU, to provide you an escape from the real world and, when you're ready, some inspiration to return to it.

Made in the USA
Columbia, SC
05 August 2017